EDEN.2

EDEN.2

Margaret A. Babcock

Queer Space
New Orleans

Published in the United States of America by
Queer Space
A Rebel Satori Imprint
www.rebelsatoripress.com

Library of Congress Control Number: 2020950739

To my darling Chuck,
with deep gratitude for life's journey shared with you.

Oh, God, the sea is so wide
And my boat is so small.
Have mercy on me.
Amen

—*The Breton Fisherman's prayer*

CONTENTS

CHAPTER 1
ORBITING PLANET KOI-3284

DATE: 2073 CE/1

The recording of jungle birds quarreling high and bright amongst the rustle of leaves brought Jerry out of sleep. He lay for a few moments, cocooned in a warm nest of soft sheets and dispersing unconsciousness, thinking how strange it was to wake to the sound of creatures millions of miles away. The sterile atmosphere of the spaceship could adapt to anything humans inserted into it, but now it orbited their destination planet. Soon, other sounds would take precedence over the imports of Earth.

Beside him his husband stirred, twisting around to bat at the alarm. The birds ceased their debate, the constant hum of the ship filling the void. Jerry settled his back into the curve of Rob's body as they began their waking up routine.

"You had the dream?" Rob breathed in his ear.

"Yes. You?"

This had become their morning litany. A communal dream, one that haunted most everyone on the Glenn—what did it mean? Did other human communities share a chimera night after night? Jerry had scoured the data banks trying to discover a precedent. Some groups experienced re-occurring images, but the whole sequence which first troubled Jerry's sleep months before their voyage now visited the entire ship:

1

The sleeper enclosed in fog. A wind without effect. A child's plaintive singing. Desire to find the source. The dreamer rooted in place.

This small mystery, minor compared to other conundrums of space life, felt personal, almost intimate. Jerry treasured the visitation.

Rob sighed. "I thought I could move this time, but then those damn birds started chirping."

"Hmmm. It's always something. Coffee?"

"God, yes. Isn't it my turn to get it, though?"

"I have to go, anyway. Back's killing me. You snuggle in for a while."

Jerry shifted his legs over the hard edge of the bed's side and leveraged his six foot three frame vertical, stretching until his fingertips brushed the ceiling. The cool air of the cabin chased the last of his sleep fog away as he pulled on his coveralls and a took the two steps needed to exit the bedroom door. He accessed the tiny bathroom niche off the common area, mindful of the woman and child sleeping in the next room.

The entrance panel swooshed open as he approached and Jerry ventured out into a hallway usually deserted and silent at this hour. Today, though, a mom holding a sleepy toddler in her arms stood at the elevator and his neighbors, the Andersons, waved as they entered their quarters. The lift signaled its arrival with a mellow chime, and he stepped in.

"Hey, Jerry," the mother greeted him, tightening her grip on the little girl she carried as she got into the silver booth. "Are Lily and Xander up yet? Alice can't sleep. This new schedule is killing us."

"They're still tucked in, Shelly. I think we're getting used to it." He smiled at the child and gave her a wink.

Twenty days ago, when the ship dropped into orbit, they had given up Earth's circadian rhythm to practice the longer thirty-two hour rotation of this larger planet. In theory, a month of simulating new sleep cycles—one "normal" eight hour period and another nap of two to three hours—would get them ready for the reality they were entering. They should have adjusted when they still orbited Earth, but in the frantic first days after their premature departure, nobody had the energy to enforce the unfamiliar discipline. Now, eight years later, the crew struggled to adapt. In fact, the only ones taking to the foreign routine were the seven children born in space.

As if on cue, the tousled head lifted from her mother's shoulders and the little girl piped up. "Mommy won't stay asleep. She keeps talking to Daddy."

Shelly sighed, pushing fingers through her blond hair which matched the disarray of her daughter's. "She's right. Maybe I'm too excited about the possibility of the shuttles landing. I'll be working the weather data after breakfast this morning. We're hoping to find a window in the storm pattern today."

"I hope you succeed. It will still be awhile before most of us crunch dirt beneath our feet though. It's not like the movies. Checking details three times over kills the thrill. In fact, I've got a meeting in an hour to sort out a landing schedule for the plants and fish. We've only been over these issues every day since we arrived."

As the elevator settled and the door opened, little Alice squirmed. Her mom set her down to run across the hall into the dining room, then turned to Jerry, her eyes dark with worry. "Do you think we can really live on this planet, Jer? What will we do if we can't survive here? People are talking about trying to find somewhere else."

"I don't think there's anywhere else to go, Shelly." Jerry spoke the words as gently as possible. We're all scared, he thought. This is such a huge change. The odds of finding another world capable of sustaining human life though were slim. "We'll adapt. If people could live in Siberia and Alaska on Earth, we should be able to figure out how to exist here."

Shelly gave him a shaky smile as they entered the cafeteria, joining several other bleary eyed early risers. "Well, coffee should boost my courage."

Jerry poured her a cup and helped her get Alice settled with a breakfast tray before he filled two sturdy white mugs and headed back to help his own little family start the day.

An hour later, Jerry sat with the xeno-agriculture crew going through construction plans for a smaller bio-dome on the planet surface to house half the contents of the ship's aquaponics garden. Details awaited decisions: What species had the best chance to thrive? How many fish should they risk? What about containment? Until they understood the ecosystem on this new world, they didn't dare introduce any Earth plants outside. A mild-mannered pea plant might, in the alien environment, take over, killing extensive native vegetation. Important stuff, Jerry thought, stifling a yawn. Important and deadly boring. He wished he was with Rob at the briefing on the landing sites being considered. Now that would be interesting.

Three other full-time workers, John Jackson the supervisor who had first introduced him to xeno-agriculture, Jim Selby and Helen Green, leaned over their com-pads in the small greenhouse off the main dome. The humidity in the room had reached the ninety-eight percent it was designed to maintain, now that they had restored water on their eleventh ISRU, the 'in situ resource utilization' pauses that marked their progress through space as they stopped to mine planets and asteroids for fuel. Jerry wiped his screen with his sleeve. He'd forgotten how moisture beaded up on the viewing panel, but felt only thankfulness for its presence.

"Helen and I will go to the surface as soon as possible to start construction on the planet's dome," John said. "They promised extra workers when the basic living quarters and kitchen are finished. While we're picking a site and getting ready, I need Jerry and Jim to stay here and prepare the plants and fish we choose for transit."

"Sure, Boss." Jim looked up from his note taking. "When should we start, though? We don't want to wrap the big trees too early."

"Yeah, I wish I knew what the Steering Committee is planning. Rob promised me at least a week's notice before landing, and it will take a few weeks for the construction. Let's look at it this way: the minute we get that heads up, we figure another month before transport."

John's forehead crease had deepened to a furrow in the last eight years. He had yet to celebrate his thirty-fifth birthday but the stress of life on board, the number of lives depending on his making good decisions when no precedent guided him, took its toll. Thin to gauntness, his hair a dull gray, on Earth Jerry would have guessed him to be at least fifty.

Jerry's wristband buzzed. He excused himself to take a call from Rob. Stepping out of the small room into the larger enclosure, he breathed in the cooler, drier air, raising his hand to open the link.

"What's up, man?"

"Hey, Jer. We're sending recognizance flights to check out three possible settlement sites. I'm piloting the one to the northern zone. I wanted to keep you in the loop."

"Do you have room for a passenger?" Jerry said, with little real hope. It was always worth a try though.

"Nope, got my quota of miners. If it looks like the right place, they'll stay behind and set up shop."

"When will you be back?"

"Good question. The weather is stable now, but these storms move around. We don't know enough about wind and rain patterns here to predict where they'll go next. We can't take chances on losing the shuttles, so if a storm moves in, we'll hang out until it passes."

"Sounds like a plan. Be careful, dear. I admit to envy. You'll be the first people to set foot on our new home."

"Well, either Bob or Dawn might beat me to their sites, but yeah—I'm jazzed."

Only Rob's face showed in the tiny hologram hovering above his band. Jerry heard the noise of heavy machinery, whirring with occasional sharp bangs and scrapes, in the background.

"Are you in the hanger? Can I come and say goodbye?"

"No, the miners think it's bad luck. That's why I'm calling. Most of them aren't even talking to their spouses, just texting them."

Jerry sighed. There would be worried faces at dinner tonight, with hushed conversations, and joint prayers afterwards. A trip to the surface of the planet was safer than mining asteroids in space, but the unknown still held power to frighten. "You be careful, Rob. I'll be holding you in my heart."

"And I'll take you with me in mine."

The hologram clicked off, leaving empty air above the blank gray of the band. Jerry went back into the meeting where the others were outlining steps to secure the fish and soil at various levels in the bio-dome.

"We may not have too long to wait," he told them. "They're sending three shuttles to make a final decision on a landing site."

Smiles and cheers filled the small space releasing new energy for the planning.

When Jerry got back to his quarters, he checked the weather planet-side, using his com-pad to call up the various locations where the three shuttles were attempting to land. He zeroed in on Rob's site and saw with concern clouds spinning towards it. He considered calling up the scientist manning the control center, but hesitated to bother her. *They'll alert me if he's in danger, won't they?* The debate in his mind just started heating up when the outer door slid open, spilling in an excited Xander.

"Uncle Jerry, guess what we learned today."

He looked up and, abandoning his internal argument, focused on the exuberant seven-year-old who plopped on the couch beside him, his round face grinning. Before he managed a hunch or even a comment, the boy leapt to another subject.

"Oh, I know what that is," he said, looking at the video feed on Jerry's tablet. "We saw that in class today. It's Goldilocks, isn't it?"

Ever since being introduced to their destination world, KOI-3284, the non-scientific crew referred to it as their goldilocks, the generic description for habitable planets-not too hot or too cold but just right for humans. When the children began talking though, Goldilocks became a name more than a definition. Now Jerry heard even the scientists using 'Goldilocks' as they would 'Earth'. It had become the planet's pseudonym. Goldilocks, he mused-a little girl trying to find a comfortable place to rest in a world filled with dangerous bears. Naming the planet after her seemed appropriate for their quest.

"Yup. Uncle Rob is landing there right now. He's taken a shuttle to scout out a good territory to colonize."

"How will he figure out if it's OK?" The child frowned, his face taking on the appearance of a much older person.

Jerry winced at this abrupt change of emotion, wondering—does he realize what's at stake? He tried to make his voice cheery. "Well, we need to consider many factors. Right now they're looking to see if there's a flat space big enough to land our science orb. They'll also assess sites for shelter from the weather."

"You mean, like to block the wind?"

"Yeah, that's right."

"We learned about wind in school today. You guessed it." The boy bounced with joy as he made this pronouncement and Jerry laughed.

"Easiest riddle I've had in a long time."

"Well, that's not everything we learned. There's more."

"Give me a clue."

"What means wind, and breath and spirit, all in one?" Xander's face wore a smug grin, his eyes twinkling. Word puzzles were their favorite, a special game he and Uncle Jerry loved, while Mom and Uncle Rob ignored them.

"Wind, breath and spirit, huh? It wouldn't be 'ruah' would it?"

"How did you guess?" Xander headed towards a pout, indignant at having secret knowledge uncovered and not being able to tell his uncle himself.

Jerry reached over to tickle him. "First, 'ruah' isn't even an English word. It's Hebrew, so I'm not sure that's a fair riddle. Second, I bet Rabbi Sarah was your teacher today, right?"

"Yeeeees." Giggles got the best of Xander as he succumbed to the tickling.

"What else did you learn about wind?" Jerry asked when the boy collapsed breathless beside him again.

"When the planet heats up and hot temperature meets cool air, it makes wind."

"Hmmm, I didn't know that."

"Yeah, and Goldilocks is very windy so she must be heating up a lot, but no one knows why yet. It could be this sun's rays are very hot, or she might have volcanoes."

"I hadn't considered that." Jerry shared his ignorance, rewarded by Xander's beam of pride in teaching an adult something.

"You should go to school with us." The offer was serious—a generous gift of inclusion.

"I have to do my work, kiddo, but I like it when you come home and teach me stuff."

The boy settled back, content with a task accomplished, and sighed. "But you know what, Uncle Jerry? I think wind might be from other things too."

"Yeah? You have a theory?"

"Well, not a real scientific theory." His Uncle Rob taught him what constituted a rigorous hypothesis and how one went about setting them up and testing them. Even at this young age, Xander could tell the difference between theory and speculation. "I wondered—if 'ruah' can mean wind, and breath and spirit, why can't wind be the planet breathing or the planet sighing, or something?"

Jerry turned to look at Xander. The child, staring into the middle of the room, felt his gaze. He shifted, turning his serious eyes, fathomless brown, up to his uncle's.

Jerry said, "You, my friend, have the heart of a poet." He draped his arm around the boy and drew him into a half hug, kissing the shiny black hair. "How about we find your mom and have dinner?"

"OK," Xander agreed.

As they left the room, Jerry made a mental note to share this conversation with Rob. It would tickle him to discover their child already thought in abstract terms.

Rob's landing site proved the best of the three potential areas and he left his miners there, setting up temporary shelters to house other workers. The crew would clear the acreage needed to set down the navigation orb. A frantic atmosphere enveloped the Glenn. People realized that this was it—the final countdown before they moved out of the limbo of space into their future on the planet below.

Grabbing his morning coffee the next day, Jerry wasn't surprised that a much bigger crowd had already settled in the cafeteria for breakfast. He surveyed the scene as he waited his turn at the dispenser. Several men had their heads together, speaking in tight, hushed voices. He noted with concern that Conner, one of the three captains who had tried to take over the ship in '66, held the other five guys' attention. At a table across the aisle sat Lily, small and neat with her black hair pulled into a loose bun. Four other nearby women talked as she sipped tea, watching Xander show little Alice the marvels of his toy truck. Jerry called her name and she looked up, giving him a lazy wave and grin. Shelly, facing away from him, noticed the greeting and turned. A minute later, she separated herself from her clutch of friends and wandered over to join him.

"Hey, Shelly. You're up early again."

"Yeah, no one can sleep in today." She quirked her mouth into a wry smile, nodding toward the table she had just left. "Jerry, do you mind if I ask you a question for all of us?"

"Shoot."

"Do Rob and the Steering Committee have a back-up plan if this doesn't work—you know, if we can't survive on Goldilocks? Because people are stressing about landing the navigation orb. They're speculating that we'll be stranded if we make a full commitment."

She looked past him to the group of men and Jerry followed her glance. At the men's table, her big Texan of a husband, Stuart sat next to Conner. He shook his head, scowling at her.

"Rob and I haven't had time together to talk about the

landing, or anything else, Shelly. But I hear your concern. I'll mention it to him before the separation procedure. Maybe we can get a briefing set up for everyone."

"That'd be great. Thanks, Jer." The woman's face lit with a real smile, she lifted her chin at the men, then pivoted on her heel to rejoin the waiting women.

They had cause to worry, Jerry acknowledged to himself. He thought back to the first time he had seen the models of the twin space ships, the John Glenn and the Neil Armstrong, that launched together on this mission. He and Rob had been at one of the endless briefings before their voyage began when 3-D replicas were handed around for the rookies to admire. They were nothing like he imagined. Instead of a sleek aerodynamic arrow, these crafts emulated lopsided barbells. Heavy mining equipment was mounted under a sphere on one end, which also held the shuttle bay, navigation bridge and laboratories. A larger globe containing living quarters and an aquaponic bio-dome weighted the other end. A shaft connecting the two orbs housed not only offices and laboratories but the collapsible radiation sails, too. When those wings unfurled, the vessels resembled rotund dragonflies.

During the briefing, a civilian volunteered that this shape looked ridiculous. A scientist, one of the original designers, laboriously explained these ships didn't need to be built for speed. They traveled in a series of hops across space, jumping instantaneously to a region light-years away and then spending months finding and mining ore to fuel their next hop.

At home, Rob had expanded the explanation. "It's not actually hopping," he said, getting out an old fashioned textbook from one of Jerry's seminary classes. He let the tome fall open on the kitchen table and continued with a demonstration. "Imagine space as a page in this book. We bend the edge back and tuck it into the center by the spine for less than a second before it comes loose and returns to its original flat state. We manipulate just a tiny bit of space, for the barest sliver of time. The real trick, though, is to position an object on the edge of that page when it's bent. Then, in the instant it springs free returning to its normal state, it deposits the object at the outer edge."

"So the energy that gets the bent space to rebound takes the ship forward?" Jerry's tentative voice made the statement a question. "Wow, that's a hell of a jaunt."

Rob laughed. "Well, yes and no. The rebound moves the ship, but it's not like a county fair ride where you whip through the universe at a billion miles an hour. There's no actual movement. One moment you'll be here (he pointed to the book's inner spine) and in the same moment you'll be there (touching the outer edge)." He traced his finger across the width of the page. "You skip the in—between time and space that the paper itself represents. Get it?"

"You're making my brain hurt," Jerry snorted, brow creased with concentration. "So if we use the springing back motion to move the ship, why do we spend months mining ore to make fusion energy?"

"Ah," said Rob. "It's not for the spacecraft, that's true. But bending space—that takes a lot of power, even for a nano-second."

Now, as the tension in the cafeteria nagged at him, Jerry realized the anxiety sprang from this problem of power. The Steering Committee's plan to set the smaller globe on the surface would cut off any escape route and doom them, if living planet-side proved untenable. Their navigation orb, designed to separate from the mother ship as well as lift off from a stationary platform, was unwieldy. So much propellant was needed for the landing procedure they would have to discover oil fields like Earth's and build a refinery to get her up into orbit again. They had counted on a failsafe—another Earth originated flight rendezvousing with them carrying extra fuel. That wasn't happening soon, if ever.

Jerry shared Shelly's concerns with Rob over the coffee he brought back to their quarters. He hated to add more stress to his husband's load. He sat on the floor of their cramped bedroom and looked up at Rob, leaning against the pillows on the bed with his mug held in both hands. The curls of his brown hair hadn't regained their spring from the night's sleep and lay flat on one side of his face. His hazel eyes, still shadowed with fatigue, stared deep into the steaming liquid. Jerry's heart ached with his beauty.

"Shit, you're right." Rob said. "We didn't follow our own rule for complete transparency. We've been moving too fast. You'd think we learned that lesson with all the crap we've gone through."

Jerry stretched his long legs even further towards the opposite wall, easing his back. "You know, Conner sat with that group kvetching in the cafeteria. I wonder if he's stirring things up again?"

Rob sighed, and the sigh turned into a yawn. "OK, I'll gather the Committee together and plan a briefing. We better have a ship-wide vote on this, too. I don't want a mutiny before we even build the housing."

Both men sipped their coffee in silence until Rob drained

his mug. Then he swung out of bed, planted a kiss on Jerry's head and laid his cheek on the thatch of dark blonde hair. "Thanks for saving our butts again. I don't know what we'd do if people didn't trust you enough to complain to you. Spread the word, OK? We'll brief everyone as soon as possible."

In the cafeteria later that afternoon, it was Kathir who stood on a small podium made of kitchen crates. Tall and muscular, with a balding head but full black beard, he commanded the attention of the room and waited for the crowd to quiet. Jerry noticed Ayisha, an equally imposing woman, standing in the back, tracking her husband while monitoring Hailey, their 4-year-old. The little girl, unconcerned by mature subjects, pranced a carved pony between the feet of the surrounding adults. Several grown-ups indulged her with smiles, offering their shoes as miniature mountains.

When everyone hushed, Kathir opened the meeting. "We want to share with you today what our options are and how we decided to set part of the Glenn on the planet," he said. "I've asked Rob to outline the pros and cons of the alternatives. He'll clarify what the issues are and then we'll take your questions and comments. While we're preparing to land the orb, there is time to change plans. We'll vote at the end of this gathering."

Up went a hand. Kathir indicated with a nod he would allow the interruption.

"What about the people already there? Don't they get a vote too?"

Jerry recognized the speaker as the wife of a miner Rob had ferried down the first day.

Kathir reassured her. "The work crew on Goldilocks is

taking a break right now to view this town hall meeting." He raised his voice to attract the attention of the communication officer on the bridge. "Hey, Abby, can you patch in the guys on the ground?"

In a second, the three screens around the room showed various shots of twenty men and women in work overalls, holding steaming cups and watching the same feed. When they realized they were on camera, their faces erupted into grins and they began waving and hamming it up. The mood in the cafeteria lightened.

Rob stepped up and said, "Abby, leave the shot of the camp on the other screens but put my graphics up behind me, OK?"

The party scene back of the podium faded and a graph with a blue line descending from the left upper corner to the right lower corner appeared.

"We plan on landing the navigation orb because it's impossible to fit the 3-D printer in a shuttle. The communications equipment is more accessible from the ground, too. I'm hearing concern, however, that once we have part of the Glenn on the planet, we won't be able to take off again. That's a frightening scenario, because we're not certain how habitable Goldilocks will be long term. We can't know until we spend time there.

"Let's consider the variables: We're worried about the amount of fuel we have with us, since we can't generate more. Remember—back in 2066 the radiation sails were damaged in the accident. That means the engines are necessary to keep the Glenn in orbit. The graph here shows the rate at which she's now burning propellant. It's not a lot, just enough to correct our trajectory. We could maintain this fifteen years, maybe twenty.

"But the same fuel that keeps us up here is what drives the shuttles. This is how much juice a round trip shuttle run to the surface burns, not taking into account maneuvering or scouting planet-side."

A thin red scratch raised from the graph on the right, intersecting the blue line near the bottom of the screen.

"It doesn't look extravagant, does it? However, when we factor in the twenty-five trips we need to get everyone to the surface, plus rides for small equipment, we'll be using this portion of our limited fuel." Another thin wound appeared crossing the blue slant half way up.

"Landing the orb will take up a significant amount of fuel, too—not to propel it but to slow descent so it doesn't break apart at touchdown." Now the red caught the blue near the top of the chart.

"Note that we've got a small margin of extra propellant here, but not much."

The crowd, silent until then, stirred and murmured. A man's voice called, "It looks as if we have a couple of years we could keep her up before grounding her. Why not wait and see what happens?"

Rob nodded as he made eye contact with the questioner. "We tried to figure out how we might do that. The problem we ran into is that we'll still need fuel to shuttle back to the bio-dome here as we experiment with different plants and fish. We struggled to devise a scenario allowing an escape route but none gave us a way to use the shuttles to explore our new environment. That ability to fly over Goldilocks' surface without the hassles of walking or sailing may be key to our survival.

"The best case outcomes we foresee require either a commitment to stay in space and look for another habitable planet or to put every resource we have to work in settling this one. The Committee feels that Goldilocks is our leading chance for long term success."

The crowd began murmuring again, but no more questions surfaced. Sarah, the rabbi who guided the Jewish congregation on board, came forward as Rob stepped back. "This is no different from the choice the Israelites faced when God called them to leave Egypt for the promised land," she said. "Remember how they had to melt down all their gold and take with them only the things they could carry, burning their bridges behind them?

"There's no doubt in my mind we have difficult days ahead when, like those wanderers, we may look back on this little space ship and think of it as paradise. But God calls us to go forth and find a place to begin anew. The events of the last eight years confirm this call. We may be the only humans left. I say we need to follow God's lead and commit everything we have and all we are to this journey."

Imam Ahdam and Tamara, a confident but quiet representative of the Christians, came up and stood on either side of Sarah. The Muslim leader spoke hurriedly, biting off his words to project his voice into the crowd "I also believe the time to follow Allah's call into a new wilderness has arrived. I trust that Allah is with us."

Tamara nodded, her calm demeanor neutralizing his nervousness. She added, "This defines profession: Throwing in our lot with God even though we don't have all the answers. Trusting they'll unfold as we progress hand in hand with Christ."

Jerry saw Sarah's eyes narrow as she calculated the crowd's mood.

"Take a minute now," she said. "Turn to your neighbor and speak what's on your heart. Listen carefully, too. Then we'll invite more comments and questions."

The buzz in the cafeteria increased as neighbors turned toward each other and shared their reactions. Eight years ago, Jerry reflected, the people in this room would have retreated to their religious silos, willing only to talk to those of their own faith. Today, a stranger couldn't tell that three distinct religions were represented here. The small groups crossed the lines of demarcations established on Earth.

After ten minutes, Kathir came forward and calmed the group again. "What do you have to share?"

Sally Jantz, Reuben's widow, stood up. Of all the crew, she suffered the worst loss when her husband committed suicide. Her face, once round and jolly, had shriveled into permanent sadness. Jerry held his breath.

"This journey has cost the life of the person I loved most. Others have died as well. They believed in the goal of settling Goldilocks. Reuben understood it was an all-or-nothing gamble. He couldn't see it through to the end. I travel now for both of us. I say, let's quit talking and just do it."

She sat, her neighbor reaching out a hand to pat her shoulder as tears streaked her cheeks.

Jill, whose little girl was one of the third ISRU babies affectionately known as the triplets, stood. "I'm concerned for the children and the dangers they'll encounter on the planet. But it's better for us to face trouble with all our resources here than gamble on the chance of finding somewhere more suitable. There aren't any safe choices, only faithful ones."

With the women willing to throw everything into the effort of settling Goldilocks, no man would dissent. Jerry smiled as he thought of the guys he had heard second guessing the Committee in the last few weeks. None of them stepped forward with objections. Soon they counted the vote. On the Glenn and on the planet, it was unanimous. They would go ahead with the landing.

CHAPTER 2
EARTH

DATE:2062 CE

The last thing on Jerry Nichol's mind was space. He'd woken from a nightmare and was still shaking off the feeling of premonition as the auto-drive on his hauler pulled up to the driveway of the house where his landscaping crew labored, planting the cacti and drought-resistant plants favored by new builders. The dream had visited him three nights in a row: a crying child hidden somewhere in the fog. A wind that blew to no effect. His struggle to move unfruitful.

What the hell did it mean? It led him back to another issue haunting his life right now—the phrase 'Children are proof of God's hope for the future.' Was his unconscious trying to convince him to get moving on adoption?

The vehicle stopped, engine whirring, and Jerry punched in the command to back up.

'Children are proof of God's hope for the future.'

Jerry shook his head. The jumble of paper, spreading over the console of his truck matched his mood completely. Contracts and bills littered the cab mirroring the mess of his soul. He stewed in the heat, the air conditioning not up to the job of cooling him and hauling the palm tree at the same time. This phrase which dropped into his consciousness less than a month ago refused to dissolve.

He groped under the captain's chair for his ultra-shades, as the hauler began the intricate maneuvering required to back up and align its load in the driveway. Rob gave him the expensive sunglasses on their first anniversary last week. Folks developed cataracts at younger and younger ages now. He slid them onto his face and told himself he needed to appreciate his husband more. The jerky movements of the rig ground to a halt. Instead of jumping out, he slumped in his seat, staring out the front window at the unflinchingly bright sky, dimmed by the brown tint of the glasses.

The group had met two weeks ago in St. Anne's library, a small room off the main sanctuary with abandoned books on cases lining one wall and cast off chairs and sofas circled in the middle. They named him the nominal leader of the class because he was studying to become their local priest. Actually, they came together to find comfort and meaning in their lives. Of the eight people present, none had read the assigned book.

Hank and Dawn sprawled on a worn out love seat, his arm slung over her shoulder. Young, fit, and carefully groomed, they might have been models. He worked at SpaceTech, a scientist like Rob, while she clerked at the local bank. In the dim lighting of the second hand lamps, Jerry thought she looked annoyed but then she snuggled in close as if claiming Hank. The conversation stumbled onto their struggle with deciding whether to have children.

"So I know it's not right for everyone, but it's important to me to bear a baby. Maybe, you know, that's God's calling to us." Dawn's pale face flushed.

Her boyfriend glanced down his nose at the top of her head, "Honey, I don't think God wants any little kid subjected to the future the Earth has coming. We'll be lucky to escape the crisis if we live beyond sixty." He looked around at the shadowed faces.

Letitia snorted. "Yeah, that's what all my men say when we start talking marriage commitment. People have been offering up that chicken shit line to avoid the hard work of love since the Garden of Eden."

"No really, I'm serious," Hank took his arm from Dawn's shoulder and leaned forward into the group. "Check out the facts. The outcome is unmistakable. Earth is this close to disaster. If the civil and religious unrest doesn't blow us up first, the ozone layer will erode in forty years and then we're toast. Right, Rob?" He glanced at Jerry's partner scowling at him from the corner chair. "All I'm saying is, if we produce a baby we can't protect it, can't give it a future. Why add to our own inevitable grief? It makes more sense to take what pleasure we can now, 'cause the good times ain't gonna last."

As Hank settled back with a smirk, the room erupted in several voices offering counter theories to his pessimism. The newscasts always featured experts on both sides of climate change stories and quotes from the optimists peppered the conversation.

"I heard an MIT scientist yesterday say pollution levels are dropping and the greenhouse effect could be reversed in five years."

"Yeah, and a new desalination plant came on-line last week. That will give the world water to live on for a century," Frank offered.

Jerry observed the interplay noting Rob's deepening frown, his lips pressed together. He noticed Dawn had dropped out of the discussion, fighting back tears as the debate swirled around her.

In a pause, he asked, "Dawn, what is important to you about having children?"

She shook her head as if to clear it. "It's hard to talk about this. Hank says it's only an instinct, an animal urge making sure our species continues. He's probably right, but there's this pull deep in my gut..." She raised her gaze from the frayed carpet to look Jerry in the eye. "The feeling is precious to me. I want to follow and see where it leads. I remember all my life, my mother saying, 'Children are proof of God's hope for the future.' I need to hold that hope in my arms."

The moment she said this, Jerry understood. He didn't have the biological urge, but still he yearned for children. Marriage gave him happiness and security. Commitment to the Church, re-established after years of absence, connected him with a larger family and a wider meaning for life. But parenting a child would bind him to the future in a way not achievable by spouse or congregation. He too wanted to hold God's hope in his arms and live the possibility of creation.

Outside the windshield, a flash of red caught his attention. An old model family van, with semi-auto pilot, pulled up to the curb. Manny, his landscaping foreman, appeared and trotted over to the car at once. Jerry recognized Manny's wife in the front seat and tensed, knowing she wouldn't interrupt the work day without an important reason. The morning news of the Sugarland gang attacks at the middle school in a nearby town flitted through his mind. He leaned out his side window, cocking his head to catch the tone of their conversation.

Their rapid Spanish sounded upbeat though Jerry couldn't identify any of the phrases. Out of the passenger side popped a little boy, seven or eight years old—a miniature Manny, square and solid. He held a golden trophy, two-thirds his own size, in front of him offering it up to his dad. The big man squatted to wrap his arms around both child and prize at once. Then they walked up to Jerry's truck.

"Hey, boss, see what my Joe won. First place in the regional soccer play-off. Each kid on the team got one. Pretty neat, huh?" Manny's great weather-beaten hand ruffled silky black hair on the child's head as he beamed his pride. Under the caress, wide eyes considered Jerry.

His throat tight with longing, Jerry managed a small smile back. "That's cause for celebration, man. Better break out the sodas. Help yourself to whatever you want, Joe."

As the boy ran to the cooler by the side of the house, Manny murmured, "Thanks, boss. It's the first thing he's ever won. He wanted to show me before anyone else."

"No problem. You need some time with them?"

"Nah, Didi's taking him to school. I've got to get that palm planted before its roots dry out."

Jerry eyed the rear-view mirror, watching two other workers unload the young tree. "Yeah, well I hope it survives. I'm giving up planting palms if this drought lasts another year. I'll see you back at the yard, Manny."

Heartache edged into anger as Jerry started up the hauler. Why the hell couldn't he have it all? Other gay couples had children. While New Mexico wasn't the most liberal state, it was better than the southern bastions of conservative ideology. Even if no one else in the Mirage schools had two daddies, children were resilient and adaptable.

The outside community hadn't thrown up the real barrier, though, and he knew it. He needed Rob on-board.

Jerry hadn't been thinking of kids when they first hooked up. The miracle of finding someone to love took all his attention. Later they talked of children, but Rob sounded like Hank minus the cynicism. He'd said he required proof that the world would turn itself around before encouraging more people to populate it. They turned their focus as a couple to other joint ventures—acquiring a house, negotiating a common schedule, creating a balance of give and take. A year into their marriage, neither of them had mentioned adoption again. It appeared out of range given Rob's interests and the number of hours he put in at SpaceTech.

'Children are proof of God's hope for the future.' The saying beat in his head, insistent and clear despite the fact Dawn and Hank had separated soon after that meeting. Maybe I can make him understand, he thought.

Half an hour later, the truck arrived at the nursery, pulling up in front of a line of saplings wilted and drooping in their tubs. Not even noon and the exposed young plants looked like they were on death row. Opening the door, Jerry cast a baleful glance at the cloudless sky, sweat slicking his forehead. He grabbed the invoice for the job he had just visited from the litter on the console, then activated the windows' reflective shades. Sometimes it felt as if every invention in the last five years involved outsmarting the sun.

Who knew how long he could keep the landscaping business going as the climate deteriorated? Jobs continued to come in as new builds and frustrated homeowners hired him to tear up their irrigating systems and design xeriscape yards. At some point, though, people might give up and let everything bake. What would he do if he lost the nursery?

Unfortunately, the answer led him back to Rob. If the

company and his job collapsed, they'd have to cut corners, but his husband's paycheck was rock solid. Rob's position as a biologist with one of the top three most innovative companies in the world meant they didn't worry about layoffs for him.

However, it required them to remain in Mirage, the little backwater town which existed to support SpaceTech's population. Well, if set free from outside work, the opportunity for parenting became even more appealing. Jerry could see himself as a stay at home dad. But what about Rob?

He pushed open the door to the greenhouse, breathing in air twenty degrees cooler. The humid, rich smell of fertilizer and top soil mixed with soft notes of rose and lavender. The fewer green trees and shrubs people grew outside, the more greenery they brought inside. Flo, managing this part of the business, masterfully re-potted and trimmed stock to meet the market. He offered up a prayer of gratitude for her skill.

A grouping of small wrought-iron tables and matching chairs with bright striped cushions took up most of the entryway space. As he negotiated his way around them, Jerry nodded a greeting to the six elderly men and women sipping iced coffee. "Hola, padre," a gnarled little man with liver spots on his bald head said.

"I'm not your padre yet," snorted Jerry. "Don't rush me. Soon enough you'll wish you left me in the pews."

A round grandma in a pastel muumuu eyed his battered jeans and dirt streaked tee-shirt. "I could sew up that hole at your knee if you want. Wouldn't take me but a few minutes."

"Eleanor, not even you can make me look respectable."

The group issued good natured protests and banter, but Jerry waved and moved on. He learned from experience that if he stopped for conversation, they sucked up the work hours before he realized it. These seniors were refugees from the hot weather. Not rich enough to run air conditioning continually, they bounced between the nursery, the library and St. Anne's, dropping in to spend the worst part of the day in a cool environment. He made a mental note: Check with Flo about our water supply.

He rounded the empty sales counter, filing his bill before heading to the back. A com's cheerful ring tone played in the distance, then cut off abruptly. Flo's tobacco raspy voice shouted, "That you, boss? Rob's calling." She emerged from his office, handing him his wrist communicator with a conspirator's smile on her tanned and wrinkled face. "I didn't tell him you left it on your desk again."

"Yeah, but I heard that," Rob laughed, sounding tinny on the speaker. "No wonder I couldn't get hold of you."

Jerry bemoaned his forgetfulness, even though they both knew he overlooked the com on purpose, craving silence and his own thoughts. He realized his spouse wouldn't criticize his habit as he apologized for once again having to stay late at work. One argument avoided, another part of his mind debated: Should I say something now? Is it better to give him a heads up or talk to him later? Only when he signed off did he realize, he'd once again held his tongue to sidestep conflict. Crap, he chided himself, I'm twenty-eight. I've got to stand up for myself.

He went into his cubicle, cluttered and unkempt as his truck, and sat on a high stool in front of the drafting table he used as a desk. He called up his computer and then touched the marker for the adoption agency he found last night, lingering over the picture of a happy baby shown on the home page. Clicking on the button for interested adoptive parents, he saw a list of needed forms. This was just the start. Background checks, psychological exams, interviews would invade their lives once they started. Rob had to desire a child too or, no matter how suitable their family, no match could be made.

What will I do if he says no? Jerry thought. What if he can't stretch that far?

No answer dropped from the universe. Like most things, he chose the road he saw most clearly, trusting the path to unfold. He sensed the pull towards parenthood as if a compass needle urged him north. Well, he told himself, the first step is to talk with Rob. And every step after that, he knew, would fall forward into the next one.

On Friday nights, Rob usually made it home for dinner so Jerry planned the next night's meal to please him. Somewhere in the maze of his unconscious he equated gastronomic success with easing his husband down the path into parenthood. He left work early, depending on his crew to finish up their projects and Flo to get the greenhouse ready for the weekend, and went shopping for fresh vegetables and fish.

Good fish presented a challenge in New Mexico. It also made up their favorite meal, one of those little points of total agreement which binds a couple together. Three stops into his quest, Jerry scored trout that had just arrived from the aquaponic farms in Idaho. He hurried home to begin his preparations.

The small, southwestern townhouse they bought before their wedding formed another link in the chain of their relationship. They both reveled in the sense of permanence owning their own place gave them. Rob embraced the light-filled space as a respite from the institutional grayness of his office. Jerry used his skills as a landscape artist in the tiny courtyard, amazed at how good it felt to create a corner of peace for them both.

He plunked his shopping bags on the kitchen counter, reaching to pull the cord opening vertical shade panels on the sliding glass doors. They swished back; the sun pouring into the yellow and white room, warming the cooled atmosphere. A twinge of guilt about pushing up the air conditioning nagged at him, but he loved looking at the small patio. Whenever he cooked, he wanted to view the cacti and mesquite trees around the brick pavement. He made a mental note to fill the hummingbird feeders, tuned his com into his favorite jazz music station, and turned to his task.

Cooking soothed Jerry. The attention needed to chop and sauté, to bread and bake, kept him occupied enough that he didn't brood over dark possibilities. His simple plan unfolded with little conscious thought. When Rob got home, he would show him the adoption information over dinner and then they would go to the concert at church.

He heard the front door open and shut with Rob's characteristic restraint. Intent on slicing an onion, he didn't turn around, waiting for his husband to announce himself. When the silence drew long, he shifted to glance over his shoulder, and saw Rob gazing at him from the hall archway. He stood there, hands at his side and his mouth crooked in a little smile, looking half his twenty-nine years—a junior high kid dressed in his father's button—down shirt.

"Hey, you're home. Great. I thought we'd eat early and catch the quartet at St. Anne's. Marjo says they're really something."

"Yeah, that's fine," Rob replied.

Jerry looked again, setting his knife aside. The words were right, but a dinginess muddied the tone. Rob's warm brown eyes sagged tired and sad. His body turned in on itself. A warning chill pricked at Jerry's intuition. He'd seen this before in his partner, brilliant with ideas but slow to process emotion. Had something happened? Or was this just fatigue?

Jerry wiped his fingers on a towel and crossed the space between them. He wrapped both hands around the back of Rob's neck and bowed his head the few inches it took to gently bump their foreheads together. "You doing all right?" he asked.

Even before Rob answered, he sensed him relaxing, leaning into the embrace. An odor of floor wax and old metal, the SpaceTech office bouquet, lingered on the tight curls of his close-cropped brown hair.

Rob reached up to gently and precisely trace the angle of his spouse's jaw. "All shall be well, and all shall be well."

Jerry eased back and smiled. That's so Rob, he thought. He can't explain his emotions but he can quote the passage of a book I read to him a month ago. "Go get changed. Dinner will be ready in half an hour."

As he returned to his cooking, an unsettled atmosphere

lingered, as if a monsoon was brewing. He questioned his plan to bring up adoption tonight, wondering if he should delay. But as he set dark blue plates on yellow mats, he solidified his resolve. Better to speak now. Rob might take days to share what was eating at him. To wait meant that the moment, and his courage, would pass.

He placed a printout of the adoption agency's information by his fork. It showed the picture of two beaming men standing close together cradling a baby festooned in pink on the top page. Then he sought out his husband. He peered through their bedroom doorway at Rob sitting on the bed, jeans, a green polo shirt and right shoe on but holding the left suspended in the air. His eyes focused on a vision Jerry couldn't see.

"Hey man, dinner's ready," he ventured. Was he intruding on a prayer?

His partner startled and looked over at him. He didn't smile. The breeze off a glacial premonition touched Jerry again, but Rob shook his head and gave a self-deprecating laugh. "Yeah, coming... I'm spacing out here."

As they sat for the fish and grilled vegetables, his husband chatted about office gossip and asked how Jerry's day had gone. He never glanced at the papers lying on the table, as oblivious to the hope they represented as to their physical presence. Jerry tensed. He tried retreating from annoyance at his partner's lack of empathy, until irritation spilled over into action.

He picked up the printout and handed it to his husband. "Take a look at this," he urged. "Remember when we talked about becoming parents someday? This may be the answer for us... adopting a child who really needs a family."

Taking the brochure, Rob sat back in his chair and Jerry experienced the intimacy between them drop away. Rob's eyes lost focus. His hands gripped the paper, so the edges crumpled. That this man, always precise in his actions, mangled the article confirmed the atmosphere of tension hanging over them. Something shadowed their conversation now, maybe their whole relationship. No longer able to ignore it, Jerry clenched his teeth against words of challenge or conciliation. Wait, he told himself, willing his husband to speak. Wait until he lets me in.

Rob laid the printout aside and smoothed out its edges. Then he spoke in a flat tone, not meeting Jerry's eyes, "Why don't we skip the concert tonight, Jer? I want to walk in the garden."

A long pause sucked at the air between the two men as Jerry processed this suggestion. The desert park of the local community college was their safe place where Rob, always slightly paranoid about being bugged and spied on, felt secure. They used it early on as they fumbled toward partnering when Rob wasn't sure of his employer's approval of their courtship. It turned out, he needn't have worried. There was great tolerance for any personal living arrangements at SpaceTech.

Jerry nodded assent. While it troubled him that his partner thought such privacy necessary, the usual buoyancy of his nature promised they could handle it together. Rob always sees problems more often than opportunities, he mused, at least in relationships.

The rest of their mundane dinner talk skittered over the surface of all that wasn't being said. They stacked dirty dishes in the sink and headed for the car. Jerry breathed easier now they were moving towards conversation, but still teetered on the edge of uneasy anticipation.

Rob maintained silence until they arrived. As they got out of their vehicle in the deserted parking lot, the day tipped into evening, the stultifying heat turning down a few notches to make walking bearable. They struck out on familiar paths, passing by the saguaros and barrel cacti, the mesquites and Palos Verdes in this unique garden. The trail, smooth and wide, allowed them to walk side by side. Jerry, breathing deeply, restrained his urgent questions. He knew enough to let his husband find his own pace.

Not looking at him, Rob began. "Jer, I need to share this with you. It could damage my career if it gets out before it's announced. I want to tell you though. I can't decide without you."

Okay then, something work related has him stirred up, Jerry thought, watching his partner, listening for emotions under the matter-of-fact words. Rob met his eyes, but dropped them before continuing.

"You understand there's only a fifty/fifty chance Earth will survive the current environmental crisis with the ability to sustain life, right? Well, the percentages lower dramatically if you add in the civil wars in the Middle East and India over their power grids, epidemics popping up in Canada and the continuing drought in Africa. Here in the States our standard of living, even our democracy, may not last if we can't deliver more water to both urban and rural areas. The desalination projects have yet to produce enough to warrant their cost."

As he went on, Jerry recognized a familiar professor mode, but with an angry edge he hadn't previously detected.

"Bottom line is this: I've been working with a team for

over a year, putting together a plan to send a remnant of humanity into space. We found another world, a goldilocks planet." Rob darted a quick look up, but then focused again on the path. "It has just the right conditions to sustain human life. The technology to get us there exists. We have ships that, with retrofitting, will make the trip. Until this morning though, we didn't have a realistic way to gather enough money to pull it off. But now... Now I'm sure we really can succeed. Dagmar's convinced the appropriations committee to recommend that the government sponsor our experiment. With the private donations already in hand, we could launch in two years, maybe sooner."

Jerry's vision darkened as he tried to comprehend Rob's report. "So you'll be too busy for a family as this comes together?"

"No, Jer," Rob breathed out, slowing to a stop, eyes still on his shoes. "I want to go. I want you to come with me. I want to live and give any children we have a chance for a future. Hell, I want to offer humanity a future." He raised his face and looked at his spouse.

Jerry realized that he had lived together with this man for a year with no dissensions greater than grumblings over toothpaste brands and how often to water the plants. Now Rob's words revealed a landscape to his inner reality he had never shown before. As Jerry considered him, his heart balanced precariously on a high cliff above that unknown and god-forsaken country. What could he do with this challenge confronting his most basic assumptions, not only about his life but about all Life?

He jerked his eyes away from his spouse, keeping them unfocused as he strode down the path, scuffed work boots crunching on the gravel.

Rob trotted to keep up, a professor turned supplicant. "Jer?" He reached out. "C'mon, talk to me."

"What should I say?" demanded Jerry, still charging ahead. "I told you everything I wanted, everything I need, and now you tell me you want to leave Earth? What kind of crazy shit is that?"

Even as his words left his mouth, he knew them to be false. The last thing Rob suffered was craziness. When he gave any bet a fifty percent chance, Jerry backed it one hundred percent. He understood in his bones that his husband's nature tended towards caution and understatement, not frantic hysterics. If Rob believed the odds for earth's survival had devolved to this extent, well... Rage and panic twisted his gut and his senses—sight, smell, hearing, touch—all retracted, leaving him isolated on the precipice he had labeled reality, terrified of slipping off.

An urgent voice reached him in his blindness. "Jer, stop and listen. Hear it all. I'll tell you everything: everything I understand, everything I'm afraid of, everything I think might be possible. Just listen and then, if you can't go with me, I'll stay with you. I promise."

It was the promise that brought his feet to a halt. That, and Rob's openness to children... Jerry turned slowly, taking a deep breath, and managed a nod. "OK. I'm listening."

Many hours later they came back, hand in hand, to the dark house where the warm scent of grilled onions and fish was just a faint fog, a memory dispersing. They paused for a moment, easing the door shut, not ready to turn on the lights. Standing there in the hallway, Rob circled his arms around Jerry and rested his head on his shoulder, holding him steady.

In the darkness, Jerry felt weariness settle over his body, the fatigue of a traveler who has come far, but has still farther to go. The major conflict he avoided throughout his life with all his cunning, all his strength, had at last found him. Love is such a dangerous thing, he thought. If I choose to understand this man, to look honestly at the interior landscape of his soul, I have to give up the cozy fiction that he's like me. All I can do is move one step closer to the stranger and one step away from my own certainty.

He breathed in the scent of his lover, still warm with the garden's air, and hugged Rob back. He would pass over this first chasm, submit to change, remain faithful. Yet deep in that place where truth hides, Jerry knew: There would never again be smooth ground under their feet. The world itself had become transitory, ephemeral—a being liable to death.

CHAPTER 3
ORBITING PLANET KOI-3284

DATE: 2073 CE/ 1

On the Glenn, Jerry climbed the steps into the shuttle, following Lily. She paused, looking back at the cavernous bay.

"I never thought it would be so hard to leave."

Jerry smiled into her sad eyes. "It's been home a long time."

"Yeah, this is the last place I saw Alex."

"And where your baby was born. It holds a lifetime of memories."

The engineers hadn't built the mining shuttle for comfort. The interior, gutted of equipment, still reeked of sweat from miners who had daily risked their lives to bring them the fuel and water sustaining them those years in space. Jump seats, hard squares of metal folding down from the walls, were the only places to sit. Six people already claimed the ones near the front, so Jerry and Lily made their way to the back and strapped in.

Rob's face appeared in the cockpit door as he surveyed his cargo. "Hey, there you guys are."

He disappeared as quickly as he had come and then seven-year-old Xander preceded him into the main cabin, dragging his feet.

"We'll get going in a moment, folks," Rob said as he walked hunched to the back of the shuttle, herding the boy in front of him. "Be sure your harnesses are tight against your bodies. It tends to be a bumpy ride. Find your airsick bags on the underside of the seats."

"You make a cute stewardess," Jerry teased him, as his spouse adjusted Xander's belt, tightening the straps that anchored him to the wall of the craft.

Rob grinned, reached under the seat and handed the child a long narrow bag. "It's a short trip, but the wind when we hit the atmosphere whips us around a lot." He leaned over to examine Lily's harness, tugging it tighter and then adjusted Jerry's. "OK, my dears. We're ready to roll. Next stop Goldilocks."

Jerry watched him tunnel back up to the cockpit, testing other passengers' harnesses and reassuring them as he went. Before he ducked through the door he turned, met Jerry's eye and smiled.

The shuttle ride to the surface progressed smoothly. Travelers looked at each other's apprehensive faces for the whole hour and a half trip, but the planet relented in their case. A few bumps caused them to brace but nothing awful or sustained followed. Even the landing, screaming through the atmosphere until the wheels hit with a thump and jolted over a wash boarded dirt road, wasn't terrible. When Rob returned to spring the outside hatch, he beamed at them. "Smoothest run I've had yet. Goldilocks must be happy to have you."

Xander wriggled, trying to undo the harness and get out to meet his new home, but Lily held him back saying, "Wait your turn."

Jerry, freed from his own constraints, reached over to help him and whispered, "Go out easy, kiddo. Take time—see and hear and sniff. Not many people experience an unexplored planet. Make this first contact count."

The boy nodded and smiled. "You too. Then we can compare notes later."

"Right you are." Jerry released him as the doorway cleared and he bounded up to it, pausing before stepping out. Lily, on her son's heels, admonished him to be careful. And then it was Jerry's turn.

Light reached out and surrounded him, drenching the world in a tint golden as honey. It reminded him of something—a hue that infused New Mexico at dawn. He'd seen it many times at sunrise on Earth, but it was sixteen hundred hours here—halfway into the thirty-two-hour cycle. He marveled, will the sun's rays always be this luscious?

In front of him a paler yellow spread right to the horizon. After a moment, Jerry's brain caught up with his eyes and saw it as knee high grass of some sort. He descended the stairs of the shuttle and moved around to the other side of the craft. There he glimpsed five long rows of Quonset-like huts, curved roof lines forming a large pentagon he knew anchored the transparent plastic canopy over the main kitchen and dining area. The hastily constructed bio-dome, waiting to receive plants and fish, stood half a mile away from the habitation zone. What direction is that? he wondered. He'd have to readjust his internal compass, unused for the last eight years in space.

The human structures were easier to recognize than the natural landscape markers of Goldilocks herself. In the distance, behind the bio-dome, mountains rose. The peaks of land appeared familiar even though the colors looked off, a turquoise haze settling over them. He squinted, but couldn't decide whether they were far away or very near. He could discern the details of sharp valleys running up their sides, and yellow vegetation growing up to a definitive line on the steep slopes. That indicated they weren't tall. Kind of like miniature Tetons, Jerry mused.

Up close, the landscape disturbed him even more. A group of towering plants he took to be trees on inspection looked similar to broccoli. Each rose in a sweeping arc of deep green from the ground up to a crown of purplish tiny buds. On one side of the makeshift town, these trees grew in circular patterns of ten to twelve in a group, each one averaging twenty to thirty feet tall. The saffron grass flourished right up to the edge of the strange forest but terminated at their roots. No hint of the yellow intermixed with the dense, dark viridity.

Jerry took a breath and relished the crisp air. It smelled rich, laden with a familiar scent. He tried to pin it down: vanilla and a whiff of that spicy bouquet that rises from a pine woods on a hot afternoon. The breeze ruffling his hair felt warm and inviting. He realized he was smiling. Maybe, he thought, just maybe we've landed in the garden of Eden, after all.

The illusion of paradise held only about the time it took Jerry to wade through the swaying yellow grass to the habitations. As he ducked through a round portal, following Xander and Lily up the hall that opened into a space the size of the Glenn's cafeteria, the wind picked up. The opaque industrial grade plastic arching five feet above his head shivered. A wavering sound, like uneven waves on a distant beach, resonated through the room. Near the entrance a work crew, gathered to review directions before heading out to do more construction, moaned and cursed as the racket increased.

"We thought you were bringing us good luck," Aiysha called. "Can't you get this wind to die down, just until we finish this last bath house?"

"Sorry, I don't have that kind of influence here yet." Jerry had to raise his voice to carry above the commotion. He turned to Rob coming in on his heels. "Is it always this loud?"

"Oh, this is mild. It becomes white noise after a while. Wait until the storms really howl. They keep everyone awake at night. We've been printing out earplugs, but the parents don't want to use them in case their kids need something. It does get on our nerves."

Sarah, welcoming each of these late comers with a hug, said, "Eli's inventing a device to protect us when we have to go outside in the worst wind. It's a kind of force field. I vote for taking him off any other job until he gets it up and running."

Eli, hurrying by on his way to join the construction crew, caught the remark. He frowned at Sarah. "I'm working on it every spare minute I've got. I'll have a prototype for you to try out by next week. This pressure doesn't help, you know." Without a glance at the newcomers, he ducked into the hall that led to the portal and disappeared.

"Wow, what's with him?" Lily said, as Sarah blushed.

"We've all been a bit on edge," she admitted.

Her face brightened as Tamara joined her, com-pad at ready, to assign them their quarters. The little crowd dispersed, dividing between four of the five long low halls that surrounded the shared space. Jerry hoisted his duffel to his shoulder and between them Rob and he carried Lily's bulging bag while she held Xander's hand and his backpack.

"So how did you decide who went where?" he asked his spouse as they hiked single file through the narrow hallway. "Are we in religious ghettos?"

"No. We decided that the children needed to be near each other so we put everyone with kids in the blue hall where we are. Then we tried for a balanced mix in the others. The fifth hall holds workspace right now. We'll be able to expand more when we land the Glenn's orb. Here's the bathroom for our section."

They squeezed past the swinging door to let Shelly and her daughter squeak out into the passageway. "Hey, welcome home, guys," she said, as the little girl grinned up at them. "Are you ready to start school again, Xander? Alice has been missing you."

Xander scrunched up his face at the mention of school. "Alice should go to classes but I'm big enough to help with building, right Mom?"

"I don't think so," came Lily's quick reply. "No worries, Shelly. He'll be there tomorrow. Where are you setting up?"

"Our room's in the red hall. We're only doing a few hours a day, Xander. You'll have plenty of time to help the adults. But remember to take it easy, all of you. It takes a while to get used to the gravity and length of days."

"That's right," said Rob, herding on their little family. "I should have reminded everyone about the stronger gravitation here."

Jerry could sense the pull, now he was thinking about it,

as if the planet tried to fasten him to herself. At each footstep she only reluctantly gave up his sole and seemed eager to embrace his foot as it touched down again. The sensation resembled running up a slight hill.

Their rooms were in the middle of the hall. They had grown accustomed to conserving space on the ship, so the small quarters didn't distress them: Two minuscule bedrooms flanking a bit of common area. It was the most luxurious suite the site offered. Workers had cannibalized desks, sofas and beds from the Glenn and arranged them in the same order here. Only the convenient bathroom was missing. Lily and Xander headed into one bedroom to organize their stuff while the men investigated theirs'.

As Jerry swung his duffel onto the bed and unpacked his clothes, Rob sat and watched. "I'm glad we had a smooth ride today, Jer. It's been rough down here, though. Six weeks is too long to be apart. Now that everyone is here, maybe we'll be more positive."

His husband paused in his chores and cocked his head. Rob had mentioned no community unrest on his flights up to retrieve crew and materials. "Yeah, I noticed that exchange with Eli. He's usually the best natured of us all. What is it? This should be a happy time. Is the wind getting on everyone's nerves?"

"People blame the weather, but I suspect it's something else, too. The children love this place already, but the adults... They feel let down not finding the Armstrong here or any message from Earth."

When the Glenn finally made it to Goldilocks, discovering that their sister ship had not yet arrived was more than a disappointment. Some had even fantasized that a SpaceTech drone would be waiting for them with news that all was well at home and a rendezvous ship was on its way. Sorrow at losing these improbable hopes tempered their joy in completing the difficult eight year journey.

Jerry sighed. "We've been orbiting Goldilocks for three months now. Haven't we gotten used to being alone?"

"You'd think, right? But I sense it too. The fact we might be the only humans left just wasn't real until our feet hit the ground. Being on a world with other living things, plants and fish, birds and bugs, may trigger it. I guess we realize we're not only the first people to see them but the only ones who will. It's as if this planet is asking us to forget who we were and start over."

Jerry sat beside his partner, silent for a moment. Then he said, "I remember when I moved to Mirage, I spent a lot of time longing for California. I talked about how I missed the cities, the ocean, the music scene. I complained so much that at a party one night this guy, Mickey, told me to quit kvetching and get to know New Mexico and the gifts it offered. He was right of course. I did finally suck it up and become a true New Mexican—but I needed to grieve where I came from first."

"Yeah, maybe that's it. I wonder, though..."

Jerry peered at his husband's face as Rob bit his lip, staring at the floor. "What do you wonder, Love?"

"There's a different atmosphere on this planet." Rob hesitated as he spoke, frowning. "The gravity, the time, the way it doesn't tilt and so there's no change in the seasons— everything contributes to the strangeness. But, Jer, there's something else too. I don't know how to explain it. It's like it pulls at the beat of our hearts."

The next morning, Jerry got up to find that Xander had woken early and Lily, just rising herself, asked him to go check on the boy. On his way to the commons, he found Shelly and primary teacher Golda Malaki with the space-born children in the hall which led to the outside portal.

"Don't worry, Jerry," Golda said. "I made sure Xander ate a good breakfast. We're headed out for games before we start our studies."

Xander waved at his uncle as the younger seven-year-olds, Saphir, and Isaac, vied for the older boy's attention, arguing and jostling to get close to him. The six-year-olds, Liam, Marnie and Hailey, tugged at the women, urging them to hurry. Little Alice ignored them all as she skipped on ahead.

"Are you taking the kids out today?" Jerry asked, his voice tinged with worry. He saw the view screens in the common area from where he stood. While the wind wasn't as strong as the gale which had blown all night, it still tossed the broccoli trees' branches around.

"Wait up, Honey," Shelly called to her daughter before turning to answer. "Yes. These kids need to work off some energy so they can concentrate."

"We say hello to the day." Marnie, the most serious of the six-year-olds, said. "It's only polite."

Jerry smiled at her. The little girl's ability to articulate seemed precocious, but he recalled that all the children had so many adults interacting with them that their language skills developed early. "Well, I guess you're right about that. Please greet the day for me too, Marnie."

She nodded. "OK. I will, Uncle Jerry. But you should go outside soon too. The world is happier there."

Still smiling at this diminutive philosopher, Jerry wandered through their walled city's center connecting with the other religious leaders. He asked each to gather with him in a corner after they finished their breakfast so they could talk about how to address the tension brewing in their community. Sarah, the rabbi, agreed, looking relieved to have the problem named, and promised to round up her assistant, Aaron. Ahdam, the imam, nodded his assent and Kathir the Muslims' cantor said, "Great. We should have thought of that."

Then Jerry approached a small group of diners gathered around the Christian leaders, Steve and Tamara Smith. As he came up, he realized Steve was complaining about living conditions on the planet.

"I don't know how we expect to exist on this miserable rock. I can't even stand up straight when I'm outside ninety percent of the time."

As usual, his wife tried to smooth over his discontent. "It is hard but we've made amazing progress so far."

She looked up and saw Jerry on the edge of their circle. "How great to see you. I'm so glad we have everybody down from the Glenn now. Would you like to join us for breakfast?"

Jerry smiled back, warmed by her graciousness but noting the scowl on her husband's face. "Thanks, Tamara. It's good to be here, finally. I won't sit. Rob and Lily will be here soon. I just wanted to ask if you and Steve would meet me and the rest of the religious leaders after your meal. We need to talk about designing some kind of service to say goodbye to our old life and help get us ready for our future here on Goldilocks."

Steve snarled. "What gives you the right to call any of

us together. You're not even technically part of the Christian congregation."

Shocked silence met this remark, his dining companions glancing between the two men. Shelly sitting across the table said, "Steve, what are you talking about? Of course Jerry is part of our community."

Tamara stood up, blocking out direct contact with her husband as she murmured to Jerry, "Yes, we'll come. Please excuse my husband. He's had a rough night. You know—having trouble getting used to the new sleep pattern."

"OK, then." Jerry said, nodding to the group as he turned to leave. "Let's gather by the coffee machine in half an hour." He glanced over his shoulder and saw Steve frowning at him as he left.

Rob and Lily arrived, grabbing a table on the other side of the room. As Jerry threaded through the diners, he recalled a conversation with his mentor Marjo back on Earth. The politicians controlling funding for their mission had insisted that the three major faith traditions in America—Muslim, Jewish, and Christian—be represented in the settler population. They weren't picky about which denominations should be included, as long as they were mainstream enough to shore up ratings with their various constituents. The scientists, though, needed a crew they could work with—people open to collaboration. Marjo noted that they should choose groups receptive to mystery, ready to discover new insights about God as their experience of the natural world expanded. "Mystics", she had declared. "You need to find sects in these religions which respect and teach wonder—an openness to the divine which admits to not knowing."

Rob passed Marjo's wisdom on to the committee vetting

potential settlers, but the scientists remained prejudiced against the thought of religious groups fostering inquiring minds. Then, when the plague hit Earth, they had been in such a hurry to get a crew on the ships to avoid contamination, they hardly screened the applicants. Had that been a fatal mistake? wondered Jerry. On the Glenn, they forged a community where these three expressions of faith were equal to each other and the scientists, but it took great effort. Would that tentative respect hold in this new environment?

Steve still bristled with hostile energy when they circled up with coffee cups in hand half an hour later. Tamara clenched her teeth, her usual sunny face glum and rigid.

Jerry decided to dive right in. "It's been a long six weeks. As part of the last group to come down, I didn't realize how difficult the transition was for those of you who transported earlier."

"You just got here," Steve said, his frown deepening with his words. "You have no idea how irritating this planet is."

"Yep, you're right. I'm wondering though if the seven of us could ease the tension by addressing the trauma of finding the Armstrong still missing."

"They're all dead, like we'll be dead in a year or two." The Christian leader focused on the ground in front of him. His wife put her hand on his shoulder and leaned toward him, but he shook her off and crossed his arms on his chest.

Sarah said, "We're all afraid of that catastrophic scenario, Steve. But Jerry's right. We can confront our fear by facing what we now know must have happened to our sister ship."

"It's more than just the Armstrong," Kathir added, his deep voice thick with sorrow. "Since we haven't heard from Earth, we need to accept the fact we may be the last remnant of humans in the universe. That's a devastating thought and a heavy, heavy responsibility."

"Right," his Muslim companion, Adham said. "All the more reason to hold tight to our humanity, our traditions, and morals."

Tamara sat up straighter, glancing at her belligerent spouse. "But don't new circumstances, and a foreign context, require innovative responses? I think being human is a matter of considering our reactions and then adapting. We need to transform ourselves to thrive in this strange place."

"Yes," Jerry said, nodding. "If we can somehow lay our past hopes and dreams aside, we'll be see the future more clearly. I hope some kind of ceremony would set that up."

Sarah nodded, "Good idea. Let's also help people get ready for such a service. We could sit Shiva for the dead."

Steve roused, scowling again as he looked around the group. "If we're going to mourn humanity, let's just do our own thing. I don't want to blunder through some Jewish ritual."

Tamara leaned away from her husband. "Cut it out, Steve. This isn't the time to retreat into little silos. Call it a wake if you want, but we can all sit and grieve together. That's what being human means."

"Yes," Kathir said. "Our future depends on us collaborating. How fitting then that we lay the past to rest in unity."

Steve's arms clenched across his chest and he looked at the floor. Jerry feared he might get up and leave, so he blurted, "God isn't finished with us yet, Steve. I'm sure God has a hand in the mix of evolution. The question isn't whether we should change our ways. The question is how do we align our growth to God's pattern, to become more connected with our creator."

"You say that like you know what you're talking about." The scorn in Steve's voice poisoned the air. "But all we really know is that if we don't adapt we die. Maybe that's what God wants us to do—die."

For a few heart beats everyone's mouths hung open and silent. Then Ahdam spoke, facing the tortured man, "My friend, I so often agree with you, but this time I'm bewildered. Our God, the God of both our religions, is the Lord of Life, not Death. We're challenged to find life on this new world." He reached out and placed a hand on Steve's shoulder. "There is light in this darkness, my brother. We must search for it together."

Jerry found he was holding his breath, waiting for the inevitable brush off and angry outburst they all expected. Instead, the gentleness of his colleague seemed to have broken through a barrier. Steve ducked his head but not before they saw his eyes brim with tears. Tamara moved close and touched his hand, murmuring, "It's all right, Babe. We're among friends here. It's all right."

He took a shaky breath. "Ahdam's right. Sorry to be such a downer. The wind's messing with my mind."

Jerry offered, "Steve, would you like to collaborate with Sarah to create a synthesis of a Shiva and a wake to take place before the commemorative service? The rest of us could concentrate on the liturgy itself. We should wait until the Glenn's orb lands anyway, since that's the symbol of our final commitment to staying on Goldilocks."

Heads nodded, and the group made plans to gather resources and begin their planning in the evening after completing the main work of the day. As they left, Tamara reached for her husband's hand and smiled over her shoulder at Jerry.

It wasn't until later in the evening, returning to the commons from the new bio-dome for second supper that Jerry understood what his husband meant the night before. The half mile path between settlement and greenhouse lay in front of him, shimmering in the deepening darkness as the pink moon, the smaller of Goldie's two satellites, set. No one else was in sight. The wind tossed the long grass shadows back and forth across the bare dirt line which the colonists' feet had recently etched on the meadow.

As Jerry bent into the gusts, the rush of air pulsed in a pattern, teasing his ears, entering his blood. He paused for a moment, taking in the strangeness of his surroundings that appeared oddly familiar. What is this sensation? he thought. Maybe déjà vu? He concentrated on the wind. What was that rhythm?

Then hairs on the back of his neck lifted. The pulse of the air matched the music of his dream, the common dream that everyone on the Glenn shared. The shock of realities colliding unnerved him. They split him in two, the Jerry on the path and a Jerry asleep in a distant bed dreaming himself. His whole body shaking, he sped up, trying to throw off the weird sensation. His empathy for Steve increased a hundred fold. By the time he reached the portal, only a wisp of unease followed him in but he could feel it tugging, as Rob said, at the beat of his heart.

CHAPTER 4
EARTH

DATE: 2060 CE

The evening was just settling over the New Mexico landscape as, in separate cars, Jerry and Rob entered the deserted parking lot of the community college gardens, crunching gravel and throwing up dust. They parked side by side and approached each other. Jerry reached out past Rob's extended hand to initiate a half-hug. Rob smiled, returning the gesture awkwardly.

It was their third date. They had seen a science fiction movie together, a remake of *The Forbidden Planet*. They also went to a classical guitar concert and out to dinner. They had not acted yet on the passion Jerry felt building between them. Rob asked him to go to a friend's wedding but Jerry had to turn him down. To assure them both of his interest in deepening the relationship, Jerry offered an intimate walk.

"So, this must be like a busman's holiday to you," Rob said, referring to the fact that Jerry owned and managed the local plant nursery.

"Well, not really. There's no paperwork or billing when I'm here. I get to enjoy nature that someone else cares for. It's a relief."

"Yeah, I can understand that." Rob breathed deeply. "I've never been here, you know. You'll have to give me a lesson in what these cacti and trees are."

"I'm glad to share."

The men walked in silence for a few beats. Then Jerry said, "Actually, I wanted to talk to you about why I couldn't go to Alicia and Tom's wedding."

"That's OK, man. It's no big deal."

"Well, it is, to me at least. I have an appointment with the bishop and the standing committee of the Episcopal Church up in Albuquerque on Saturday. They're deciding whether to support me as a postulant to the priesthood." Jerry gazed at the horizon, focusing on the threads of cloud straight lining up above the jagged mountains in the distance. The setting sun tinted them a dull orange.

"Wow. So what does that mean? Will you go away to a monastery or something?"

"No," Jerry smiled at the question, pleased that Rob was concerned he might leave. "I'll stay here in Mirage and do on-line seminary education. In the Episcopal tradition priests don't take a vow of celibacy. The track I'm on is known as the local priesthood. Parishioners of St. Anne's identified me for the calling. It's that little white church on Temple Avenue. If I'm accepted by the diocese and get through the training, I'll volunteer my time with them."

"I see."

The two walked on in silence. Jerry had found that religious conviction and an active love life rarely mixed well. He didn't dare look at his new friend, afraid that this fascinating man might arrange his features into neutral 'I have to leave' mode. His shoulders tightened.

Rob said, "So how did you get into this?"

The words weren't snarky. The voice sounded interested.

Jerry stole a quick glance and saw only wide eyed sincerity on his face. He took a shaky breath and began.

"I guess my curiosity hooked me." The reds in the sunset deepening before him gained a liminal quality as if the color opened onto another dimension. "First there was a mystery of a dying tree. That led me to a riddle of an old woman, who put me on the path of wondering about God. It all kind of hangs together."

Rob laughed. "Maybe you'd better tell me the whole story."

So Jerry told him about Marjo.

When he first met Marjo, he dismissed her as one of those old ladies trying to escape the twin boredoms of retirement and widowhood. She came to a gardening demonstration he gave at the greenhouse and sat in the back row of cheap folding chairs with a yellow legal pad and poised pen.

It wasn't until after the session that Jerry found out how clueless she was about anything plant related. She waited for him and as he walked out of the room asked him to tell her what 'acidity in the soil' meant. Somehow, the explanation led to him offering to come out and check on a dying tree which, he discovered, did not grow at her place but in the churchyard of St. Anne's. Her job wasn't to care for trees, she explained. The Jr. Warden had landed himself in the hospital and she couldn't stand to see living things wither away because she was too stupid to know what to do for them.

When the parish secretary interrupted their consultation under the shade of an over-watered acacia tree, it took Jerry several minutes before he realized he'd been talking to the rector of the church. He remembered priests as dull old men in black suits and stiff dog collars or youth pastors trying to look cool in blue jeans. What did an unimposing white haired woman in khaki pants and a camp shirt have in common with them?

It may have been this contrast with his memories, or because she didn't ask him to come to church, which compelled him to show up in the sanctuary that first Sunday. He slouched into a back pew, prepared for the flare-up of anger and shame triggered in other religious settings. But as he sat in the stuffy self-satisfied atmosphere of St. Anne's, so like the parish he attended as a child, a message slipped into his mind: "Welcome home." He looked around to see who whispered to him before realizing he hadn't heard this with his ears.

Marjo, he discovered, was not a riveting preacher. However, her tone of voice, the sincerity with which she spoke the graceful old words of prayer and consecration, and the confident joy she conveyed conspired to pull him in. The people of the congregation, an older crowd whose faces bore the stamp of religious survivors, shuffled around to make a place for him. They included him without questions or need for credentials.

"So saving the tree led me to finding a friend in a priest," he confided to Rob. "Then, I felt like this family of off-beat characters adopted me and set me on a track to finding God. It all seems connected somehow and keeps leading me on."

Rob smiled at him, nodding. "Sounds like what happens to me when I'm tracking a mystery in the bio lab. I start with one unknown and figuring that out, or just investigating it, leads me to another and then another issue. It's what I love about my job. You get glimpses of the universal pattern, and each step brings you a sliver of truth. Fractals, you know."

"Fractals?"

"Yeah, the repeating patterns of life. We identify them on every level-micro to macro. Sounds like you find them in plants and people."

They walked on, the cooling air surrounding them with the astringent scent of recently watered creosote bushes. Jerry's shoulders relaxed, the dread of judgment dissipating. In the space vacated by anxiety, a tremor of hope vibrated, blossoming into intense longing. He gets it, Jerry thought. This guy is not only smart, kind and gorgeous, but he understands what I hold most dear. The sunset before them glowed with fierce red and orange striations across the darkening sky. Soon they would have to turn.

Rob asked, "So, if Marjo is their priest, why do they need another one?"

Jerry blinked, trying to come back to the conversation as the sharpened edge of his desire scraped his insides raw. "Well, insurance really. She's in her seventies and will have to retire sometime. St. Anne's is nowhere near being able to hire a full-time seminary trained priest, and part-timers like Marjo are scarce. The congregation explored alternative ways to keep going. Reorganizing as a baptismal community with everyone doing volunteer ministry and supporting each other seemed like the way to go."

"They must think you're pretty special to want you ordained."

He attempted a nonchalant shrug. "I suspect a good part of their enthusiasm is my age. At 26, I'm the youngest of the regulars there. The older generation wants assurance that a priest will be around to bury them."

"Surely it can't be just that."

Rob half laughed but Jerry recognized concern in his dark eyes.

"Well, maybe it's that fractal thing, you know?" he said, venturing again into vulnerability. "When I came into the congregation, I wanted to figure out everything about spirituality and God that I could. I began a study group and, to my surprise, younger folk showed up along with a few of the older members. Marjo recommended various reading and video courses. It took off, even with people who didn't belong to St. Anne's. Just doing that small thing enlivened the whole church. It was like they had stalled out on their path and without meaning to, I kick started it into following the pattern again."

"So they see you as someone who can lead them into the future?"

"I'm not sure, really. At least I have the chutzpah to wrestle with it and that gives them hope."

The two men continued walking side by side. They talked of work, family and friends until the clouds burned down to a dull gray with only the faintest outlining of neon orange on the edges closest to Earth.

"Let's head home," Jerry said, reaching out to take Rob's hand.

They went to Jerry's apartment that night. They had been together ever since. In Jerry's heart, Rob became one with the pattern begun by the dying acacia tree, and rooted him in all that mattered in the world.

In the three years following that evening in the garden, life's pattern continued to unfold with Jerry and Rob walking together. They married a year and a half after their first encounter. Until the mission to settle a new planet became a possibility, Jerry thought he perceived the design of their future. Now though, he struggled to see coherence in the path of its development. Was it possible that the fractal was unraveling? Did the impending space travel embraced by Rob really include him?

These questions haunted him at sunrise on an October morning as he stood outside a gate set in a chest high adobe wall surrounding a small patio oasis of desert plants and trees. He looked over it at a woman sitting Buddha-like, perched atop a pillow on a low platform. She faced away from him, but he saw she contemplated something in cupped hands resting in her lap, although he couldn't tell what it was. A blanket draped about her rounded shoulders fended off the early chill, but her head had lost all its thick white hair. Jerry shivered imagining how exposed her scalp must feel. From the back, she appeared old and frail, her neck thin and her ears translucent shells in the dawning light. Her shadow lay behind her on the ground, a dark pool bleeding the life out of her.

He spoke to break the horror of that vision, but gently, reluctant to intrude. "Hey, Marjo."

The woman straightened her back and looked over her shoulder towards him. "Jerry. Come on in. Are you playing hooky this morning?"

The gate swung silently and he strode across the flagstones, settling on a pillow opposite her. In her hands, still lying open in her lap, rested a single deep blue juniper berry. Following the gaze of his eyes, she said, "I was trying Julian of Norwich's meditation. You know, 'seeing all the world in a hazelnut.' I didn't have a hazelnut."

"So how's it going?"

"Not so great. Sniff." She rolled the berry with her finger and offered it under his nose. A pungent scent hit high on his palate. Grinning, she told him, "Smells like the gin and tonics I gave up thirty years ago. It kind of destroys one's concentration."

Then she was up, swirling the blanket around herself, inviting him into the house for tea. As they entered together, the Jerry's wristband pinged.

"Anything important?" Marjo asked.

Jerry peered at the tiny screen. "Looks like they're shutting the Mexican border, trying to delay the spread of that flu that's hitting South America."

"The Argentine Bleed?" Marjo used the lurid term newscasters came up with for the disease which caused bleeding from the eyes before terminating its victim's organs. "I heard it was developed in a lab, like a biological weapon." She squinted at his band.

"Yeah, that rumor was going around SpaceTech too, but Rob says it's more likely a mutant virus insects are spreading as they migrate north with the heat wave. He worried that they might call him off the mission to look into it, but Dagmar promised he wasn't lending out any of his scientists. They're too close to launch to get involved."

Marjo sighed. "Well, that's a mercy. Maybe you all will leave before it hits the States."

"It's probably nothing to worry about. That small pox scare from the melting permafrost in Canada didn't amount to much."

"True. Come on in, dear."

Her kitchen, like the patio, radiated intimacy and invitation. Jerry perched at the counter island, marveling at her vitality while she put the kettle on and shook loose herbal tea into a pot. He knew she got three weeks off in between chemo treatments and on this third week of the third round, her strength surged. Fourteen days ago she couldn't even roll off the sofa. She'll be right back on that couch, sick as a dog, next week, Jerry reminded himself. He looked down to see his hands playing with a teaspoon, tracing the outline of its handle, following the scroll of its inlaid pattern.

Marjo puttered around, reaching up for mugs, locating the honey. She sighed and rested on the bar stool beside him and said, "So, tell me."

"Rob and I both passed the physical and psychological tests. They'll let us go."

"No problem with the gay issue, then?" she asked.

"Nope, we're golden—responsible child-loving adults with no ability to have our own. We'll be the safety net for any children who lose natural parents. They're figuring a need for three or four grown-ups to every new kid, at least in the beginning, to ensure survival rates for the babies."

The irony of what he relayed still astounded him. This big problem in his life, the impediment to acceptance and happiness in his native society, had literally become his greatest asset. SpaceTech scientists didn't need a landscape artist on their expedition. His bishop hurried to ordain him so an established Protestant Church could claim a leadership role on the historic journey, but that didn't impress them either. No, it was his committed relationship with one of their own, and his suitability for adoptive parenthood, that made them enthusiastic to include him.

It also emphasized the risks involved in this enterprise. A staff doctor had pointed out mortality rates of mothers might increase without the prenatal and delivery care common on earth. They planned to encourage a few pregnancies during the space journey itself—risky, but important to confirm its possibility. After arrival on Goldilocks, they hoped the environment would be conducive to reproduction. Everything they didn't know about the home they headed for though, loomed over their future, shadowing any plans they created.

Marjo poured the boiling water, steaming her glasses and giving her a vague faraway look. An exotic smell of cinnamon and cloves tinged with something orange-y and sweet wafted out of the teapot, before she sealed on the lid. She settled again, letting the tea steep. "You've made up your mind then," she said, tilting her head to make it a question.

Jerry nodded slowly, concentrating on weaving the spoon in between his fingers. "Yeah, I think so. It's dangerous, but it's also the place where Rob's dreams and mine connect. It feels right—most of the time."

Marjo poured the tea out, shoving a mug towards him along with the honey. She looked up with a warm, sad smile. "Sounds like a calling to me, sweetheart." No head tilt now, just the direct gaze and open face of a dying seventy-five-year-old woman.

His fingers tightened on the spoon as he met her eyes, trying to stem the wave of grief and gratitude closing his throat. She'll let me go without a scene, Jerry realized. Just when he thought he had her figured out, she astounded him. The spoon tapped the place mat rhythmically. Am I growing up and leaving home, or am I betraying my best friend? He didn't dare speak the question aloud.

Marjo reached out and covered his hand, quieting the

nervous beat. "What is it?"

Jerry sighed and carefully relaxed his fingers. "I asked if you could come too." He admitted. "I thought... I still think they need wise leaders for these religious communities. The politicians have maneuvered SpaceTech into recruiting groups of American Christians, Muslims and Jews as settlers for the new planet, but they see them as competitors. It's a publicity stunt for them, trying to prove one religion's superiority over the others. The scientists understand that everyone will have to learn how to work together on this trip, but they're not letting anyone over thirty go as a settler. Forty years old is the limit among the experts. I'm just squeaking in myself."

"Jerry, I couldn't have gone anyway," Marjo said. She kept her hand over his, tightening her grip. "I've got my own journey to travel and we both know it. Don't ignore reality. That doesn't help either of us."

She smiled then, catching his eye and holding his gaze. "You need to be the wise one now."

"Well that sucks—both for the space mission and St. Anne's. I've only been ordained three months. I finally commit to the Church and then I leave the parish in the lurch."

Marjo snorted. "Get over yourself, Jerry. The Ministry team will either call someone else to be priest or they'll find another part-timer when I'm gone. If you're worrying about St. Anne's survival, give it up. In all my ordained years, fretting about a congregation's long term viability did nothing to sustain them. It only reinforces fear and selfishness."

"But you love St. Anne's." Jerry exclaimed, "Everything you've done here has laid a foundation so they can carry on.

Before I got caught up with Rob's mission, I pictured that as my calling too—saving this church."

Marjo reached for her tea mug and sat back on her stool. She deliberately breathed in the steam and blew out gently before taking a sip. He waited, knowing her habits of deliberation, of needing silence to pull her thoughts into words and her words into speech.

"I don't love the Church as an institution, Jerry," she finally said. "Look through this lens: you know the little orange tree you bought for me several years ago that we put in the sun room? It stood in that beautiful dark green urn. It was perfect for the porch, but one day you told me it was growing root bound and needed to be planted outside.

"You found a place in the yard for it. Remember? We tried to save that pot, but it had cracked and fell completely apart as we pulled the roots out. I threw the pieces away. It was worth losing the planter to preserve the tree, the living thing it held."

Marjo shifted on her stool, shaking her head. "I don't love the Church, Jerry. It's just a pot, a beautiful receptacle to hold the relationship between God and humanity. It's been cracking a long time. We need to let it go and find a bigger container to thrive as God's people."

Jerry frowned, eyes narrowing as he tried to get his mind around what she was telling him. "So why spend your energy on St. Anne's?" He asked. "Why encourage me to study for ordination? Why stay in the Church at all?"

Marjo gazed at him, and he could tell she hadn't missed the edge of anger and disappointment in his words. He frowned, picking up the spoon again. When she spoke, Marjo's voice sounded calm and warm as ever.

"Would you throw out the tree with the pot just because it's root bound? I don't think so. I do love God. I do love the people of St. Anne's. I love you, too, dear. There isn't anywhere else I've seen that's bigger or better to plant us.

"Now, though... You're going to that place, Jerry. Think about what being a priest means. It's not about saving the Church. It's about choosing a different future and helping people evolve into who God created us to be. All of us—even those who don't wear dog collars. Even those who never sat in a pew."

Marjo leaned forward resting her elbows on the counter, clutching her mug. "For God's sake, don't spend your time making old mistakes. Leave the baggage behind, all of it: the pews and vestments and precious little chapels. Plant yourself in the dirt of that foreign planet and let it change you. That's the only chance the Church has, Jerry. There's no untainted soil left on earth, no place wide and deep enough to nurture us."

He sat still, the silence between them echoing with her fervor. Something shifted in him as she spoke. The room grew smaller, the universe more frighteningly real. He set down the spoon and reached for her hand. Wrapping it, warm and fragile, in both of his, he said, "OK, I'll try. I promise, I'll try."

Jerry left Marjo's house the way he came, through the patio and little gate. As he walked to his truck, he paused at the juniper tree bordering the garage. He picked a dusky blue berry and rolled it in his fingers, the scent of gin filling his senses. Will junipers grow on that distant planet? He wondered. Or for that matter, will hazelnuts?

Time collapsed on itself as Fall progressed to Winter that year. Within two months, the cancer in Marjo's body was finally defeated not by radiation or chemicals but by her frail heart surrendering to death. Just after Christmas, the bishop preached at her funeral speaking of all the good this woman had done in the world—the congregations she served and the groups she helped.

"What a model of Christian service," he said, his dispassionate voice filling the shadowed sanctuary, while in the pews her family, the old people of St. Anne's, trained their damp eyes on Jerry.

He sat beside the altar, face white as his alb, eyes wet as theirs, the symbol and a further cause of their pain. They had not lost a good worker, a person defined by what she did, as the bishop seemed to believe. They mourned someone much more precious: a friend, a mother. One who loved them. The wound of her passing would not heal soon. They knew Jerry would leave them, too, deserting them for space as she had for death.

Two weeks after Marjo's funeral, Rob called to ask Jerry to meet him on the Space Tech campus for an afternoon coffee. Jerry had gone to work, determined to fight through the miasma of grief still engulfing him. This request was so unusual though, that he dropped the paperwork he was plowing through and drove over. At the gate, he waited ten minutes while the guard who knew him and had previously waved him in, phoned for permission to let him enter. As he pulled into the parking lot fronting Rob's office, he saw his husband waiting in the shade of an old mesquite tree that graced the dirt yard.

"What's going on?" he asked as he clambered out of the truck and headed over to meet him. "Security's really beefed up. Is everything OK?"

"Let's get coffee and I'll tell you all about it." His face was set to careful blandness. Jerry's heart beat harder.

Only when they settled in a quiet corner of the company's cafeteria, sipping iced cold brew, did Rob open up.

"It's the Argentine Bleed," he said. "Word is that it's spreading quickly and the governor will shut all the state's borders soon. Other states have already closed highways and prohibited any travel into their territories."

"But I thought they had it stopped in the Texas. Just this morning the news reported that it was contained."

"Yeah, south of us it's fading out, but here's what they're not sharing: Somehow the virus jumped to Europe, probably by airlines that didn't quarantine early enough. No one noticed until now because it mutated. The bleeding eyes don't happen right away in this version. Instead, victims have mild flu symptoms and by the time the hemorrhaging starts, they've been contagious for several days. It's moving fast, Jer."

"God." Jerry looked at his spouse's pained expression and felt the chill of the future he perceived. "What about your work, Rob—the mission?"

"We need to get the whole crew up on the ships as soon as possible so we don't take this plague with us."

"How soon?"

"Dagmar wants both scientists and settlers on campus within two weeks, and then on board in a month."

"How can he do that? Have you even finished the checks on the colonists you're considering?"

"Yeah, that's a problem. We can't be picky. That Jewish kibbutz in Iowa we've been negotiating with will join us right away. We promised all their older members and anyone with kids can stay at SpaceTech when we go into quarantine. Same with the Muslim group from Idaho, but we need more of them. There are only thirty people eligible in that population and we planned on a full hundred—that's fifty for each ship. The Christian congregation we had pegged as most suitable is in San Jose and California has already locked down, so we're back to square one with them."

Jerry's heart skipped a beat. "Rob, my family—they're all in California."

He nodded. "I know. And my mother is in Boston." He reached across the table and took his husband's hand in his. "There's nothing we can do for them, Jer. It's already too late. The travel ban has begun. You'll catch it on the news in a few hours."

The room held too little oxygen. Jerry pulled his hand away and stood up. "There must be a way. We have to get them here. Can't Dagmar pull strings?"

"He's calling in all his debts just to bring the settlers and scientists here. We can't take the chance of becoming contaminated. No one from either coast is being allowed into the interior of the country."

"I could go to San Francisco and get them. If I left now, I'd be there by tomorrow morning."

"Listen to me, Jer." He didn't look up but his hands on the table top curled into fists. "You won't make it past the New Mexico border. If you somehow sneak by the guards, you'd never return, with or without your family."

"Aren't you worried about your Mom?" Jerry's voice sounded shrill even in his own ears. He looked down at the brown curls of Rob's head unable to see his face and realized that his husband's shoulders were shaking. The heat infusing his face flipped and became ice in his heart. Sitting down abruptly, he saw tears streaming down Rob's cheeks. "Tell me," he said, scooting his chair around until he sat next to him. He leaned in close, his arm circling his spouse's bent back.

"I called her right away, after I heard about the quarantine. She says she's got the flu, Jer."

CHAPTER 5
PLANET KOI-3284

DATE: 2073 CE/1

Two weeks after moving to the planet's surface, Jerry shuttled back up to the Glenn to help with the selection and removal of plants and fish. Only a third of their stock would fit in the planet-side dome. They planned to test which specimens could survive the conditions on Goldilocks. Ultimately, they had to be self-sufficient on this new world.

Jerry spent his time dragging netted trees and potted vegetables to motorized carts. He then drove them through empty halls to the smaller science orb retrofitted for its separation from the Glenn and the trip to the surface. As he worked, he noticed the silence of the ship compared to the windy planet. Already the settlers were assigning earth words to the different winds that daily kept them company. The day he first touched down had been merely breezy. The much more common 18-20 miles an hour wind, with a temperature around 70 degrees, the crew called 'chinook'. This type blew for the two weeks he'd been part of the team building the mini bio-dome. He had yet to experience the force of a blinding wet 'gale' or even the freezing dry 'mistral' which the initial work party labored through their first month planet-side. Naming the temperaments of Goldilocks didn't make them more bearable, but it helped the colonists complain more accurately.

In the hollow halls of the Glenn where the air didn't stir, the gusty atmosphere of Goldilocks seemed a fairy tale. Jerry straightened and shrugged his shoulders, reminding himself that here he didn't need to hunch against the wind, a habit being acquired by the crew living below.

Jim came up to help him shift the plants and fish, but even with both, the job took four days. Jerry slept alone in the old quarters overnight, surrounded by quiet, stale air. Meals for breakfast, lunch and dinner were sandwiches which Lily packed up for them. They tasted of home. He lingered over them, pressing his fingers to pick up any stray crumbs, licking up each bit of memory.

As company, Jim didn't contribute much. Although a hard worker and a fine Midwestern farmer in his former life, the foreignness of their plight brought out his natural pessimism.

"Oh man, this apple tree will never survive on Goldilocks. The weather will dry her out, for sure. We'll need to plant wind breaks, but who knows how long they'll take to grow. Those tilapia might not make it either, Jerry."

On the fourth day, as they secured the last of the tanks in the smaller science orb, the maintenance crew judged conditions favorable (or as good as anyone predicted in the near future) for a landing. They would leave when Jerry and Jim had the fish locked in.

As they hurried to complete their task, Jerry nearly missed the beeping of his wrist band, and was tempted to ignore it. He glanced down, saw Xander's face in the hologram, and called for a break.

"Hey, Kiddo. I'm kind of busy now. We're launching

soon. I should be home for dinner tonight. I'll talk to you then, OK?"

"No." The boy's shrill voice crackled with panic. "I tried to tell Mom but she wouldn't listen. I don't think the planet understands. She may blow harder if you try to land."

"What? What are you talking about, Hon?"

"Goldilocks. I don't think she trusts the Glenn. She can't hear inside the science orb. She won't know you're in there like she knew we were in the shuttle."

Behind him, Jim had gone back to wrestling the tops onto fish tanks. He clearly needed a hand and Jerry struggled with the pull that sucks at parents when they have a job calling them away from their children.

"Sweetheart, can you explain this later? Jim needs my help. If it's really important, tell Uncle Rob, OK? He should be around somewhere."

"But Uncle Jerry..."

"I love you, buddy. I'll be home soon." Jerry broke the link as he moved to give his colleague a hand. His mind, though, retained Xander's words. As they banged the temperamental lids shut, he worried over the boy's propensity to anthropomorphize the planet. Was Goldilocks becoming his invisible playmate? *Shit, I wish I'd read more child psychology,* he thought. He'd ask Doc about it if it went on too long.

Finally, Jerry and Jim strapped down with the fish and plants in the cargo hold. Eli Dahl stuck his head through the hatch and yelled, "All set here to detach and fly." Red-haired Abby Bennett flashed a smile as she climbed past Jerry and made her way to the bridge door, disappearing inside. As the communication specialist on this trip, she would strap in next to Eli, their engineer.

Conner Newman piloted the orb for this landing. He was the only one with the necessary experience and stepped on board confidently. Janice Rice followed to copilot position. Conner and Janice stayed close friends after partnering in a power struggle which threatened the mission early on, but they had never again bid for control. Still, Jerry felt a twinge of anxiety, wishing Rob had drawn the copilot slot. He promptly rescinded his wish. If anything goes wrong, he thought, at least Rob will be safe to take care of Xander and Lily.

The pilots disappeared onto the bridge, newly configured to fly the orb. Jim and Jerry, alone in the big interior, sat on hastily constructed jump seats on opposites sides of the room. Jerry discovered he couldn't see his colleague through the clutter piled in the bay. He leaned his head back and stared up through the leaves of the poplar sapling tied in next to him.

Jim called across to him, "I'm going to miss the peace and quiet up here."

"Yep, me too. But I'm anxious to get home." Jerry said.

A crackling sounded over the intercom. Conner announced, "The wind is at 15 miles an hour, south by south-west. It's now or never, kids. Hang on. Commencing disconnect in 5, 4, 3, 2, 1."

A deep throbbing began, shaking the steel flooring under Jerry's feet and the concave wall at his back. Then a roaring whoosh blasted outside the room, plastering Jerry to the curve with its force. Conner's voice over the intercom confirmed, "Unlocking successful. Setting a course to planet."

After the graceful maneuverability of the shuttles, even

the passengers stuck in the interior of the orb sensed how awkwardly it flew. Jerry reminded himself that they just needed to fall to the right place on the surface below. This section was designed for it.

"Firing thrusters." The intercom stayed open letting Jerry and Jim listen to the play-by-play. A second later another roar and push.

"OK folks, hang on back there. We'll be entering the atmosphere in fifty seconds. It might be a rough ride and get hot too. I'll try not to boil the fish alive though."

From his hidden seat, Jim called, "Forget the fish. Don't roast us to death."

"I copy, Jim." Evidently the communication system worked both ways. "No worries. Contact with atmosphere in 5, 4, 3, 2, 1."

The jolt pulled Jerry forward this time, throwing him against the harness, digging into the meat of his shoulders. A scream and curses resounding through the intercom told him everyone experienced the same. The orb quaked. He put a hand out, trying to check the seal on the tank closest to him. Water slapped on the lid. They would lose some fish to shock if nothing else.

"Hang on back there." Conner's voice hardly registered over the metallic vibrations. Somewhere a tree broke free and crashed to the floor.

With a pop, the shaking stopped. "OK, sound off. Is everyone still with me?"

"Janice, check."

"Jerry here."

"Jim, OK."

"Abby survived."

"Eli here."

"All right then, cowboys and cowgirls. It should be smooth sailing from here until touchdown."

"How reassuring." Abby was not enjoying this ride. Jerry smiled at the sarcasm.

Just as he took a deep breath and tried to relax his tense muscles, another jolt threw him forward, followed by a blow that slammed him back against the wall. The floor tilted, rolling up and over his head as the orb spun. On the speaker he heard Conner yelling to ground control and his copilot, who responded only "shit, shit, shit."

Someone's scream on the intercom pierced the air. Blood rushed to his now upside down face. The tree which had broken free came sailing by, narrowly missing him. He spent a nanosecond worrying whether Jim was in its trajectory before realizing that water was dripping on his forehead. The fish tanks...

"Conner, get us upright." He yelled at the top of his lungs, trying to communicate over the mayhem. "The tanks are leaking."

For a moment he thought the pilot had complied with his wish. The room rolled up. He pulled as far as possible into the wall, remembering the loose sapling. But as his feet reclaimed their accustomed place beneath him, they continued on and up the other side. They were spinning, out of control.

The next time his shoes revolved under his body, another jolt caught and banged him against the wall. He realized that by some miracle the pilot deployed the landing chute when the orb was in the upright position. Thank you Conner, he telegraphed in his mind.

Still, they accelerated. Friction from the atmosphere heated the room. The floor swung back and forth under his feet in diminishing arcs, water sloshing against the tank sides. A shrill whining filled the space between the bumps and rattles of objects trying to break free of their restraints.

"Jerry, we're going too fast." Jim's voice, panicked and sharp, penetrated the chaos.

Thank God, he's still talking. "Hang on, Jim. At least we're not rolling anymore. I think the chute deployed."

"Too fast. It'll burn up."

Jerry looked around, but saw nothing helpful. A smell— the scent of a catalytic converter overheating, sweet and heavy, oozed up from the floor.

Just as he registered this, the orb smashed into the ground, throwing him so hard against his harness the world went black before his eyes. Then he bounced back against the wall and breathed again, air hot and thick around him.

"Jim. Jim, are you all right, man?" he called, struggling to undo the straps holding him in place. As he got them off, he fell forward, the floor angling away instead of level under his feet. Disoriented he yelled again, "Jim?"

"Yeah, give me a hand. I can't get this stupid harness off."

Jerry, relief flooding him, slithered downwards and around a fish tank to find Jim and help him unlock the restraints. Together they climbed over plant beds to reach the bridge's doorway.

"Conner," Jim shouted. "Open the damn door." Nothing moved. No one hailed them.

Jerry fumbled for the manual release on the wall and pulled the lever. With a metal moan, the doors unlocked and shifted an inch apart, giving room to insert their hands and pull an opening wide enough to slide through.

They had hit the ground on the side of the orb occupied by the bridge. The viewing screen, shorted out somewhere, flickered a picture half black and half a horizon of yellow grass. For an instant, Jerry saw boots running towards them, far away. Then a loud pop and the display died.

Conner was slumped over in the captain's chair, head on the console. Janice had gotten out of her seat beside him but lay with her face on the deck, tilted down against panels. Jerry scanned the bridge. He located Eli to his right, unconscious or dead, strapped in his fallen seat, ripped from the floor. Then he spotted Abby, who was feebly trying to extricate herself from her chair's harness on his left.

"Jim help Abby," he said and stepped over to check Eli, who was breathing shallowly. Not wanting to move him until he knew what injuries the big man might have, Jerry moved forward to the main console to examine Conner.

Blood spread over the screens where the pilot's head lay and close up Jerry saw the unnatural angle of his neck. He reached over, avoiding the glassy eyes staring up at him, and groped for the artery. Holding his own breath, he prayed for a flutter telling him there was hope. Nothing.

"Conner." He called, "Conner, stay with us, buddy. We need you." But the pilot had left. He felt the emptiness.

Behind him, Jim knelt to lift Janice into her seat, which he had turned around so that the back now faced the downward slope of the cabin. She slumped sideways, threatening to slip to the floor again, and both men grabbed to support her body. There was blood smeared across her face, but Jerry couldn't tell if it was hers or Conner's. Again he sought the beat of life at her throat, and this time a tiny movement rewarded him. He stopped his own breathing, closed his eyes and concentrated. Yes, there it was again.

"She's got a heartbeat. Lay her on the floor, against the console. I don't think she'll stay in the chair."

"OK, but the smoke's worse down there."

Smoke? Jerry raised his head and sniffed. "Oh, God, where's the fire?"

"Push the alarm." Abby's voice, strained and breathless, barely registered.

"What?" Jerry turned toward her. "Where is it, Abby?"

"On the console, to the left."

He looked at the blood splattered buttons and screens, completely dark. He pushed at one but nothing happened, tried another, zilch.

"I think the computer's dead. Nothing works."

"Manual override. Help me."

Jerry climbed up to her, leaving Jim to monitor Janice. The communications officer had remained in her chair, bracing herself with her arms to stay there.

"Can you move?" Jerry asked.

"Something's broken. Pelvis or hip. Get me to the door panel."

He slipped an arm around her back and hauled her upright, her breath hissing with pain.

"You'll have to carry me." She tightened her grip on his neck as he gingerly bent and caught up her legs in an awkward lift. Luckily she was on the light side.

Jerry edged forward, fighting to stay upright as he moved toward the door. Abby showed him a panel at shoulder height on the wall which he pried open, and she entered a code on the pad.

"Pull the bar," she instructed him, but with her in his arms he couldn't get the leverage he needed to budge it.

He set her legs down, keeping her weight on his other arm, but the lever still didn't move. Smoke clouded the air, blurring his vision. Abby coughed, choking and sagged lower.

"I've got to lay you on the floor, Abby," he said, kneeling to ease her descent. There was no reply. He looked at her—eyes shut, pale face ashen. He stood up again and with both hands tugged, sinking low to take advantage of his weight. With a snap, the lever broke free, and Jerry found himself sprawled beside Abby, a fine mist spraying over them. She moaned and turned her head, gasping "Don't breathe it." Jerry leaned his body over her to shield her face, yelling to Jim. "Don't breathe the water. Protect Janice's face." He peered at Eli and hoped he was resting at an angle that would screen him.

The drizzle stopped, smoke settling out of the air. Now what? He rocked back on his heels and looked at Abby who had passed out again. A buzzing began and Jerry realized it was his wrist band. Dazed, he tapped it on and saw Rob's face, focusing on him. "Jer, we can't access the main door. Where are you? Can you move to the hatch in the shuttle room and open it for us? We're getting ladders."

"We need medics. Get Doc. Hurry, Rob. I'm on the bridge but I think I can make it to the back door," his voice rasped.

"Right. The emergency team's on its way. How many hurt?"

"Three badly. Conner's dead."

"OK. I'll meet you at the door." And he was gone.

Jerry looked at Jim, still bent over Janice. "Is she

breathing?"

"Just barely."

"Stay there, OK? I'll go open the hatch."

He rose on legs that seemed far away from the rest of his body. Willing them to move, he skirted Abby and stumbled through the narrow passage back into the shuttle bay, pulling himself up the sloped floor with whatever came to hand. As he passed a fish tank, he noticed it was leaking, the water pooling against the plant beds.

Finally, he reached the portal and found the manual release. He punched the button, and then grabbing the wheel on the door with both hands, tried to turn it. Like the fire lever, it mocked his efforts. Bangs sounding from the other side urged him on. He pulled up his legs and crouching, swinging his whole body into the effort, yanked hard. "Oh, God, thank you," he breathed as the wheel budged and spun.

From the outside, fingers reached around the opening and a medic swung herself in over the ledge. She turned to examine him as her partner followed her in, but Jerry waved them both on. "Go to the bridge. I'm fine. Go, go, go."

Doc, climbing in behind them gave a nod, and patted him on the arm. "We'll be back for you." She said as she hurried after her helpers.

Jerry slumped against the wall, his legs wobbly. I should go help, he thought. And then Rob was there, pulling himself over the edge, on his knees beside him, wrapping him in his arms. His warm breath was on his neck and Jerry felt his husband's heart beating against his chest, as frantic as his own.

The dream seeped into his consciousness. Like the fog, it seemed sluggish. Maybe, he thought, it's reluctant to come? He found himself as always standing upright. Feet on solid ground but head muffled. He looked around, missing something familiar. No wind blowing and no singing. He felt a panicked moment of disorientation. Was this his old dream, beloved dream? And then a gentle zephyr started. With it, a small child's voice sang. The song, however, was no longer playful. Now it wept so piteously, his heart broke. If only he could walk to it! He strained to move. On a far pillow, his head tossed.

Pain shot through his side scattering the dream. Jerry's eyes opened, squinting against a bright glare. Each breath he took radiated a sharp slice of agony around his chest. He panted shallowly trying to ease it.

The room swam into focus—a make-shift infirmary, planet-side. Light, diffuse from the curved and opaque wall, filled the space. Lily stood over him, watching as he came back to consciousness. He looked at her, dazed.

"Jerry, you all right? Do you need Doc?"

"What happened?"

"The orb crashed, Jerry. You're safe now."

"Hurt. My chest hurts."

Xander's head appeared over the bed rail. "You broke three ribs," he said, impressed. "But don't worry. It won't kill you. I asked."

"I'll get Doc and Rob." Lily touched his arm. "Don't talk, OK? Xander, you sit here, quiet."

Then she left and the boy, ignoring his mother, came closer. His small hand found Jerry's laying on the sheet and he gripped it hard.

"I tried to tell you, Uncle Jerry. Please don't be mad at her. She didn't believe me. I couldn't get her to understand."

A vague memory of Xander calling before take-off brushed his mind. What had the boy said? He'd been upset about something. It was his imaginary friend, wasn't it? A shiver of fear pushed the pain aside with the urgency of a premonition.

"Xander, did you know the ship would crash?" The words, even whispered, brought on the stabbing sensation.

"No." Xander's voice sounded shocked.

He paused, and Jerry supposed for a moment the child had retreated into silence. But then, he leaned in so Jerry saw his face.

"You have to believe me," he hissed with an intensity beyond the ken of an seven-year-old. "She couldn't hear you in the ship. She thought we were in danger, like from a meteor."

"Who?" Jerry managed the question.

"The singer. You know, from the dream." Xander glanced toward the door and then focused back on Jerry's face. "She's Goldilocks."

"The planet?"

"Hey, no talking." Doc strode into the room with her com-pad in front of her, checking his vital signs. "Xander, we've got to let your uncle rest so those ribs get better. Why don't you head to school, now he's awake?"

The little hand in his gripped hard.

"It's OK. He can stay." Jerry managed to whisper.

Doc sighed. She came to the bed side, glowering at them. "Well at least move so I can examine the patient."

Xander released Jerry's fingers and slunk into a corner. For the first time Jerry noticed only one wall around him was solid. Drawn curtains composed the other three. Someone rustled their covers behind them and he saw the shadow of a person sitting near the fabric.

"The others?" His voice croaked.

Doc, examining the wrap on his chest, paused, looking into his face. She pulled up the blanket and murmured, "We lost Conner and Janice. Jim survived with only bruises. Eli has a concussion but should be OK. Abby broke her pelvis, but she's young and strong. She'll recover." She nodded toward the curtain. "Darren hasn't left her side since she came in."

With a glance over her shoulder at Xander, in a louder voice she continued, "And you, my friend, have several broken ribs, and a dislocated finger on your left hand. You're going to hurt like hell for a while."

"Hurt like hell now."

"OK, I'll get an injection. The best thing for you is sleep."

Rob stepped through one of the curtains. "Let me say hi before he goes under again, Doc. How are you doing, dear heart?"

The doctor ducked out to fetch medication and Xander joined Rob at the head of the bed.

"Tell Rob what you were telling me, kiddo."

"About Goldilocks?"

"Yeah."

"She didn't know people were in the orb. It's hard to make her understand."

"Who?" Rob frowned at the child and then at his husband. "What are we talking about?"

"Xander's communicating with the planet. Somehow, they're connected. Could we be, too?"

Rob, lips pursed, took a breath and let it out. "You've got to rest, Jer."

"Seriously, Rob. Listen to Xander. I had the dream just now. The singer was weeping."

"She feels so bad. She didn't mean to hurt you." In the child's voice the implications sounded improbable.

"Xander, let's not worry Uncle Jerry, OK?" Rob was gentle but firm.

"I'm serious. Listen carefully to what he's saying." The effort to be convincing cost Jerry much and he bit his lip to keep from moaning.

His husband caught the gesture and anxiously reassured him. "All right, all right."

Doc came back with a syringe which she plunged into the IV plugged into Jerry's arm. "Out—both of you. Let this man rest."

Rob bent to kiss his forehead and whispered, "I promise, I'll listen to the kid. You get better soon."

"Think this through with me," Jerry begged Rob after his husband had, for the third time, tried to change the subject. "We had a theory that the dreams might be attempts of an alien to contact us. Why can't that alien be our planet?"

"Great chunks of dirt orbiting a star don't talk to people. It's a known scientific fact." Rob grinned, trying to tease his spouse out of the determined sincerity he kept displaying around this ridiculous subject.

"Just because planets haven't before, doesn't mean this one can't. We might be witnessing an evolution, the development of a sentient world."

The conversation was taking place in their new quarters, the cramped set of two bedrooms with a small common room between them. Lily and Xander had retired and the men tried to keep their voices low so as not to disturb them. The outer wall, bowing out in a curve from floor to ceiling, darkened with the night outside. Usually the wind provided white noise blocking out conversations, but tonight it died to a gentle breeze that teased the ears but didn't obscure sound.

Xander peeked around the bedroom door.

"Oh man, did we wake you up?" Rob asked.

"No, I need the bathroom."

The toilets and showers lay down the hall, one set to each of the long housing units.

"Which uncle do you want to go with you?" Jerry asked, smiling.

The boy tilted his head, considering the question. "I'll take Uncle Rob tonight, please."

"At your service, my dear." Rob levered himself off the pillow and stood. "It's good of you to let Uncle Jerry rest his poor ribs. Be back in a minute."

As they left, Jerry caught Xander's voice. "Why don't planets talk?" He smiled to himself. Rob was in for a long conversation.

When the two of them wandered in half an hour later, Xander beamed like a gold medal winner.

"We're going to do an experiment," the boy announced.

"An experiment?" Jerry exclaimed, smiling at Rob who rolled his eyes. "What kind?"

Xander plunked himself down beside Jerry with Rob joining them. "So there's four things that prove something is alive: Metabolism (that's eating and pooping), growing, and reacting to stuff like being poked. And reproduction—that's having babies."

"Wow, you got a science lecture on the way to the bathroom. You'll need at least four experiments to test all that."

"Uncle Rob says, start with the hardest to confirm and the rest will be easy."

"So which is the most difficult?"

"Ummm..." Xander frowned to consider this question.

Rob said. "What about reproduction, Sport? I never heard of a planet having offspring. How are we going to prove that?"

"I guess that is the hardest. We don't know if Goldilocks is old enough to reproduce. I'll be much older when I become a father." Xander furrowed his eight-year-old brow. "But there're different ways to get babies, right? Not only a man and woman getting married. Uncle Jerry's girl fish lay eggs and then the boy fish swim over and put their sperm there."

"Yup, and lots of single cell creatures, amoebas for example, divide themselves and become two," Jerry said, wondering if they were teaching the kids sex education too early. *Did I know this at his age?*

"Still, I can't imagine the planet breaking off bits of herself and throwing them into space," A speculative tone shaded the scientist's voice.

"What about bees?" The idea visited Jerry like a revelation. He sat up straighter on the couch, suppressing a groan as his ribs reminded him they weren't healed yet.

"I think bees lay eggs, Jer." His husband shot him a bemused look.

"No, I mean the way flowers use bees. How they entice insects to gather nectar and when they show up, the sticky pollen gets on their legs and they take it to other flowers. That's how plants reproduce."

"So what's the parallel situation here?" Rob asked.

Xander, looking at Jerry replied, "We're the bees, right Uncle Jer?"

"Could be. The dreams sure appear to be inviting, calling us to come, even if we don't understand them very well." He paused, lost in the weirdness of what he was contemplating. "I wonder if bees ever realize why they're attracted to flowers. Do they just go because they're hungry? Do they comprehend at some level that the plant needs them too?"

"We came because we needed a new home." Rob, intrigued, still played the voice of reason.

"Yup, that's what we thought. It would be great to find out if someone else on earth had the dream before we left, besides me. I wonder if Goldilocks contacted Dagmar."

"I don't see how our coming here will help the planet reproduce though." Rob had on his lab expression now, eyes narrowed, focused on nothing, turning the problem over in his mind, looking at it from every angle.

"What if she's like you and Uncle Jerry?" said Xander.

They both looked at the child, puzzled. "What do you

mean, kiddo?" Jerry asked.

"Well, two men can't have a baby but you wanted a family, so you helped Mom. And now you have me, your child. Maybe Goldilocks will do that. She'll help us live and be the mother to us people, because she can't get her own babies."

Tears welled in Jerry's eyes. God gives wisdom to the innocent. He glanced at his husband, sitting stock still, looking with a stricken expression at the boy. "Well, clearly he somehow inherited your brains, Rob. Xander, that's brilliant."

Rob nodded. "That is a possibility. Consider this too: it's possible to inject DNA from one species into another to create a hybrid offspring. It could be we provide new genetic material or some other element for the planet's systems. I wonder how we could test any of these theories though?"

"We should ask her." Again Xander left them speechless.

"So can you talk to her that easily, Love?" Rob asked, after a pause.

"No, not really. Not yet. She doesn't use words. It's more like she sings pictures and feelings and then I try to sing pictures back to her. Sometimes we don't understand each other very well."

"Like when you tried to tell her the orb was landing?" Jerry said, shifting at the painful memory.

Xander's face fell into sadness. "Yeah. I sang a picture of it coming to the ground by the housing and she went wild. I saw lots of rocks falling down and big dents in the dirt and fire and stuff."

"She must have remembered her early days when asteroids crashed on her," Jerry said.

Rob was obviously thinking of something else, his eyes scrunched with concentration. "When you get quiet and your mom says you're being dreamy, is that when you communicate with Goldilocks?"

Xander looked surprised. "Sure. I told you guys. Well, I guess I said it was the singer, but I didn't understand the singer was Goldilocks yet. I was just a kid when she started talking to me, you know."

Both men laughed and Rob reached around the child's shoulder, gathering both Jerry and him up into a hug. "We're dopes, Xanda Panda. Uncle Jerry was right. I should have listened to you. Can you teach us how to talk to Goldilocks? If we learn to understand her, she might tell us the answers."

Several drinks of water and another trip to the bathroom later, they got Xander back to sleep and went to bed themselves. Jerry's ribs throbbed and his left forefinger, bound in a splint, ached in syncopation with them as he tried to find a comfortable position. Rob lay still beside him, but there was no sound of deep relaxed breathing.

"What's keeping you awake, Hon?" Jerry asked in the darkness.

"I'm thinking you're right—that Xander is somehow connected to the planet. It's scaring the crap out of me."

"Wouldn't that be a good thing?"

"Shit, Jer... It would be a miracle. To find life on that scale—sentient, conscious, let's sit and talk together life. It'd be a discovery on par with fire. But aliens are intimidating enough if they're our size or even big as Godzilla. We're talking here about a living, breathing, reproducing planet."

"Don't forget eating and pooping."

"That's what scares me. I'm not forgetting eating. If

Goldilocks called us, we don't comprehend why. She could be fattening us up for lunch, for all we know."

"If those were her intentions, why continue to talk to Xander? Why keep sending dreams?"

"Jer, she nearly killed you. Janice and Conner are dead. If what Xander says is true, she intentionally generated enough wind to knock a space ship out of its trajectory. That's huge."

"If Xander has it right, she was protecting him and the people already here. She didn't understand that the orb had us in it and could land without harming anyone."

Rob lay still for a moment. "So much depends on Xander. Jer, he's just kid."

"Yeah." Jerry sighed and wrapped himself around his husband, spooning him into the curve of his body, ignoring his painful ribs. "'A little child shall lead them....' It says that somewhere in the Bible. Old Testament, so both Sarah and Ahdam should be good with it. Don't dismiss the miraculous. This feels good. Scary, but in a sacred way."

Rob breathed, blowing warm air onto Jerry's chilled fingers, kissing his splint and each of his palms. "OK dear. I'm going to try to sleep on that note: scary but sacred. I'll figure out how to test a planet for reproductive capabilities in the morning."

"A child's faith in you depends on it." Jerry smiled and kissed the back of Rob's head before he too drifted off.

CHAPTER 6
SPACE

DATE: 2069 CE

When Jerry brought a mug of coffee to Rob, as he had every morning now for over four years, it surprised him to see his husband still sleeping. Usually the day after a jump stoked him. He could hardly wait to discover what asteroids the overnight crew had mapped, wanting to find that wet one which would relieve the restraints of their depleted water supply and speed them on their way.

The twelfth inter-stellar transition sent them unerringly into another star system as had the others before it. The thin hope they might rendezvous with the Armstrong, or at least retrieve a message buoy from her, died before they went to bed. There had been no sign of their sister ship since their fourth jump. No one shared conjectures of what could have happened. Instead, they focused on their own survival, the search for water and getting coordinates right each time they hurled the Glenn across Space. They had come more than halfway. Surely they would make it to Goldilocks now.

"Rob. Hey, Love, it's time to get up." Jerry sat on the mattress, careful not to spill the precious cup of caffeine. His spouse lay on his side, eyes shut. Was he twitching? He reached out and set the mug on the dresser before half turning and touching Rob's shoulder.

"What? Move!" Rob jerked up with a yell and Jerry grabbed his other shoulder to restrain him.

"Hey, take it easy. Are you OK? Having a bad dream?"

Rob grasped his forearms hard and his staring eyes gradually focused on him. Jerry smelled the tang of sweat and noticed stains of dampness on his T-shirt. Evidently it was a doozy of a nightmare.

"It's all right. I'm here. It's morning. You with me, man?"

Rob shook his head. "Yeah, sorry. I had the most vivid dream. I couldn't wake up."

"Want to share it with me?"

"Give me coffee first."

Jerry smiled. His analytical husband held onto certain weird superstitions. He never shared a nightmare before he ate or drank something in the morning. Long ago his mother told him that if he did, the dark dream might come true. Some beliefs defied logic. He handed over the mug and waited for the story.

"There was a fog all around me." Rob held the thick sided cup in both hands, taking small sips of the hot liquid. "At first, it was kind of peaceful. But then I heard a child singing. I needed to go right to it. I tried to move my feet forward. They stuck like they were in quicksand. I heard a storm come up howling. Good, I thought, I'll blow free now. But that high wind didn't touch me. The mist didn't dissipate. I don't know why I was desperate. I felt the child was in trouble."

He took another sip and looked at Jerry, who was staring at him, not moving a muscle. "What?"

"That's mine. You had the same dream I've been having since, well, before we left Earth."

"You never told me."

"Right. How weird. If I had shared it, I would suspect your subconscious was reliving my story."

"Have you had it recently?"

"I had it last night, or actually this morning. Before I got up. It's always a dawn dream. At first, I'd react as if it was a nightmare, but I'm used to it now."

"It's truly the same?"

"Sometimes, like before Xander was born, I detect more children's voices. But there's usually only one. I can't make out the words of the song and I never reach it."

Rob shook his head and drained the last drop of his coffee. "I wonder if this is an effect of the jump. Or are we such an old married couple even our dreams coincide?"

He gave Jerry a peck on the cheek as he swung his legs over the edge of the bed and got up. "Let's ask Doc what she thinks. This might be an obscure psychological phenomenon. Are Lily and Xander up?"

"Up and out. The bathroom's all yours." Jerry stood too, giving him a quick hug. "I'll catch you at dinner, OK?"

Four years and that same dream keeps coming back to haunt me and now Rob? Jerry wondered why he hadn't ever told his husband about it, or anyone else for that matter. He looked forward to Doc weighing in on it.

This day had challenges enough, though, without another mystery to unravel. He headed to the bio-dome where once again the gunked up pumps needed major cleaning. Long ago he had loved a fresh trout dinner. Now he fantasized a juicy steak, a nice pork roast, even stewed chicken. No good imagining those dishes though. It only makes the walls move in, he thought. Soon they would find sufficient water to get the 3-D printers on line again. Then, he hoped they would revamp fish protein into something tastier.

At eleven hundred hours, Lily beeped him. Her miniaturized face, hovering above his wrist band, held no clue to her emotions but her voice, curt and tense, sounded annoyed.

"He's doing it again. Can you come?"

Jerry wiped his hands, wet and smelly from dumping trout back into their cleansed home. "Yep, I'm just finishing up. I'll be there in five minutes." He grabbed a squirt of sanitizer from the pump next to the ponds and hurried to their quarters.

As he entered the common area, he registered Lily on the couch, her com-pad in her hands, flat-lined mouth and stern eyes. Xander, in the middle of the room, spun round and round. His chubby three-year-old legs tottered, little arms flung wide open. His face, Jerry noted, bore an expression of pure happiness. He didn't waver when the door opened, or even notice his uncle.

The tableau of the three of them lasted a minute. Then Lily reached out and caught the boy's arm. "Stop it. Go play with your toys now."

Xander, shocked out of his serenity, began crying before she got the words out of her mouth. He looked up, and seeing his uncle Jerry watching, increased the volume to a howl. His mother let loose a torrent of Chinese which they both understood as a rebuke. The child pulled away and stomped off to his bedroom.

Lily sat back frowning. "See, it's getting worse every day. Spinning and spinning. Even when other children are here."

"Why's he doing it, Lil?"

"I can't tell. Maybe just to bug me." She looked down

at her tablet and tapped at the screen again, continuing the work she had been doing.

From the distance came the sound of little feet unevenly stepping, and humming in a high childish voice.

"Stop it, Xander," Lily yelled.

Jerry rose, going to the bedroom door. Xander, ignoring his mom, twirled round the room narrowly missing the bed in his gyrations. His feet tangled in blocks scattered on the floor and he stumbled to a halt.

"Hey, kiddo," Jerry crossed the space between them and crouched beside the boy. "What's with all the spinning?"

"Whoosh!"

"Whoosh?"

"Yeah, wind—whoosh."

"So how does he know about wind?" Lily now stood in the doorway, her arms clenched across her chest.

"That's a good question. Do you think someone compared the fans in the bio-dome or the shuttle bay to wind?"

Since Xander had been born on the space ship, it was impossible for any weather to be in his personal experience. Comparison to mechanical fans seemed a stretch though.

"How did you learn about wind, little guy?"

The child's face lit up. He ran to his toy box. Bending over so far he nearly disappeared into it, he dug around, throwing out balls and blocks until he let out a happy cry. He marched his treasure back and put it into Jerry's hands: a battered children's book featuring the alphabet.

"Wind," he said.

Turning to the page with 'W' on it, sure enough the word 'wind' appeared with the illustration of a duck in a mackintosh holding an umbrella being blown inside out.

"Wow, you learned 'wind' from this picture? Good job, Xanda Panda."

"Not good job. Stop spinning. There's no wind here." Lily's annoyance now spread to both.

"Come on, Lil. It harmless enough. Why are you worried?"

Her mouth settled into the slight downward curve which Jerry recognized as her 'don't argue with me' frown. She turned on her heel and stomped back to her seat in the common room. He stood, and after ruffling Xander's hair, followed her.

As he sat on the couch beside her, they caught the sound of him whirling again.

"It is kind of strange, but kids do weird things, Lily. It could be because he's never felt the wind, it intrigues him."

She looked at him, her eyes hard and bright. "Doc says maybe it's autism."

"Autism?" What the hell was Anne Price thinking? Jerry wondered to himself. A bubble of fear rose in his gut, but he pushed it down. "Oh no, Lil, that can't be it. I've seen autism. Xander's emotionally connected to all of us. Autistic children don't look people in the eye. They don't hug you. Do they even talk? Xander's speaking."

"He's not talking like Ben or Saphir and they're six months younger."

"Yeah, but that's because you're speaking Chinese to him, right? Anne said it would take longer for him to verbalize because he's exposed to two languages."

Lily's frown increased, and she looked at the com-pad grasped in her hands. "Doc says there's a kind of autism that comes later. He could go back, you know—stop talking, stop hugging." The knuckles on her fingers turned white.

"Regress?" Jerry wanted to either run out of this terrible room or shake Lily for scaring him so. The trouble was he realized she might be right. His mother had cared for such a child in her day care center. That little boy had faded in front of them. The bubble in his gut reached his chest making it hard to breathe.

Lily watched him. "You think it's autism?"

Her voice softened, reaching for hope. Her eyes scrutinized him. He looked at the floor. In the inner room, the sound of Xander's twirling became unbearable.

"Stop it, Xander," he shouted.

Lily turned her face away.

They went together with Rob to see Doc that afternoon.

"Look," Anne said as they huddled on chairs in her tiny sick bay office, "there's no way to ascertain what's going on with your son. My tests indicate he's completely healthy. His behavior is anomalous but not that far out of range for normal toddler actions. Why don't you keep an eye on it. I'll do more research and see if we can devise preventative therapy to push him back into the norm. I've got to say, though, even on Earth, they couldn't do much to help autistics."

"What symptoms will tell us if he's sick?" asked Jerry.

"Well, notify me if he develops any other obsessive behaviors, like staring at lights or banging his head. If you see him pulling away from you, not wanting to be touched anymore, that would also cause concern. I don't recall how many words he's saying now, but if he stops speaking in sentences or regresses in language skills, that's a red flag."

"Do you think some food in his diet is missing?" Lily asked. "Not enough vitamins?"

"No, Lil. The best studies on autistic kids indicate

something goes wrong with genetic development very early in the fetus's gestation. There's this range of chromosomes on our DNA. Autism isn't a specific disease. It's a whole slew of problems that vary in severity, linked to combinations of affected chromosomes."

"That first jump we took... Lily was only five or six weeks pregnant." Rob wore his analytical scowl which Jerry sensed hid his terror. "Are you thinking genetic damage happened then?"

Anne, sitting behind her cluttered desk, looked at her fingers intertwined before her and sighed. "We understood that jumping while women were pregnant posed an unknown risk. Perhaps it was a good thing we stopped letting anyone else conceive."

"You mean you think that the other children may develop autism too." Jerry offered his fear, laying it before them for consideration.

She looked up, frowning at the three. "We don't know Xander is autistic and we can't predict that whatever is bothering him will affect the others. This is not the time to be spreading rumors which might cause panic among parents, OK? We have to sit tight and see what happens. This may just be Xander's personality developing in a quirky way."

The two men nodded, unhappy but accepting the doctor's orders. Xander's mother—not so much.

She stood up, as tall as her five-foot frame could stretch, leaned over the desk and said, "No. This is my baby. We need to do something now."

"Lily, come on." Doc shifted away from the tiger mom's anger. "What do you want me to do? It's too early to tell. We have to wait."

"What would you do if he was your kid?" Lily threw the challenge in her face. "Only sit around?"

Anne looked for help from Jerry and Rob, both of whom raised their eyebrows. "OK, Lil, how about this? We can't treat Xander medically because we don't know yet if it's a medical problem. But we could get Darren to assess his brain function. He might have more specific ideas of what we should investigate."

Lily frowned. Their neuro-scientist wasn't her favorite person. They had brought in him to consult with Doc on her emotional breakdown after her husband's death. She found him both a reminder of that tragedy and an unsympathetic character.

Rob said, "It's an avenue we should explore, Lil."

Darren often collaborated with him in the bio-lab, so Rob had a good handle on the young scientist's potential. He was brilliant, no doubt about that. Darren just didn't connect well with other people, speaking over their heads and hiding behind the shock of dark hair which always hung in his thin face. He had difficulty putting other people's needs before his own agenda. In many ways, Jerry thought, he remained his fourteen-year-old self—thrown into adulthood at Harvard, completely ready for the intellectual challenge and equally unprepared for the social life.

"I'll get him up to speed on the tests I've done and ask him to work you into his schedule soon," Doc said. "Please remember though, the less we mention autism to the other parents the better. If they're afraid, people see problems with their kids when nothing is wrong. Let's not start a panic here."

"OK," Lily agreed. "But I'll give Xander more vitamins

too."

As they left sickbay, she turned to Rob. "Can you talk to Darren? Let him know how important this is?"

"I will, Lil. He's coming in this afternoon and I promise I'll get him to see this as urgent."

Jerry put his arm around her shoulders in a traveling hug. "Try not to worry. Remember, Doc thinks this might simply be a phase Xander's going through."

Even as he said it, he looked over her head at Rob, who met his eyes with concern in his own.

Jerry made a point of being with his husband when Darren stopped into the lab to check on his experiments. As Rob raised Xander's strange behavior, the neuro-scientist showed no interest at all in examining him.

"If Doc's done the tests, there's nothing more I can do." He looked around Rob to the shelf which held the electron microscope and reached for his samples. "Autism isn't my field."

"C'mon, Darren. With no psychiatrist on board, you're the closest we've got to an expert on the human brain."

"I am an expert. I could tell you a lot about a person's brain but I need to dissect it. If we had a loaded CAT scan like they have at UCLA, I could investigate without killing him, but we don't."

Rob sucked in a breath, but before he snapped at the annoying man, Jerry discreetly held up a finger. He suspected that much of Darren's arrogance hid deep loneliness. How could they keep him engaged? He grasped the first idea that came to mind.

"OK, here's another riddle for you, Darren. How do two people dream the same thing at the same time?"

"Explain." He looked up, not at Jerry, but at Rob who breathed out and, with a nod to his husband, began the story.

"I had a weird nightmare this morning. When I told Jer about it, he admitted he'd been having the same one since before we left earth. It's as if I caught it from him, like the flu."

"Describe it."

As Rob recounted the nightmare, Darren sat on a high stool, fixating on him.

"I had this dream, too." He said the words without surprise—just a matter of fact.

Both men stared at him. "How can that be?" Rob asked.

"You say Jerry had it before?"

"Yes, regularly, since before we launched."

"Hmm... Wind might be the bridge."

"What?" Rob, no intellectual lightweight himself, looked confused. Jerry felt the disconcerting free fall of being left in the dust as Darren leapt ahead with a theory.

"The boy's playing at being in the wind and we're having dreams which feature wind. There may be a link. Maybe the kid's having the dream."

"That's a stretch, don't you think?" Jerry scanned Rob's face as he spoke and saw his brow contract into his 'focusing now' look.

Darren shrugged. "Two weird things happening, both involving a common element. I'd check it out."

"How?" Jerry asked. "Xander's only three. If we describe the dream to him, he might think he should just agree with us."

"No idea. Ask Abby. She's excellent at coming up with experiments.

Rob glared at his flippant colleague, stopping his move to leave. "OK, but you have to work with us, man. You and Abby have collaborated before. She's good, but she's a sociologist, not a brain specialist. We need you involved too."

Darren hesitated a moment and then gave a sharp nod.

Abby Bennett, their sociologist who cross trained as a communications specialist, was one of the few 'soft' scientists on the Glenn, as Conner would say. She orbited the outskirts of both the scientific society and the religious communities, making friends with everyone. Her bright red hair and snub nosed round face sprinkled with freckles gave her the air of a teenager which invited many to initially discount her abilities. No one made that mistake after four years in space. Abby perceived the big picture of a situation better than anyone else on board. Somewhere along the line, she had found the confidence to stand up to being ignored and insisted that other scientists take her viewpoints seriously. While Darren used to ignore this personable young woman, Jerry knew they now worked together regularly creating models of communal living units designed to ease adaptation on the anticipated new world.

As Darren tinkered with an experiment in the bio-lab, Rob called Abby and invited her to join them. When she arrived, Jerry pulled four of the stools into a rough circle and they sat. He noticed that before he took his seat beside her, the awkward young man brushed his unruly bangs out of his face and quirked a small smile in her direction. Abby's response, "Hey, Brainiac. Are you in on this conference?" brought up a flush under his brown cheeks.

"Yeah, these guys need help with a dream, so I thought of you—our woo-woo scientist."

"A dream, huh? Sounds right up my alley. Tell me all about it."

Rob, shaking his head, took the lead in explaining both Xander's strange spinning behavior and that the three men had an identical nightmare. "Darren thinks because wind plays a significant role, Xander might have had it too and is acting it out."

"OK, stop there a minute." The young woman looked up from taking notes on the com-pad balanced on her knee. She frowned at them. "You guys all had the same one? That's kind of weird. Tell me what it was."

Before Rob answered, Darren said, "No. Think for a moment, Abby. Did you have a dream early this morning just before you woke?"

The red head tilted and her turquoise eyes met the intensity in Darren's dark face with humor. "Well, yes. As a matter of fact I had a vivid nightmare. Do you want me to share?"

"No. Let me tell you what you dreamed: You were surrounded by fog. Somewhere a child was singing. You wanted to find the kid. But you couldn't move your feet. Then the wind came up howling. You could hear but not feel it. The whole scene scares you."

The room fell silent. Abby stared at Darren and then at Jerry and Rob, who nodded their heads. She exhaled, pursing her lips. "The child sounded so sad and I was helpless. I couldn't get there. It makes me want to cry even now."

"Have you ever heard of people dreaming the exact same thing?" Rob asked.

"No. There are symbols universal to humanity and I guess there might be specific cultural themes in dreams.

I've never seen or studied anything like this, though." Abby paused and then said, "Each of you tell me in detail what you dreamed."

Darren nodded, absorbed now in the presenting problem. "Let Jerry go first. He's the only one who had this dream previously."

The men shared the details of their nightmares as the young sociologist listened, unconsciously chewing a hangnail. Then, her brow contracted, and she ventured, "Well, the setting— fog, wind without movement, a child's voice and the need to move but not being able to—those matched. I notice we each reacted differently though. I looked up, trying to see the sky and get my bearings. Rob attempted to gauge the distance to the child and the solidity of the ground. Darren freaked out most around the immobility. Jerry focused more on his feelings about the singer, but he's been having the dream for a long time. He even moved a little once, which none of the rest of us accomplished."

Rob summarized for her. "So the environment is the same, but we have our own individual reactions during it. That's so strange. Could it be a sleeping hallucination?"

"We're far from home, guys." Darren said. "Who knows how space affects our brains."

"I'll put together a survey to see if anyone else has dreamed this." Abby turned to look at Jerry. "I think Xander can answer a couple of questions too, don't you?"

"What about the rest of the kids?" Darren interrupted.

"Hmmm, you're right. We need to test all the children. I wonder if they might be more sensitive to whatever initiates the nightmare. Obviously Jerry is since he's been having the dream for so long. What's different about him?"

Three sets of scientific eyes scrutinized him, and Jerry squirmed. "Hey, guys, back off. No dissecting a living crew member, OK?"

Abby laughed. "I'll make Darren take that option off the table."

A week of interviews uncovered eighty people on the ship who remembered having a similar dream the night after their twelfth interstellar jump. Some of them had already discovered they shared the phenomenon, and it provided a topic for conversation trumped only by speculation on whether they would find water this ISRU. As more nights passed, fifty percent of the dreamer group continued to have the nightmare regularly.

Abby determined that Xander also dreamed a similar scene but, like Jerry, he appeared long familiar with it. While the dream elicited yearning, frustration, and even fear in adults, Xander looked forward to its regular visit. He expected to feel the wind and find the singing child any night now. His spinning was an attempt to connect with what he heard and had only recently identified. Lily bounced between relief and worry about this new development. Jerry pointed out that the phantasm visited him for over four years with little side effect and gave thanks that autism no longer threatened.

The next step was to assess the younger children's experience with the dream. Abby and Darren collaborated to devise an experiment which put them into a simulation of the scene while they observed their reactions. Jerry and Rob set up a mister in a tiny office close to the bio-dome. They filled the room with fog, using dry ice, and ran a fan which made a blowing noise, but didn't so much as ruffle the air within. Abby took the children in one by one. Jerry stayed outside, singing plaintively, "Jack and Jill ran up the hill to fetch a pail of water, Jack fell down and broke his crown and Jill came tumbling after." They all agreed this song most approximated the singing in their dream.

Abby reported their results to the steering committee. "Xander went in first and was delighted. He obviously recognized the experiment as reconstructing his dream. The three-year-olds also reacted favorably to the 'game', laughing and jumping about in the fog. Then they moved confidently toward the singing. Saphir told me the voice was wrong.

"I speculated that the youngest children might be afraid, so I let their mothers come in with them. But even they presented confidence and appeared at home in the setting."

Jerry had joined the steering committee as they faced each other over the table in the briefing room off the bridge. While the issue with the dreams didn't seem dangerous, curiosity was growing.

"What does this demonstrate?" asked Doc.

"While not the most rigorous test," said Darren, standing behind Abby and avoiding eye contact with them, "it's the best we could do under the circumstances. It may prove nothing, but it leads me to believe all the children are familiar with this dream. What we can't know, given their level of communication, is if it is exactly the same for them. And it still doesn't explain why it's happening to so many of us."

Abby nodded. "None of them seemed frightened, though. I take that as a good sign.

Ahdam said, "Allah speaks to us in dreams. This may be a message to his last people. We must ask what it means."

Sarah leaned forward, elbows on the table. "I agree that dreams are vehicles for God to communicate, but have you ever read of more than one person having the same one? Is that in your scriptures? Because I don't remember it in the Torah anywhere."

"No, I know the Old and New Testament backwards and forwards, and I can't recall this." Steve's assertion came across as a brag, but those gathered accepted his authority in biblical knowledge.

Jerry spoke. "Let's look for both the scientific reasons behind the dream and its metaphysical message. It doesn't have to be an either/or answer. There's another question we should ask, too."

Kathir leaned forward, watching him. "What might that be?"

Jerry, rubbing his hand over his cropped hair, took a breath before venturing an response. "I asked myself, if not God, who else may try to communicate with us?"

"Who else? What do you mean?" Adham's frown deepened as if offended.

Rob picked up Jerry's line of reflection. They had gone over this alone several times. "We've speculated for centuries about whether the universe has other intelligent beings. Scientists sent out messages on radio wavelengths, in satellites, and with deep dish antennas at SETI. Just because we never made contact doesn't mean that no one listened. In fact, those communications took a long time reaching their targets. What if someone did receive them and is just now responding?"

"Or maybe," Kathir said, "it has nothing to do with our history. This may be a new communication sent from this area of space. That might be why people received it after our twelfth jump. We're only now in range."

"Except Jerry and Xander tuned in much earlier," Abby pointed out.

Jerry sensed the energy in the room increase by several notches. This was the most alien event they had encountered in outer space. Every other experience mirrored everyday happenings back home. Traveling between the stars, mining asteroids, the daily chores of staying alive all had new and exotic components, but they also connected with what they had done on earth. This shared dream caught them off balance. It was outlandish—a mystery haunting them all.

Three years later, Jerry stood by the observation deck's door waiting for the children. He heard them long before they appeared—seven little pairs of feet thundering down the hall punctuated by happy shouts and squeals. They raced around the corner, Xander leading the way. Jerry crouched to catch the seven-year-old before they collided, swinging him to his side while the others gathered round. Even the youngest, Alice, caught his serious mood, watching him with big eyes, while still panting. They all wore identical new navy jumpsuits, with a bright yellow and blue SpaceTech patch on one shoulder and the American flag on the other.

The Glenn would jump within twenty-four hours. If all their calculations were right, this was the leap to Goldilocks—their destination, the planet where their journey would end. Jerry smiled as he recalled several weeks ago when Abby and Darren asked him to preside over their marriage on this day—the day before the rest of their lives. It presented the perfect celebration for the crew, a container for all their hopes, as they faced this unchartered chapter of their mission.

Ayisha Hassani, Jane Dahl and Rob trailed the kids around the corner talking amongst themselves as they joined the little mob. Jerry noted the boutonnieres and brides' maid bouquets they carried. Thank God, this ISRU had provided enough water to erase the worries of scarcity and put the 3-D printers back on line. They hadn't had moisture to grow real flowers for years now. He was glad he had squirreled away packs of seeds though. Perhaps roses and lilies would bloom on their new planet soon. He raised his hand to catch everyone's attention.

"OK, you guys. Let's have the girls come help Abby get ready. All you boys, go over to the gym where Darren's waiting. Xander, you're the oldest, so I need you to remind the younger kids what to do. Make sure Uncle Rob remembers, too." He added the last sentence with a wink to his husband.

Xander nodded as he accepted his duty and took the hand of the youngest boy while Rob led them across the hall to the gym. Jerry and his entourage entered the observation deck.

As they came in, Abby turned from the round window looking out over star studded black space. They would leave these constellations behind as they had done twenty-five times before, to find another pattern of stars to claim as home. Her red shoulder length hair curled around her pale cheeks. The same white daisies and lavender irises which the little girls now clutched in their hands crowned her head. She could have dressed in an elaborate wedding gown but, being Abby, she opted for a new jumpsuit in the same dark blue she wore when she boarded the Glenn seven years ago. "I look good in navy," she'd told Jerry. "And anyway, Darren wouldn't even recognize me in a dress."

Ayisha, still mourning the lost opportunity to dress up, slumped down on one of the pillows scattered around the polished floor. "It's amazing how stunning you are in these godforsaken overalls, Abby. I feel like a pole ready to hold up a circus tent. You know, when I first got on the Glenn, they made us wear these. I took mine off the minute I could."

"I see you found high heels to make you an even taller pole," Abby teased, shaking her head at her best friend.

"If you're a tent pole, I must be a tent stake." Jane Dahl, the other bridesmaid and nutritionist for the crew stood a good six inches below Ayisha's nose. Over the last seven lean years, she had lost the plumpness which she once feared might disqualify her from the mission. Her husband complained there was hardly any of her left to hug, but Jerry suspected it was their marital devotion which prompted Abby to select her for her second attendant. This would not be a wedding for magazine layouts, but their sociologist realized the ceremony affected everyone on the Glenn. She had given careful consideration to the symbolism of the moment.

"Jane, you're the most beautiful woman on board. Just ask Eli. Oh and look at these girls." She opened her arms to gather in Alice, Saphir, Hailey and Marnie. "I'm the luckiest woman in the universe to have four gorgeous flower girls lead my procession."

Jerry rounded the bride and attendants up into a tight circle and prayed a blessing over them before he left to

organize the congregation waiting for them in the cafeteria. He hugged Abby. "I'd tell you not to be nervous, but I have to admit to being jittery myself. This is the first time you've gotten married, but it's also the first time I've ever conducted a wedding. Everyone expects the bride to be on edge but I'm supposed to know what I'm doing."

"Don't worry, Padre," she whispered back. "I have complete confidence today. If we stumble, someone out there will pick us up."

A makeshift stage stood at one end of the cafeteria. All the crew who could be spared from their jobs crowded in to witness while the others, stuck at necessary chores around the ship, tuned in on video feeds. They used the simple elegant liturgy of the Episcopal Church. Jerry had offered to alter it a bit, knowing Darren avowed no religious beliefs and Abby had left her Roman Catholic roots behind with childhood. They surprised him by insisting they wanted the traditional service. The soon to be groom gave him a conspirator's grin. "Hell, I don't even understand why it's important for us to get married, so we might as well use the Church's incomprehensible language too."

Abby had jumped in. "But the ceremony is meaningful to us, Jerry. We're not just throwing a party. We take this commitment seriously and we want the crew, our family, to witness our vows."

Looking over a sea of blue coveralls crowded into their dining area, Jerry realized that the crew was making a statement of solidarity with Abby and Darren. He'd never heard of a wedding where everyone wore the same outfit. Individuality wasn't dead, but commitment to live in community was the theme of the day, he decided. He draped the white stole, a final gift from his earthbound congregation of St. Anne's, about his neck. The satin shone sleek and brilliant on the navy of his own jumpsuit. The ancient words weaving humanity into God's immortal love rolled smoothly from his mouth. At the end of the ceremony, he wound the stole around Darren's and Abby's joined hands, securing them to each other with a blessing, while the crowd held its breath. Then, as the bride and groom kissed, the crowd erupted into cheers and clapping.

Several men dismantled the stage as bride and groom recessed and the reception party began. The plan was for the couple to have this evening before the jump free for a mini honeymoon. Ayisha, Jane and a few other women snuck into the couple's spartan apartment just before the ceremony, decorating it with rose petals, satin pillows, champagne and chocolates. The newlyweds only had ten hours before needing to be back on deck, preparing for the Glenn's last interstellar transition. It didn't surprise anyone that as soon as they had eaten a slice of cake, Darren took his flushed bride by the hand, trying to whisk her away.

Jerry helped clear a path to the door as well wishers gave hugs and kisses. When the pair stepped over the threshold into the hallway, a small figure darted through the crowd and slipped out with them. Jerry found himself out in the hall too, saying one final good night, when Xander inserted himself into the love fest. He tugged at Abby's sleeve. "I need to tell you something important. The dream—something changed about the dream last night."

"Sweetheart, why don't you tell me after the jump?"

Darren put his arm around Abby's shoulder, claiming her even as the boy clung to her.

"But it's important." Xander's face was a study in anxiety, lower lip trembling.

Abby leaned into her new husband and looked down at the demanding child.

"Honey, could you share it with Jerry? Then he can enter it in the file and I'll check it as soon as I have time after the jump."

"OK, but don't forget."

"You know I won't. Jerry, the pass word is maerd—dream spelled backwards. Clever, huh? See you guys later."

With that, she disengaged Xander's hand, kissing him on the top of his head and scampered with Darren toward the elevator.

"Uncle Jerry, can I tell you about the dream now?"

Jerry looked at the cafeteria door but, knowing Xander wouldn't let this subject rest, he gave in to the inevitable. "OK, kiddo. Let's go onto the observation deck and talk."

They settled on the pillows in front of the great round window that provided the only unaided view to the outside of the ship. A lone daisy, escaped from one of the bouquets, lay on the floor and Jerry picked it up, twirling it as he concentrated on the boy's story.

"When I dreamed last night, it was different. I got a picture—a feeling—that the singer is like Abby."

"Like Abby? You mean friendly and warm?"

"No... Well maybe yes. It's more like the singer is a girl."

"Oh. Why is that significant, Xander?"

"That's the thing—it's big to her. She wants us to know who she is when we find her. She really hopes we won't give up looking for her. Or she thinks we'll get to her pretty soon. Anyway, she's excited and worried about something."

"Can't she help us move in the dream, then?"

"I don't think so. She can't move even more than us, so she really hopes we'll find a way to her."

Jerry considered the earnest young face in front of him. "You get a lot out of the dream that none of the rest of us do, dear. Why do you think that is?"

Xander shrugged. "I don't know. But Abby says to give her all the data. She and Darren are potting varies."

"You mean 'plotting the variables'?" He smiled. This was one way to teach the scientific method.

"Yeah. So will you put this in the journal, Uncle Jerry?"

"Yep. Right after the party's over, OK? Let's go and see if there's any cake left."

Later that evening as Rob and Jerry were getting ready for bed, Xander poked his head in to remind his uncle of his promise. With a sigh, Jerry kissed his husband good night and went back into their tiny common room to access the computer. He entered Abby's password and sure enough, up popped an extensive list of the ways they were tracking the common dream. He marveled at the amount of material there. Not only were the notes of the original accounts recorded, but it seemed Abby had meticulously listed when members of the crew began to have the nightmare. Her chart showed that ninety percent of the crew now shared the dream. That meant people who thought it gone had been revisited by it, and recently.

Jerry saw she had also documented all the crew's theories on what this phenomenon might be. His comments about the possibility of alien contact, the speculation about God's message and a common hallucination appeared on the earliest date. Later someone had offered the theory that space radiation initiated the episodes. That's interesting, he thought. I wonder if this will stop when we set down on a planet again.

He opened the file for changes observed in the dream and found Abby kept track of two kinds of variables: One was when people reported something out of the norm occurring in their particular dreams. His own name caught his attention when he saw she had noted that he moved a few steps, which no one else had yet accomplished. She also seemed interested in how an individual's understanding about what was happening in the nightmare evolved. Jerry saw that most of these entries came from Xander. I wonder, he pondered—is it right to encourage the boy to think so much about this strange phenomenon? Sure we all share it, but perhaps he's imagining a lot of this stuff.

After adding the latest episode of Xander's perceptions to this category, Jerry closed the file and went to bed. As he shut his eyes, he thought, tonight could be the last time I'll hear the singer. Instead of relief, his heart ached with sadness.

CHAPTER 7
PLANET KOI-3284

DATE: 2073 CE/1

"Come with me to the steering committee meeting today, Jer."
Rob, arriving at the small table with his tray of scrambled
eggs and toast, plopped onto a seat. "The rest of the members
will want to hear Xander's story from you."

"What story?" asked Lily. She had finished her meal, but
lingered, sipping her tea.

Jerry looked at her, considering for a moment telling her
of Xander's conviction that Goldilocks was talking to them.
He glanced over at Rob and saw a reflective gaze on his face,
so he said, "Has Xander told you he thinks the singer in the
dream is the planet?"

"Huh. He didn't tell me that. He's being dreamy a lot
now, though. Maybe that's why?"

Rob cocked his head at her. "What do you mean—
dreamy?"

"Oh, you know—he gets quiet, stares at nothing and
doesn't answer people when they talk to him."

"Has he been doing that a lot? I hadn't noticed." Jerry
grimaced. How could he have missed signs that Xander was
struggling?

"Shelly says all the kids are doing it. She said it's normal—
something about the new environment."

Rob nodded. "Yeah, that might explain it. Or the other children tune into Goldie too." He glanced up connecting with Jerry's eyes. "We should check that out. When Abby recovers she can help us test them like she did with the dream."

"Right. So what are you telling the Steering Committee today?"

"Well, I'd like you to tell them exactly what Xander told you, both about contacting the planet before the orb launched and how he receives messages from her."

Jerry's stomach soured. He set down his fork. "Sounds like you're more skeptical this morning than you were last night."

His imagination jumped ahead to dealing with Steve's constant need for exact and detailed information and Ahdam's insistence that every move be in line with Muslim law. Yes, his belly definitely hurt.

Rob's eyes softened, and he smiled at his husband. "I'll back you, Jer. Don't worry. Something unusual and special happened to our kid. I'm just not sure what. It's my job to ask the right questions. I need your witness to events because I don't want Xander harried. If he suspects we doubt him, we could lose his trust."

"So you do believe him?" Jerry wasn't certain why, but he needed confirmation.

"Yeah, I'm convinced he's getting some kind of message he interprets as coming from the planet. It's evident that something is reacting to our presence. Our seven-year-old didn't create wind which knocked the shuttle out of the sky, yet he knew a disaster might happen. We need to investigate, but discreetly."

Lily, listening to this conversation, asked, "Is Xander in trouble?"

Rob looked at her in surprise. "No, not at all." He took a steadying breath and then said, "We think he may be communicating with our new planet."

She stared hard at them both. "That's crazy."

"See why caution is necessary?" He addressed Jerry, who was smiling at Lily, trying to reassure her.

She persisted. "Has he been telling you stories? 'Cause he's got a great imagination."

Jerry said, "I assumed he had a fantasy friend, too, Lil. But what if this playmate is real? Remember when we feared he had autism, but it turned out he was having the same dream as the rest of us? Xander may understand that dream better than we do. He's a smart kid. He might be right."

Rob nodded and reached out to pat Lily's hand. "Whatever is happening, we need to assure Xander that we trust and stand by him. He knows we have a lot to learn about the phenomenon he's uncovered."

"Just keep him out of trouble," the tiger mom growled. "Or he'll have to deal with me."

The Steering Committee established a routine for overseeing development of their colony after the last of the crew landed. They convened twice a day. The first meeting after breakfast dealt with assigning new jobs and assessing the big picture—problems which had arisen and challenges that lay before them. This gathering often lasted an hour. Sometimes, though, they stayed until the second meal, wrestling with the dilemmas of existence on foreign soil. Then they headed out to join the rest of the colonists, helping on whatever projects had priority.

After the communal meal they called 'first supper' (the third of four meals in their thirty-two hour rotation), the leaders assembled again to check the day's progress. While other settlers chatted, listened to the latest composition of one of their musicians or played endless rounds of bridge and poker, the leadership team went over the events of the day, planning the colony's work.

Membership on the Steering Committee rotated every two Earth years. The eight elected members now included Rob and Eli as the scientists' representatives. Sarah, the rabbi, chaired the meetings this year and the Jewish contingent had recently chosen Hadith to join her. The Muslim community always sent their imam, Ahdam, and Kathir, their cantor. The Christians also regularly re-elected their pastor, Steve, but on the last rotation replaced Tamara with Shelly. Steering Committee meetings, even during their time in space, were open to anyone who wanted to attend. Early on, though, they established that only those elected could weigh in during the sessions. Non-members had to catch a leader's ear to be invited to speak.

This morning the leadership team gathered as usual, pulling together the white plastic cubes serving as all-purpose furniture to sit on and hold their mugs. Only Eli, being nursed in sickbay, was absent. Jerry sat with a handful of other spectators on the periphery of the team's loose circle. Behind them in the main hall the kitchen crew busied themselves with washing off tables and sweeping the floor. He heard the sharp clatter of dishes being stacked in the side room which served as the food prep and storage area. The coffee maker remained on its table. He thought about grabbing one more cup, but then Hadith, who had been leading the conversation about schedules for laying water pipes to the lake, put down her com-pad signaling a readiness to go on to the next item on the agenda.

Sarah turned to Rob with a smile and said, "That's all the short term planning we can do today. You had something with long-term implications you wanted on the table?"

Before he could begin, a stir behind the spectators caused him to hesitate and Jerry saw Doc making her way across the dining room. She waved to be sure she had the committee's attention.

Sarah sighed, shaking her dark curls. "Sorry, Rob. I forgot Doc needed a few minutes this morning too. Do you mind letting her go first?"

"No, not at all." Rob got up and moved another cube into the circle. "Have a seat, Anne, and tell us what's on your agenda."

"Thanks." Doc perched on the block, wrapping her lab coat around her as if chilled. She quirked a wry smile at them. "I know Goldilocks has been home only a little over a month, but we've been lax in creating a reproduction policy. The birth control implants in a third of our women expire next week. It's time to decide how many pregnancies can be supported at a time and how many children we can nurture. And I'll say this again: we must reach an understanding of how we will optimize combining our genes. Better to wrestle with it now than to get entrenched in our traditional childbearing and rearing ways and not be able to change later on."

As she spoke, several members of the committee shifted uncomfortably. Adham frowned and turned away from the small feisty doctor. Sarah looked around, assessing the mood of the group. "You're right. We all remember your instruction on genetics. I'm afraid it strikes to the heart of our fear though, Doc. We don't want to lose the very cultures we've been fighting so hard to preserve."

Still facing away from her, Ahdam said, "Why do you harass us on this subject, Anne? We agreed that we would let our married couples have at least one child together without challenge. Let's get that done and worry about DNA later."

Doc looked at the imam and each of the other leaders. Jerry saw her fingers tighten as she held the fabric of her lab coat. "You all think we have plenty of time to decide this—that it can wait until after every woman who is able bears a child with her husband, but I'm worried. If we don't commit now to the most extensive recombination of DNA possible, it's going to get harder down the line. For example, the mothers who gave birth in space should consider having second children now. Will you deny them that or let them have two offspring from their marriages while everyone else has to mix it up for their second born? See how sticky it gets?"

"Wait, wait, wait." Adham's discomfort showed in every line of his body, from his clenched fists to his stormy brow. He turned to glare at Doc. "How do you suppose this genetic mixing will happen? Are you suggesting we ignore our marriage vows and sleep around with anyone else to get our DNA combined adequately?"

Anne sighed. "We talked about this on the ship, remember? There are several options, but simple artificial insemination, a procedure called intrauterine insemination or IUI, is a possibility. It doesn't take much equipment. A woman could do it in her own quarters although the conception rate would be higher if she agreed to let me help her with the sperm placement."

Hadith crossed her arms in unconscious imitation of the doctor's stance. "I thought we were going to wait until the children grew up and allow them to marry outside their religious communities if they want to. Why won't that still work?"

Heads nodded around the table but Doc shook her's. "That was a possible solution if the Armstrong's crew met us here. Now we know we're alone. Look guys, we are in a very precarious position. We barely have enough of a population to hope to avoid extinction in the next generation."

They all knew she was right. At the ship's capacity of two hundred adults, divided between males and females within the age range of fertility, they teetered on the edge of viability as a species. In fact, they had not begun their journey with a full crew and had lost twelve people already. The present population was one hundred and sixty-eight grown-ups and seven children.

Steve shrugged. "OK, then—I don't think we have any moral problem with artificial insemination. Let every couple have their own kids first. Then the gals can get pregnant with different men's sperm."

Sarah sat up very straight, her eyes fiery. "We will not be going back to an era when men use women as receptacles for children. This committee may suggest options, but women will maintain the right to decide what's best for them. And I have grave concerns about IUI. What might it do to the sacred relationship between parents and children? Will families with artificially inseminated children love them less than their naturally conceived first-born?"

Doc met her look with steel in her own eyes. "Sarah, I share your concern on both counts. That's why we can't wait to cope with this issue. Science tells us that to preserve our species we must have as many babies as possible, and that we need as great a variety in the gene pool as achievable. Our history as humans on earth warns us that if we produce second-class citizens, using women as chattel or creating children who are under nurtured, we set ourselves up for a society full of strife and pain. Somehow, we have to create a different scenario."

"Anne's right." Rob said. "We have to face this now. We should plan our future before we mire down in a pattern here. And it's not just about genetics. How many children can we support? How many women dare we lose from the workforce while they recover from delivery or are caring for infants? We planned on up to ten births a year, but that would mean some wait up to five years to get pregnant. We have to remember, our women are aging out of the possibility of parenthood quickly."

Now all the committee members were frowning. Hadith tapped a finger on her lips while Shelly's eyes darted to the group sitting behind Jerry where her husband and their little Alice played with a rag doll. Other leaders squirmed on their blocks.

Kathir, glancing at his wristband, held up a hand. "Friends we've been at this for ninety minutes now. I need to get out to the building site. I know you all have responsibilities, too. We're not going to solve this issue today. Let's think and pray on it. When do you want a decision, Doc?"

Her shrewd eyes scanned the gathered group, and Jerry felt her measuring their capacity for the truth. "The efficacy of the implants begins to decrease in about one week, but that doesn't mean someone will get pregnant right away. It also doesn't mean someone won't. The uncertainty is what I prefer to avoid because we don't want to face asking parents to abort."

"Right," Sarah said. "Let's sleep on this and revisit it tomorrow. We may need to schedule a longer meeting once the science orb is functioning. Rob, I'm afraid your issue must wait too. Are you OK with that?"

"Sure." He glanced at Jerry, who nodded his compliance.

The group stood, gathering up coffee cups and moving off in different directions to their day jobs. Rob joined his husband, waiting on the periphery and said, "John brought in another example of that little bug that looks like an armored car yesterday. This one is bright red instead of green."

"Did they find a nest?"

"No, they only discovered about twenty of these in various places around the building site. They attach themselves to stems of the yellow grass, but John couldn't tell if they're feeding. He said they seem content to hang there. I should go out and look for myself."

"I'm headed over to help Jim with the seedlings. Do you want me to bring you anything from your office?"

"No, but I'll walk with you. I can grab some insect traps and a magnifier before I head out."

Together they started towards the bio-dome. Doc fell into step beside them. Jerry, surprised but not wanting to seem rude, said, "Are you coming out to the dome for some R and R, Anne? There aren't flowers yet, but the greenery is soothing."

"Soothing sounds good. Committees drive me crazy. They talk and talk but nothing gets decided."

"It can be frustrating," Rob matched his pace to her

shorter stride. "Just remember, the settlers are coming from worldviews different than ours. They'll need time to adjust."

"Seems like Jerry doesn't feel the same qualms as the others. You're religious, Jer. Why is it different for you?"

"I'm not sure I'm unique but being gay means I've known for a long while that any children I have won't share my DNA, or Rob's. I also come from the perspective of being an outsider for most of my life, so I'm more used to questioning the central beliefs of my religion. That doesn't scare me as much as it does someone who has no ambivalence about their faith."

The three of them exited the main structure, bowing low to pass through the portal, and abandoned any attempt at conversation. Outside, a thirty mile an hour gale hit their faces, and they bent into the force to keep from blowing over. When they reached their destination, Jerry wrestled the door to the vestibule open, dug in his heels and held it as Rob and Doc scuttled in. Then he too ducked inside, the door slamming shut behind him. The receiving area to the bio-dome was cramped but as soon as his husband stepped in, Rob pushed through the entrance to the dome. They spilled into the still, warm air, which smelled of damp earth and home.

When they built this bio-dome, they knew it would be a refuge for homesick colonists, just as the garden on the Glenn served that function in space. So, between the spindly trees and new beds of tender shoots, a path meandered punctuated by small benches inviting people to sit and chat or meditate. Jerry halted the trio near the first seat they approached. Wind buffeted the thin translucent skin of the structure. He could barely hear Jim putzing around on the far side, putting in the bean plants that needed transferring. "Some thing's on your mind, Doc. Why don't you share it with us?"

Anne Price was a small woman but so vital and confident that no one perceived her as little. Now, though, she sat hunched over as if desiring to take up no space at all. Jerry, perching on the retaining wall across the path from her, wondered if she might be ill. Rob must have had the same thought because he dropped beside her, reaching out to touch her shoulder. "Are you all right?" he asked.

Doc laughed—a short, derisive burst. "Oh, it's not me that's in trouble. It's us. All of us. The problem's keeping me from sleeping but if we can solve it, I'll be fine." She lifted her head to look at the man sitting next to her. "We don't have time. Rob, you know this. We have barely enough people to renew the human race. If we dither around trying to make our morality fit the present circumstances, we are doomed. This isn't the season for compromise. We must force a new way of reproducing so the community survives."

Rob tilted his head, keeping his eyes engaged with hers. "What are you suggesting, Anne?"

"We need babies now—right away. It's clear the committee will put off deciding. They'll opt to allow all the married couples to bear at least one child, before they deal with the fact that more genetic variations are imperative."

"I think you're correct." Rob glanced over at his spouse, who nodded his agreement.

Doc shot Jerry a glance and then looked at the gravel between her feet. "By the time that first crop of babies arrives, we'll be so settled into repeating our heritage, that the crew will reject mating across religious lines or providing out-of-wedlock parentage. Either that or a caste system favoring legitimate children over second class bastards will develop, just as Sarah predicted."

Jerry leaned forward. "Do you have an idea? Can you see how to avoid those pitfalls?"

"We must force the committee's hand—do something to make this problem concrete here and now."

"So we need a catalyst—an event to focus everyone's energy on finding a solution now instead of reacting later to unpleasant situations." Rob said, nodding.

He also bit his lip, Jerry noted—a sure sign of stress. He turned his glance to Doc. "With so many other urgent decisions and projects to follow through on, I'm afraid if we rush the committee to resolve this they'll react badly and choose the easiest path possible."

"Jer's right, Anne." Rob frowned, still chewing. "You feel the solution is clear, but in the minds of the settlers this dilemma is a huge issue. Pressing them too hard may not be the wisest thing to do."

"I agree. We need a gentle catalyst, not a catastrophic one. Something which can highlight the need to alter our society while providing impetus and practice for that transition."

Jerry studied Doc's intense face. "You have a change agent in mind. Why don't you tell us?"

She nodded, looking up at him and then glancing at Rob beside her. "I have an idea and it involves you guys. I hope you'll forgive me if I'm too personal here."

She hesitated a second but when neither of the men spoke, she continued. "Lily already had a child with her husband and unfortunately, unless she marries again, won't get another chance to conceive under our present circumstances. You two have a loving relationship with her not currently sexual in nature, am I right?"

They glanced at each other and nodded, Rob flushing and Jerry growing paler as they anticipated where Doc was leading them.

She directed her eyes to the gravel under her feet again and spoke rapidly. "My plan is that, either by intrauterine insemination or by intercourse, Lily should conceive and the three of you become a model of a different sort of household. With your acceptance of Xander, you're halfway there already. A child with a biological father in your trio will be a concrete example of a way that mixing genes can happen. He or she will force the issue by making an unconventional family a reality and therefore a possibility for everyone else too. I hope that where one alternative exists, people find it easier to consider others."

Nobody spoke for a moment. Jerry heard the watering system kick in across the dome. He glanced at his husband, noticing that his slight flush had turned a deeper red and he focused on his hands clasped in front of him. Jerry took a breath, attempting to steady his voice. "So you want Rob to father a child with Lily."

"Rob?" Doc looked up-surprised. "Well, I suppose that would work, but I was really thinking of you, Jer."

Both men viewed her with astonishment.

"Me?" Jerry asked.

Rob smiled. "Of course. It has to be you. You're the priest, the trusted counselor of everyone on the Glenn. If you father a child out of wedlock, it gives every other faithful member the right to consider it."

"That's exactly what I was thinking," Doc said. "Plus, Jerry often talks about ethical matters and he's a respected religious leader. After the fact, he can explain why he did this and others won't discount him for simply being, you know—horny."

Jerry stood and paced up and down the path. "So we could use this, what did you call it? Intrauterine insemination, right? If Lily agrees?"

"Yes, the conception rate with IUI isn't as high as with intercourse but I'll help Lily monitor her cycle and catch her most fertile days. She doesn't have any physical problems to make this difficult, except for increasing age. We need to test your sperm levels and motility, but you weren't exposed to as much radiation as, say, the miners, so I bet you're OK."

"Any blow back by the community will affect Lily and the baby more than me and Rob." Jerry came to a halt. "We can't tell how people might react. Should we ask a child to bear that burden for us?" He sounded angry even to himself. He forced himself to take a deep breath and sit down again.

Doc leaned towards him. "Can you think of anything else that would push the committee to create guidelines on ways to mix our DNA and the treatment of children born outside of a traditional marriage?"

Jerry shook his head. Rob said. "I've got nothing. If we do this, it challenges the committee. They'll have to figure out how to treat both adults who make this difficult decision and how to protect the children. Even if we stall in setting up guidelines, other colonists will have permission to act in the best interests of our communal future."

Doc's wristband pinged, and she stood, stepping away to answer it. Jerry and Rob listened to her conversation with an assistant in sickbay and her directions to attend to what sounded like a sprained wrist. She ended her transmission with, "OK, hang on. I'll be there in ten minutes to check it. Be sure to get Eli up for his walk before second meal."

She turned toward the men and shrugged her shoulders. "I've got to go back. Can you guys talk to Lily about this, or do you want me to bring it up with her?"

"No, it will be better coming from us, don't you think, Rob?" Jerry looked at his husband.

"Yeah, then you'll have to explain how IUI works, and what you need from her."

Doc, already heading toward the door, gave them a stern look. "Please don't put it off, OK? We have to start trying right away."

Both men nodded, watching her exit, neither moving from their seats across the path from each other. Jerry heard Jim humming amongst the beans. The wind rattled at the roof but he thought it was dying down.

Rob sighed and hung his head. "What do you say, Jer? Will Lily go for it?"

"I'm not sure. She'll probably dislike the whole IUI thing. You know how she is about anything medical."

"So, would you have intercourse with her if that's her preference?"

Jerry considered this, looking at his spouse. "I could try. She might wish for you though."

Rob shook his head. "God, you saw this coming, didn't you? Years ago. And I promised you it wouldn't come to this—that I'd always be faithful."

Jerry left his seat on the wall and moved to sit beside his husband, wrapping an arm around him and bending close. "No one will be unfaithful, dear heart. We're just going to expand the parameters of faith. I've grown a lot since we talked about this in space. No matter which of us fathers a child with Lily, no matter what method we use, you and I belong to each other. No one else can break our relationship. That's what you promised me. That's what I promise you. Lil understands that."

Rob took a deep breath. "You're right. It'll take time to live into this. Let's go see what she says."

They intended to talk to her right away, but Lily, like every other colonist, was serving double duty. She worked on a crew building new shelters between cooking and cleaning up after meals. They caught up with her, eating first supper with Xander, but then Rob left for the Steering Committee's wrap-up session. Lily was putting the boy to bed when he finally returned to their quarters. Waiting in their tiny common room, Jerry looked up from his reading as he entered.

"How was the meeting?"

"Not bad. We're reconsidering where to put the gardens. Eli wants the landing field for the shuttles right where John requested a plot for vegetables."

"Good thing we have the whole planet to play with." Jerry smiled as Rob collapsed on the couch beside him.

"So did you tell Lil we need to talk to her?"

Jerry's smile dissolved. "No, she's pretty tired tonight. Maybe we should wait until tomorrow."

"Wait for what?" Lily emerged from her bedroom, clutching her toothbrush and paste with a pink towel slung over her arm.

Rob stood up. "We need to talk, Lil."

"Sure. Xander's already asleep so I have time."

She dropped onto a cushion, tucking one leg underneath

her, as Rob pulled up the desk chair to form an intimate circle. Jerry sat up straighter, easing the tension on his still sore ribs. The men eyed each other vying to see who would begin. Jerry decided he lost the toss and took a deep breath.

"Doc came to the early Steering Committee meeting today to say we're ready for colonists to have more babies. She's worried about the need to mix up our DNA though. Do you remember those lectures on genetics we had back on the Glenn?"

"Sure, but settlers won't be happy about that. They're scared it ruins their marriages."

Rob nodded. "That's the sentiment now, too. Doc fears she won't be able to change their minds in time for us to produce a healthy population. You know how close we are to the minimum number of people needed to restart the species, right?"

"So, what's this got to do with me? I'm single—a widow woman."

"True." Jerry leaned in toward her. "You're not married but you can still bear children. And you are in a relationship although not a marriage relationship. The three of us—well, four with Xander—are a different kind of family. Doc hopes if our unique configuration gives rise to kids who are healthy and loved, the rest of the crew might change their ideas about how to have children too."

Lily looked at Jerry and then at Rob. "But maybe someday I'll marry again. I'm not so old, you know."

Jerry sat back. "Have you been considering that, Lil? Is there someone you're interested in?" He flipped through the list of eligible bachelors in his head. He could call up only a handful—all of them scientists. They had lost none of the women settlers.

Lily sighed and frowned. "Not really. It makes me sad sometimes. I think, this woman might die and then I can be with him—but I don't want any of them dead. You're right. You guys are my family now." She cocked her head considering the men before her. "Do you want another baby?"

They looked at each other and smiled.

"Yes. Yes we do." Jerry relaxed into the truth of the statement. He and his husband wanted this. If Lily did too, a radical family might take root in this new world.

The woman before them squinted, focusing in on their faces. "Which of you will be dad?"

Rob said, "Doc wants Jerry to be the father this time. She feels it will help the other settlers see this as a valid moral choice and not just a scientific experiment."

"But that doesn't mean Rob couldn't father a child with you too." Jerry added.

"So how do we do this, Jerry?" Lily, as always, drilled into the problem. "You and I are like brother and sister. It must be hard for you to make love to me. Rob might be jealous, too."

"Doc suggested intrauterine insemination, if that's OK with you. She'll put the sperm I donate inside of you. Evidently it's easy and she considers us both good candidates."

Rob made eye contact with Lily. "If you want this, Lil, we'll make it happen—one way or another. The three of us may need to adjust our relationship, but I'm sure we can do it without too much discomfort. There are other complications to consider though. Repercussions might be hard for you, and the child—even for Xander, if the rest of the settlers don't accept our arrangement. If someone you like becomes available to marry, it will complicate things."

"Oh I'm not worried about that." Lily dismissed the dark future Rob painted with a wave of her hand. "I don't care what others think. A brother or sister would be good for Xander. And I'm getting old. I better get more babies while I can."

"OK, then." An impossible bubble of joy rose in Jerry's heart and he beamed at these two people he loved. "We'll make a family."

CHAPTER 8
SPACE

DATE: 2066-2067

A taxi delivered Jerry to the space shuttle's processing center early in the morning four weeks after Rob told him about the spreading plague. His husband had promised to drive him but he phoned at the last minute to cancel. Once again, Dagmar called an emergency meeting of the SpaceTech scientists and Rob, indispensable to this group, would miss the shuttle launch. "Don't worry," he'd said, in a voice which sounded very worried, "I'll come up in two weeks—sooner if I can swing it."

It hardly matters, Jerry thought as he pushed through the center's double doors with a duffel slung over his shoulder. I haven't spent over thirty minutes with him in the last month. He swallowed his loneliness, determined to engage with his future. There had been no contact from either his family on the west coast or Rob's mother and sisters. They faced the probability no one was left to say goodbye to, but it was too early to accept.

The room in front of him looked like the small airport of his hometown—a utilitarian holding space of cement floors and functional chairs bolted to the ground. About twenty young adults, all dressed in dark blue coveralls like his and clutching SpaceTech duffel bags, filled the area, huddled in groups of two to four.

Jerry found an empty spot and slid down to sit on the floor, back against cool metal wall panels. There was something unnerving about the scene. In a moment he figured it out:

Rob had pulled strings to get him assigned to the last shuttle taking settlers up to the Glenn. These passengers, members of the three religious groups, all volunteered for a historic journey of at least fifteen years—to become the first colonists on an unsettled planet. They planned to journey five years to reach KOI-3284, spend five years creating a settlement—planting crops, having children, sinking human roots into alien soil—and then return heroes to their native land. There should have been excitement, but none of the little clutches of travelers speculated on their pending adventure. No one here spoke above a murmur. They sat or slouched in near silence as if waiting for a funeral.

We're in limbo, Jerry realized. All of us have lost friends and family. We have no idea who we'll find gone when we return. He lowered his eyes, not wanting to connect with the sadness of the scene in front of him. His own grief overwhelmed him so he tuned out everyone and everything else, and missed the announcement scratching over the intercom giving instructions for boarding the shuttle. He looked up and noticed people gathering their satchels and moving with purpose in different directions. He realized he didn't understand what he was to do and levered himself off the wall to look around for clues. A touch on his elbow drew his attention to a petite Asian woman standing beside him.

"Hey, we're seat partners. We go into that line, there."

Her voice, with its lilting accent and off-beat accentuation of words, tugged at his tired brain. Who is she? he wondered. Jerry tried to focus as he followed her across the room. Only five feet tall, she looked more like a child than a grown woman in the SpaceTech uniform. He noted a bright beaded barrette held straight bangs out of her eyes.

"I should remember your name. I'm sure we've crossed paths but I can't recall where."

"Don't worry. I'm Lily... Lily Jensen? We met at that dinner when they got the scientists together. My husband is Alex from the university. He told me I would sit with you."

"Oh. How did he know?"

"I was supposed to go earlier and so were you. So they made seats for us on the same flight. Alex is already on the Glenn."

Her brusque, matter-of-fact manner burned through his fog, providing a solid framework to latch onto. The room came into focus, his chest relaxed and he breathed easier. It appeared he had a guide to help get him through this. Grateful, he engaged her in more conversation as they took their place in line.

"Has Alex been up there long? Any word about what it's like?"

"Oh, you know, he's too busy to send many messages. He went two weeks ago, but I had to go back to my hometown in China to say goodbye. Lucky the plague hasn't gotten there yet."

"That must have been hard."

"Not so bad. I didn't visit for three years. Not so different to be gone longer if they stay well. My parents could have come to SpaceTech but decided China's safer. My grandmother's there, too. The whole family stays together."

Flight attendants motioned the line forward. Lily and Jerry shuffled along with the rest to board a van going out to the elevator. With standing room only on the small bus, he caught an overhead hold with one hand and steadied his companion with a grip to her elbow. There was no ring within her reach.

At the launch pad they rode the lift in groups of four, up to the nose of the shuttle poised on its tail like a salmon ready to leap upstream. They climbed off the platform and two men in orange coveralls met them at the hatch door. These attendants ushered them in, then maneuvered them onto an open lift running down the inside of the plane itself. As it lowered them to their row, Jerry saw other passengers eying them from below, reclined on cushioned seats. He had a brief vision of his father leaned back in his lazy-boy, watching a football game. Then it was his turn to scoot across and settle into his space by the hull. Lily slung herself into the chair beside him.

They achieved this boarding without more conversation, bombarded first with the noise of machinery and then with instructions on how to strap in, vomit into ready-seal bags, and signal for assistance. While the lecture was rather terrifying, the craft itself looked like any commuter plane with rows of two seats on either side of a central aisle except it faced straight up. No windows punctuated the smooth rounded curve of the wall, and the wait for lift off proved long.

Jerry closed his eyes, inviting the fog of grief to claim him again. Lily didn't notice or pretended not to see his retreat. As the elevator ascended to receive four new passengers, she restarted their dialog. "Do you want to go?"

He looked over at this small stranger, engulfed in the seat's padding, surprised at her question. He realized he assumed he was the only one launching with questions and regret. How self-centered I am, he chided himself. Everyone on this flight is dealing with similar emotions.

Aloud he admitted, "Well, I guess I want to go more than I want to stay, but it's a conflict. My family's on the west coast. I don't know what happened to them. I feel guilty leaving."

He thought at first she wouldn't respond to him and wondered if her English was sophisticated enough to understand him. After a pause, she said, "Me too."

Then the elevator descended, loudly whirring and clanking, and the recorded warnings played for the four people struggling into position in front of them. Jerry welcomed the interruption. Lily's frank question hit home, pressing at the painful bruise of the last month's emotions. Her curiosity pushed a mirror too close to his face when he wanted to avoid looking at himself.

The rhythmic ascending and descending of the elevator, delivering directions and passengers, punctuated the rest of their conversation. Lily, however, kept talking but Jerry relaxed as he gathered that all she was asking for was a listening ear. He bent his head toward her, focusing on what she told him next.

"When I was in hometown, my great-grandmother, very old, went to temple to check my fortune. The monks tell her; this is very lucky time for me to travel. They say it is very lucky time for my husband too."

"That must make you feel good."

"Well, I don't know. Do you believe this stuff? My great-grandmother and grandmother do, but my mother even never goes to temple anymore."

The elevator made its trip allowing Jerry a minute to reflect on his answer. What did he have faith in? He could claim no vision of the future. Hope was obscure right now. What truth could he give that would not be cruel?

Quietly he said, "I guess I'd go no matter what the monks predicted. I'm going because I trust my partner and what we have together as a family."

She looked up into his face and smiled, a jab of brightness in the dusk. "Me too. We want a baby. Well, I do and Alex will."

"What are you doing, until you become a mother?"

The elevator again, and then—

"That's a problem. I don't do anything they need. I was in marketing before I married Alex. So, they taught me cooking for the space ship. Maybe I'll cook on the new planet, too."

"I'm glad to connect with you then." Jerry smiled, trying to pump warmth into his response. "It's always good to be buddies with the chef. You can slip me extra rations."

"Yes, double desserts. That makes many friends." She laughed, and he sensed the bubble of it echo deep within him, pushing at his darkness.

"What will you do?" She asked "Do you want to cook with me?"

"They assigned me to the aquaponics lab on the ship and I'll help the biologists and farmers when we get there. Also, I'm a priest, so I'll be working with the Christian group as well."

The elevator interrupted again as Lily looked startled. Ah, Jerry realized, Alex didn't find out about my ordination, did he? SpaceTech must have kept that kernel of information from the outside scientists.

He decided she was more than surprised though. Disappointment registered in her lips pressed together and the slightest of wrinkles between her brows. When it became quiet again, he named it. "You don't like Christians or priests?"

"Oh no, no. It's just, I thought you were the same as me. You know, without a group."

Of course, he realized. She's isolated. Not being a scientist herself, she doesn't belong to Alex's tribe. And if she isn't Christian, maybe she isn't Jewish or Muslim, either. "You sound lonely. The cooks could form a group."

"Oh sure. It will be all right."

But Jerry heard anxiety in her voice, the fear she had lost a tentative but coveted connection. It tugged at his heart. "I think we should be a gang, you and me. The late arriving spouses club. We'll let others in later, but for now it could be just us."

"OK, but I don't believe in God."

"Yeah, well, I do—but I don't always want to." Jerry realized with a start he spoke the truth. A good part of his sadness masked anger. The bitterness of his words spread bile on his tongue. He looked up to see her frowning in concern.

He said, "Let's make that our secret, OK? The first skeleton in our group closet."

The elevator whirred again. Lily laughed, but he couldn't hear it. He only saw her mouth bow up and eyes warm. It was enough.

The procedure of exiting the shuttle after docking with the space ship turned out to be easier than entering it. The hour-long ride after the noisy, bone rattling take-off proved anti-climactic. Nothing to see, nothing to do but wait. As the hatch opened, and the attendants prepared them for departure, Jerry anticipated his first encounter with weightlessness. Like so many glamorous experiences, the safety rules and restrictive protocol leached out much of the excitement. The passengers lingered, waiting their turns. Then, assisted by an experienced astronaut who guided them to the door in pairs, they swam through the air by pulling themselves forward using handholds on the aisle seats. Lily's hair, a dark cloud billowing around her face, distracted them both until their turn came. Then Jerry plunged in: a whale shadowing an agile, graceful minnow as she fell upward and out, a wiggle of joy propelling her toward the unknown.

Alex met her. The moment Lily's feet dropped through the hatch and she stood upright on the ship that would be their home, he caught her up in a hug of welcome. As Jerry locked onto gravity again, he took in their reunion, the backwash of their happiness highlighting the loneliness of his own position. He frowned and balled his fists at his side, disgusted by his own self-pity. Taking a deep breath, he focused on his next steps, tying himself down to tasks.

He found his duffel bag in a nearby pile, slung the strap over his shoulder and let himself be pushed along by the passengers behind him. In the hall outside, he watched as Lily and Alex headed off to their quarters. She started to wave goodbye to him and then spun around and returned to stand in front of him, pulling her husband with her.

"Alex, this is Jerry. Remember? Rob's partner—you met him at that party. We sat together on the shuttle, just like you said. He's my first friend in space." She beamed at

Jerry while her spouse, towering a foot above her, extended a hand in greeting.

He was a handsome man, with serious gray eyes and, although under thirty-five like all the scientists on board, Jerry saw matching silver sprinkled throughout his thick brown hair. He smiled but with none of his wife's exuberance. "Glad to meet you again."

"Good to see you, too." Jerry managed a polite grin. "It was kind of you to make sure Lily and I could sit together."

"No problem. Well, catch you later."

Although Alex broke off the conversation, Jerry sensed natural reserve rather than any animosity. "You bet. I'll check in with you tomorrow, Lily. I know where to look for you."

"Yes, I'll be in the kitchen. I'll save you something special to eat. Double desserts."

Her enthusiasm battered against his depression and with surprise, Jerry realized he felt better, more hopeful than he had in ages. Was God signing that indeed 'all shall be well'? At least, he thought as he schlepped his duffel bag to the lift, I have someone else to think about—someone who needs a friend as much as I do.

T

Over half a year later, Jerry watched as Lily, now six months pregnant, lowered herself to the floor in the observation deck, leaning back against the wall supported by pillows. Other women also drifted through the door and settled, cross-legged or sprawled on cushions, into a circle which included him as the only man present. Their precipitous first jump left behind the psychiatrist scheduled to join them on the Glenn. Jerry, with a few psychology courses under his belt and a natural skill at listening, had become the ship's de facto counselor.

They had recently entered their second ISRU: the In Space Resource Utilization phase, when miners deployed to new planets and asteroids harvesting the rare thorium which fueled inter-stellar transitions. On the jump from Earth, three of four barely pregnant women miscarried. Miraculously, Lily's fetus hung on and now two others confirmed their expectations and four more waited in hope. Jerry called this circle together daily to keep spirits up and prepare the young mothers-to-be. They came from all groups on board—Jewish, Christian and Muslim, with Jerry and Lily attached to the scientists. Abby Bennett also attended at Jerry's invitation. The young sociologist not only knew a lot about family systems, but he detected her increasing isolation from her colleagues and figured she could use a circle of friends too. It was the Glenn's first real gathering across tribal lines. Motherhood, it seemed, trumped even divisions of faith. They settled in and sharing began.

Shelly Lundgren spoke her news so quietly that those sitting across the circle from her had to lean in to catch her voice. Her hands rested on a belly with no discernible bulge, but her words spoken through both tears and a shaky smile confirmed hope. "They heard the heartbeat this morning. Doc says everything is all right—that the baby was just lying in a weird position yesterday. I guess it happens this early. They think I must be barely eleven weeks along."

The woman on her left leaned over to hug her while everyone else, including Jerry, exhaled in relief. That made four viable pregnancies. Shelly must have conceived just before the last cutoff date. Learning from the first disastrous experience, they changed guidelines to allow for conception only in the initial months of a mining rotation. The theory was that if a fetus could achieve at least two months of growth before the next inter-stellar transition, fewer spontaneous abortions would occur. So far, the theory held.

Lily, the most rounded of the women, leaned against her wall pillow, arching her back to find comfort. Well into her sixth month, her small frame struggled to support its growing load. "Your husband must be very happy," she said.

Shelly shook her head. "Stu had to leave with the mining crew. I don't think either of us slept last night. I can't wait to tell him the good news."

"Oh, Alex left early too. Four a.m. Woke me up and I couldn't go back to sleep. I never get enough sleep now."

Murmurs of sympathy swirled around the room. Everyone present knew the toll mining took on the whole crew. Extraction proved a painstaking job, full of carefully made calculations, long stretches of meticulously adjusting machinery, and then a few frantic hours of moving rocks in a weightless atmosphere. Although only twelve people went to the asteroid to set up and run the operation, the support squad involved over thirty other jobs. One group supervised their flight and landings, and several teams were responsible for receiving and processing the ore they brought in. A third of the Glenn's population engaged in the production when mining was under way, requiring the rest of them to fill in other critical tasks. Everybody either assisted or provided back up. Today Rob flew the shuttle while Alex oversaw the operations team. Besides Shelly's Stuart, Ayisha's husband also manned heavy equipment on this shift.

During the first ISRU, the two ships had gone to separate areas of nearby space, seeking to find the most fertile fields for their endeavors in the least time. The Armstrong, needing help with a broken conveyor, had called them to come to its assistance. They lost not only several days of mining but the whole asteroid the Glenn had been working on—their effort squandered it as it spun out of their reach.

On this second ISRU they determined the ships should stick together, backing each other up on one job at a time. They hoped to work two sides of the biggest space rocks, doubling their take before moving on to the next operation. The first week had gone well. They found an asteroid near their arrival site and maneuvered to engage it, on opposite sides of the giant boulder.

Jerry sighed quietly to himself. He missed Rob when he worked with the mining crew. He could imagine how anxious Shelly was to have Stuart back so she could share the good news.

The rest of the women now finished checking in, each of them reporting on how she was doing physically and emotionally. Then com-pads came out, and they explored stages of fetal growth—following a book they were reading together. Jerry had helped Lily through most of this text and followed the conversation with interest. Just as Ruth Schulman, their most avid researcher, reported on helpful nutritional supplements, a loud thump shook the ship throwing them off balance into each other's laps, tablets dropping to the floor.

Before they could react with more than frightened looks at each other, static fried the air. Then words came, rushed and breathless: "Prepare for propulsion in five minutes. Medical teams report to sickbay STAT."

The speaker hesitated, intercom still on and crackling. In

that distant place, other voices shouted indistinctly, calling for instructions, giving coordinates. The announcer asked, "Do we need both teams? How many injured?"

A gruff voice responded, "At least Alex. Maybe more. Better scramble both teams. Get them down to launch."

The original speaker came on again, louder with authority: "All medical personnel to sickbay. Emergency medical teams to launch bay alpha, STAT. Repeat: emergency medical to launch bay alpha and all other medical personnel to sickbay. This is not a drill. I repeat, this is not a drill."

Jerry looked towards Lily. The color drained from her face, her mouth opened gasping for air. Her wide eyes met his as she twisted her swollen torso to push up from the floor. "Oh my God. Alex. Something's happened to Alex. Help me get to him, Jerry."

The other women began to move and Jerry, now on his feet, reached to grab Lily's upper arm, helping her unwieldy body up. "Breathe." he said, "Take it easy. It might be nothing."

But he knew it wasn't nothing. His thoughts flashed to Rob, piloting the shuttle. He had been in bed when his spouse left this morning, murmuring goodbye from a warm fog of sleep. His breath and heart beat skipped out of synch. He staggered with Lily's weight.

A loud thump and the floor beneath them bucked, causing screams and oaths as the women struggled to stay standing. Jerry just barely held onto Lily, keeping her upright. He looked across the ragged circle to see Shelly's sick look of fear. Another woman supported her.

"Jill, can you get Shelly back to her room?"

"I'm on the med team. I need to go to sick bay."

Abby came up and slipped her arm around Shelly's waist. "I've got her."

Everyone moved towards the door, time thickening about them until Jerry sensed he ran in slow motion. He tightened his grip on Lily, pulling her to the side of the hall as a squad of emergency medics hurried by with a stretcher. One carried a plastic briefcase with the defibrillator. A sound like erratic hail on a pane glass window made it hard to hear footsteps behind them. When had that noise begun? Again, a loud thump—the shock causing them to stagger.

Under the racket Jerry noted the dull roar of the engines engaging. A vibration in the floor signaled that the ship was moving. Lily clutched at his shirt, pulling him onward as she jumped back into the middle of the hall to run after the medics. "Oh God, we're moving. Don't leave him behind!"

"Lily, hang on. The shuttle must have landed." Because we never leave anybody behind, right? He thought. Just like Marines in all those movies... He picked up the pace striding forward on his long legs, matching Lily's speed.

Someone propped the door to launch pad A open and as they approached, they saw that indeed the shuttle had docked. The first of the mining crew were exiting the craft, climbing down the ladder, met by medics who led them off for review. The second man hustled away was Stu Lundgren. Jerry registered that Shelly would be so relieved, but felt nothing. His emotions had deserted him.

Doc appeared at Lily's side panting and flushed. She looked across her to Jerry with a scowl. "What are you two doing here? Get her to sickbay, Jerry."

Simultaneously they asked, "Rob?" "Alex?"

Doc's face froze in a mask of pique. "Neither of you

should be here. I'll meet you in sickbay."

But Jerry, searching for a sign of his spouse, had spotted movement in the cockpit of the shuttle. Is that Rob? His feet rooted to the spot as his eyes struggled to bridge the distance and the glare on the window.

Anne had a hand on Lily's other arm now, pulling at her and bringing Jerry's attention back to the bay floor. "Come on. Let's go," she insisted.

"But where's Alex?" Lily tried to pull away from them both, moving towards the shuttle, her darting eyes searching the descending men.

Then Doc took a long step, putting her wiry body in front of Lily, blocking her vision. Something was being lifted out of the craft—a heavy limp form in a space suit. Jerry realized the helmet was still attached and wondered, why haven't they taken off his bubble?

The next moment, as they eased the body onto the waiting stretcher, the head flopped to one side. He saw the shattered back of the globe, shining jagged sides framing darkness inside. In a heartbeat, the reality of death sucked the air out of the room creating a silent, stunned vacuum. In the next heartbeat, Jerry tore his eyes away from the obscenity, straining towards the shuttle cockpit again. Yes, someone moved. Rob appeared, solid and alive, staring back at him with a white face, hands on the glass. Their eyes locked on each other in a connection so strong it held Jerry upright. Somewhere, a scream pulsed over and over. In the nightmare, Lily's weight sagged on his arm. He kept his eyes on the man in the window. Rob was alive.

Alex, however, was not. Losing a member shook the crew to their foundation. For Lily, the shock of her husband's death threatened not only the child she carried but her mental stability. She shut down for several days, ceasing to speak or interact with anyone. Their neuro-scientist, Darren Evans, warned them that the condition might be irreversible. Doc, with her no-nonsense approach to any illness which couldn't be treated with a cast or antibiotics, advised the simple passage of time as the remedy—that and a baby to fill empty arms.

After Alex's funeral, though, when the pregnant widow remained silent and non-responsive, Anne was reluctant to let her leave sickbay and equally unwilling to isolate her there. On his daily visit, Jerry caught her persuading Lily to move in with her. She crouched in front of the tiny woman sitting on the edge of a narrow bed, trying to make eye contact.

"Lil, it's not good for you to be alone. Why don't you stay with me at least until the baby's born? We can shift one of the inner walls and create a private sleeping room."

Lily shook her disheveled head. Doc sighed. "What do you want to do, Hon? You shouldn't be by yourself right now. You might need help when the baby comes. Is there someone else you'd rather stay with?"

Her patient didn't respond and Anne stood, turning to Jerry leaning on the door jamb. "Hi there. I didn't see you come in."

Jerry stepped over the threshold and sat next to Lily on the rumpled sheets. She turned a fraction towards him, and he reached out to hold her hand. Doc crossed her arms and looked at the two. "Would you rather live with Jerry for a while?"

"Yes." She whispered, but both caught it. Jerry folded her small fingers in both of his hands.

"Do you think you and Rob could take her in, just until the baby is born, and she feels better? I can speak to maintenance about increasing your living space."

"I'll have to talk to Rob, but I'm sure he'll agree."

In fact, he considered, this might go a long way to helping Rob recover from the survivor guilt that haunted him. Every day since the accident happened, he reviewed the story. It boiled down to this:

When the incident occurred, the Armstrong's crew was working on the opposite side of the asteroid from the Glenn. It was a big rock. The geologists anticipated no problems. The Glenn's miners arrived late and were setting up equipment, floating their massive pipes into place, when a warning call came from their sister ship. An earthquake, set off by fluid they were pumping into the ground, destabilized their mining zone.

"This shouldn't be a problem." Rob remembered the other shuttle's pilot radioing. "We're pulling our rigging off and heading back to re-calibrate, but go ahead with your work. We'll coordinate before the next shift."

Rob told Jerry how peaceful the universe appeared, holding his craft steady in the void as he watched his miners float their machinery into place. He saw the other shuttle propel away, coming out of the shadow of the asteroid, headed back to the Armstrong. That's when he noticed chucks of rock beginning to litter the black deepness of space in the vessel's wake.

And then the entire world fell apart in front of him.

"It just disintegrated," he told Jerry. "I have no idea how anyone outside survived. Alex was in charge of the set up and I heard him yelling at them to grab the parts and get back to our shuttle. They didn't want to lose any equipment. Alex floated closest to the bay door, but he went out again, towards the chaos, to help with the biggest pipe. By that time, rocks were pinging off my sides and I knew we only had minutes, if not seconds, to escape."

The others hailed Rob as a hero for holding his nerve and keeping the shuttle steady as the last of the miners scrambled on board with the equipment intact. But in his mind, he kept going back again and again to when he saw Alex's helmet jerk, the lifeless body pirouetting through the shining chips of glass and blood droplets, before they hauled it aboard with the lifeline.

"If I had ordered them to abort right when the Armstrong called me..." he told his husband, head bent into the palms of his hands, staring at the floor. "If I left a minute earlier..."

All Jerry could think was, You're alive, you're alive. Alex's death didn't put a dent in that one real fact. He sighed. Maybe having Lily with them would help his guilt too.

Rob agreed without hesitation to help the young widow. The Andersons graciously shifted out of their next door quarters and they merged the apartments to make a unit of two bedrooms with a bathroom and bigger common area. The uncles, as Lily designated Jerry and Rob, became daddies to her baby Xander, born ten weeks after his father died. Just as Jerry imagined, he now had a child to love and nurture. Rob too embraced parenthood, finding a reserve of curiosity and fascination with the newborn which led him to interact much more than Jerry had expected. Through this unanticipated arrangement, three adults revolving around the bright sun of a needy infant, they all reclaimed a sense of balance.

Their bubble of stability lasted six months.

How can I be so busy and so bored? Jerry wondered well into their third ISRU. He scooped another fish out of the tank he was cleaning, transferring it to a holding bucket where thirty others churned. One more to catch and then he would stream the pond's water through the recyclers while he scrubbed the black plastic by hand. He had to have everything clean in forty-five minutes or the tilapia became stressed in their makeshift vacation villa.

"Shit." The last fish eluded the net once more. "I'm trying to do you a favor, you moronic pest," Jerry muttered as he attempted to trap the slippery creature in the curve of the tank. The bright flash in the water slowed to a quiver. He swept up, transferring the frantic slip of silver into the crowded bucket. "At least you guys don't have to stay there for the next six years," he told them as he reached for the valve to empty the pond.

The design of the aquaponics guaranteed that a slow but steady drip of fish-poop polluted water nurtured the vegetables and then returned cleansed and re-oxygenated to the fish. But the same accident which took Alex's life had also sheared off a tank on the Glenn's outer hull, spewing more than half their water supply into space. Now there wasn't enough liquid in the mechanism and it broke nearly every week. The buildup of impurities could kill their main protein providers if human intervention didn't help. It was just another chore in the struggle to stay alive. Hopefully one of the repair techs would come by soon and get them up and running again.

The Glenn faced another month or two before her next jump. Rumors circulated about several asteroids with potential—more chances to find water to replenish their stores and release them from tedious disciplines imposed by their virtual desert. They had been so optimistic in their last mining foray but that ice formation turned out to be only a few feet thick—hardly worth the effort. The hope they might catch up soon with their sister ship, the Armstrong, faded.

As Jerry stepped over the side of the tank and scrubbed off the slime, he sighed. Over the past six months they had survived the crises that the accident spawned, both physical and social, and the joyful challenge of birthing Lily's infant. Now that life settled into a more normal pace, mundane tasks left his mind free to wander. He turned his ruminations to Xander.

Lily decided early on that she wanted her son raised primarily by herself and his two 'uncles', even though plenty of other willing hands offered help. That meant arranging schedules so that one of them was available for baby care round the clock. Because Lily nursed, she had the least flexibility, but she didn't want to let the kitchen crew down. After a month of what she called 'lying around and milking' she missed interaction with her work team.

Rob, struggling to keep up with the demands of a new steering committee's endless meetings to resolve daily problems on the ship, had little time to spend with Xander. His fatherhood hours became the time Lily prepared for sleep and the early morning interval after the baby woke, but before the tired mom dragged herself out of bed. Jerry hung around for those times too, valuing the feeling he and Rob shared this parenthood gig.

When Lily returned to afternoon shifts on Xander's one-month birthday, Jerry loaded the kid up in a front pack and went to work in the bio-dome. He loved the closeness, the beat of the tiny heart against his chest. He found that if he meandered around, doing some clipping or hoeing—things that didn't jiggle him too much—soon the heavy head drooped and the baby fell asleep with little fuss. Peace didn't last long. He might get forty-five minutes to an hour before the child woke up and wanted more attention or cried until Jerry took him to nurse. The inefficient arrangement comforted him, though. Time with Xander softened the grim facts of the Glenn's condition.

Remembering this, Jerry thought ahead to the evening. He and Rob promised to watch the baby while Lily attended the latest lecture in the cafeteria. Tonight, as on three earlier weeks, the presentation involved genetics.

Jerry reached over the side for a smaller bucket of clean water to rinse the tank, wrinkling his nose at the fishy smell, his mind still on Rob. As it became evident that they might never connect with Earth again, his husband and Doc raised the concern that the human race was in danger of extinction. Jerry considered it too early to warn the crew about effects of inbreeding and the necessity of mixing up the genetic pool of the two hundred humans left in space. After all, they had agreed on no more pregnancies until the water shortage eased. Anne, however, was adamant that the crew plan for the inevitable as soon as possible. Rob convinced her to first teach everyone how genes combine, so that when the time came to discuss the limitations of their DNA, they would understand the science involved.

It was a good theory but flawed. Some crew members intuited the goal of Doc's intentions and already speculated on how to save the moral values of the religious communities. An affair between a Christian man and Jewish woman, only a few weeks cold, fueled speculation that scientists might take advantage of moral lapses, forcing dramatic shifts in their ethics. Given the narrowly defeated attempt by the three ship's captains to claim total control over the Glenn's population just a few months before, such nervousness was understandable.

He swung brushes and bucket over the side of the pond, climbed out and turned on the spigot. Cleansed water gushed back into the tank. Luckily most of this arrangement worked on gravity. Once lifted to the raised beds, the liquid filtered back to pond level on its own. "Hang in there, little flippers," Jerry said to the swirling fish. "Your home will be ready to inhabit again in thirty minutes."

Later that night, Jerry hit the cafeteria, one of the last to eat dinner. The technician who knew how to fix the pond pump finally had an hour to spare and Jerry waited late to capitalize on his availability. As he mopped up his spaghetti sauce with a slice of soy bread, he looked forward again to an evening in his quarters with just Rob and the baby. Hopefully Xander would go to sleep early giving him and his husband precious alone time in their own space. He hurried to finish his meal, handed in his soiled dishes and headed home.

The minute the door swooshed open, the scene struck him. Lily and Rob sat together on one of the two small couches forming the living room. Lily stretched out the length of the couch, resting her back on its arm, her feet in his husband's lap. Rob faced Lily, his eyes soft and happy. His hands, the strong confident hands that caressed Jerry, now massaged Lily's tiny toes. He heard their laughter, intimate and warm, even before he registered their actions.

Jerry stood still, disoriented as fear slithered into him. It couldn't be—he refused to think it—but the seed of suspicion rooted in his gut in a nanosecond, tendrils curling around his heart, reaching for his brain. His pause, the door open at his back because he hadn't moved into the room yet, suspended the animated conversation in front of him. Rob looked at him, registered his hesitation, and tilted his head, frowning. Lily, seeing Rob's reaction, glanced over her shoulder to check out what was happening.

Their expectation of normalcy forced Jerry to speak. "Did you get the baby to bed already?" His words came out breathless and clipped.

"He's snoozing away. Come on in. It's drafty." Rob spoke without putting the dainty foot down.

"What's the matter, Jer?" Lily twisted her torso more to look at him.

"Nothing, nothing... I've got to go back... Back to the bio-dome. I mean, Lily, are you still going to the lecture?" His brain tried to convince him that his gut instincts were wrong. Behind his conscious thoughts, it screamed that what he sensed wasn't true, couldn't be true. The conflicting messages churned within, making it hard to know what to do.

"Oh, I'm so tired. I guess I'll skip it tonight."

Rob said, "Hey, I'm giving free foot rubs. You want yours now?"

His husband looked at him, but... Why so wide eyed? Wasn't that a philanderer's strategy? Jerry felt faint as if sucked into a black hole. "OK, I'll just go and do—you know—that thing."

He turned, bolting down the hall, hearing the door swish shut behind him. As he hurried through the corridor, his hands shook and he folded his arms across his chest, tucking them under his armpits. He entered the waiting elevator, grateful for its emptiness, letting out a quavering breath as the panel slid closed.

Don't think about it, don't think about it, he thought, trying to hold his soul together. When the lift came to a stop at the third level, he made his way back to aquaponics, head ducked, watching the painted floor in front of him. The lectures drew a big crowd. Most people congregated on the level above tonight, listening to Doc's explanation of how DNA combined to make babies.

In the dome, he paced the path around the perimeter, willing the fog that enshrouded his brain to stay so he wouldn't have to face the monster lurking there. Then the protection blew away and Jerry sank to sit on the small retaining wall, folding himself into his arms, covering his head and wept. Minutes ago he looked forward to an intimate evening with his beloved. Now the image of Rob and Lily on the couch threatened to annihilate the possibility of any such bliss. Such sharp descent from hope to fear gave him the emotional bends. How could I be so stupid? he thought. Why didn't I see this coming? Rob's obsession about genetics should have given me a clue. It wasn't just a clinical interest in healthy population growth that concerned him, but laying the groundwork to father his own child. Jerry rocked his body back and forth, trying to absorb the shock.

He heard the crunch of gravel only when it was too late to move and hide. He didn't bother to look up. Jerry knew Rob had come.

"Hey man, what's going on?"

Jerry focused on the shoes his husband wore, the ones he tripped over every morning as he got out of bed. They lined up with his own boots as Rob settled on the wall next to him. He clenched his teeth, trying to get a grip on his tears. The familiar arm circled his back, warm and steady pulling him into a half hug. He might be wrong. Oh God, let me be wrong, he prayed.

He took a deep breath and sat up, rubbing his face dry with one hand. He looked at tomato plants across the path as he tried out in his head several things to say. Beside him, Rob waited. He had a gift for stillness. Jerry inhaled again, struggling for calm.

"I don't know, man. It hit me when I got home. I expected we'd have the evening together and then—you and Lily on the couch. I didn't realize..."

"What? You suspect something sexual going on between us?"

He said it so brutally, Jerry clutched at a shred of hope. If Rob named it without shame, it must be a mistake.

"I don't know... God, I'm so stupid. It's just that you both were laughing and her feet are so elegant and..." He couldn't explain the certainty that even now he tried to refute.

Rob rubbed his back, but made no comment.

"So it's not that way, right?" Jerry despised himself—the quaver in his voice, the neediness that forced him to ask the damning question.

His partner remained silent, stroking Jerry's shoulders in a circular pattern. As the pause lengthened, Jerry turned his head to look. Rob stared at the same tomato plants he'd been looking at, lost in thought. A chill settled on Jerry's heart. He shrugged off his husband's hand.

"Rob?"

A sigh before Rob faced him with a smile on his face, sad but genuine. His eyes steadied Jerry. "No, dear heart, I promise you. I haven't screwed Lily."

OK, this is where relief should hit me, because I believe him. I've always been able to believe him. But no wash of solace occurred. He bent over and covered his head with his arms again, mumbling, "What's the matter with me then? I was so sure. I'm so scared. Am I crazy?"

Rob reached out to capture Jerry's near hand in his own. "You're not crazy. Give me a minute."

They sat silent together, sadness and fear dissipating with the warmth of his beloved's fingers around his. Rob wasn't driven away by his insecurity. Maybe it would be all right.

For a brief instant, Jerry transported back to himself as a small boy, huddled in despair over his father's rejection. What was it that time? Surely I was too young to understand I was gay, he thought. Was it when I brought home the abandoned kitten? Or when I blew the try out for peewee football? It doesn't matter. It was always something.

Rob shifted beside him, taking a firmer grip on his hand.

"Remember that I love you. I'm committed to you. But I need to tell you something I haven't shared with you before. I'm sorry, Jer. I should have come clean with this earlier but at first it was so confusing for me, and then... Well, after I realized I loved you and you loved me, it didn't matter. I decided I'd made a mistake."

His voice sounded fragile. While the words poked at the fear strangling his heart, Jerry responded to Rob's vulnerability by sitting up straighter, putting his free hand over his spouse's. "It's OK. Tell me."

"You remember I told you I only had one other love affair before you? And that it had ended badly?"

"Yeah, with a guy named Andy, right? You lived together, six months or so?"

"Yeah, I was asked to leave because I was too boring. I assumed I'd never have another relationship—that it was my grand shot at romance and I blew it."

Jerry recalled the night Rob shared this story as the moment he realized he wanted to be with him the rest of his life. He felt again a rush of affection enveloping him for the bruised and defeated man.

"The thing is, Jerry—Andy is, or was, a woman. Andrea. Everyone called her Andy. I didn't lie to you. I let you make an assumption and never corrected it. I guess I lied passively. I'm sorry."

Silence stretched between them, but neither moved nor even shifted.

"Jer?"

"So why didn't you tell me? Lots of gay men try to connect with women before they accept their orientation. It's no big deal."

"Right. Exactly. That's what I decided, that it wasn't a big deal. But Jerry, have you ever made love to a woman?"

"No." His answer was faint but unambiguous.

"See? You're so confident in your sexuality and I—well I wasn't. I didn't want you to reject me."

"I get that. But how does this connect with Lily?"

"Jer, you are so far over on the gay scale you've known since you were ten what you wanted. But other people aren't so certain. Most of us live closer to the center of the continuum. What I realized tonight is that I'm right smack in the middle, attracted to both men and women."

The tendril of fear squeezed and panic rose in Jerry's gut again. He pulled his hands away and clasped them together. "So you were flirting with her?"

"This is what's so hard. I didn't mean to, didn't do it intentionally or even recognize what I was doing. But damn it, Jerry, you're so sensitive. You comprehend things about me before I do. I saw what you suspected the instant you stopped in the door, and the next moment... The next moment, I understood it was true."

"Oh God," Jerry rocked back and forth now, hunched over his knees which he had drawn up onto the wall. "I knew it. I knew we were too good to last. What am I going to do, Rob? What am I going to do?"

"Well, first, you're going to quit catastrophizing." Rob's arm circled his back and halted the rocking. His voice, warm and sure, said, "I'm here. Married to you. And until you kick me out that's where I'll stay."

Jerry didn't resist. Instead, he laid his head on Rob's shoulder, too hungry for affection to brush even crumbs of it aside. He couldn't tell how he felt now, much less sense his husband's mood. Heavy hopelessness enveloped him.

"Rob, do you remember Simon and Belinda?" He breathed out in a whisper.

Of course he did. He must have recalled them as he left to find Jerry. Simon and Belinda were a couple who orbited on the edge of their friendship circle on Earth, coming to plays and concerts, often seen at dinner parties. But sometimes only Simon showed up, and when alone, he flirted with any gay guy that appeared unattached. Rob complained once to a mutual acquaintance how uncomfortable this made him, how sorry he felt for his wife. Jerry was present as their friend explained:

Simon was bisexual. His wife hadn't known when they married. They split up initially when he admitted he was hooking up with guys, but Belinda still loved him. Simon claimed to be miserable without her. They made an uneasy pact—he would never be unfaithful to her with another woman and she agreed to ignore the gay affairs. Simon flourished in the arrangement.

Jerry and Rob had seen Belinda once without Simon. They ran into her at their favorite grocery store and greeted her warmly. She said the right things, but her smile when she recognized them had been brittle. She looked at the floor and then over her shoulder signaling her discomfort. They speculated on the way home she assumed one of them had succumbed to Simon's advances. They never saw Belinda in that store again, nor ever by herself.

"Yeah, I remember, dear heart. We won't be Simon and Belinda, OK?"

"How can we be Rob and Jerry again?" The sadness in his soul could get no darker, he decided.

They remained silent for a while, Jerry marveling at his spouse's ability to take a challenge and sit with it. He always wanted to respond right away. His partner, though, could spin a conundrum in his head, examining it from all sides, before venturing a response. That's what he was doing now. Rob's arm stayed around his shoulder but he'd gone off to that laboratory in his mind, dissecting this problem and investigating its every aspect.

Finally, Rob said, "We've been married nearly three Earth years, right? I'm not sure where that puts us on the relationship scale. I suspect that running into a bump about now is common. I'm sorry it occurred. I'm sorry it's my fault. But that's how relationships evolve."

"So just ignore it and act like it never happened?" His voice sounded sanctimonious even to his own ears, but hope nudged Jerry. Maybe they could turn back the clock.

Rob craned his head around looking into his face, frowning. "That's not how evolution works. You know that. Evolution takes you to a new level, a new normal. It's never healthy to regress."

He sounded so detached that for the first time in this little drama, anger jolted through Jerry. He pulled away from his husband and stood up. "Is that all we are to you, Rob—a god damned clinical trial, an experiment to conduct in the best scientific manner? My heart's breaking here, and all you can do is speculate on evolution?"

Rob stared up at him wide eyed, startled. Then, with slow deliberation, he said, "I guess it's better for you to be mad at me than depressed. Before you stomp out of here, though, listen: I don't love you any less today than I loved you yesterday. My reaction to Lily took me by surprise. I'm trying to figure it out. That's what I do. I take problems and analyze them. I can't ignore facts, even when I wish they were different.

"But, dear heart, facts are only little truths. They're not the big Truth. So, while it's a fact that I'm attracted to Lily, the bigger truth is that I'm committed to you. I don't have to act on my feelings for Lil. I just have make you comfortable again."

Jerry loosened his crossed arms and sat, hanging his head. "If she moved out, would it change things? Would you lose desire for her then?"

"I don't know, Jer. I suspect I need to pay attention to myself differently. Even if it helps me and eases your jealousy, moving won't be easy for her and Xander. She depends on us to help with the baby so much. They're not ready to live by themselves, yet."

Jerry nodded, accepting that they needed to consider others as well as themselves. "I supposed this trip would be the last place I'd have to worry about infidelity."

Now Rob's voice sharpened with irritation. "Why is that? You could hook up with an unattached scientist or married man behind my back. Fidelity isn't something you engineer. It's an agreement, a value of both partners in the marriage. And I treasure that ideal, Jer." It sounded like a dare.

Carefully, because he couldn't judge how far he stood from the brink of disaster, Jerry said, "I sense a 'but' in that sentence. What aren't you saying about this evolution you envision?"

Ignoring the question, Rob leaned backwards, his elbows resting in the damp earth of the bean bed contained by the wall they sat on.

"Man, you're going to get your shirt filthy," Jerry warned him.

"Yeah? Might as well go whole hog then." He lay flat, bending his knees to set his feet on the embankment, and scooted back until he stretched out, facing the bio-dome's ceiling. Little lights twinkled far above him in the gloom. "Wow, it's magical here in the dark. Why didn't you ever tell me? What are those stars up there, anyway?"

"Sensors, you goof. The white ones measure humidity, the red ones oxygen."

"What's that big blue one?"

Jerry had to go down on his elbow, craning his neck to see what his spouse saw.

"Hmmm... That must be the timer on the second level water pump." He cradled his head in his hand and stayed there, watching Rob's face. The smell of dirt, rich and moist, rose around them like a promise of life. "I don't want to be Simon and Belinda, Rob," he murmured.

"We won't be, dear heart. We'll figure out a way to be ourselves."

"How?"

"That's the question isn't it? The evolution quandary. You don't get to fall back. You only have choices about how you'll move forward."

Though Rob's face, obscured by the shadowy pattern of leaves, looked alien, his voice sounded as familiar as Jerry's own. He whispered to him, "I thought the issue might be children. If you hook up with Lily, you could have your own kid and get those genes circulating."

"Ha." Rob's snort may have been laughter or exasperation. He reached up and traced the outline of Jerry's face from forehead to chin, then gently touched his mouth. "You always guess what I'm thinking. How do you do that?"

Jerry bent and brushed a kiss against his lips. "Enlighten me." he said. "I may perceive the subject but I don't see the details. Tell me what's going on inside."

Rob sighed and turned his head to gaze up at the ceiling. "We didn't plan on losing Earth. All the scenarios we ran— we had the ships blowing up, we speculated one or both might get lost and never make the planet, we even factored in getting stranded. We never considered these two boatloads of people would have the responsibility of resurrecting humanity."

His hands made a pillow for his head, elbows sticking out. His eyes, staring upward, blinked. Jerry realized he had shifted and was looking at him.

"In the end, it may be only us here on the Glenn, just one hundred and eighty genetic copies, left to reignite the race. It's barely enough, Jer.

"We didn't bring the tools for artificial insemination, but we can print them when we get more water on board. I keep wondering, though—is that the best way to manage the problem. When we face this, will it be better to donate sperm and carry children conceived in a doctor's office, or is it time to look at the foundations of marital love?

"That's what you were thinking when you were rubbing Lily's feet?"

"No, I wasn't thinking anything. But before she sat down with me I'd been stewing about it."

"So you're speculating on not just marrying across religious lines, but other kinds of unions, right? Three or four way marriages? Back to polygamy?" Jerry tried to imagine this future.

"No." Rob answered, his frown barely visible. "I guess I believe monogamy is good for a relationship. You said it once: you get a choice between going wide or going deep. Certain people will go wide, having multiple partners either all at once or serially, like half the humans of Earth were doing by divorcing and remarrying. But I'm sold on going deep."

"God, I'm glad to hear that." Jerry laid his head on Rob's chest, relaxing for the first time that night. If Rob committed to their marriage intellectually, he would find a way live into that promise.

"Yeah, well keep listening, man," Rob put an arm around him holding him pressed to his heart. "What if children were so precious it didn't matter who fathered them, like Xander is to us? What if a community accepts and nurtures any child and has a vested interest in making sure that each one is healthy and happy? Would that ease the taboos we have on creating kids outside of marriage relationships?"

Jerry frowned into the dark, but kept his head pillowed on his husband's chest. The regular thump of Rob's heart warmed his cheek through the thin fabric of his shirt. "So you're envisioning a culture where sex isn't the measure of fidelity, where people accept intercourse outside a marriage as non-threatening?"

"Yes, to create healthy children. There may be other reasons, too. I read about a man who stayed married to his impaired wife for years until she died. He considered himself faithful to her, even though he had sexual encounters with friends. That sort of development might happen if boundaries shift."

"I don't know Rob. How do you define fidelity in a relationship if it doesn't include sexual exclusion?"

"I'm wondering that, too." Beneath him, Rob's body tensed, and he curled up, looking at Jerry, trying to see his face. "I need to understand: what does it mean to be faithful, really, at the center of our lives?"

Jerry lay silent, the challenge weighing him down into the soft earth. Rob relaxed and looked upward again. Then Jerry rolled over on his stomach, reaching to hug his husband and whisper into his ear. "Being faithful means telling your Beloved the darkest, hardest secret you find out about yourself. It means speaking the truth. You have been faithful, always. I hope to God I can be as true to you."

CHAPTER 9
PLANET KOI-3284

DATE: 2073 CE/1

"Are you serious, Rob? How can Xander's fantasy about Goldilocks being alive affect us? The boy's just eight years old. He's a little immature but he'll grow out of it."

Shelly, Jerry realized, discounted the possibility of the planet's sentience so completely she didn't comprehend what Rob was saying. Looking around the circle, he saw baffled expressions on most of the steering committee members' faces—Eli, Sarah, Steve, Ahdam and Hadith exchanging glances of concern. He leaned back onto the translucent tarp creating the wall behind him and welcomed the beat of the wind against the taut material. For a moment he felt as if someone looked over his shoulder as troubled by his friends' obtuseness as he was. Well, what did we expect? he thought. It took a crash and two deaths to convince Rob and me. Who would believe a child talking to a planet?

The sharp snap of plastic at his back seemed to rebuke him. On a whim, he set the palm of his hand against the pliable wall, and focused his mind: Don't worry. It takes time for humans to accept new ideas. All shall be well and all shall be well and all manner of thing shall be well.

Somehow it didn't surprise him when the wind calmed to a whisper, insistent but no longer battering.

Eli knit his eyebrows together trying to fathom the radical shift in reality being postulated. "Rob is very serious, Shell, and it has nothing to do with Xander except he's caught on quicker. He's asking us to look at the planet in an entirely new way. Right now we assume worlds exist for humans—we explore them, catalog them, colonize them. We should put that lens down and try to see Goldilocks through the glass Xander's picked up."

"I don't understand." Shelly frowned and crossed her arms in front of her.

"That's the first step." Eli smiled. "You're right—we don't understand. We need to admit our limitations. The question is, should we reconsider our assumptions about planets considering what Xander experienced or is it a waste of time. For me—well, I trust that if Rob and Jer think this planet may be alive in a different way, we should be open to the possibility. The effort won't hurt us."

"It's fine to consider the possibility of sentience." Sarah leaned into the conversation. "But is that all we are being asked to do? Isn't there more?" Her gaze settled on Rob as she posed the question.

He nodded. "Eli's right about having an open mind, and yes—I'd like to experiment with this notion of Goldilocks' consciousness to see if we can prove it. I also want to know if adults are able to connect with her." He turned and glanced at his husband who sat beside him. "Jerry's theory that the common dream is a rudimentary attempt on the planet's part to establish communication leads me to imagine we should start there. Can Abby continue the research she did on the Glenn? For years she cataloged who was having the dream, how it changed over time, and looked for differences between those who dream and those who don't. Since the children access the phenomenon most comfortably, I'd especially like her to monitor them now."

"I knew you were taking us there, man." Steve rolled his eyes, attempting a balance between contempt and humor to diffuse his critique. "It's one thing to consider this intellectually but another to divert resources needed to produce a tolerable quality of life here. Take Abby away from jobs she's doing and who will fill in? We don't have an inexhaustible work force."

"Steve's got a point," Sarah said. "And Abby's still recovering from the crash. Can we keep this possibility in mind and come back to it when more personnel are available?"

Jerry spoke up even though he wasn't on the committee. "We came here with the perspective that we could colonize this planet because no other sentient life form inhabited it. If we're wrong in that assumption, it changes our whole relationship to this place. We know we need to be careful with the natural balance of life but, if Goldie herself is a conscious entity, that's a variable we didn't consider. Ethically, we can't just ignore it."

"Not only that, but we may miss the most important asset for our survival." Rob spread his hands on his knees, angling forward to emphasize his point. "If Xander is right, and the planet increased the wind to bring down our science orb then, as our partner, she could mitigate the winds as well. At least we would be more informed about the weather, which would help our planning."

Kathir spoke up, frowning as he worked out the implications of what Rob said. "So if we don't make friends with the planet, we might regret it. What if she objects to being colonized—sees us as intruders and thieves of her riches?"

People shifted on their cubes as they considered the unpleasant scenario the young cantor suggested. Jerry thought, well they've opened their minds enough to spot the bogeyman. Perhaps they'll consider a positive outcome eventually.

"If the planet wanted to get rid of humans, she could have done us in already," he said. "I wonder if the dream serves as an invitation. I believe we're here because she wants us. We need to understand what we can give her in return for the home she's supplying."

There was a silence while those in the circle digested Jerry's theory. He watched their faces and recognized bewilderment with concern. On Steve's face, this expression resolved into annoyance.

"So what are we supposed to do?" he said, pursing his lips around the sour words. "Are you suggesting we pray to the planet? Build it a temple and sacrifice to keep it happy?"

"As far as I can tell she hasn't asked for worship or sacrifices." Jerry frowned and shook his head. "Why do you assume she wants adulation? Maybe she's just lonely."

Rob added, "The problem with dealing with something so alien is that we want to find a box to put it in so we can manage it. A sentient planet is so big, so different, naturally we pull out the biggest box—the God box—to contain it. But, Steve, Goldilocks made no claim to divinity. We don't have to treat her as a threat to our religions unless our faith depends on never discovering new aspects of God's creation."

Sarah sat up straight. "I admit this sounds so weird

my initial reaction is dread. But, I wonder—if we put fear aside, can we consider other ways of relating to such a strange being? Xander isn't scared and because he's not, he's learning to talk with it. That's an obvious first step towards a relationship."

Rob smiled at the rabbi. "You're right. We need to work on establishing a bridge of communication. She may tell us more about herself than we could learn by any experiments we can devise."

"Why do you keep calling it 'she'?" Ahdam's arms still crossed over his chest and he scowled at Rob from across the circle.

"Xander mentioned even before we landed that the child in the common dream was a girl. If his theory that the singer and Goldilocks are the same is correct, it would make sense that the planet identifies as female in some way."

Jerry grinned at the Imam. "Since our boy always refers to her in the feminine, we got into the habit too. But you're right, Ahdam, we need to understand what that means to Goldilocks because clearly it's a different experience in her form than in ours. Isn't it interesting to speculate though, why humans referred to our Earth as Mother for millenniums? Perhaps all planets are female."

Hadith, silent through the whole discussion, spoke up. "I'm still having the dream, but the singer isn't as sad. It's a more coaxing song. I'm never able to move, but now the child seems nearer. I expect to meet it, her, every night."

"Me, too." Jerry laughed. "I keep feeling like she's sneaking up on me. It may be Goldie trying to communicate with us."

"So, how do we help her?" At last Shelly seemed to buy

in. Jerry figured it was just a matter of time before everyone else on the committee joined her.

Rob smiled. "Let Eli and me work on outlining a few experiments. We'll get back to you soon."

It turned out that Rob had to develop most of the experiments to determine Goldie's sentience by himself. Eli's attention in off hours, after tackling the myriad of diverse tasks needed to get the colony running, focused on one thing and one thing only: Inventing a device to mitigate their exposure to the incessant wind. He'd been working on it since they arrived on the planet, cheered on (and sometimes prodded) by his fellow colonists. During his recovery from the concussion he sustained in the crash, he broke through a major barrier in the problem, but still had a long way to go to completion. Even Rob concurred though—he should keep pursuing this dream of providing relief from the turbulent atmosphere.

At first supper, four and a half months after they settled on Goldilocks, Jerry looked up to see Eli entering the crowded commons as people sat down to their meal. He held up a fragile—looking tangle of wires and straps announcing, "Friends, I think I've got it."

Excitement trumped hunger as everyone circled up to witness the test of Eli's invention. As he strapped it to his head, Ayisha pointed out, "It looks like those halos we made for the children's Christmas pageant."

"Yup," he replied. "That's what inspired me." He struggled to get the thin fabric strap snug around his forehead. A stiff piece of metal connected to a small black box on the rear of the headband held up a horizontal circle of wire so it hovered about three inches from the crown of his head. When he had it secured, he said, "OK folks, back up." Then he reached and fumbled with the switch on the case.

Nothing happened. Jerry couldn't help feeling the letdown mirrored on everyone's faces. But Eli just kept fiddling with the toggle until his face lit up in a smile. "Xander, go find something soft to toss at me."

The boy who had scooted between adults to get a good look at the contraption, backtracked to a nearby table and scooped up a neglected napkin. He hurried back and stood five feet in front of the chief mechanic.

"That's right. Now throw it like you're trying to hit my stomach."

Xander wound up and with all his strength pitched the wadded square of fabric at him. It bounced off an unseen barrier about a foot from Eli and dropped to the floor. A slight pause ensued as people realized what this meant—then they erupted into cheers.

Eli held up his hand. "It projects a low level force field in a cone around my body. It should protect us from all but the strongest of the winds. Let's see it work outdoors."

Jerry led the way down the hallway, opening the hatch to the outside and stepping through before anyone else. The light wind which had blown most of the day had increased as night approached, building to an evening gale. As the colonists spilled out onto the unprotected lawn, their hair whipped around their faces and shirts, pants, even necklaces all pressed hard against straining bodies. Some put their hands over their ears, and all but the children ducked heads and pulled in their arms, huddling together for protection.

Eli stepped out to stand before the crowd, the halo perched on his head, buffeted back and forth. He reached up to flick on the switch. The wire circle stiffened, stopped moving and Eli, who had been hunching like the others, stood tall and smiled. His thick brown hair, still in disarray, lay quiet on his forehead. His clothes hung straight down. Even in the gale, people clapped in joy and excitement.

"Let me try it, Eli."

"Can I have a turn?"

With calls coming from every side, Eli beckoned to his wife, Jane. She stepped forward, and he transferred the apparatus to her head. Immediately, her shoulder length hair settled into place around her beaming face. But as she reached out to hug him, the surrounding quiet dissolved and she nearly blew over.

Laughing, her husband pulled her upright and adjusted the switch on the headband again, taking care to stand clear of the force field. "Don't touch me," he shouted. Then he turned to the mesmerized group staring at Jane, standing in her pool of stillness. "It needs a few adjustments. You can't put your hands into the energy grid without the whole thing shutting off. Same with your feet. At least you can take a walk. Try it, honey. Move around."

Jane, holding rigid in front of him, nodded, turned and took a few steps away from the group. Jerry noticed that as she moved into the grass, the blades parted for her. It was as if she wore an invisible bell which started at the peak of her head and blossomed out to about three feet around her on the ground. He smiled as he thought, this changes everything.

Rob and John Jackson, the supervisor of the bio-dome, requested the first replicas of Eli's invention. Always on the lookout for nutrition compatible with human physiology, they had been planning an expedition to the forests to explore the plants there. So far, they found they could boil and eat the seeds of the prolific yellow grass as a sort of oatmeal substitute but it wasn't very palatable. The tiny bright beetles which attached themselves to the stems and tapped sap for nourishment might be a protein source although no one had tried them. Rob wanted to see if anything in the woods could compliment the fish they already harvested from the neighboring lake, and John craved a closer inspection of the broccoli trees.

A month went by before Eli could construct four more of the force field halos, but the expedition members gladly waited for them. They understood when they had to gather a specimen or put up the tent the device couldn't protect them, but at least some relief from the wind was possible. On the day they set out, Rob, John and the bio-dome workers Jim Selby and Helen Green, got up early. They loaded up two open-air all-terrain vehicles which Eli's team had modified from the mining equipment to be their ground transport.

"Uncle Rob, why can't I go?" Xander wailed with disappointment as he helped carry sleeping bags out to the ATVs. "I could help you know what Goldie is up to. I wouldn't be any trouble."

"Sweetheart, your middle name is trouble." Rob faced into the ever present wind that graced the planet and lifted a case of empty specimen containers into the back bed of the nearest ATV. Then he turned, taking the bags from the pouting boy. "Besides, I only have four halos for our team. You'd blow away."

"I don't even like those things. I can't hear with them on."

In fact, none of the children were enchanted with the halos, but Rob just shook his head. Jerry, who followed out on Xander's heels with a box of dry food rations, tried to coax him out of his temper. "C'mon, kiddo. I have to stay home too. Next time it's our turn."

"But the forest is special. I want to go now."

Rob crouched in front of the boy, putting his hands on his shoulders. "Xander, this time I need to travel with just adults. We can't be sure what's out there. But I promise, if it's not dangerous, I'll take you next trip."

The small arms remained crossed, the brown eyes stormy. "It's not dangerous. She would tell me if it was dangerous."

His uncle sighed. "I believe you, but not enough to risk it. Next time, I promise." He stood and faced Jerry. "Hug me goodbye and then I'll put on the halo. We're ready to go."

They only planned a three-day trip. The first day they would meander out to the forest which covered the lower slopes of the mountains north of the settlement, collecting samples as they went. Then they would spend an evening and day observing nature in the woods, heading back after a second night. Rob and John assessed the danger as minimal. It was the first of many expeditions as the colonists explored their new home. Jerry made himself remember these things as the two vehicles lumbered out of the yard in front of the compound and swam their way through the swaying grass. He watched until even the silver circles floating over the four heads disappeared into the yellow horizon.

In theory, the expedition would have uninterrupted contact with the colony. However, the crash of the science orb four months earlier damaged much of the equipment needed for the network. Abby, their communications expert, still struggled to recover from her broken pelvis. Eli patched up the system, but it wasn't reliable yet. The long range connection which the explorers attempted at intervals proved intermittent. They got through a text when they arrived at the forest early in the afternoon, so Jerry and the rest of the settlers knew they were safe, but reports of their findings would have to wait until they returned.

On the third day, the expedition due home mid-morning was late. Jerry, on the lookout for the ATVs since breakfast, found reasons to pace the path between the living quarters and bio-dome between meals, scanning the horizon in the north. Eli assured him they were on the way. He'd had a message they left camp just after sunrise.

Perhaps they decided to gather samples as they drove home, Jerry thought, when after lunch there was still no sign of the travelers. Maybe the ATVs broke down.

Speculation grew darker as the colonists mingled at first supper with no new bulletins. Everyone drudged through their duties, scanning the screens to see if the cameras showed movement in the yard before the hatch. The children, catching the mood of the adults, whined and teased more than usual. Shelly and Ayisha gathered them up, taking them outside for games in the dusky light of the Rose Moon rising before the sun set.

Jerry stood with the women watching the kids run around in a game of Duck, Duck, Goose while talking over what might be keeping the expedition. While their adult supervisors huddled out of the wind by the structure, the children appeared oblivious to the cool breeze which ruffled their hair and blew their laughter in Jerry's direction. Xander, the goose in this round, circled the only playmates he had ever known, tapping them on their heads. His uncle heard him calling, 'duck, duck, duck,' but before he got to 'goose', something out in the grass caught his attention. He stopped and stared, his hand poised above Isaac's head. Jerry followed his gaze. Two black dots on the horizon grew bigger by the second. The explorers were returning.

The vehicles trundled over the plain, moving more slowly than they had left. What was wrapped around the roll bar of each of the jeeps, warping the smooth outline of the metal? Had there been a crash? Jerry began walking out to the border of the yard where the trail into the saffron grass started, the children following close behind. The colonists, alerted by Shelly, spilled out of the hatch, ready to welcome the travelers home. But as they got closer, it became obvious everything was not all right. The ATVs slowed to a crawl and Jim, the passenger in the front car, stood up waving for people to move back.

Jerry turned to herd the kids towards the settlement. Even as he retreated though, he looked over his shoulder, and the scene resolved into coherence. Whatever was on the roll bars perched there. He could see several necks stretching out and the hunched outline of small bodies. The expedition, against all guidelines, brought home animals.

Jerry stopped and faced the ATVs, which halted at the edge of the clearing in front of the settlement. The creatures— he now realized there were four, two to each vehicle—were about three feet long. They had sinuous bodies ending in fleshy tails suggesting snakes or lizards. He made out their heads weaving back and forth on lengthy necks. The skulls were flat and round—with faces blunt nosed, wide mouthed, and hooded eyes ridged in dark bumps. He saw the nostrils on one flare pink.

There was a collective gasp from the group behind him. A creature on the first ATV, perched just behind the crown of Rob's head, produced a high note of clear beauty and leapt into the air spreading what appeared to be four back legs. Unfurling between those limbs, bent up and behind its spine, were wings—dazzling rounded sails of yellow, blue and red, veined with a delicate net of black. The colors, so vibrant they looked iridescent in the setting sun, swirled above them as the wind lifted this fantastical butterfly up and up. Jerry craned his neck with the rest to watch in amazement as it circled and then, with another cry, dove straight down at him.

"Stand still."

He heard Rob call, and he had no time to duck, lost in wonder at the outlandish beauty above him. It hit his chest hard, and he staggered a step. Forelegs grasped the collar of his coveralls, the stained glass wings disappearing as they folded under its dark body. The strange head leaned back and twisted and Jerry stared into one bright eye, the color of gold foil. It knows me: the incongruous notion leapt into his mind—and then the moment was over. The heavy lid came down in a slow blink, extinguishing the discerning gaze. The weight of the creature pulled at his clothes as it clambered, all six feet engaged now, onto the horizontal surface of Jerry's left shoulder. There it settled, tail wrapped around his neck, and the wide face tipped to assess him again.

Before Jerry had time to react, the crowd in front of the colony's hatch gasped again. All three of the other creatures launched themselves in the air and the colors—the wings varied and exquisite—lit up the darkening sky. Just as the first creature had, these gave little one note cries, plummeting down to land on various individuals—all of them children. Jerry saw a green winged animal clutch at Xander's chest and the boy's response of reaching around to hold it on. Isaac held up his arm for a tan and pink to settle on and Saphir, slipping out of her mother's restraining grasp, ran forward to meet an orange one.

"Stay calm. They won't hurt anyone." Rob got out of the ATV and hurried toward the nervous colonists. "They're just curious about us."

"This guy may be eating my hair." Jerry's laugh shook with nervousness as the creature butted its nose against his head. He reached up and stroked the tail looped around his neck. It felt cool and smooth, but tougher than human skin. A smell of musty cinnamon emanated from it.

The children, entranced, cooed to the beasts as if they were long lost pets. The younger kids pulled their parents towards the trio of their older friends, reaching up to pat and stroke the strange creatures. For their part the bird/lizard/butterflies peered at each human that approached, extending their clawed foreleg paws to touch as well.

"What are they?" Shelly held out a tentative hand to the creature her daughter Alice was petting and which Saphir cradled in her arms. It stretched out its head to meet her fingers, sniffing and emitting a chittering sound.

Jerry noticed other adults approaching cautiously. A compelling attraction emanated from these little creatures.

Jim, John, and Helen all now joined the crowd at the front door of the settlement. Their halos hung on their belts and John held the video recorder so it took in the scene before them. Rob paused by his husband, asking, "You OK?"

"Yeah, I may have a new best friend." The creature on his shoulder gave hop, angling its body over to Rob, its tail still curled around Jerry, forming a bridge between the two. "I guess he's your buddy too."

"They seem social." Rob pried the grasping paws from his collar and settled the beast back on Jerry. "Curious and unafraid."

They walked the short distance to the main group, the creature riding Jerry like a parrot in a pirates' movie. Bill, channeling captain mode, was questioning John as he recorded. "They're wonderful, but why did you bring them here? We're not supposed to do that. You don't even know if they can survive on the plains."

Helen stroked the neck of the little beast now sitting on Xander's shoulder. "They wouldn't take 'no' for an answer. We tried to disengage them from the roll bars, but they kept returning. Finally we thought, they'll probably fly away when we start driving... But they just hung on."

Jim laughed. "We decided that if they wanted to come with, we should at least make it comfortable for them, so we drove as slowly as we could. We didn't want to hurt them."

As Rob joined the group, he added, "If they show any distress, we'll drive them to the forest again. We took the precaution of bringing some branches from the trees home with us. The buds and leaves seem to be a food source."

"Then we can keep them, Uncle Rob?" Xander's specimen had moved around to hang from his shoulders like a school backpack. His alien face tilted up under the boy's left ear, looking at him as he begged. "This one can sleep with me. I'll clean up after it."

The other children pleaded too, and Lily frowned. "Do you think they're safe? I don't know if they should go inside. What are they, anyway?"

"Yes, that's the question, isn't it?" John raised his voice, quieting the rising clamor. "We can't fathom what these little guys are—insect, reptile, or bird. They don't seem to fit any category we have on Earth."

"It's fairer to say they don't conform to a specific classification but share qualities of the three that John mentioned." Rob coaxed the beast on Isaac's shoulder onto his outstretched arm and lifted a stunning wing, colors ranging from light sand to deep fuchsia, connecting its two back left legs. "They look as fragile as butterfly wings, but these membranes are much tougher. Yet the limbs themselves bend out in ways only insects' do on Earth. They don't flap their wings like birds but use the wind more effectively than flying squirrels."

"Maybe they're fairies." Alice, the youngest child, beamed and cuddled Saphir's creature in her arms.

"I think they're more like dragons." Isaac grinned. He kept a hand on the pink one, claiming it as his.

Helen mirrored their smiles. "Yes, the kids may have a point. These are definitely magical beasts."

"What are we going to do with these fairy dragons?" Bill, again pointed out the presenting problem. "Are you keeping them to study, Rob? Will they stay in the bio-dome?"

The night, descending into darkness now, surrounded them and the wind was rising.

"You're right. We need to have a plan. I guess the bio-dome would be the safest place for them."

"No, no." The children united in their objection to being separated from the creatures.

"Please let them stay with us." Saphir's deep blue eyes pooled with tears.

"We could sleep in the gardens with them." Xander's diplomacy had a frantic edge. "We promise to be good."

Shelly snorted. "Now you've done it. We'll never get them to sleep tonight."

But as the scientists and parents engaged in working out a compromise, the wind blew harder, shifting from the north-east to blow from the south. The creature on Jerry's shoulder straightened its tail and stood erect on its hindmost legs. Jerry craned his neck around to see what it was doing. With a clear single note cry, the fairy dragon leapt up and snapped open his magnificent wings. A gust bellowed them out, and it circled up over the colonists' heads. The three others detached from their human perches too, bounding up into the now dark sky, illuminated only by the soft light of the Rose Moon. Then all four leveled out on the rising gale, disappearing into the night.

Helen started for the ATVs. "C'mon guys. Let's make sure they're all right."

John caught her arm. "What are we going to do? We can't follow them in the night."

She shook him off and kept moving. "But we're responsible for them. What if they don't make it back to the forest?"

Rob shouted into the wind, "They'll be fine, Helen. They're headed the right direction. Listen to John—there's nothing we can do for them tonight. We'll be up with the sun and send out a drone to check between here and our camp site. If they're stuck on the plain somewhere, we can rescue them then."

Helen fumbled with her halo, her pale face set with determination. "I'm not waiting hours to find out what happened to them. We should have secured them in the bio-dome. Jim, will you come with me?"

The colonists had moved indoors seeking shelter and, of the children, only Xander remained by his Uncle Jerry's side watching this drama. As Helen strapped on her halo and strode toward the vehicles, Jim trailing behind, he ran to catch her. "Wait. Goldie has them. She's taking them home. They're OK."

She stopped and cocked her head. "Goldie?"

"Yeah, Goldilocks—the planet. She sent the wind to get them. They need to be in the trees tonight."

"That's right. They roost in the trees."

"They'll be there soon. It's OK." The earnest young face tilted up at her and he took her hand. Jerry held his breath, but could see by Helen's softening eyes she was having doubts about her impetuous move. Jim looked relieved, too.

As Xander led her back to the settlement Helen glared at Rob and Jerry. "Really?"

Rob nodded. "You can trust him. But I promise—I'll send a drone out first thing in the morning."

"The equipment?"

"Jerry and I will unload. You and Jim go on with Xander. Get something to eat."

John and Eli already had the plant specimens and headed out to the bio-dome to store them. Rob and Jerry moved the camping gear and left-over food supplies into the hatch, and then caught their breath in the hallway. Jerry grilled his husband. "Is it strange for these creatures not to fear humans? After all, we aren't like anything they've ever seen before."

"I wondered the same thing." Rob lifted a box of trail mix onto a stack of MREs. "When we got to the forest, I had the uncanny feeling that they were waiting for us. They reminded me of a welcoming committee."

"Do you think Xander is right—that the planet is blowing them back home now?"

"Well, he's been accurate about all his other readings of Goldilocks. It makes sense she's tuned into these creatures who are part of her biosphere. If we're serious about her being sentient than we have to take into account that she may have a closer relationship with the components of this world than we comprehend. Consider, dear heart: if you stick out your hand to touch something, after you feel it you bring it back to where it's comfortable."

"So Goldie might have used the fairy dragons to connect to us and now is withdrawing them?"

"Fairy dragons—is that what we're going to call them?" Rob snorted in mock dismay. "I was hoping we'd name them after me."

"What? Ander's Lizards? No, I think Alice and Isaac trumped you. Fairy dragon describes them perfectly."

His spouse sighed. "Well, OK." He sat on the box he had just stacked.

Jerry stood, leaning on the wall next to him. "When the one that landed on me first looked at me, I got the distinct impression it knew me. I wonder if that's how Goldie sees— by looking through her creatures' eyes."

"It occurred to me that Goldie might use them to check us out, but I didn't say anything to John or the others. I can't figure out a way to verify it, yet. Those fairy dragons have amazingly sophisticated eyes. As far as I could tell they have the acuity of an owl's or eagle's sight. We need to observe them more closely to really understand them." He looked over Jerry's head toward the hatch.

"Don't plan your next expedition just yet, old man." Jerry reached out and hauled his spouse up. "Let's at least get some food in you before you run off again."

Rob paused before heading for the common room and faced Jerry. "If Goldie uses her animals to experience people better, perhaps we can come to understand her in the same way."

"What do you mean?"

"We might extrapolate from her creatures her personality, her disposition. You know—they are her face, her hands and feet and her ability to express herself. Since the fairy dragons are curious, unafraid and highly social, I speculate Goldie has those qualities too. What have you learned through this encounter?"

"Hmmm—I think she likes vibrant colors and is kind. Presumably she didn't have to either visit us or help those creatures get back to their beds tonight."

The scientist shook his head as he laughed. "Colorful and kind? We can't verify those traits."

Jerry shrugged. "Still, colorful and kind sounds like someone I'd like to know better."

A month after the expedition Jerry came back to his quarters after lunch looking for notes he promised the bio-dome crew about oxidation rates in the fish tanks. He'd left his com-pad by the bed, and when he picked it up, he noticed that a message had come for him.

As he sat in the common room to retrieve the note, the door opened and Lily stormed in. She had shared with him last night that it was time for her third round of intrauterine insemination, and he'd dropped his contribution off at the clinic earlier that morning. Now, an aura of anger and discouragement surrounded her, clouding her face, held in place by her arms crossed around her stomach. Seeing Jerry on the couch, she turned and headed toward her bedroom.

"Lil," he said. "What's the matter? Did something go wrong?"

"Something go wrong?" She parroted back. "Everything is wrong, Jerry. This whole IUI thing is wrong. I hate it." She moved to enter her room.

"Hey, don't go away. Stay here and tell me. Come on, Lil." Jerry reached out and caught her arm as he spoke, pulling her down beside him on the couch. He saw her face crumple, and she dashed at the tears in her eyes. He held fast to her hand.

"I didn't realize it was so bad. What happened?"

"Nothing happened. The whole thing just feels awful, like I'm being used because no one really loves me. Spread your legs and let's get this goo inside you and then you go make a baby for us. Nobody caring about me."

What could he say? He felt completely out of his depth facing her unhappiness. He put a hand on her shiny black hair charting the curve of her skull under his palm and wiped a tear with his thumb.

"Tiger Lily, you're the most beautiful, strong woman I know. I love you very much."

"Not enough to give me more than a test tube of sperm a month." She bent her head away from him, staring at the floor. "It's been eight years, Jerry. What I want is Alex and for eight years I can't be with him. No, Jer. I love you too, but you are my brother, not lover. If we have a kid together, you'll still be uncle."

He kissed the part in her hair and gathered her into a hug, willing his warmth and care to surround her. "Maybe this time it will take."

"No one else is pregnant either. Maybe we can't get babies on this planet, even the regular way."

"Doc said she wouldn't worry about that until six months had passed."

"Believe me—she's stressing now. She doesn't know what to do. She told me, better not eat food from outside. Only eat bio-dome stuff."

He sensed her relaxing, letting her anger dissipate and shifting into problem solving. He held still as he could, giving her space to decompress.

"What kind of life will Xander have if we don't make any more children, Jer? What will happen to him, to all of us?"

"Those are pretty dark thoughts, Lily. It's too soon to go there. Think about what happens if you conceive this time. Do you want a boy or a girl?"

This elicited a snort of hopeless laughter against his chest.

"Oh, I don't care. I'll take anything I get."

She lay quiet for a few moments and then whispered. "Xander might be more happy to have a brother, but I hope for a daughter. Would you like a girl, Jer?"

"I'd love a baby girl, Lil. One like you."

She sighed again and snuggled closer. In a minute Jerry recognized the even breathing of sleep and repositioned to hold the weight of her tired body more securely. He yawned, allowing himself slip into a nap too.

The dream wrapped around him. Fog, with wind high overhead. But now the singing drew near. He couldn't move his feet though. Lily was still in his arms. The song surrounded them both. The mist glowed with golden light.

"Jerry?"

He woke with a start, tightening his hold on Lily who shifted in his arms. Rob stood looking down at him.

As their eyes met, he smiled and whispered, "Everything OK?"

Jerry held up one finger, asking for a moment, then tried to disentangle himself from the small woman who slept on top of him. As he slid out from underneath her though, she roused and sat up. Her eyelids, he noticed, were still red and swollen from weeping, but her face had regained its peacefulness.

"Hi guys," she said, half yawning. Then her eyes opened wide, and she faced Jerry. "You were in the dream. And light—light was everywhere."

Jerry nodded. "Yes, I remember. A brightness infused the fog. I thought the singer might appear. And you're right—somehow we were together."

"Wow," Rob said. "Sounds like a major dream shift to

share with Abby."

His husband stood up, joints cracking as he stretched. "I didn't mean to fall asleep. What time is it?" He glanced at his wristband and moaned. "Oh shit. I completely missed my meeting with John to do the fish assessment."

"I saw him at the bio-dome, Jer. He asked me to tell you he had to go out to the lake after all so he couldn't meet today. You get a pass."

"Why didn't he call?"

"The communications network is down again. Eli's working on it. Says it should be back on line by tomorrow morning. John thought he got a text through to you, but you didn't respond."

Lily, stood up too and moved toward her bedroom. "Only an hour before first supper. I'm going to go finish my nap." She paused. "Thanks for listening, Jer. It will be all right. I'll keep doing the IUI."

It wasn't until the next meal that Jerry glimpsed what the real implications of the changed dream might be though. As the little family gathered with the rest of the colonists, Xander joined them from his day at school bouncing up and hugging each of his uncles. When he embraced his mom, he stopped and drew back to look at her, and then hugged her tightly again.

"What is it?" She asked. "You OK, kiddo?"

"Yeah," Xander beamed up at her, whispering. "You've got a baby. I'm going to have a sister."

Six weeks later, the Steering Committee delayed their evening meeting waiting for everyone to arrive. Rob hurried in last and, as he sat, Jerry followed and shoved a bowl of stew and a piece of bread into his hands. "They're closing the kitchen, dear. If you don't eat now, you'll only get trail mix for dinner."

"Thanks," he replied as his spouse perched on a seat behind him, outside the circle. Then he turned to the waiting members. "Sorry. I got back from the lake late. We found another species of fish and I wanted to catalog it while the information was still fresh in my mind."

"Go ahead and eat. We've all had a long day. I hope we can move through these reports quickly." Sarah glanced around and nodded. "Looks like everyone is here. Who wants to lead? We'll let Rob wait until he finishes dinner."

Steve and Ahdam, who had been whispering together during this exchange, now looked up. The Imam said, "Before we start, I'd like to check out a rumor that's going around. We hear we might have our first pregnancy on Goldilocks, but it's not one we expected."

"What do you mean?" Sarah's puzzled face mirrored the rest of the committee members'.

"My wife overheard several colonists whispering about it. Someone claims Doc gave Lily directions for taking prenatal supplements this morning. They concluded that she, of all people, has conceived."

Adham looked hard at Rob who put down his bread. "What do you know about this? Could it be correct?"

Rob met his eyes, a small smile growing on his face. "It's possible. Lily is a healthy woman still in the range of child bearing age. And if true, I'll rejoice to welcome another baby among us."

"But who is the father?" The Imam's voice sounded demanding, but the other man didn't respond with equal heat.

"That's not the question we need to ask, Ahdam. The issue we, as the Steering Committee, must consider now is how we can support both mother and child. Will we set ourselves up to judge relationships which produce children? Can we trust our women, and our men, to keep the good of our colony in mind when they conceive?"

"We didn't agree to encourage out-of-wedlock offspring." Steve zeroed in on Rob too, his face growing red.

"If I remember correctly, this board did nothing—neither encouraged nor discouraged—despite Doc demonstrating the genetic Russian roulette we're playing with our shallow gene pool. If Lily has chosen to have a child that's her business—not ours. She doesn't belong to your faith community and isn't subject to your moral criticism. Even those of us who are members of your groups aren't accountable to your judgment. Involvement with a religion is completely voluntary. As a Steering Committee of the whole colony, we must support our people whether or not the congregations do."

Steve took a deep breath, ready to dive into conflict, but Shelly cut him off. "Who cares who the father is. If Lily got pregnant than others can too. Is it true, Rob? You know we love her. We'll take care of her."

"Yes, she doesn't need to be afraid," Hadith chimed in. "A baby belongs to everyone. We'd never shun it or the mother. You realize that, Rob. We'll help. Lily is one of us."

Sarah, looking at Steve's scowl, chuckled. "Well, I'm with Shelly and Hadith. The women of the committee at least agree. If Lily is pregnant, she'll get our blessing and so will her child. The bottom line is, Steve, that she provides a huge gift by taking this step. She invites us to embrace the reality we must someday. I say, let's accept the challenge and make it part of our charter to commit the colony to full support of all children no matter what their parentage."

"But who is the father?" Steve sputtered the words, his anger erupting. "Whose marriage will this compromise? How can we hold together when we can't even fulfill our wedding vows?"

Jerry stood up from behind Rob. "I am the father of Lily's child." He put his hands on Rob's shoulders. "I promise you all that in becoming a parent I have not broken faith with my husband. We may be an odd sort of family, but try to understand. The three of us choose this together. We make this commitment not only to each other but also to you—this colony and this world."

The stunned silence reverberated for seconds before Sarah cleared her throat and said, "Maybe you'd better join the circle, Jerry."

Kathir, sitting next to Rob, scooted his block over making room for Jerry to move his seat in beside his partner. As he sat down, Shelly beamed. "Congratulations—I guess to both of you."

"Yes." Rob returned her smile. "But Hadith is right. This is wonderful for all of us. The baby will belong to the whole colony like our other children do."

"But how..." Hadith started and then stammered to a stop.

Jerry laughed. "Don't be embarrassed. We debated the how quite a while, too. We settled on intrauterine insemination and it worked."

"Could that be the key to conceiving?" Kathir, his eyes brightening, sat up straight. "Does Doc have a special technique that could help the rest of us?"

"I don't credit the IUI or anything Anne had to offer. We wanted to wait before we talked to you all about this. Lily is only about six weeks along and we want to make sure everything is normal—that the pregnancy holds." He glanced sideways at Rob who shrugged and nodded.

Sarah said, "C'mon guys. Whatever you're speculating, you need to share so we can explore possibilities too. There are people, like me, panicking at the thought humanity might be at a dead end."

"Yeah," Eli jumped into the conversation for the first time. "Spill the details and let us sort it through with you. One baby is great, but we need a lot more to put ourselves on track for continuing our species."

"You're right." Rob looked at Steve and Adham sitting silent across the circle from him. "But I don't want to get away from the central question of how we define the relationship of all our children to the colony."

Sarah held up her hand. "Give me a moment and I'll put together a motion." Her fingers flew over her com-pad while the other members sat waiting. Rob took a bite of stew.

"OK, how about adding this to our by-laws?" She hit a button and the computer's voice, flat and high, sang out: "We commit this colony to equal support for all offspring, whatever their parentage, health status, gifts, or weaknesses. We acknowledge that all children belong not only to their biological parents but to the colony as a whole, and their welfare, nurture and education is our duty."

"What about the rights of fathers and mothers?" Steve asked. "My children should be my responsibility, under my care. And I'm not sure I want to manage anyone else's kids."

"You wouldn't protect Alice if something happened to me and Stu?" Shelly sounded shocked as she faced her fellow Christian.

"Well of course I would. You know that." Steve's voice grew peevish and his scowl returned.

"And what about Xander, Isaac, Saphir, Hailey, Liam, and Marnie?"

"Shelly, I care about them all."

"Yes, you do. That's all this resolution is asking us to commit to, Steve. That we, as a wider community, must work hard at nurturing all the kids. We'll always have a soft spot for those of our own bodies. Mothers understand that even better than fathers. But we also appreciate that every one of our offspring need to belong to the greater family of this colony. A big part of our problem on Earth was we didn't care for all our children, so we forgot how to love all the adults too."

"OK, I guess I can agree with that."

"A vote then," Sarah said.

It was unanimous—with the caveat from Ahdam that they would work on the specifics of what offering support at different ages meant.

"Now," the chair directed her gaze at Jerry, "if you have the assurances you need that we'll back you and your family, let us in on how Lily conceived while we remain sterile."

Jerry drew a big breath and looked at his husband who smiled encouragement. "I realize you haven't come to consensus about the question of Goldilocks' sentience," he said, "so I'll just tell you what happened and you can draw conclusions."

He recounted the story of the day Lily came home from Doc's so discouraged and they shared the dream—but a changed one where they were together with the singer, wrapped in honey colored light. Four weeks later, the pregnancy test displayed positive. Now six weeks later, it still held and Doc was sure Lily was with child.

"You think the planet somehow involved itself in this conception?" Kathir's question sounded more like a statement, but both Jerry and Rob nodded.

"How?"

"We don't have a rational hypothesis yet." The scientist in Rob always spoke the truth.

Eli bent forward, holding his right fist in his left. "OK—speculate."

Jerry put his hand on his husband's thigh, forestalling a technical discussion between the two, and continued his story. "Lil and I were at the end of our ropes that afternoon, tired and frustrated and wondering if we should continue to try to conceive. When we fell asleep, we both stayed in that vulnerable state and then... Well, I suspect our openness allowed Goldie to join us. Remember, Lily had recently returned from an IUI procedure so the physical conditions all lined up. What Goldilocks gave us amounted to permission—you could say a blessing. Maybe some development occurred in her womb-women's bodies are sensitive to the influence of the moon back on Earth. It might only be emotional, though. Lil says she woke up knowing something inside her had shifted and everything would be all right. I had a sense of calm too."

Ahdam shook his head. "No this is all wrong. You're describing a mystical experience. Are you saying the planet is God?"

"Not at all. It felt holy, set apart from normal everyday happenings. But it also seemed limited. How can I explain it? When I woke I experienced awe, but it was wonder at the variety and magnitude of God's creation that included a being like Goldie. It blew my mind that we landed here, to meet this magnificent and strange creature and become part of her." Jerry hesitated and looked around the circle. "Yes, that's a frightening idea, but wondrous too. We can't go back to Earth, but this planet desires us, wants us to be part of her."

The conversation paused as members considered the import of Jerry's words. Then, shaking his head, Kathir asked, "What does this mean for other potential parents?"

Rob glanced at Jerry. "We've wondered about that, too. Our hypothesis is that communication with the planet is key and the way she connects is through the common dream. So, welcoming the dream, giving yourselves permission to invite it, think about it, share with your spouse what shape it takes in your psyche, all could open you to Goldie's influence.

"You might get outdoors more, too. The halos are great, Eli, but the kids sense that Goldie communicates through the wind. It would be helpful to note what you try and how it works out. I'd encourage us to keep sharing, even though it's uncomfortable at times."

Sarah gave a short laugh. "It sounds like we have our work cut out for us. I wonder—before we call it a day, do we need another motion expressing permission or encouragement to consider having children with partners other than our spouses?"

"Why can't we keep quiet and let people decide what they want to do?" Shelly concentrated her gaze on Rob and Jerry. "Don't you trust enough of us to make the right choice?"

Rob shook his head. "I'm sure it will be easier if leaders actually lead in this matter. Cultural norms and religious injunctions maintain strong constraints. Jerry and Lily have opened a conversation about specifics, but we need to encourage our people to live into that experiment to change significantly."

"Yes," Eli said, eying Steve and Ahdam. "Everyone must be open about who they're choosing to mate with. Someone—probably Doc—needs to keep a record of physical parentage so we can track genetic information."

"So we're all going to breed like horses or dogs?" The scorn in Steve's voice curdled the air, and several members sat back, squirming.

Sarah tilted her head as she addressed them. "You all know how I feel about forcing any woman to bear children she doesn't want. The picture Steve paints is of regulated and enforced procreation. But Jerry and Lily—and Rob, you too—have given us a concrete example of another way. They expanded their family deliberately, in an effort to benefit our colony.

"What if we set out the facts and possibilities, pledge the Steering Committee's support to all parents and children, and let people both struggle and choose for themselves? Eli's point, that we need a public recording so we have data to help us with future planning, doesn't mean that we are regulating it. It just shows we must accept it so completely that no one will be shamed. The information about genetic combinations can benefit the whole settlement."

Shelly nodded. "And Rob is right in saying that leaders should lead. The members of the steering committee need to consider if they can walk down this path first."

"Easy for you to say," Ahdam, usually so gentle, sneered at Shelly. "You have a child with your husband already."

Her eyes opened wide in surprise. "But I didn't mean you shouldn't conceive with your spouse. I'm only suggesting that people with children already consider having IUI, like Lily. Even those who aren't parents yet can support couples who choose that."

The Imam sank into himself, misery rather than anger on his face. "We've been trying for over four months and only Lily has been blessed. Perhaps none of this is up to us. If Jerry's right, the planet determines our fate."

Sarah leaned in, looking into his sad eyes. "Ahdam, I share your sorrow and even your despair. But let's focus on what we have control over. If we take a step in this direction, the next step may become apparent."

"I don't know." The Imam looked toward Steve. "I hate to say this but I'm so uncomfortable with the notions of allowing parentage beyond married couples and an alien being influencing conception... I wonder if my people would be happier in a neighborhood by themselves. We could live near enough to share food and work but not these other ideas."

A shocked pause hit the committee. Jerry sat up straight, his hands curling into fists. "Ahdam, would you really consider a split? The last time a group went their own way—well, remember how awful that got."

They remembered. For a moment, the painful history

swept them all away.

CHAPTER 10
SPACE

DATE: 2066 CE

The day they broke orbit from Earth began as every other one had for three months on the Glenn. The crew of scientists and settlers—Jewish, Christian, and Muslim recruits—worked on learning their roles and perfecting the skills essential for not only completing the mission but staying alive.

A hierarchy of management established the work flow. Members of the scientific team headed each department necessary for the spaceships to function. On each ship, three captains were responsible for both maintaining route and flight schedule. They dealt only with other scientists. The other division heads—nutritionist, mining supervisor, chief engineer and an aquaponics manager, etc.—trained and used the religious settlers who made up three quarters of the two hundred person crew on each vessel. Although the plague had forced everyone up to the ships six months sooner than planned, Dagmar Sorenson, mission director at SpaceTech, hoped this apprenticeship strategy would be a benefit.

Every member had at least two functions on board, a necessary development on the small ships. They assigned Jerry to care for plants and fish on the aquaponics team and he had wished for a slot as a shuttle craft pilot, like Rob. Soon after boarding though, Dagmar appointed him to the role of counselor. The plague had caught the Glenn's psychologist in California and she never made it out of quarantine.

This morning, like every other one so far, Jerry completed his shift in aquaponics, washed the soil and fish smell off his hands, and then ducked into his husband's lab bordering the greenhouse. They often went to lunch together before Jerry met with Abby Bennett, the ship's sociologist and communications expert, who taught him counseling strategies to round out his sketchy pastoral care training. Jerry liked to help feed the hedgehogs which Rob kept for the experiments he ran. On this day, as he finished putting the last little ball of spikes back in its cage, the overhead speakers sputtered to life. "All senior scientists report to the bridge conference room, ASAP. Repeat—all senior scientific staff, we require your presence now."

Rob paused for a second, his brows contracted, then waved his spouse to his side as he hurried out the door. "C'mon, Jer. Let's see what this is about. If it's routine, you can go to lunch without me."

It was not routine. When Jerry glimpsed Dagmar Sorenson's face on the viewing screen in the middle of the conference table, pale with a sweaty sheen and his eyes sagging, he knew they'd reached a crisis point. The unspoken dread of sixteen weeks in space, removed from but not immune to the knowledge of the chaos churning on the serene looking planet they circled, descended on him. He stayed at the back of the crowded room, but angled himself so he could keep an eye on the display.

Connor, one of the captains, looked around. He saw Jerry, but let his glance run over him without comment. "We're all here on the Glenn, sir," he said.

A voice on the open microphone from the Armstrong confirmed they also gathered their scientists and listened. Dagmar nodded, reaching up to sweep unruly gray hair off his high forehead. "I'm giving the command for both the Glenn and the Armstrong to break orbit and begin your journey to KOI-3284. You will make your first interstellar transition in two hours."

Dagmar paused, and the only sound was the sharp inhale of breath by everyone in the room. Then, an avalanche of protests filled the air:

"You can't be serious."

"We need at least three more months to prepare."

"We haven't run all the disaster scenarios yet."

The man on the screen bent his head and waited. Conner's voice rose above the rest. "Quiet down. Let's figure out what the problem is."

An uneasy hush settled in both the Glenn and Armstrong conference rooms. The mission's director looked up and took a shaky breath. "This won't be easy for you. We thought we could keep SpaceTech safe. Your extended families were promised sanctuary. We've failed."

He continued in his calm, succinct manner to detail the events that had transpired in the last few days. Unknown to the senior staff, the guards let in relatives fleeing from the plague. The illness came in with them, taking down those guarding the facility first and spreading to the crew's families and the scientists. As security collapsed, gangs of desperate refugees roaming the country had discovered the treasures of SpaceTech: stored food and medicine, shelter and the generators which kept them from dependence on external sources of electricity. As many of the compound's residents as possible had taken cover with personnel in the buildings which housed equipment for the technicians working on the space mission. That morning they had to face the truth of their situation: They had no supplies. They couldn't access the generators and feared that someone might cut them off from the grid at any moment. Half the people gathered showed signs of illness. No outside help had yet answered their frantic calls.

"It's just a matter of time before we can no longer coordinate your departure," Dagmar concluded. "We'll keep trying to find a solution here. Even if we can't preserve SpaceTech, some of us may escape. We might be able to reach you from the Peruvian bases, or perhaps the Russians' space communications are still intact. I'll try to contact you in a month. But now, you need to be on your way."

A woman in front of Jerry began to cry, her shoulders shaking as she stifled sobs. Her neighbor put his arm around her. Conner asked, "What are the odds that humanity will survive this, sir."

"Hard to say. Our best estimates were that we had a forty percent chance of making it through, but that was before we found out the government shut down in Albuquerque. New Mexico was one of the last areas to succumb. I don't know of any country or any of our states which have functioning police. I'd guess our chances are down to twenty percent now." He looked up and rubbed at his tired eyes. As he took his hand away, Jerry saw the telltale smear of red staining his cheek, marking Dagmar as doomed. "Get ready," the director said in his gentle voice. "Go with our hopes and blessings."

As the countdown to the jump commenced, the crew worked together to secure the contents of their quarters and labs. The speaker had reached ten minutes as Jerry locked in the last of the hedgehogs and Rob, looking around at the clean, hard surfaces of his lab, gave a nod of satisfaction. "OK, let's get buckled in."

They embraced as if saying goodbye before going off to work. Then they separated to sit in chairs bolted to the floor but swiveling from their bases. The two men fastened the restraints and adjusted the seats, positioning them so that they faced each other before anchoring them in place.

Jerry thought about the explanation that Rob had given him of the interstellar transition. "I remember you said that space moved, but the ships don't, so why do we have to take so many precautions?"

"The jump won't bounce the ship around, but we may run into something on the other side that shakes us up. We can chart the stars and planets to avoid crashing into them, but a comet or ion storm is always a danger. The odds of a smooth landing are high though. Don't stress."

"Shit, I should have checked on Lily before I came down. Alex has to stay in engineering so she'll be alone."

Rob shook his head. "Don't worry about her. She's in sickbay with the rest of the pregnant women."

For a moment, Jerry lost sight of the fact that they were about to do something never before attempted. "Pregnant? Who's pregnant?"

"Your friend Lily, for one. Also Mary Anne Larsen and Hadith Goldsmith. They won the lottery. We removed their trans-dermal birth control about six weeks ago."

The overhead voice interrupted announcing that they had just five minutes to the jump. Jerry felt his heart race. "Will they be OK?"

Rob shrugged, eyes on the floor. "We shouldn't be jumping this soon. We conducted tests on pregnant animals and... Well, this early there's a good chance they'll miscarry. Doc knows the odds." He looked up at Jerry. "Don't worry. She'll take care of Lily and the others."

The countdown continued in the silence between the two men. "Three minutes to interstellar transition. All personnel must be secured."

It occurred to Jerry, examining his husband sitting so calmly in the face of the unknown, that he had a courage much greater than he ever gave him credit for. This mellow scientist squared off every day with mortality, looking extinction square in the eye and refusing to shy away from the possibility of death—his own, his beloved's, humanity's.

"How are you doing over there?" Rob's voice broke into his revelation.

"Snug as a bug..."

Rob snorted. "Who says 'snug as a bug' anymore?" he teased.

"Listen, man," Jerry's words tightened with urgency and he stared into his spouse's eyes. "I had a dream last night, different from the one I usually have. It was the middle of winter somewhere in the Midwest. I looked out a window, and it was just like I remember, snow up to the porch. I was thinking, as if I was still a kid, that soon my mom would tell me I had to go out and shovel. And then this whole flock of robins swooped down and landed on the snow. Robins! Their orange breasts flamed against the white as if they would melt it. And I thought of you, Rob. I wasn't a child anymore. I thought of you."

Silence stretched between the men while the mechanical

voice chanted numbers: "ten, nine, eight, seven."

"I love you too, Jer."

"Three, two, one."

The light shimmered, as if a heat wave passed through the room but, instead of a rise in temperature, Jerry shivered with a sudden chill. His ears hurt on the inside, as if listening to violins pitched too high, a tightening in his head trying to avoid a sound he couldn't quite hear. A small but significant jolt, bounced both men in their seats like running over a speed bump in a school zone. And then, nothing.

Jerry, whose eyes had never left Rob's face, raised his eyebrows. "Is that it?" He whispered, not wanting to upset the balance of the ship if they still traveled.

Rob nodded. "Yeah, I think so. Kind of anticlimactic, isn't it?"

They both looked at the ceiling as the automated voice announced, "Interstellar transition complete. Recalibration of internal systems complete. Personnel are now safe to move freely."

"Let's go to the observation deck and take a look." Jerry said, and he held out his hand to his husband.

Lily's fetus was the only one that survived the jump. The elation at the success of the first interstellar jump floundered in face of two miscarriages and the growing dread as each day brought no message from Earth. The crews struggled to learn their jobs amid strange stars in a foreign galaxy while wondering what fate their families and friends back home suffered. Perhaps that's why, on their off hours, the settlers kept to their religious communities. Other than the mother's support group, organized by Jerry when three other women conceived, little mingling happened between the groups on board.

Finally the captains of both ships agreed—they could wait no longer to hear from SpaceTech. They assumed the worst and put all their resources into finding and settling a new world. There were fifteen jumps to make in the five years allotted for the journey to KOI-3284. When they successfully mined the asteroids in this first area, gathering the required thorium, both the Glenn and the Armstrong made the second interstellar transition. Again—success. And then the accident happened...

Two weeks after the asteroid they were mining disintegrated, just days after Alex's funeral, Lily prepared to move into her best friend's quarters while she waited for the birth of her baby. Jerry went looking for Rob to tell him they were ready to roll. It had taken a while to shift the Andersons out of their adjacent apartment and re-configure the walls. They designed the inner divisions of the ship for such renovations as the architects had planned on growing families. The new configuration provided Rob and Jerry with a private bedroom mirroring a room set up for Lily with an adjoining shared bath. Between these rooms was a common area, now holding three built-in desks and a couple padded benches which faced each other across a fold-down table. In its stored position, there was space for Jerry to stretch out his long legs.

He wanted Rob to be present when their new family member stepped over the threshold, welcoming Lily home. Jerry believed in such rituals, hoping that a staged display of happy inclusion would set them on the path to making it a reality. As he approached the door to the genetics lab to fetch his spouse though, he overheard raised voices. He paused uncertain to the side of the opening. Rob seldom let himself get angry, but tones now striking Jerry's ears sounded furious. He held his breath, listening intently to the argument, getting his bearings before interrupting.

A man's voice he didn't recognize, baritone yet shallow, spoke. "We will tell them, Rob, but later. Don't you think there's been enough trauma this week?"

"Conner, they're not children. They have a right to participate in decisions about our future. You can't dictate what happens. Nobody knows what our odds are now. Sure, give them our best guesses on what needs to take place, but if we're going to get through this, we need to work together."

The other voice, Jerry realized, belonged to Conner Newman, the lead engineer and one of the three pilots of the Glenn. He shot back, "Jesus Christ, Rob, they're either religious fanatics or complete airheads. All of them, except your husband, are liabilities. Can you imagine them understanding the depth of trouble we're in and not panicking? Fuck, those pretty girls won't be able to resist washing their hair every day much less live with reduced water rations for years. We'll retrench however possible without alarming them, before we let them in on the problem."

"And you assume you can finesse it so no one will notice?"

"Yeah, we'll hang on if the next asteroid we mine has ice, and we put in a few more shifts to bring the water level up. We have to make sure our population doesn't increase though. We can't feed more mouths."

"What do you mean? There are six women pregnant on this ship. Six babies waiting to be born."

"Fetuses, Rob. It's potential that will have to wait."

"Well, then you need to explain to the settlers why you want them to abort. You can't just notify them you changed your minds about children in space."

The silence that fell between the two arguing men crackled. Jerry felt tension roil his stomach. When Rob spoke again, he heard in that soft voice a fury he had never before witnessed.

"Shelly miscarried yesterday. That was you. You're inducing abortions without telling them."

"Not in Lily, Rob. She's too far along. Her baby will take Alex's place. We all agreed to that."

"You all agreed? Who? Are you three captains claiming the power of life and death over us? What's that called, Conner? An Oligarchy? A dictatorship? This expedition is an exercise in democracy as well as a space exploration."

"Yeah, well it's an exercise in survival now, where the smartest get to live. If you want to be part of the alpha team, fall in line with that. We expect our scientists to support us. And keep your mouth shut. We'll make sure your precious settlers survive. When we land on the planet, everyone can afford the luxury of equality again."

"Do you think I'll swallow that shit, Conner? Do you propose treat we people as inferior for years and then change back to being equal with them overnight?"

"Look, I'm not having this debate with you anymore. We made the decision. Keep your head down and we'll get through this crisis. If we ever return to Earth, you can protest all you want."

"What are you going to do when they find out you're killing their babies?"

"They won't—unless you tell them. They'll write it off as a natural result of being in space and assume Lily is the freak. We'll sell them some medical reason for why Asians have a better chance at carrying to term. And we're not killing babies. You aren't a right to lifer, Rob, so don't hang that on me."

"It's not what we believe about when life begins that matters, you jerk. This is their hope, the product of their love, that you're murdering. You can ask them to sacrifice that, but it's not fair to rip it away from them."

"God, grow up, Anders. This is a life and death situation and I'm making sure we end up alive. Us. Not some sentimental hoped for brats that aren't even kicking yet. Look, I'll get you enough water to save your fish. You help keep the lid on this state of affairs and everything will be fine. Got it?"

"Yeah, I 'got it' all right."

Conner's footsteps approached the entryway and Jerry pulled back. He ducked behind three black barrels of stored seeds which stood nearby, crouching close to their solid mass, his mouth open to breathe silently. His heart raced as this mundane guy, this acquaintance transformed into a hit man, stomped by, anger radiating off him. The door slid shut with a click.

When the footsteps receded, sharp as bullet shots in the

distance, Jerry rose. He went to the laboratory door again, signaling it to open, but the panel remained closed. Had Conner locked Rob in? He leaned against it, palms pressed against the plastic, and called softly to his husband. "Rob? Can you let me in? It's Jerry."

With a click and swoosh the panel slid open, almost spilling him onto the floor. Rob stood by the computers, face drained of color. "Sorry, Jer. I sealed the room. I was getting ready to call you."

"What's going on? I heard you arguing with Conner..."

"Did he see you?" Rob cut in, telegraphing his fear.

"No, man. I hid behind the barrels. This feels like a scene in a bad movie."

"Yeah, it's crazy. I think the captains have taken control of the ship. We lost a lot of water. They're justifying their actions by saying we're in a state of emergency, that the scientists are the most qualified to make decisions." He looked up, eyes clouded with concern. Jerry could see his hands shaking as he crossed his arms to pin them steady at his sides.

"What was that about ending the pregnancies?"

"We need to warn the women not to go to sickbay, not even for their check-ups. I suspect they slipped Shelly something that caused her to lose the baby. I can't believe Anne is in on this."

Jerry shook his head, frowning. "It wasn't Doc. Shelly told me Janice Rice was on duty, right before the miscarriage. She gave her a dose of B vitamins. Shelly wondered if that set off the contractions, but Doc assured her it couldn't. Do you think Janice put something in that shot?"

"Makes sense. She's one of the captains. Jesus, Jer... What are we going to do?" Panic thinned Rob's voice.

"I don't have any idea, but whatever we do, it's got to be quick. Conner knows you too well. He'll figure out you won't stand by and let them do this. Our only advantage is if we get this information out and expose them at once."

"But Jer, he's right about mutiny. Our circumstances on this ship are fragile and now we're even more compromised. None of us will survive a riot."

"OK, we want to be smart about this." Jerry paced, casting around for answers. The lights hurt his eyes, bouncing off the shiny surfaces of the lab counters. Damn arrogant scientists, assuming they see the whole pattern, that they control every situation.

"Let's get the support group together and brainstorm with them. Those women are bright. They'll want desperately to save both themselves and their families. And they understand how to approach their own leaders. It's possible we can forge an alliance out of the settlers and whatever scientists have their heads screwed on right."

"They won't go ballistic?"

"I think they're our only chance of avoiding that reaction. Abby's part of the circle too. I can't believe she'd collude in staging the abortions. She'll help us, I'm sure."

"Yeah, she may know what they told the rest of the SpaceTech team."

Jerry sent out a message to the women of the support group. Within thirty minutes, they all made their way to the observation deck, lowering onto the pillows circled on the floor and studying the solemn faces of the two men. Even Lily came, silently taking her place beside Abby. Since the accident, she leaned heavily on the ship's sociologist. She was her main source of comfort, besides Jerry.

"Did someone else miscarry?" Ayisha asked as she sat next to Shelly who was still pale with grief and pain.

"Not yet," Jerry replied. "but something has happened. We need to decide together how to respond."

Abby, tilted her head and looked at Rob with raised eyebrows, asking silently why he was present. Jerry nodded. Was she aware of the problem?

"You recognize my husband, Rob." Jerry began. "He wants to tell you something that affects all of us. Try to stay calm while he gives you what facts he knows. We want to decide with you how to react to this, but if we panic I'm afraid we might make things worse."

Rob glanced across the circle. "This may be old news to you, Abby. I only discovered it an hour ago after I noticed the level in the tilapia tank was low. I called the mechanic but he said he had orders not to dispense any more water, so I contacted Conner Newman, the lead engineer, to see what the problem was. Those fish must have fresh water to breed and I didn't want the system becoming unbalanced.

"Instead of changing the order, Conner said he'd come to the lab. When he got there he told me that when the mining accident happened, losing Alex wasn't the only catastrophe. A chunk of asteroid hit the Glenn, puncturing one of the water tanks. We were so busy trying to move away that no one noticed the water level dropping until half of our supply vented into space."

Abby nodded as Rob paused. "The captains gathered the scientists that evening and explained we needed to go easy on water. You were still in sickbay when we met. They didn't want to alarm anyone else on the ship though and asked us to keep it quiet. It sounded like they had it under control."

"Did they say how they would address the problem?" Rob scrutinized her. Jerry saw a muscle in his spouse's jaw jerk and realized that his anger still smoldered under the surface.

Abby glanced from Rob to Jerry and back again. "Obviously something is wrong here, but I don't remember anything sinister from that meeting. The engineers seemed confident they could regain the water on mining expeditions. No one invited us to craft solutions. They just informed and asked for cooperation. They said we should refrain from worrying the settlers about it for now."

Rob nodded, letting his eyes fall from her face. "OK. Apparently, they didn't let you in on how serious this situation is. And they didn't share their whole strategy for dealing with it."

"Who is 'they'? And what strategy? What are you implying, Rob?" Abby's broad brow furrowed as she stared at him. The other women shifted on their cushions.

Jerry reached over and placed a hand on his husband's forearm. He sensed a trembling beneath Rob's skin. "Tell them. It'll be OK."

Rob looked down, took a breath, then continued, "I'm not sure who's making these decisions. Certainly the captains are at the center: Conner Newman, Janice Rice, and Bill Jameson. Other scientists may be involved, too. Maybe even some settlers. In any event, a small group has decided on a course of action which affects everyone, and they did it without our knowledge or approval.

"What they told you is partially true, Abby. It should be possible to regain the water from mining, but it will take more time than they implied. Our ecosystem on the ship is already stressed. Conner said he didn't trust that the settlers could make the sacrifices required and that to increase our population would jeopardize the expedition."

The last words rushed out. Looks of bafflement on the faces of the women in the circle transitioned to horror as several of them instinctively wrapped arms around their middles.

Shelly, wide eyed and white faced, whispered into the silence, "My baby... What did they do?"

Rob considered the grieving woman, tears in his own eyes. "Shelly, I don't know for sure, but I speculate that whatever Janice gave you induced your miscarriage. Conner said they decided to abort every pregnancy but Lily's."

"But why?"

"How dare they?"

"Not my baby!"

Everyone spoke at once, outrage gaining the upper hand in the room. Jerry raised his voice. "Listen. We must stay calm and figure out what to do. We are stronger together than we are alone. It's our only chance to save the children and ourselves."

His words brought attention back to the center and quiet prevailed again, the sound of Shelly's weeping the only distraction.

Rob said, "Jerry's right. If we go off half-cocked there's a real possibility that we could all die. We're in a very precarious position now."

Ruth, dark eyes flashing, looked ready to levitate off her pillow. "How dare they make that judgment? Who do they think they are? "

"Wait a minute," Abby said. "Are you sure, Rob? I can

see them cutting off any more conceptions and even asking the women to consider ending their pregnancies if we're in serious trouble, but to cause miscarriages…"

"I heard this too," Jerry said. "Conner's words were: All the settlers are liabilities. Those pretty girls won't be able to resist washing their hair every day much less live with reduced water rations for years."

The precise slur, the petty ugliness of the dismissal, took their voices away for a moment. Then Miriam, clenching her fists to contain her outrage, said "What sacrifices are necessary, Rob? How can we make room for children now?"

"I'm not sure of the details. That's why this is so frightening. I don't know who made these plans or how they put together their estimates. My best guess is we'll require extra years in space. It takes time to look for water sources. We may need to ration our consumption so agriculture and mining can continue. That means fewer showers, less frequent laundry, and some limitation of drinking water. The real problem is we don't have the statistics. We didn't anticipate this situation in any of the planning scenarios—at least the ones we got to before we had to leave."

"Couldn't the Armstrong lend us water?" Kim looked shaken to the core. Since Shelly's miscarriage she had been in a constant state of worry about her own pregnancy.

"Then they would suffer the same condition as the Glenn. The agreement made on Earth was to not compromise the other ship, if one got in trouble. It appears hard hearted, but in theory at least it's better for some of us to make it than none."

"So we're on our own with this problem." Ayisha spoke calmly, her voice regal.

"Yes and if we opt to mine for water we'll get behind on schedule. We'll be alone. The Armstrong will go on without us."

Miriam shrugged. "So is this a big deal? They'll land on the planet first and the Glenn arrives a little later."

"Up to three years later. Maybe that's part of the problem." Rob scowled. "It's risky to be out here by ourselves, and the mining will take longer, but I wonder: Were these decisions made because our guys don't like coming in second? This will be the first manned expedition to reach a planet outside our solar system. Some people see it as a race."

"I don't care who wins, but three more years in this tin can might drive me crazy," Kim whined.

"I'd do it for the sake of the children." Jill, holding Shelly's hand, was emphatic.

Ruth nodded, "Yeah, I would too. And everyone in our congregations will want it that way. These babies belong to all of us."

"So how do we convince the captains they're wrong?" Ayisha brought the group back to focus.

Kim said, "Let's lock them up like they deserve and find someone else to pilot this ship."

Rob sighed. "That's part of the problem. Those are the three people best qualified to get us to our destination. We need them, especially if we're going to radically alter our trajectory and projected date of arrival."

Jerry, listening intently to the conversation, made a stab at wrapping up the various threads. "So we have to expose the captains' plan, make them admit they caused Shelly's miscarriage and planned other abortions and then figure out how to work with them again."

"It will take a big bargaining chip to even get them to listen." Abby bit her lip as she thought. "We'll have to go on strike—quit doing all the essential jobs like the mining and cooking that the settlers do. If we can enlist scientists to join us that would help. The captains may know where we're going but they depend on people like Eli to make sure the ship is running smoothly."

Jerry nodded. "If the fish and plants begin to die off, the threat of starvation will bring them up short too."

"That strategy needs to work quickly," Rob said. "We don't have a wide margin for recovery if systems start to fail in the bio-dome or in engineering."

"What about if we staged it in waves?" Ayisha narrowed her eyes, focusing on the problem. "We shut the kitchen down, and if they don't respond, the miners quit, and then as a last resort, the bio-dome workers stop."

Abby nodded. "That might work if we convince the captains enough people are on our side to make a difference. We need a symbol of solidarity—something to impress on them that the majority on the ship will strike if they don't give up control and share decision making."

Silence, heavy with desperation and grief, settled on the group. Jerry stared blank eyed into the middle of the circle. What would make the captains pay attention soon enough to avert disaster for everyone?

A voice, creaky and thin, threaded itself through the miasma. "We all shave off our hair."

It was Lily. Every member focused on her, stunned. These were the first words she had spoken to anyone but Jerry and Abby since the accident. She sat still staring at her hands which rested in her lap, oblivious to their amazement. Her mouth opened, and she spoke again, a little louder. "They want our babies. We give them our beauty. It's all we have. There is nothing else."

Abby, sitting next to her, reached over and grasped Lily's hand. Looking into her face, she said, "Oh, Lily, that's perfect. If we shave our heads, it will be a sign of protest, of solidarity. We can get everyone who agrees with us to do it. They won't be able to ignore it. They'll have to listen."

"It's a symbol of grief, too. It can serve as our mourning gift to Shelly's child." Jill's tears tracked her cheeks.

"And to Alex." Abby gave Lily's hand another squeeze.

Ruth grinned. "It'll also make us look as if we're in a concentration camp. That should shame those pricks."

Gazing at the women, Jerry felt the stirrings of hope. "Yeah, if I woke up one morning to the majority of the crew silently accusing me of being a monster like Hitler, I'd sure rethink my position. This might just work. We'll need our members to do it immediately. Then, after visual evidence of the number of people who stand against them has sunk in, we can demand to meet with the captains and outline our plans for striking. We should close the kitchen right away, but hopefully we won't have to take it any further."

Rob reentered the conversation. "The hard part may be restraining Stuart and the rest of the husbands from killing Conner, Janice and Bill."

"So what do you think?" Abby challenged the group. "Is it possible to convince your people our lives depend on forgiveness, on working together even with the captains?"

The women looked at each other, assessing the leaders in their religious communities. Finally, one by one, they nodded.

"Yeah, we're the only ones who can pull it off." Ayisha said. "We've got the most to lose."

"What about you, Shelly?" Abby asked. "Can you convince Stuart? Are you OK with this?"

"Get a razor. Let's do it now."

Miriam, a hair stylist back on Earth, got to her feet. "I'll get my shears," she said, heading for the door.

The group sat silent for several minutes, a meditative circle contemplating how their lives would change. When the panel whooshed open to readmit her, Rob volunteered to have his head shaved first. "It's the least I can do. I'm responsible for not noticing something was wrong, for letting this arrogance of scientific superiority run out of control." The razor buzzed over his scalp, flowing across the curve of his skull, as tight curls scattered petal-like around him.

Jerry watched as his spouse emerged from under Miriam's hands looking vulnerable, younger. "Hey, it's a look I could get used to," he offered to break the mood, but no one laughed.

Lily gave her locks next, long jet strands of silk floating down to lay lightly on the brown ringlets. Then, with the sound of the razor's buzz covering muted conversation, each member stepped forward, making an offering. Jerry's blonde topped off the pile. Lily fetched a broom from the kitchen and swept the hair, a mound of dark straw glinting with highlights of gold and Abby's shocking orange, into a garbage bag.

The deed done, they paused a moment. Miriam passed a small mirror and each peered in. A few reached up to stroke their shorn heads. Ruth is wrong, Jerry thought, looking at the women as they assessed their handiwork, clear-eyed and determined. They don't look like survivors of a concentration camp. These are Amazons preparing for battle. I hope the captains recognize what they're up against.

Before leaving the security of their group huddled on the observation deck, the women reviewed their timetable: Those belonging to a religious community would go together to talk to their leaders, filling them in and rounding up other members to join them for an assembly in the dining room in one hour. During the meeting they had limited time (Jerry estimated 45 minutes) to convince people of the danger and get them ready for confrontation. Success depended on those gathered at once grasping the problem and uniting around the protest. They had to act before the captains suspected a mutiny.

As the women left in pairs to mobilize their communities, Lily went to find more razors and prepare the cafeteria for the meeting. Rob and Abby left too, bent on finding scientists who might support them.

Alone in the dining room, Jerry turned his attention inward. As he filled his coffee cup and settled in the back of the room, he worried briefly about the women's ability to convince others to come to the assembly without giving specific details. Their problem, he told himself. If we're going to pull this off, we have to trust each other. These women are capable. I need to grapple with my part in this, not theirs. He breathed in the steam from the heavy mug, imagining the caffeine rushing to his brain to give him the jolt of energy he needed to get this right. He had always been a nervous preacher. This felt ten times worse. Honesty and forgiveness, he mused, those are the themes here. We can't be a community if those qualities are missing. How can I persuade them?

Half an hour later he abandoned his tepid coffee and lame notes to help Lily fashion a crude platform out of sturdy plastic crates. While only six foot square and three feet high, it would raise the speakers enough for everyone to see and hear them. Lily reminded Jerry that the intercom might be used to listen in on their meeting, and together they found the control box and turned it off.

The crew trickled in, grabbing drinks and taking accustomed seats. Jerry regretted his last cup of coffee. The acid in his stomach roiled with anxiety. Still, he made the rounds, helping people adjust their seating so they could see the stage, dodging questions, thanking them for coming. Abby and Rob entered and followed his lead.

If eighty percent of the ship's population showed up, they would pack the cafeteria. Jerry noticed separation into the three religious groups still held. A small band of scientists also arrived, isolating themselves in a back corner. He gathered the support group members as they returned, directing them to stand together behind the stage as a backdrop of bald unity. He hoped an illustration might help more than words alone.

The time came. By the door, Shelly whispered something to her husband Stuart and another tall, burly man. Jerry realized she was taking the precaution of guarding the entrance. Good for her, he thought. *I wonder if she's telling them to keep anyone else out or not to let people go before we're done?* Regardless, he felt comforted by her action. As she took her place with the rest of the support group, Jerry stepped up on the crates. He realized as he faced these people he had known for months he should start with something devotional. Crap, he snarled at himself, some priest you are, just getting around to thinking of this now. What can I offer that won't sound manipulative or trite? But consternation linked him to inspiration.

"Friends," he said, "I realize I should begin this meeting with a profound prayer, but the only words that come to mind are an ancient fisherman's plea. They sum up what I am experiencing today."

He paused just a second to take a breath, closing his eyes, trying to reach the Power with his heart. Then, into the crowd's anticipation, he prayed. "O God, the sea is so wide and my boat is so small. Have mercy on me. Amen."

He let the silence settle for a moment, then leaned forward to engage them.

"It's a desperate prayer, isn't it? But this is a dangerous, desperate time.

"I know you are wondering why the mothers' group called this assembly. We face a serious threat, but before we go into the details, I want to lay the foundation for our concern.

"This spaceship is far from home and the structures of society which protected the rights of every citizen. We undertook this journey knowing the physical dangers inherent in the mission, but we didn't reflect on the moral perils which isolation and fear can engender. Although we're members of a democracy, our practice of that most difficult form of government already eroded so much on Earth I suspect none of us has confidence in shared leadership.

"In the last months spent together, we've pulled into our own particular groups to find the comfort that only close family can give in a crisis. In doing so this crew has become an even more separated, fractured society than when we first began our journey. We don't think of ourselves as a single people with different faith expressions. We see ourselves as separate tribes. That pattern of thought has created a weakness in our midst which now threatens our existence.

"Rob will tell you the story of how that fault line came to light this morning. I ask you to suspend your questions and your judgment until Abby suggests a plan of action to address our healing. Then, together, we'll decide what to do."

Jerry stepped backward off the platform to make room for Rob to step up. His husband had practiced his speech and told the story of the morning's confrontation succinctly, ending with the conclusions the support group had agreed on: That a small number of scientists, most likely the three captains, were making decisions without sharing information with the rest of the Glenn's members. One of their choices was to terminate the Lundgren's unborn baby, with other forced abortions planned.

Shocked silence blossomed into a crescendo of noise before Rob could move off the dais. Neighbors turned towards each other to exclaim, to question, to challenge. Jerry watched the clutch of scientists most closely. They appeared more bewildered than the religious groups. A few scanned the larger group fearfully as if expecting an attack.

Abby at once jumped on the makeshift stage to address the crowd. Without her wild red hair, their sociologist's round, pug-nosed face looked even more child-like than before. The crew, however, was used to her voice issuing instructions as their chief communications officer. When she raised her hands and shouted for attention, the room quieted for her.

Jerry noticed how she accepted that silence as a gift, then acknowledged how hard it was to hear these things and how everyone suffered under this betrayal. Next she outlined the embryonic plan they had hatched:

"Our goal is to set up a democratic decision making policy group, with each of our communities equally represented. Because we don't know all the details of our status, we can't promise it won't come to asking our pregnant women to abort, but we can insist that nothing happens before we all vote on it. To force the issue, we will quit working our jobs, beginning with meal preparation and, if necessary, continuing onto mining, the care of the bio dome and finally, maintenance of the spaceship. We hope to get the captains' attention before we jeopardize the Glenn's safety. That's why having a dramatic symbol, a visual sign of our level of commitment, is so important. Our shaved heads indicate not only our grief, but pledge our willingness to make the sacrifices needed for the good of the whole community. If everyone here shaves off their hair, if you join the mothers' group in this sign of distress, it sends a message: We uncovered your plot and we stand together against it. This protest adds weight to the demands an intervention team will make at the captains' report meeting tonight."

"Who's on the intervention team?" A person up front thundered the question.

"Each of our four groups (scientists included) need to choose a member. Rob and Jerry will go too because they heard Conner admit to the planned abortions. We'll need leaders who can improvise when negotiating, because we don't know the extent of the conspiracy. We have come up with an outline of points to consider for a resolution, though.

Our leaders will settle for no less than full disclosure of the crisis on the ship as it now stands, the immediate formation of an oversight committee including representation for everyone, and the formal admission of guilt, with apology, for initiating Shelly's miscarriage. Unless other data comes to light to disprove the assumption that the three captains were in on this, even though they must continue their duties, another scientist will supervise their work at all times."

"Wait a minute. Why should we forgive murderers?" The question bulleted from the back.

"Yeah, they deserve to die!" The call for vengeance stirred a rumble of assent in the room.

Jerry strode forward to jump up next to Abby, compelled by an urgency beyond him. He looked into the mass of people before him, seeking the face of anger and finding beneath it the fear apparent in most eyes. He spoke to the fear, his focus narrowed with certainty.

"Janice is our sister. Bill and Conner are our brothers. If we punish them by death, we kill a part of ourselves as surely as if we had murdered one of our church, or mosque or synagogue members."

"You can't forgive murderers," someone cried, shrill and cutting.

"Of course you can." Jerry shot back. "What do you think Moses, Jesus, and Mohamed built their communities on? Forgiveness isn't pretending an awful act didn't occur. To forgive, we acknowledge what happened and say, 'never again.' Then we reconnect with the people who committed the sin. If judgment and punishment came into religions later, it was because disciples ignored that call to forgiveness, not finding the strength to follow where God led the way.

A community takes a step towards becoming just another institution when it fails to forgive."

"How could anyone reconnect with these captains? I say get rid of them," a man's voice boomed near the platform.

"We don't have the luxury we had back on earth of fooling ourselves about not needing each other. We may be all the humanity that's left. You think Conner, Janice, and Bill did the unforgivable? Wait until you face your worst fears and act in a way you never thought possible. Then you'll see. Everyone can do the unthinkable. If forgiveness isn't possible—if we establish that we cut off those who hurt us—then the day will come when you are exiled or killed, too. How many must we sacrifice before hope for the future collapses?

"We have a chance here, a crossroads where we can stay as we are or become a community in truth. If we extend ourselves in forgiveness, we also find the strength to cross those borders which have kept us separated into ghettos of Jew, Muslim, Christian, and scientist. We'll grow in love, knitting together a greater family here on the Glenn.

"Rob will tell you our physical safety depends on making this choice, that we cannot survive without Janice, Bill, and Conner. I tell you our souls depend on choosing to follow God in forgiveness."

An uneasy silence gripped the room. Jerry looked around at the support group women behind him and nodded at Shelly. She reached out to take his hand and stepped up on the crates. Standing crowded there beside him, the smooth curve of her shorn head accentuating the semicircles of darkness under her weary eyes, she raised her chin and spoke. "The violence was against me and mine, and I stand with Jerry and

Abby on this. I forgive." She paused a moment, searching the crowd. "Stu, dear, will you join me?"

Shelly's husband, his six-foot-four frame hunched with the weight of their loss, moved with deliberate steps through the silent people to the edge of the platform. He looked up at his wife, and taking her hand, spoke with his eyes still on her, "Seventy times seven, Christ said." The words boomed out with his Texas drawl, sounding like an old-time preacher. "I figure this covers nearly four hundred of those times we need to forgive. If Shelly can do this, I can too. Bring me a razor."

The tide turned. Jerry felt his focus soften, the room reappearing, past and future reasserting their place on his internal time line. He stepped off the crates, the support group women coming forward to invite the leaders of their religious groups to join them. Jim moved to the side and bowed his head to the razor. Others lined up behind him as if in a bizarre altar call. The blessing bestowed with a whir and a buzz left penitents changed, transformed before their peers.

Two other stations set up with clippers. Soon they finished shearing everyone and the leaders of the religious groups joined Jerry for a dismissal prayer. They hadn't completed the job. They still had to confront the captains. But Jerry had little doubt of success.

They only missed one meal. Two hours after the assembly, Bill, Conner, and Janice had seen enough bald heads to make them realize something was up. When Rob ushered the intervention team into the evening report, the captains faced them with defiant scowls, but no surprise.

Bill caved first, physically moving to their side of the

table as he protested that he never wanted to hurt anyone. When Conner and Janice understood there was no way to stop Bill from disclosing their deliberations and decisions they too agreed, if ungraciously, to the demand for a steering committee made up of representatives from all groups on board. Conner's arrogance kept him blustering for a while about the difficult choices leadership needed to make, until Rob firmly assured him that he would be relieved of that burden in the future. Anger nearly trumped fear in Conner's sharp eyes then, but a quick look around the room at frowns and lowered brows convinced him to back down.

Janice's reaction, though, turned Jerry's heart to ice. As the one who had injected Shelly to induce her miscarriage, he expected her to express the most remorse. Instead, after the first shock of the team bursting in on their meeting, she retreated emotionally. With her hands buried deep in the pockets of a white lab coat several sizes too big for her petite frame and her eyes squinting at the floor, she looked, Jerry thought, as if she were concentrating on an esoteric mathematical problem, annoyed by the surrounding distractions. When Rob laid out the stipulation that the three captains would be supervised in their work from now on, Bill made no objection and even Conner agreed with little protest. Janice made only one comment before acquiescing. "We must arrive at the planet as soon as possible. I have work to do there."

Jerry gently acknowledged her comment, saying, "Yes, arriving as soon as possible is one of everyone's goals but other considerations will be respected as well."

Later, at a ship wide meeting where the captains apologized for their actions, Bill and Conner did most of the talking. Janice came forward to acknowledge that she had been wrong and reiterated that she needed to get to the planet as soon as possible. Shelly and Stuart grimly accepted this as the deepest apology she was capable of and the assembly moved on. Jerry worried, though. How can a community heal when some of its members aren't capable of moral decisions? It would take time, he realized, for them to find out.

As the information on their condition sorted out, it became clear the captains had accurately assessed the gravity of the Glenn's situation. The steering committee grappled with hard decisions needed to keep the mission viable. They recommended delaying the next scheduled jump to save the pregnancies and give the miners time to find water on the asteroids within their reach. They also proposed a ban on any new conceptions until the crisis stabilized.

A vote of the whole confirmed this course of action. When the committee contacted their sister ship with the news, however, they had to explain the state of affairs again, this time to a resistant, if distant, audience. The crew of the Armstrong voiced as much apprehension about severing their connection as the members on the Glenn experienced. Jerry watched as Rob, representing the scientists, came home after each on-line conference looking more harried than ever. He confessed, "We've gotten everyone to agree, Jer, but the truth is we don't have enough information to make a safe decision. God, I hope this is right. We're gambling with our lives."

Jerry put his arms around him, holding him chest to chest until the beat of their hearts synchronized. Physical harmony helped keep chaos at bay, but comfort was fleeting. They both knew the odds favored them with the barest of margins.

The day of the scheduled jump, everyone who could skip their work gathered in the cafeteria to bid farewell and watch the Armstrong leave. Members on the Glenn waved and blew kisses to friends in the crowded room on their sister ship which mirrored their own. Jerry noted the haggard faces of many on the screen and thought, our tragedy marked them too. Prayers offered from both ships spoke of hope they would meet again on KOI-3284, but as Jerry whispered goodbye, others around him choked back sobs.

The moment came. Without a sound the Armstrong, their steadfast companion, winked out of existence. Black space remained unruffled as if the spaceship had never been. Now they were alone.

Not much changed in the everyday routine on the Glenn. Rationing water meant that everyone showered less and miners worked overtime searching for the valuable substance frozen on asteroids, but basically life continued. Janice, Conner and Bill slogged through their duties, followed around by bored colleagues. The most noticeable change in their behavior was that they now avoided each other. Bill was eager to reintegrate into the community and his fellow scientists gradually welcomed him to sit with them at meals and slip into conversations again. Conner nursed his pride longer until it became apparent that acting the victim only kept him isolated. He finally stopped trying to justify himself and found his way into an uneasy truce with the others. Janice acted like she hardly noticed anything had happened.

Two weeks into their solitary ISRU, Jerry relaxed. Maybe the worst is over, he thought. We can do this.

He was wrong. Reuben Jantz committed suicide that

evening. He hanged himself from the bathroom door in his quarters. His Jewish congregation, in shock, held a funeral within 24 hours. People all over the ship joined them in grief, bewilderment and fear.

Reuben had been a gregarious, even jovial member of the mining crew. He'd been part of the company on the disastrous accident, dragged to safety just before Alex died. But his wife Sally reported she'd seen no evidence of survivor's guilt. No dark depression dogged him. Many in his group and in the Muslim and Christian communities speculated in private a crisis of faith brought him down.

Three days after Reuben's funeral, Jane Dahl tried to follow him, courting death with her own hand. Jane, a smart, no nonsense nutritionist, had been on the Space Tech team from the beginning. Married to Eli, the chief mechanic, she formed half of a pair known for their dependable presence and adaptability, and their devotion to each other.

She had stashed away pain pills and tranquilizers from a long ago broken leg, smuggling them onto the Glenn. Eli, stopping into their quarters to retrieve a pair of forgotten work gloves midmorning, found his wife passed out in their tiny bathroom, lying in vomit. His forgetfulness saved her life.

Abby caught Jerry in the hall as he exited sickbay after visiting and praying with the distraught Eli, sitting hunched at the beside of his still unconscious wife. Wrapped in his own fog of disbelief, he didn't notice her until she grabbed his arm and said, "Jer, we've got to stop this."

He looked at her flushed face, red as the fuzz just sprouting on her scalp, and blinked back tears. "What do you want me to do? I can't counsel everyone. Jane never came to see me.

She seemed so strong, so together."

"You're right. This isn't a problem that counseling can cure." She kept a grip on his arm and walked, guiding him until they reached the observation deck. They slipped into the dark room, the portal shining with a million icy points of foreign stars and when the door slid shut behind them she turned to face him. "It feels like we're beginning a suicide cluster—a phenomenon where one death sets off another and another. We have to disrupt this pattern at once. We don't have enough people to absorb an epidemic of our own making."

"God, Abby, I don't know what to do. It seems like ever since the Armstrong left, everyone's falling apart."

The young sociologist crossed her arms, hugging herself. "Yeah, the depression is palpable. We need to build a deeper sense of community than just our separate tribes—to get people to reach over the barriers and create hope. I'm convinced we have a chance here, Jerry. We got them pulling together against the captains, but now we have to find a way they can work towards something positive."

"They work together all the time. Work is all we do. Then we hunker down to mourn with our friends over the families we've lost and share fears about what lies ahead—about not finding enough water, not finding the planet, not knowing whether anyone on earth is still alive." He sank down to sit on one of the floor pillows scattered across the room, putting his face in his hands. God, I'm so tired, he thought.

Abby knelt down beside him, reaching out to rub his back. "That's the problem, isn't it? We're steeping ourselves in fear and everything we do is about survival. But just keeping alive won't cut it for us. We need a reason to live."

He raised his head, suddenly tuned in to what she was saying. "You mean like, instead of banding together to fight a threat, we should orchestrate a situation where we join forces to create something."

"Or some things, right? We don't have just one type of creative person on board."

Jerry recalled the time when the call of suicide almost seduced him. After being dumped by his first lover at the tender age of seventeen, rejection and his own adolescent insecurities overwhelmed him. Even now he remembered the step-by-step plan he formulated to end the agony by sitting in an antique jalopy his father was restoring in the garage. He would close the doors, turn on the engine and wait. He lulled himself to sleep for a week with this scene playing in his head, convincing himself this was a way to cure the painful wound which life had become. If his uncle hadn't called that summer, begging him for help in the nursery, he might have done it. Instead, the kindness of an old man and the needs of seedlings and saplings redirected his thoughts, nudging him back from the brink, until he believed in the future.

He nodded, in sync with Abby's urgency. "So we could create theater and writing clubs, painting studios—stuff like that?"

"Yeah, that would be a start. And then somehow weave it into our lives so we develop a culture that belongs to all of us."

"How about instituting an entertainment hour every evening after supper? People can form creative groups and then make presentations or entertain the whole crew."

"That might work." Abby nodded, settling back on a

pillow beside him. "We'd need to be up front about why we're doing this, Jer. Transparency is important. Our leaders should understand the point is to get everyone mingling and enlarging their experience. It's an effective antidote to depression."

"I don't think anyone will resist the idea. Having something positive to try in the face of these tragedies feels like a real gift. I bet they'll all see it that way."

The Mother's Support group once again came to their aid by organizing the effort. The women already experienced the power of sharing with each other across religious boundaries as they embraced the new life growing in their bodies. With Abby and Jerry's plan in hand, they cajoled and bullied until each member of their various tribes found a place to express themselves. A barbershop quartet formed as well as a jazz band, and two theater clubs with spin offs of artists who composed plays and created sets and costumes for them. Soon evenings on the ship filled with members crossing their self-imposed borders, discovering the gifts of their neighbors. The tide of despair turned as the community coalesced. Hope crept back into hearts, until seven years later they arrived at Goldilocks as one people, diverse yet united.

CHAPTER 11
PLANET KOI-3284

DATE: 2073-2076 CE/1

Unable to contain his nervous energy anymore, Ahdam stood up and circled around the outside of the gathered steering committee. The tension in the room increased with his leonine prowling, but no one admonished him. Sarah, with her trademark calm said, "What is the greatest barrier to our unity right now?" She directed the question to the whole group, but it was the Imam who stopped in his tracks and faced his fellow members again.

"This is the point of no return for me." He sat back down on the edge of his cube, hunched as if ready to spring into action. "If we have children of mixed parentage between our congregations, or even of parents who are not religious, how should we raise them? Shall I send my seed out to become Christian or Jewish or nothing at all? Will my wife bear a child we can't teach our ways to, not lead in our faith? That is unthinkable for me."

Silence descended on the circle. Most of the members studied the floor, avoiding the anguish in Ahdam's eyes. Jerry could sense a resonance in each of them as these questions hit home. He looked around though and realized that he loved each of the people in this group, even Steve who continually challenged him.

"Ahdam," he said, willing the Imam to look at him. When he did, Jerry continued. "I would entrust any child of mine to you, not because I wanted him or her to be Muslim, but because you would teach them to be open to wonder, and so open to God. You're right—if we entwine our lives so that my children and yours never care who their 'real' parents are, but understand all adults cherish them, we won't be able to give them the religions and cultures we grew up with. But we could start something better. These kids might grow up with a faith which embraces the best in all our traditions and leads them to know God in an even deeper way."

Kathir nodded. "My family was Muslim, but we didn't observe religious traditions. I had to leave them to become a true member of Islam. The process of choosing to be spiritual for me was also a rebellion against their shallowness. Ahdam, most young people take this journey. As parents, we may have to loosen the reins early, but we should expose them to every belief system represented among us. When they grow up, they'll decide for themselves how they want to live."

Sarah's eyes brightened. "Yes, even as Rabbi, I can see that. There's no guarantee our children would have followed our religions on Earth. In fact, the odds were against that. At least here on Goldilocks, all adults commit to some faith journey."

"Well, except for the scientists." Steve said.

"No, the scientists on this mission are all capable of wonder," Jerry said, looking at his husband and Eli. "And wonder is the path which faith walks. I would commend a child to any of them. The decision before us is how to embrace the different ways of walking towards Truth our colony has and then commit to letting the kids try each of them out."

"Would you include children born of our sacred unions—our marriages—in this exposure?" Ahdam still had his arms crossed and a scowl on his face.

"Yes." Jerry gave a definitive nod. "The great challenge will be to quit assuming we own any of these kids. No matter what combination of DNA they have, we must believe and act as if they are given to all of us."

"And that they exist for none of us," Sarah insisted. "Children, in the end, belong to God and themselves. We can only be stewards, caretakers, of this greatest gift from heaven."

Steve sat up straight. "You know, it doesn't matter how often they go to one service or another, or even what traditions they learn. Kids will become who they love best."

Jerry, thrown by his nemesis' support, said, "That sounds about right, Steve. Tell us more."

With a glance at Shelly, and a flush rising on his face, the Christian leader continued. "Like Kathir, I grew up in a family who had no real religious beliefs. We had a lot of traditions, though. We always did Christmas up proud, had a classic turkey feast at Thanksgiving, and decorated to impress the neighborhood at Halloween—but every holiday felt empty. It meant nothing. Only at my grandma's house did celebrations make sense. I realized early on it was because she loved us so much that the trappings didn't matter to her. Then, when I was ten or eleven years old, I found out she followed Christ. She took me to a worship service. When I asked her why she went she told me, 'Church is where I learn to love'. Her devotion and integrity hooked me. My parents never understood. They supposed I would grow out of it. Instead, I kept growing into it."

Shelly tilted her head at him and smiled. "So you became a Christian because your grandma loved you into it?

"Pretty much. That's my point—I realize after these past eight years, if she had been Muslim or Jewish I would probably have adopted that religion. The form wasn't as important as the person I revered who embodied it."

Jerry nodded. "I know how that feels."

Steve took a deep breath and then forged ahead. "So Ahdam, I can relate to your fears, but I think Kathir's idea of raising the kids to experience all our religions is the way to go. Islam might not survive like it was on Earth. Christianity and Judaism probably won't either. Even science is bound to change. But we'll lose nothing essential, if we love the children well."

The Imam scrutinized his friend. "So how do we raise them in all our ways? How do we make time, with so much else that needs to be done?"

Hadith shrugged, saying in her gentle voice, "Aren't we already doing it? When Shelly leaves little Alice with me and its Shabbat, the child sits with us. I bet she knows all the prayers. Xander has been to every sort of worship experience we offer just because he's interested. As long as we don't forbid them and we make our services and other traditions open to all, they'll educate themselves."

Sarah said, "Yes, that's reasonable—we'll encourage a curiosity that invites everyone, adults and children alike, to inspect the beliefs of our neighbors. Can we all agree to that?"

Eli spoke up. "As long as that also means a solid education in the sciences and the scientific method of discovery, I'll go along with it."

Murmurs of assent rippled around the circle. Even Ahdam gave a curt nod, but then said, "The decision won't matter if there are no new children to raise."

Rob leaned into the group. "Yes, Ahdam's right. It's great to accept a different way of being parents, but how procreation works on this planet is still a mystery. None of us has answers—only the hope that Lily and Jerry bring."

"I need more than hope." Hadith's eyes swam. "If Goldilocks wants to be involved for me to get pregnant, I'm willing. I just don't know how."

Jerry said, "I'm not sure it's a particular action. Perhaps the willingness, the openness to Goldie is enough."

"Still, what does that mean? Is it something I think? Do I signal somehow I'd like her to show up?

"I'm not clear about what happened, Hadith. Lily and I both had the dream after coming to our wits' end around intrauterine insemination. Maybe it was that sense of needing help that got telegraphed to Goldie. I wonder—if you and Nathaniel both try to get the message of your desire for a baby across when you have the common dream next, that could be enough."

Rob nodded. "It's a place to start. We'll ask people to communicate the invitation for Goldilocks to help during their dreams and see what happens. If the conception rate goes up, we've got it right. If not, we'll have to try something else."

Sarah arched her stiff back and rubbed her neck. "OK, guys. This is as far as we can go tonight. I'll make a preliminary report at last supper about our decision to encourage IUI and the need to create as many combinations of our genes as possible. Jerry, I'd like you and Lily to announce her pregnancy too. We'll give everyone a day to absorb that news. Then we'll use tomorrow's gathering time to go into the details and discuss Goldilocks' involvement."

Three months later, Jerry entered the bio-dome for his shift. He was plotting out in his mind the steps needed to get all his duties for the day done in time to take Xander out to the lake before first supper. As he stepped into the entranceway, he saw Tamara sitting on the bench in front of the main door. "Hi. I didn't expect to see anyone out here so early this morning. How are you doing?"

As he spoke, she stood up and smiled, but her hands clasped before her as if she tried to keep nervous energy contained. "I hope you don't mind, Jerry. I wanted to speak to you privately."

"OK, but can I get started while we talk? I promised Xander an outing this evening and if I don't move, I won't be able to finish everything."

"Sure. I'll just tag along and we'll chat as you work. What's on your to-do list today?" She followed him into the main part of the dome, and Jerry told her about the project they planned to tackle that afternoon—the sowing of their first outdoor garden.

"That means I need to finish all the chores here so Helen and I have time to till that patch of ground Eli gave up as a landing strip." He chuckled. "We want to claim it before he changes his mind." He noticed that Tamara didn't laugh at his attempt at humor. Instead, her eyes focused on the path in front as they walked back to the office and Jerry realized she hadn't heard a word he was saying. "On second thought, let's sit down and you can tell me what's bothering you."

He took her elbow and guided her to a bench where they both perched, facing the tomato plants. When he looked at her face, he noticed her eyes were reddened, the lashes shining with dampness. He sat still, waiting until she was ready.

With a little laugh, she reached up to rub her face. "I stayed up all night, trying to decide how to talk to you about this." She paused, shook her head, and started again. "The thing is, Jerry, Steve doesn't want to accept the planet has anything to do with the pregnancies we're getting. He only had the shared dream once—after the seventh jump when we all discovered it. He never had it again. I suspect he's blocking it, or her, Goldilocks, out."

"So you're afraid you won't be able to have a child?"

"Yes—at least not with him. The common dream still visits me. I'm sure Goldie somehow facilitates conception. Lily and the other five women who conceived all report interaction with her. They say the dream changed for them and their partners right before they got pregnant. I can't convince Steve to consider the possibility though." She bowed her head, staring at her lap where her hands lay, knuckles white with tension.

"It's early to worry, isn't it?"

Tamara sighed. "Did you know the steering committee may start the lottery again?"

He looked up. "No, I hadn't heard. Why?"

"If all the women who are pregnant now deliver healthy babies, we'll be halfway to the number of children SpaceTech originally wanted us to produce each year. Steve and Shelly don't want to strain resources or cut our work force too drastically. They're going to bring up the possibility of restricting fertility at the meeting tonight."

"Our food sources are more abundant than we ever expected. If we find we can cultivate plants outside the dome, we don't need to worry about starving."

"Yes, that's why they didn't move more quickly. But having half the workforce out with morning sickness and small children will slow down progress on both our colony's development here and on exploration. We should be careful, I understand that. I just..." She wiped a tear tracking down her cheek and stood up, turning her back on him, addressing the tomatoes. "All those years in space the only thing that kept me going was the hope of having a child. I want to be a mother. I love Steve, but I'm helpless. Right now, I'm so angry with him."

She turned and faced Jerry straight on, crossing her arms. "I'd like to consider another partner. If Steve's pride keeps him from accepting the truth about this planet, I refuse to suffer the consequences. Could I do intrauterine insemination? Maybe when I have a baby by someone else, Steve will open himself to the reality of our situation."

Jerry gazed at her face, noting clenched teeth and narrowed eyes. "I understand. You don't want to miss the opportunity to fulfill your calling. Did you share with Steve how you feel about this? To succeed with IUI, you need to establish a significant friendship with another man."

She sat down beside him again, hanging her head.

"No. I'm afraid—afraid that he could go off the deep end, or divorce me, or convince Ahdam the two of them should leave the colony."

Jerry's brow wrinkled as he questioned her. "You know, when the steering committee grappled with the issue of kids with mixed parentage, Steve appeared OK with it. He talked about his grandma and how it was she, not his parents, who brought him to Christianity."

"Yes, he's more complex than most people give him credit for. He could love a child he hadn't fathered physically and be a great daddy." She sighed and wiped at another tear. "But Jerry, he's very possessive, even jealous. I've had to talk him off the ledge several times when he assumed someone attracted me. Steve is insecure at his core."

Jerry regarded her. "Do you think he would throw away your marriage and his place in the Christian congregation?"

Tamara sighed again and shrugged her shoulders. "I've become close to Judith, you know. She hasn't conceived yet either. Ahdam has never dreamt the singer. He tells Judith that he's open to the planet playing a part in the act of creation but won't believe it until Allah reveals it to him. She's not hopeful that will happen soon. If those couples who don't or can't have kids feel isolated and deprived, I can see a break away. It's not rational, Jerry, but it is human nature."

"Is Judith also considering another partner?"

"No, that's a step too far for her."

"I wonder..." Jerry fell into a reverie, staring into the plants on the other side of the path.

Tamara waited, twisting her hands together, until anxiety got the best of her. She broke into his quiet. "What?"

Jerry started, called back to the present and the impatient

woman beside him. "We all process new information in different ways. Lily and I hoped having a child would shake up the common assumption about how families should look. Goldie aiding the conception startled and challenged us too."

Tamara nodded. "That's often the case, isn't it? You plan to teach people one thing and then you're surprised to learn something new yourself."

"Yes, and it's harder for us to accept things we haven't experienced than to just tweak the limits of what's already acknowledged. Both Steve and Ahdam think concretely. They learn through doing things themselves—hands on. That's one reason they're such good friends. The two of them are wired the same way."

"So you're wondering, if they can't receive the dream, how can they experience Goldilocks?" Tamara tilted her head, considering her husband in this light.

"Right. What would give them a window into the reality we get a taste of in our sleep?"

She bit her lip. "I've got no idea, but you seem inspired."

Jerry nodded. "It was something Rob said. Remember when they brought home the fairy dragons? Rob suggested we could extrapolate Goldie's character from observing her creatures."

"So if we expose Steve and Ahdam to the fairy dragons it would connect them with Goldie's presence?"

"It might give them a concrete way to interact with her. I know I sensed her looking at me through the eyes of that beauty who landed on me." His excitement grew. "If we alerted Goldilocks to this dilemma some humans have, perhaps she could even help get the point across."

Tamara's face softened into hope. "There's another

exploration team going out next week. Do you think Rob would take Steve?"

"Let's look into it, OK? Before you make plans to partner with someone else."

The second expedition to the turquoise mountains already had a team of scientists in place: John and Rob went again as the senior botanist and zoologist with Jim and Helen assisting. They planned to range further into the woods this time, collecting specimens, observing the natural habitat in this special environment and tracing the patterns of life that occurred there. They also wanted to inspect a small river which ran through the trees which they discovered on their first visit. Jerry, through the long years in space, had become their fish whisperer—the human most likely to call forth the wiggling of any aquatic presence—and so he joined the company. Xander, because of Rob's promise to take him next and his unique ability to converse with the planet, claimed a spot with them too.

Rob and John weren't enthusiastic when Tamara asked them to consider Steve and Ahdam for the excursion's support crew. They had been counting on someone with more culinary experience joining them, to avoid the prepackaged food they survived on before. This trip, after all, would last a whole seven days. They relinquished the vision of traveling with Jane, or at least Lily, however, bowing to the needs of the wider community.

As they started out across the sea of yellow grass, the sun rising as the Rose Moon set, Xander captured first place for enthusiasm. Squeezed between Helen and Jerry in the backseat of the leading ATV, he craned his neck squirming to catch each fresh sight. In the second vehicle, Ahdam and Steve sat more quietly. Neither of them had expected to be included. Many of the settlers were being assigned to new jobs since landing on the planet. There was no longer any call for space mining and the recent slowdown in construction meant a greater population of available workers to help the scientists with their discoveries. The two friends knew the tasks they faced were basic grunt work-setting up and caring for the tents, cooking and, if time permitted, helping to collect plant and insect species, but they felt lucky to go. At very least, the expedition gave them a break from the monotony of seeing the same ten acres of land every day.

They made their camp at the base of the mountains, just outside the broccoli forest, where a ring of scorched dirt showed the first expedition had camped before. No fairy dragons greeted them on this trip, much to Xander's disappointment and, in truth, Jerry's too. They pitched several sleeping tents and erected a kitchen shelter—all protected by wind shielding force fields. Getting the site set up was an exhausting physical feat in a twenty mile plus gale. After a dinner of heated prepackaged meals, the whole crew turned in, eager to get an early start on their projects the next day.

In the morning, the adults woke as the sun rose. Steve and Ahdam made a proper breakfast of eggs and oatmeal to sustain the explorers as well as packing lunches for those venturing too far out in the field to return until first supper. Xander, however, slept late, oblivious to the commotion around him as people dressed and straightened out sleeping bags. When Jerry checked on him after he'd finished his own meal, the boy still snoozed.

"I hate to wake him," he told Rob. "He was so excited about coming on this trip he didn't sleep the night before we left. He's exhausted."

"Well, let him be for a while. I'm sure he can scrounge something up to eat. I'm going with Jim today to map out the exact depth of the forest. We suspect it ends a few miles up into the foothills, but need to trek up there and assess the environment."

"OK. When Xander gets up, we'll look for the stream and get acquainted with the area."

"That's a good idea. Steve and Ahdam can go with you. It will give them a chance to experience it without pulling any of us away from our work. Then tomorrow, I'll either come with you to the river or send Helen to help you—depending on how far Jim and I get with the mapping project today."

"Sounds like a plan."

Helen, listening in while filling a backpack with water and sandwiches, said, "Have you given them directions? It gets a little dense in there. We don't want them lost."

"Right. Come on, Jer. Let's go out and I'll show you the landmarks." He raised his voice to include Steve and Ahdam who stood together on the other side of the cook tent organizing supplies. "Hey, guys, would you drop that and step outside with Jerry and me?"

At that moment Xander, rubbing sleep out of his eyes, stumbled into the shelter. Ahdam laughed and ruffled his hair. "Hi, Mr. Sleepy Head. Do you expect breakfast now? Everyone else has eaten."

The boy shrugged. "Could I have a granola bar?"

"No, no—we'll make you a full meal," Steve insisted. "Ahdam's being lazy. We have to keep up all the crew's strength."

"Can you wait a few minutes while we go get directions, Bud?" Jerry asked, smiling at the child.

"Sure. Where are we going today? Will we see the fairy dragons? I want to take my backpack."

"Whoa, man. One thing at a time." Rob came over to give Xander a hug. "Let's orient you and after that we'll start the day."

Outside the shelter of the big tent, the wind blew, and the men fitted their personal halos on their heads. Xander, not bothered by the gusts, looked around, soaking in the honey colored light and searching the nearby branches for fairy dragons. Rob gathered them up in a semi-circle and pointed out distinct markers in the landscape for them to remember.

"The mountains will always give you a clue where north is, but once you get into the trees, it's hard to view them. What we've found is that there are little clearings throughout the forest where you can usually glimpse the mountain tops. You should be able to find one of those and regain your bearings if lost. Remember that camp is to the south of the mountain range.

"The river is an hour's walk from here. Notice how that tree is nearly a foot taller than its neighbors? Enter the woods there and try to walk straight north. There aren't any paths through the trees—no animals big enough to make them. You'll know you're getting close to the water when you hear the little waterfall. Tie some strips of cloth around branches as you go so you can find your way out. That's what we did. In fact, you may be able to follow our markers in and out. Let's check if they're still there."

Xander ran ahead as the men followed to the edge of the forest. As he passed the tall tree that Rob pointed out, he let out a small yelp. "I found a marker!"

Rob came up to inspect the boy's find. "Yep, it looks like they lasted. Keep an eye out for these and you'll be fine."

After the scientists' teams left for the day, Steve and Jerry gathered backpacks and filled them with food for lunch. Adham returned to the cooking shelter from his sleeping tent and saw them working. "Won't we be back before noon?" he asked.

Steve shook his head. "No, the rest of the crew won't turn up again before sixteen-hundred hours. I figure we can have a light meal by the river and still return in time to make them first supper."

The Imam cast around looking worried. "Maybe I should stay here and guard our things."

Jerry looked up from his work, noting his wrinkled brow and tight lips. "What's wrong, Ahdam?"

"Nothing. It's just... Well, we'll be gone at dhuhr, my mid-day prayer. I'm not sure how I'll manage in the forest."

Because the traditional five devotions of the Islamic faith linked to the movement of Earth's sun, the Muslims on Goldilocks had conceded a schedule in this foreign context preceding their meals instead. As Ahdam said, it was the discipline of praying, not the hours, that mattered. Having changed the timing though, the little congregation grew even more conscious of its ritual. The whole colony came to value Kathir's sonorous bass voice chanting the call to prayer throughout the day. While some just used this as heads up for the next meal, others—Jews, Christians and scientists alike—paused to open their hearts to God with their Muslim brothers and sisters.

Steve, alerted now to the Imam's concern, also stopped his packing. "Don't stress, friend. We can roll up your prayer rug and tie it on your pack. I've got my Bible and devotional on my com-pad. Jer and I will take a break and do our prayers when you do."

"Thanks." Ahdam's tight face relaxed. "I'll take a water bottle as well for wudu, in case we haven't reached the river by lunch time."

Xander, holding up his bag, said, "I'll carry your rug and water. I don't have much in my backpack."

The hour's walk to the river proved pleasant and uneventful. Wind died to a breeze, just enough to ruffle the warm air, so the halos hung from the men's belts as they waded through loose undergrowth surrounding the smooth trunks of the trees. Sunlight filtered through the close set branches with a bluish cast and a spicy smell seeped up from the fallen twigs and blossoms they stepped on. Rob was right. They heard the waterfall long before they could see it and adjusted their hike to intercept it.

The watercourse barely qualified as a river, being only a few feet wide in most places. It leapt from a cliff as tall as the trees on either side, creating a spectacular curtain of spray and a churning channel before settling into a rushing current. As the explorers wandered its banks, they found a few spots where the stream slowed and widened to create deep pools, but it soon returned to its furious linear pace.

Jerry stopped often to peer into the water's depth, trying to glimpse any aquatic life.

After another hour of wandering downstream, Xander ran ahead and called to them. "I found a clearing."

The men veered away from the river to follow his voice. Just beyond the nearest trees bordering the water, they discovered a perfectly round room, fifty feet across, walled in by pillars of trunks and roofed by a sky so bright it appeared white. Short moss—like plants carpeted the ground—brilliant green with a few buds of tiny golden flowers blooming. Even though the stream lay less than ten feet from this meadow, the only sign of it was the sound of rushing water which visited them in the still air. The woods here grew so close together it was impossible to see it. When the group looked up, they spotted mountain peaks above the forest wall, rising to the north.

"Wow, how beautiful." Jerry said, swinging his pack off his shoulder. "Let's eat here."

The others concurred. Ahdam retreated to the river to perform his ritual washing before devotions. Steve set both the prayer rug and his own blanket close to the trunks, with twelve feet between them, shaded from the high sun. Jerry and Xander joined him, relaxing into the heat of day. Steve sighed and stretched out his legs, angling his face to the light like a sunbather at the beach. "What a magnificent afternoon. Why can't our planet be this pleasant more often?"

Xander, lying on his stomach at the edge of the blanket studying a beetle in the moss, looked up frowning. "I think she's always nice. She just has different moods like everyone else."

Jerry reached for the com-pad to forestall any bickering

that might ruin the peaceful mood. "What are we reading today, Steve?"

"I'm meditating on the psalms this month. I marked my spot."

"Psalm eight-four?"

"Yes, that sounds right. Do you want to say it aloud?"

"Sure." But Jerry paused as Ahdam returned from the river bank and his ritual washing. With a nod to the group on the blanket, he stepped on his rug to begin his prayers.

As the Imam chanted, Jerry read, pitching his voice between him and Steve so as not to disturb the Muslim devotions. The mingling of holy words and distinct voices, noted by one corner of Jerry's brain, seemed to create a new form of worship in the space between them. Contentment settled into his bones. This, he thought, is how life is meant to be.

As he finished the reading, Xander, who had continued to study his beetle, suddenly sat upright. Both Steve and Jerry looked at him and then turned their attention to where the boy's vision focused, up into the broccoli trees overshadowing their oasis. Six dark shadows blurred the outline of the branches high in the foliage, hanging like gargoyles over them. Jerry's eyes narrowed, trying to make out the forms.

"The fairy dragons are here." Xander's joyous cry startled Ahdam preparing to bow towards Mecca, a direction of intention rather than a physical fact in this foreign context. He too looked up in the trees, but his expression matched Steve's apprehension, not the boy's enthusiasm.

"Don't worry," Jerry murmured just loud enough so Ahdam could understand. "They won't hurt anyone. They're inquisitive. Let's do our thing and let them get used to us."

"Right." Ahdam muttered the response but continued with his bow and the men on the blanket heard his prayers resume.

Steve took back his com-pad, calling up his devotional. He and Jerry joined in the Lord's Prayer. When the strange beasts in the trees made no moves, he whispered to Jerry, "Do you think it's safe to go on?"

"Yes, I'll pray while you read through your daily meditation. I'm sure they mean no harm." He looked toward Xander who sat gazing up into the branches. "You'll keep watch won't you, kiddo?"

"OK. I hope they come down soon though. What are they waiting for, Uncle Jer?"

"Maybe they're letting us finish our prayers." He smiled at the eager boy and composed himself, breathing deeply as he contemplated the beauty of not only the psalm they had just read, but the surrounding creation. The murmur of Arabic reached him as Ahdam continued his ritual too, now down on his knees and touching his forehead to the ground. Jerry relaxed completely.

A slight breeze kicked up, enough to cool but not annoy. From up above, a single precise note sounded and Jerry opened his eyes to see all six fairy dragons descending in lazy loops, their shining wings catching the mild updraft. They landed between the prayer rug and blanket, separating the small group. Jerry glimpsed Ahdam's face for an instant before they touched down, eyes wide and lips tight. Before he could react, Xander moved, jumping to his feet and walking into the midst of the strange creatures now folding their brilliant pinions. They greeted the child with chittering and snuffles, the largest stretching out a long sinuous neck to rest its head on his shoulder. Xander hugged it.

"It's OK." The boy directed his voice towards Ahdam, but Steve and Jerry heard him too. "They're really interested in what we're doing. They think we're wonderful."

"I think we all should continue then." Jerry tried dampen down his excitement, willing confidence into his tone. "Do you think you can carry on, Ahdam?"

"I'll help." Xander moved over to the prayer rug, one hand still on the fairy dragon's neck. Two other beasts followed him and the rest turned toward the blanket and the two men sitting there cross-legged. Jerry kept his eye on the boy as he knelt beside the tense Imam and the strange creatures arranged themselves in a semi-circle behind them.

The other three creatures settled around the Jerry and Steve. They all, like cats, wrapped their long tails about their bodies and rested their noses on them. Jerry realized that golden eyes watched them closely under the heavy ridged lids, but felt only the benevolence of nature emanating from them. With one last check on Xander and Ahdam, he prepared to his resume his meditation.

Steve cleared his throat. "Should we read another psalm before we pray? How about eighty-five? Why don't you take the even verses and I'll read the odd."

Jerry nodded opening his com-pad to the psaltery. Then in low voices, so they wouldn't bother the nearby Muslim worshiper, they began. As the stanzas traded back and forth, the fairy dragon in the middle sat up to attention, while the other two lifted their heads as if to catch the words.

When the reading stopped, the men prepared to meditate again. Steve set a timer to mark fifteen minutes. They closed their eyes, and Jerry settled into the rhythm of his breath, trying to ignore the weird and wondrous creatures sitting so close to him. As he found the expanse of his inner space, a weight on his leg startled him. He opened his eyes to see that one of the fairy dragons had scooted near enough rest its head on his thigh. He stroked its long neck, looking over at Steve who had an alien nestled into his hip too, and smiled. First contact, he thought, as he closed his eyes again and realized Goldie now shared the landscape of his meditative zone. He wondered about what Steve and Ahdam were experiencing, but then his discipline asserted itself and he let go of even that speculation.

When the chimes went off ending their meditation time, Jerry looked up to check on Xander. On the Imam's prayer rug, two of the beasts flanked Ahdam with their wings spread out—the colorful arches overlapped behind his back and fanned out to his sides. Jerry couldn't tell whether they touched his friend, but, since they weren't very tall, he could observe the man kneeling with his eyes closed between them. Xander and the third fairy dragon had moved to the front of the carpet and faced the Imam. Xander sat cross-legged, the creature nestled in his lap with its wings also unfurled over his knees and its neck outstretched, head bowed to the ground before him.

As Jerry considered this tableau, the wind kicked up, blowing the fallen leaves around them and shaking the broccoli trees. As if summoned, all the fairy dragons folded their wings and retreated from the humans, skittering on their six legs to the clearing between the rug and blanket again. Then, with the single note cry coming from each of their throats, they jumped into the air, spread their wings and soared up into the forest.

The men watched them go, Xander running after them a few steps into the trees before he turned back. Jerry brushed away tears as the emptiness of their departing beauty descended on him. Without speaking, they moved to gather up the rug and com-pads, making room for a meal on the blanket.

As they prepared to eat, Ahdam paused and looked at Steve. "Did you sense her with you in your prayers as I did?"

Steve nodded. "Yes, it brought back the dream. I can't refute this experience. I'm not sure what it means, but there it is."

Ahdam sighed. He turned to Jerry and said, "I can't deny it either. Allah works in mysterious ways and this is the most baffling. I think though I can now accept this being, this planet, who acknowledges that she too belongs to Allah. Forgive me for my cynicism."

T

Three Earth years later, the colonists prepared to celebrate their first RAS (revolution around the sun) with seventeen new children in their midst and several on the way. The gala party's special meal insured that everyone would be present. As Jerry entered the commons, a cheerful chaos reigned with families reuniting after the day's work and friends grabbing spaces at scattered tables to eat together. Steve and Tamara greeted him as they walked by, swinging their one-year-old Rosy between them. He waved at Judith who nursed baby Ben in a quiet corner, Ahdam hovering nearby. As he scanned the space to find Rob and Lily, a little body tackled him at knee height, giggling maniacally. He looked down to see the light brown hair and mischievous dark eyes of his daughter sparking up at him. He swooped Emma up with a laugh and a hug. "Where's your mommy, darling girl? What are you doing toddling about by yourself?"

Ayisha's strong voice sounded behind him. "I've got my eye on her, Jer. Xander fell in the lake when he was fishing and Lily's helping him find dry clothes."

"Thanks. I'll stake out a place for us to sit. Have you seen Rob?"

"No, but it's early yet. Come hang out with Kathir and me."

Jerry threaded his way through the crowd to get to Ayisha's table and settled down with Emma perched on his knees. Seven-year-old Hailey already sat with her mother, saving space for her dad beside her. She chewed on a piece of yellow grass cracker, snagged from the serving bowl in front of her. Little Em, squeaking with delight, reached to grab the morsel from the older girl, but Jerry pulled her back.

"You can't steal Hailey's treat, you rascal. Are you too hungry to wait for dinner?"

The toddler motioned to her mouth with the fingers of her right hand, signaling she was indeed famished.

"How do you ask?" Her father prompted.

The child circled her fist on her chest, making the sign for 'please'.

Jerry sighed. "Yes sweetheart, but can you say, 'please'?"

No sound, but a hopeful look and repeated signing of hunger got the child what she wanted. Her daddy picked out a piece of cracker and gave it to her.

Ayisha who had been watching this exchange, smiled ruefully. "Don't worry. I'm sure she'll begin speaking soon."

"I hope so." Jerry stroked the soft brown curls beneath

his chin. "Her mom is getting worried."

"Didn't Doc tell her it's normal for intelligent children to be slow to talk?"

"Yes, well—you know Lily. She never quite trusts the doctor's opinion."

Jerry had to admit, it concerned him too. None of the kids born planet side spoke yet, but information in the data banks showed they should start at least by their first birthday. Emma, at twenty-five months, hadn't uttered a word. Experts on child development noted that children only needed exposure to adults speaking to learn—and these little ones had grown-ups yammering at them all day long. Talking should have commenced, but of the ten toddlers who graced the colony, not one had said even 'Mama'.

He sighed. Doc found no physical reason for the phenomenon. At least they had healthy children now, and more on the way. If nothing else the human race could survive with sign language. The kids showed no deficit of intelligence and signed with great glee.

Rob, Lily, and ten-year-old Xander appeared at the hall entrance to the commons and Jerry waved to catch their attention. Soon they all sat in front of piled plates, tucking into a feast of both native and Earth foods. Jane had outdone herself to celebrate this turning point, serving up several fish dishes, vegetables and yellow grass muffins with delicate free-berry jam, usually reserved for birthdays. She had even gone to the trouble of synthesizing pork and chicken courses out of soy protein for this festival meal. A cheerful racket of happy people eating with enthusiasm filled the space.

When everyone finished and returned dirty plates to the kitchen, pots of tea appeared and made the rounds.

With coordination generated from long experience of team work, the table and chairs reconfigured into a theater and the colonists settled in for an evening of entertainment. The littlest babies snuggled in to nurse or nap, some fussy ones being passed back and forth. Space-born older kids lured the toddlers into a play area set up to the side, where they rolled around a carpet strewn with dolls, blocks and trucks. Adults tolerated the children's noise, and a lot of running around, with equanimity. If a parent got frustrated dealing with an offspring, an 'aunt' or 'uncle' jumped in to help. Most interruptions had no effect on the larger crowd.

The first entertainment of the night was a poetry slam. Several authors stood and delivered their efforts, one by one, to cheering appreciation. Then a short play, a comedy, written by a settler and performed by the theater group, had them all in stitches. Throughout the show, the little ones romped in their space, not sparing much attention for the adults. Jerry noted that whenever the grown-ups burst out in laughter, some kids looked up and laughed too.

The finale of the evening was a musical presentation. Kathir directed the Colony Chorus, as the fifteen aspiring singers called themselves, and they specialized in a capella numbers. The Muslim congregation's cantor excelled at making the most of his own voice and proved an able music teacher and encourager for the amateur group.

Lily got up to join them on stage. She had only been to a few practices so far, pulled in by her friends Ayisha and Abby who struggled to hold up the soprano section. She left Emma with Jerry or Rob on those occasions, knowing the toddler, while loved by all, would prove too great a distraction for her.

Now Jerry held the little girl up so she could see her mother on the stage. "Look Emmy. Mommy's going to sing a song for us."

'Swing Low, Sweet Chariot' was the initial number in the series of old Earth folksongs Kathir showcased tonight. The singers hummed, warming up and filling the common room with the melody. Emma, who had been squirming on her daddy's lap, trying to convince him to set her down, froze with the first note. Jerry bent down to check what caused her to become so still and saw her laser focused on the musicians. He settled her on the floor between his knees and she stood leaning against him, never taking her eyes off the stage.

As the cadence of the old spiritual opened into words, Emma gripped the fabric of Jerry's pants. He glanced around and noted that all the children in the play area had left their games to watch the singers with an unnerving intensity. The tiny fists at his knees pounded with the beat of the music. Rob caught his eye and smiled uncertainly. Jerry shrugged his shoulders. Then he noticed that Em's mouth was open and her voice had joined the melody. It disrupted nothing. Although thin, the tone held true, and the notes were right on target. Emma warbled with the chorus as if she knew the number well. Both men bent to catch the sound. They looked at each other, awed by this tiny miracle.

The piece ended but before they announced the next song, the little girl preempted Kathir. Distinct and pure, she sang to the tune of the song they had just performed, "Mommy Mom, sing sing sing. Emmy girl sing sing too." A low murmur ruffled through the crowd. On stage, Lily stepped out of the front line of singers and jumped off the platform, running to her daughter. "Emmy, did you talk?

Did you say 'Mommy'? Can you say it again, darling?"

The two-year-old pulled back from her mother's embrace, her round face flushed and mouth pouting. Right on note, she sang, "Sing, Mommy, sing sing. Emmy wants sing sing sing."

"Honey, you're talking. You're saying words." Lily beamed at the annoyed toddler in front of her, but her daughter was having none of it.

"Sing, Mommy, sing."

Xander appeared at Lily's side and said, "She wants you to sing your words, Mom. You know, like Goldie. Remember the dream? She always sings."

Lily stared at him in bewilderment.

"This way, Mom." Xander turned from his mother to the frowning toddler and sang. "Emmy girl, Emmy girl, what a great thing. You're growing up and learning to sing."

The child brightened and responded. "Emmy girl sing. Emmy girl sing."

"Why won't she talk, Xander? Why is she only singing?" Lily torn between exasperation and joy, squatted to study her daughter's face. "Can you say 'Mommy', honey? Say 'Mommy' for me."

"No, Mom, sing it to her—like this:" He found a tune. "Emmy sing 'Mommy' now just like before."

"Mommy. Mommy. Mommy." The toddler's two notes sounded high and delicate.

"You sing back to her," Xander instructed Lily. "Do this: Emmy girl. Emmy girl."

Lily took a breath and tried to imitate her son's instructions, a wavering but similar phrase. The toddler's face lit up again. She held out her arms to be embraced. The crowd around them burst into applause as the duet between Mommy and Emmy girl continued, finding new words and tunes.

Overnight, Emma's vocabulary grew by leaps and bounds. In a week, she was caroling demands for food, calling to her favorite people and naming the colors and numbers she had formerly signed. Her trilled 'no' confirmed that a two-year-old had arrived in full throat to take her place in the colony. With her example, the children close to her in age began vocalizing too—all singing their words. The planet's influence, it appeared, extended well beyond conception.

CHAPTER 12
PLANET KOI-3284

DATE: 2078 CE/2

Sarah blew through the bio-dome's door, six-month-old Asher on her hip and Xander tripping on her heels. Jerry, planting soy bean seedlings halfway around the circumference, watched her snap off the force field which kept her hair in place even through the current gale. Xander simply ran his hand through his shiny black mop, clearing it out of his eyes.

Jerry smiled and waved them back, glad to catch a break in his workday. As the little group came closer, mother and baby leading the way down the narrow path, Jerry noted with surprise that Xander now surpassed Sarah in height by half an inch. He saw the boy's forehead above the crown of her head. When had that happened? Almost a teen, the kid had stood taller than his five-foot mom for several years but this was ridiculous. He must be five-feet seven-inches.

"Hey, Jerry." Sarah smiled her greeting and her step had a spring in it even bearing Asher's weight. "We came to ask you something."

"Shoot." He shook off the dirt from the tender sprouts he'd been replanting and, wiping his hands on a rag tucked in his belt, gave them his full attention.

Sarah moved to the side and nodded to Xander who stepped forward.

"May I have a bar mitzvah, please?"

"What?"

"I'll be thirteen next week and Rabbi Sarah said I can do it first if Mom and Uncle Rob and you are OK with it."

Jerry looked at Sarah who shrugged.

"He knows more Hebrew than Saphir. Actually, Isaac knows more Hebrew than Saphir too, but the fact is that Xander turns thirteen first so he's the one ready to go."

"Is Kim going to let Isaac have a bar mitzvah?" Jerry couldn't contain his glee at the thought of that boy's mom, who had been the strictest of the Muslim mothers, allowing her child this honor.

"We've been talking about it."

"Well, Xander," Jerry beamed, "I'd be proud if you read the Torah and led the congregation in prayers. I think it's a wonderful way to celebrate becoming a real teenager and..." He faltered seeing a familiar faraway look take over the boy's eyes.

Xander no longer was with them. He stared out past their faces and then moved closer to the curved wall, putting his palm on the opaque plastic the wind beat against.

"Xander?" Sarah's voice sounded worried. The baby on her hip whimpered, and she shifted him to a body hug while concentrating on the older boy.

Jerry stepped behind the youth and put a hand on his shoulder. Then he closed his eyes and tried to let the planet connect with him as the children taught him to do. There it was—the swirling fog, the wind blowing and a sound like a child singing a song imbued with urgency. Clearly, Goldilocks was upset. He perceived darkness, bright dots of light, but what message was she sending? Asher's whimper grew to a full-fledged cry and Jerry listened to his mom speak soothing words to calm him. The image retreated into the mist and the baby hiccupped into silence.

The shoulder under his hand twisted around and he opened his eyes to see Xander staring at him. "Did you hear her, Uncle Jerry?"

"Yeah, but I can't tell what the problem is."

"A space ship is coming. It looks familiar."

"Could it be the Armstrong?"

"She doesn't know names, but it's like the Glenn."

"OK, buddy. Is it in orbit, yet?"

"It's starting to circle her."

"Let's go find Abby and Eli. We never fixed the communications array, so we'll need to rig something up quick to connect with them."

They turned in unison as Sarah, forgotten behind them, said, "Is everything all right?"

"Looks like we may get company for Xander's bar mitzvah."

Bill talked to leaders on the Armstrong after Eli souped up the range of the wrist coms. He set the time for their first shuttle landing on the next day, then called the Steering Committee together. Rob gave Jerry, elected as a Christian representative at the beginning of their second RAS, the message with an apologetic smile. He himself had just finished a term and could pass on the stress of planning a reunion.

Jerry came into the meeting room, followed by Sarah and Tamara who still represented their congregations on the board. He stopped inside the door, watching Bill pace back and forth behind the table. The two women, chattering about preparing a welcoming party, sat without engaging either of them.

Jerry intersected Bill's steps. "How did the call go?"

"They'll set down tomorrow at 08:00. Do you think you could ask Xander to connect with Goldie and dampen the wind?"

"No problem. You look worried, Bill. What's up?"

The big man looked at his feet and chewed his lip, hands deep in his pockets. "I don't know, Jerry. It felt weird talking to them on the Armstrong. It might be harder to reconnect than we expect."

"Yeah? How so?"

"I wish you had spoken with them. I'm not good at getting the sense of a conversation."

"They wanted to touch base with you first, right?"

"Yes, that's part of it. They're working with the old vertical hierarchy model. They assume the 'captain' is in charge and since I'm the only one of Glenn's three captains left, they think I have more authority than I do."

Bill peered over Jerry's shoulder. Glancing around, Jerry saw Eli, Ahdam, and Kathir enter and take seats with the women.

"Is Miriam coming today?"

"Yeah, she's getting back from scoping out possible settlement sites, so she might be late, but she promised to show up."

Like an incantation, the mention of her name brought the Jewish hairstylist turned enthusiastic trek organizer to the door.

"OK, Bill. Don't worry too much. Just tell us how it sounded and we'll be here for you."

Bill sighed. Jerry knew he hated speaking before even this intimate, positive group. He sat beside the nervous man as they took their places around the table.

At the end of the meeting, they agreed on a loose plan for greeting the members of the Armstrong arriving the next day. The steering committee refused to have their spirits dampened by Bill's premonition of trouble. They decided a celebration was in order for this first landing party.

They organized the shuttle's arrival on Goldilocks through Xander. At his request, the planet made the effort, a complicated juggling of different functions, to suppress the natural wind of her atmosphere. The children explained it as "holding her breath." She could restrain it for only limited amounts of time—and no one understood what those limits were.

It was enough to set the shuttle down gently. As the hatch opened and the five Armstrong crew members exited though, a mistral kicked up. It almost blew the thin figures exiting the vehicle off the steps.

Eli, crossing the landing field with the other Steering Committee representatives, whipped off his force field halo and settled it on the first visitor's head, flipping the switch. The effect looked like someone had dropped a giant fishbowl over the pilot's whole body. He stood stunned in a calm atmosphere while Eli now bent into the howling wind, grinning with delight at this introduction of his invention to a new audience. Others in the welcoming group stepped forward, setting halos on the other travelers, and the procession crossed the lawn of yellow grass to the rounded rows of huts which still formed the center of the Glenn's colony.

Ken Branson headed the landing party. Rob, remembering him from Space Tech, had commented earlier to Jerry, "He's a good guy, resourceful. He got impatient over little things though. I remember when he tried to take Dagmar to task for working with the politicians. Boy, did the old man berate him. Told him to grow up and learn to play nice with others. I imagine he learned that skill over the last few years."

"I hope so," Jerry had replied. "If he didn't, their life must have been miserable up there."

Phoebe Miller, the Armstrong's geneticist and a colleague of Rob's, came down on the shuttle with Ken, as did three other scientists, Philip Newton, Brent Briarwood and Tom Snodgrass. Jerry, walking with them back to shelter, read the story of their thirteen year separation from the Glenn in their sharp cheekbones and hollow eyes. He registered how Phoebe limped as she made her way through the grass.

They entered through the portal, moving single file up the hallway until they emerged into the calm buttered sunlight in the commons. Once there, helpful hands reached to flip off halos and hug the Armstrong's band with enthusiastic excitement. The gathered Glenn settlers pressed around, cheering and calling greetings. All the children on hand for this great event added their shrill songs (and some crying) to the jubilation. At the sight of toddlers and babes in arms, the shuttle crew slowed to a halt.

"How old?" Phoebe stammered, her eyes glued to chubby Asher, just handed over to his mother.

"Six months. Would you like to hold him?" Sarah asked and held out the wriggling child.

"Oh, not until I sit down. I'm afraid I might drop him." The yearning in her face betrayed how much she wanted this honor, but the crowd pulled her forward to a laden buffet.

"Don't worry," Jerry murmured. "I'll make sure you meet all the children when we get seated."

Phoebe smiled wanly at him, looking overwhelmed and bewildered. He put a hand under her elbow and steered her to a seat, signaling Lily to bring her a plate of food.

The kitchen crew had out done themselves preparing delicacies: the tiny fish fries and delicate fruit of the broccoli trees that tasted like almonds, plus banana and eggplant casseroles and the "birthday" muffins. The travelers struggled to maintain a sense of dignity when laden plates appeared before them, but as conversation swirled around them, it became clear they hadn't had enough to eat in a long time. They responded curtly to avid inquiries about the Armstrong while shoveling food into their mouths as fast as possible.

Lily, seeing their conflict, scolded the questioners away. "Let them eat first. Then we'll have tea together and talk."

The colonists pulled back to allow them to savor their dinner. Philip smiled at Lily, whom he had known from her husband's university days, "I'm so glad you're here, Lily. Where's Alex?"

Lily sat across from him. "Alex died, Phil. He was the first of our losses." She registered his distress and added, "It's OK. We have a son."

"You married again?"

"No, my son and I live with Rob and Jerry now."

Jerry, overhearing this conversation, watched the man's face as he digested the information. Before he could respond with more questions, a colonist came up to ask if he knew what had happened to a friend of hers, a woman named Nancy Gleeson. Phil glanced at Lily as he mumbled, "I'm afraid we've had our losses too. Nancy died several years ago. I'm so sorry."

When the shuttle crew had eaten their fill, more people came forward with inquiries about special friends on the Armstrong. Jerry noticed how many times the answer was that the person hadn't survived. The travelers appeared unwilling to say much about the deaths though. Ken said, "We'll share the official account of our losses with your captains. We won't go into details right now."

News of the casualties put a damper on the celebration. Ken leaned over to whisper to Rob. "Maybe we should make our report and then we can decide how much to tell your settlers."

Rob frowned, but then shrugged, "I guess the group you want to talk to is our Steering Committee. We've set up a room in the science orb and, if you're ready, we'll go over there for a private meeting."

"Yeah, that sounds good."

As the visitors rose, Phoebe looked around and waved. She raised her voice to carry, calling, "Thank you so much for this bountiful welcome. You can't imagine what your generosity means to us or how anxious our crew is to come down."

The crowd clapped as they exited but Jerry, following

them out of the room, heard shocked murmurs commenting on the obvious hunger and uneasiness of their guests. "Did something awful happen on our sister ship? Why are they so reluctant to share?"

Jerry had the same questions, but he also felt the trust of his group. The Glenn's settlers knew they would eventually hear the details. They had confidence the members they elected would include them as decisions and plans were made.

"What do you mean, the planet is sentient?" The Armstrong's captain sounded both shocked and sarcastic. "Are you guys worshiping nature now?"

Absolute silence met this outbreak. The Steering Committee members eyed the Armstrong crew somberly. Jerry thought, how can we explain what's taken us five years to accept and still keeps us up at nights trying to figure out? Ignoring the wisecrack, he said, "It's hard to comprehend that an entity as big as a planet could be alive in the sense of having individual consciousness. Consider the differences in scale between other forms of life, though. To a tiny amoeba, the fact that a whale exists must seem incredible."

"OK, it's nice of you religious types to welcome us, and we loved the food, but really, we need to meet with just the scientists now. Right, Bill and Eli? Wouldn't that be better?" Ken's chilled smile dismissed Jerry.

The Glenn's scientists looked at each other and their colleagues. Bill's cheeks reddened, and he stammered, "That's not how we do things, Ken."

Eli was firmer. "And we're not going to start. Jerry knows the planet more thoroughly than any adult here and he's trying to help you understand. I suggest you pay attention to him."

The Armstrong's captain refused to back down. "Where's Rob, Jerry? Shouldn't he be here instead of you?"

Sarah stood up and leaned on the table. "Listen up, Ken, and all of you from the Armstrong, too. We established a democratic leadership that has worked for over ten years. Jerry is an elected member of the Steering Committee as am I and the rest of us in this room. We will be the ones deciding when you can land your settlers from the Armstrong. We will be the ones you negotiate with for space on this planet. We will determine how members of the Glenn will work together with you. The bottom line is, if you want our help, you deal with us-respectfully."

"No need to be so touchy, Sarah. I only want the scientific facts." Ken rolled his eyes at his crew. The three men smirked in response. Phoebe shook her head and looked at the floor.

"It is a scientific fact that Goldilocks is alive." Xander stood in the doorway, flanked by eleven-twelve-old Isaac and Saphir. "We did experiments to prove it wasn't just in our heads. We still don't understand how she reproduces, but she meets the other criteria."

Phoebe sucked in her breath. Jerry realized this was the first time she had noticed the older children.

"Honey, how old are you?" she asked.

Xander cocked his head, studying this foreigner. Then he

flashed his warm smile and said, "I'll be thirteen in earth years five days from now. I'm going to have a bar mitzvah."

"Thirteen?" The woman's eyes abandoned him, seeking confirmation from the other adults. "You had children in space?"

"Xander is our oldest." Miriam nodded at the other two youngsters. "Saphir and Isaac were born sex months later. Altogether we had seven in space and another thirty-seven since we landed."

Phoebe's eyes teared up. "The radiation hit us hard when we got lost. We gave up trying after five pregnancies ended in miscarriages. It was too dangerous."

Again there was silence in the room. Jerry scanned the newcomer's faces. These people went through hell, he thought. Are they ready to find peace?

Ken turned in his seat and frowned. "Why didn't you produce more children by now? How long has it been? Five earth years? Shouldn't your population be at least doubled?"

Tamara gazed at him. "Every child is precious. We increase our numbers very deliberately, so we can give each one attention and care while they're young."

"Please try to understand," Kathir added. "We're still getting to know Goldilocks. Our experiments are teaching us how many crops and fish to we can raise without stressing her ecosystem. We don't want our presence to be a burden to her life, but a blessing. We're searching for the right balance."

"So you're waiting for the planet to give you permission for more children?" Again, Ken's lips twisted into a sarcastic smile. He sniffed as if he smelled something rancid.

The members of the Steering Committee sat still, noting his disdain. His own contingent shifted uncomfortably.

Phoebe tried to cover her captain's discourtesy by calling attention to the children, standing in the doorway. "Do you kids want anything?"

Xander took in the tense scene calmly. "No, Goldilocks wanted a look at you. She's having trouble connecting with anyone on your ship. She likes Jaime though."

"Jaime?" Phoebe asked.

"Do you mean Jaime Rodriguez, from the Christians?" Tom Snodgrass offered illumination.

"I think so. He has the best dreams."

Phoebe scrunched her brows. "What do dreams have to do with it?"

Jerry said, "Goldilocks communicated through a dream even before we knew who she was. On the Glenn—before the first jump—she touched me that way. Then later, we discovered many of us were having the same dream. We didn't understand what it meant until we got here."

"God, I can't believe you are into this crap."

"Ken." Phoebe hissed. "We're guests here."

Xander and the other children eased further into the room. Saphir stepped forward and stood next to Phoebe, her hands on the arm of the chair. "You've had the dream."

"What do you mean, dear?"

"The one with the singer—there's fog and wind and a singer, but you can't see her."

Phoebe's pallor deepened and Jerry feared for a moment she might faint. "I've had a dream like that for years. How did you guess?"

The Steering Committee's attention rested on Phoebe now. Ken fidgeted beside her, tapping fingers on the arm of his chair.

She tore her gaze away from the girl and spoke to the room, "You don't understand the level of stress we've been living under."

"Tell us," Jerry said.

"When we jumped in 2066, we found ourselves in a star system we hadn't expected. We had no maps, no orientation, and we panicked. Only two alternatives presented themselves: we could go forward and try to find the next jump coordinates from where we were, or go back, where we might land on you guys or worse, miss the coordinates and become even more disoriented.

"We went forward, as we practiced in the scenarios on earth. We miscalculated and hit another uncharted system. This time we entered the vicinity of a planet giving off high levels of radiation. We had three pregnant women. All of them miscarried. We lost members to radiation poisoning, too. We had to keep mining. Our lives depended on getting more fuel so we could jump again. The crew on that rotation—well, none of them survived long. We jumped again as soon as possible, retracing our steps to the last foreign but safe spot."

"That must have been terrible," Miriam said.

"The settlers were the ones who panicked. They blamed us for the deaths." Ken's voice was harsh.

"They couldn't comprehend what was happening," Phoebe countered. This sounded like an old argument revisited. The three other men on their crew kept silent, avoiding eye contact.

"Why didn't they understand?" Sarah leaned forward to see Phoebe's face but Ken jumped in to answer.

"There wasn't time to run seminars and explain everything. We worked as hard as possible to figure out the safest thing to do next."

"Why don't we tell them?" Phil spoke, swiveling in his chair to make eye contact with each of the Committee members. "The religious groups rebelled against the scientists and tried to take over the ship. They boycotted mining. They stranded us for a whole year in that godforsaken system."

Xander moved to his uncle's chair and draped an arm over the back, resting his hand on Jerry's shoulder. Jerry reached up and grasped it as inconspicuously as possible. Sarah glanced at them, but no one else noticed. Jerry closed his eyes for a moment and concentrated. Yes, he sensed Xander's concern and behind that Goldilocks' intelligence pulsed. What is she feeling? he thought. It tastes like a mixture of curiosity and caution, with a sharp edge of something else—but what is it? His breath caught in his throat as he realized: It's dislike. Goldie is negative about someone here. He'd never known her to exude such distaste.

Suddenly he was observing the Glenn's Steering Committee through the emotions of the Armstrong's crew, via the planet's perceptions. These people judged him and his friends as undisciplined—a motley group thrown together with no discernible order or clear lines of authority. It wasn't just that the colony functioned differently than a normal hierarchy. They were perceived as less competent and should have been less successful. Envy snaked around in the critique's morass.

In the brief time spent in the commons, the visitors had already noticed the boundaries between the Glenn's religious groups and scientists had dissolved. It hadn't escaped their notice that people formed relationships in new ways, too. Lily living with Rob and Jerry. Two women obviously partnered.

They suspected other combinations. The casual but complete inclusion of children everywhere, even here, bothered them, too.

The Armstrong's leaders had expected to find common ground with a population they understood. Instead, they met as aliens and the disillusionment stunned them. Ken's response, at the top of the Armstrong's pyramid, was to wonder how to manipulate and get control of the established colony. It came to Jerry as a clear-cut fact: even now he's planning a coup.

Jerry's heart raced. Goldilocks' insight became his own: if no mutual respect exists, it will be dangerous to allow them to descend and live amongst us. Yet, the conditions on the ship must be awful and disintegrating fast. What can we do?

As he focused again on the conversation going forward, he noticed Ken looking at him. He smiled weakly in his direction, confused for a moment at the blandness of the captain's gaze when he had just perceived him plotting to overthrow them.

Ken turned and addressed Bill and Eli. "The bottom line is that it cost us a hell of a lot to get here. We've lost a third of the crew and have been on survival rations for what—nine months, Phoebe? We need to land everyone and integrate our people with yours as soon as possible."

"OK." The Glenn's last captain nodded. "We'll start building more housing right away. How many are we planning for?"

"Wait a minute, Bill," Jerry said as calmly as he could, his heart pounding with anxiety at the threat he glimpsed. "We probably should establish boundaries first. It's clear that the Armstrong functions under different expectations than we have here on Goldilocks. I'd hate to see us get crosswise with the new settlers before we have a chance to bond."

The look Ken shot him now was anything but bland. It sparked with anger. "Are you saying you don't want us here?"

The Steering Committee members sat quietly watching the confrontation, but the Armstrong's crew tensed. Phoebe reached over to calm Ken, the three other men scowling. Isaac hovering near the door, now came in and hoisted himself into a chair next to Miriam. He looked small and vulnerable. The Jewish representative smiled and squeezed his knee. Saphir, still standing by Phoebe, reached out and patted her on the shoulder, startling her. Xander remained behind Jerry, in contact with him.

Phoebe said, "Perhaps the children should go. This isn't a discussion they need to hear."

"Goldilocks wants us to stay." Xander's voice sounded high but confident. "It's easier for her to see through us than the adults."

The five people from the Armstrong froze. "Man, this is just too creepy," said Brent Briarwood—the first words he uttered during the meeting.

"It's not creepy, it's insane—a mass hysteria." Ken stood. "Maybe our ship should leave, but we don't have resources to find another planet."

"We don't want you to go." Sarah looked pained at the possibility of losing these new partners. "Goodness, if we're the only humans left, we need to work together."

"Yes, but there's no reason to crowd ourselves," Eli offered. "The Armstrong's settlers can set up shop somewhere else— say at that area to the north where we've explored. It's only a six day walk. We'll help them build and let them discover their own connection to the planet. Later on, it will be easier to mix."

Sarah nodded. "Why don't you sit, Ken. Let's consider how we can get you started with your own colony and encourage our relationship to develop at a slower pace."

Ken glowered at them, considering for a moment. As none of his followers offered to stand and stomp out with him, he settled back in his chair.

Phoebe picked up the conversation. "Tell us about this possible site."

As they talked through the logistics, a plan formed for a sister colony.

Jerry suspected members of the Armstrong might be glad to escape from under Ken's thumb. "What about letting people choose which village they'd like to live in, after we have time to know each other?"

"Well, we can't lose many people and maintain a workable settlement," said Phil, "although it'd be good to have members from the Glenn join us. Do you think any of you might want to join our colony?" He looked around the table.

Sarah tried to respond diplomatically. "We're used to more equality here. Also, there are the youngsters. I don't know anyone who would leave them."

"You said only thirty-seven babies had been born here. People without kids yet might come. Or maybe folks would bring their children to live with us." Phoebe sat up straighter, looking hopeful.

"Their children?" Sarah echoed, bemused. Then she nodded. "I see what you mean, but we don't look at parenthood that way anymore. They belong to everyone. We feel a deep commitment and love for each one. It would be like deserting our physical sons and daughters, for us to leave them. And to send them away—that's not an option."

"Yeah, that's the reason we have such a hard time creating other settlements," Eli said. "Nobody wants to be separated from the kids."

Phoebe looked at Saphir who had dropped to the floor beside her, sitting cross legged on the carpet. The young girl grinned up at her. The older woman smiled. "I can see why it would be difficult to leave," she said. "I suspect our colony will be in much greater danger of losing people to you."

After the shuttle crew left, the Steering Committee conferred.

"So you think this will work?" Kathir posed the question they all chewed on.

Jerry shared his premonition of Ken's intention to seize power.

Tamara crossed her arms on her chest. "I felt threatened too."

"Should we let them be here then?" Bill frowned with worry.

Jerry looked up at Xander still standing over him. "What they don't believe, but what we know, is that Goldilocks is here and we're part of her. We're not in much danger. If they try, in their desperation, to undermine or attack us I'm afraid they're doomed. Hopefully, they'll make friends with the planet soon."

Xander, his eyes clouded, gave a nod.

CHAPTER 13
PLANET KOI-3284

DATE: 2079 CE/3

Five months after the Armstrong landed, Jerry sat at dinner with Rob, Lily and Xander, and Xander's current best buddy Saphir. Saphir's mom, Miriam, joined them. Intent on their conversation and food, Jerry didn't notice when a group of people entered the dining area returning from a trip to the outback, still carrying their knapsacks and halos. He looked up only when others called greetings. That's when he noticed the travelers' serious faces, eyes shadowed and mouths straight-lined with concern.

As they walked into the room, it became clear that food wasn't the first thing on their minds. They made a beeline to Jerry's table. Helen Green, who had become one of the Glenn's best explorers and guides, bent close to address him. "We need to talk to the Steering Committee, as soon as possible."

"I think every member is here tonight. Do you want to get something to eat and we'll gather after dinner?"

Helen looked over her shoulder at the small group of travelers huddled behind her. All three gave slight head shakes, and she turned back to say, "We should speak to the Committee before anyone else. If we sit down, someone will ask questions."

"OK." Jerry assessed how much tension an emergency meeting might generate in the colony. He looked at Xander following the exchange closely. "Hey kiddo, would you and Saphir tell each of the Steering Committee members to meet me in the briefing room right away?" As the children jumped up to run their errand, Jerry and Miriam rose too. They nodded reassurances to the rest of the table. Jerry said, "I'll be back to fill you in as soon as possible, but don't wait for me if this runs long."

"We'll make sure Saphir gets to bed. Contact us if you need anything else." Rob's brow creased in concern, but no one panicked. They'd had lots of experience with crises these past years.

In the bridge's meeting room, the travelers shrugged off their packs and tugged halos from their heads before sinking into cushioned chairs around the oblong table. The rest of the Committee members filtered in carrying mugs, some still chewing hastily made sandwiches. Tamara entered with a pot of tea and cups which the new comers received with gratitude. In just a few minutes, everyone settled and got ready to attend.

As the expedition's guide, Helen began by outlining the reason for their trip. "You remember that we were to go to the Armstrong's colony and help them put up the communications unit. We took with us the basic equipment they need and the coordinates of our own tower."

Heads nodded around the table. When the Armstrong arrived, they brought their settlers down to the agreed on village site without the gala homecoming celebration the Glenn's people wanted so badly to throw. Their leaders said they needed time to heal on their own, to get their feet on the ground. They isolated the workers sent from the original settlement to help set up living shelters and a bio-dome, so not even they could mingle with the new immigrants.

Grumbling surrounded this enforced segregation, especially amongst the scientists who had good friends on the Armstrong. Jerry suspected that Ken and his cronies didn't want to contend with the fact that the Glenn's colonists accepted the phenomenon of a sentient planet who related to them. He didn't worry over this behavior, though. They had time. No need to force the issue. Their sister ship's people would experience Goldie in their own way and then they would compare notes. This next step, the new communications setup, would make sure the two settlements could speak with each other. Conversation, he was convinced, would ease the tension.

"They're building a wall." Helen's words, clipped and loud in the silent room, brought frowns of confusion. "And they took our equipment without letting us into the village."

"OK, back up and give this to us step by step." Jerry kept his tone as neutral as possible while a shadow of unease crept up his spine and settled around his shoulders.

Eli, the senior mechanic on the traveler's team spoke. "Helen's given you the basics. We traveled three days to the new village. As we got close, we noticed a stone wall going up on either side of the path. It's approximately six feet high and about that wide. They're actively working on it. The plan is to wrap it around the whole site. They've fashioned a gate in the middle from doors salvaged from their ship."

"Yeah, and after our long trek this creep comes out the door and asks us what we're doing there." Abby, their communications expert, didn't even try to keep the indignation out of her voice. "They treated us as if we were strangers or servants who weren't using the right entrance. They didn't invite us in, didn't offer us food or drink—nothing. It's lucky we took plenty of supplies."

"Did they forget we were coming to help with the communications array?" Sarah shook her head as she spoke. Even she didn't believe this.

"No." Eli crossed his great arms and scowled. "They wanted the instruments. Ken came out and thanked us for bringing them but said they would take it from there."

"I asked him point-blank if we couldn't come in and rest up before starting back." Helen picked up the story again, calm but stern. "His exact words were, 'No, it's better if you go. We're fine by ourselves.' We were so taken aback that we turned around and came home." She stared at the table now, her hands gripping the edge. "I hope we did the right thing. It didn't seem productive to quarrel about it."

Kathir leaned into the circle, resting on his forearms. "What do you think this means? Why separate themselves from us so completely?"

Jim, who had traveled with the party to check in on the Armstrong's bio-dome progress, radiated gloom. "I don't know what they're thinking but I'll tell you this: the guys at the gate didn't like us. I've known Tony Richards since grad school and he looked at me as if I'd become a monster."

"This is crazy." Miriam said, wringing her hands together in her distress. "Don't they understand we have to join forces to survive? Don't they want their children to have a future?"

Her anxiety fanned the tension growing in the group, and conversations began to overlap, escalating fear and frustration. For a moment Jerry gave into its pull, sensing himself sucked towards a vortex of panic. As blood beat at his temples, he had a vision of Marjo on her mat in the old walled garden back home. What would she have offered? he wondered. He pulled away from the quagmire of angry feelings, groping for higher ground.

"Wait a minute guys," he spat out. "Let's not transfer our nightmares onto the Armstrong until we figure out what their fears are."

"What do you mean by that?" Jim's face reddened as he directed his gaze at Jerry.

"Only that Kathir has the right questions. We know what you and the others felt when they didn't let you in, Jim. That's valuable information. What we don't understand, and can't discern until they share, is what they're feeling and why they're shutting us out. We need to go talk to them before jumping to conclusions."

"I don't think they want to talk to us," Helen said. "That's the problem."

Sarah nodded. "Yeah, but Jerry's still right. We have to make it safe for them to interact with us and discover what's triggered this impasse. Our relationship with the new colony is too vital to our future to let it disintegrate."

"You know, maybe they're paranoid because of their awful experiences in space the last few years," Bill offered. "We had shaky times and some of us weirded out—at least I did. They might still be in crisis mode."

Faces around the table softened from angry to reflective.

"Good point, Bill." Jerry said. "I wonder how we can create a secure environment so the Armstrong's leaders will engage in a real conversation?"

As the group considered this conundrum, the meeting

room door eased open a few inches. The inquisitive face of two-year-old Billy poked through.

"My Dada-o, Dada-o play me now." He sang in a high wavering voice.

Jim's unhappy appearance transformed, the tight creases around his eyes melting, as he caught sight of his child. The door opened more, the toddler squirming to gain release from a restraining hand. A weary mother's head and shoulders came into view. "Sorry, guys. He escaped. He's getting too fast for me."

Jim was already with her, scooping the little boy into his arms and planting a kiss on his wife's flushed cheek.

Watching the family reunion, Miriam smiled wearily. "There's nothing we can do tonight. Why don't we sleep on Jerry's question of how to get in dialog with the Armstrong? Then tomorrow we'll decide how to approach it."

T

The next week, Jerry found himself preparing to be part of a conciliatory expedition to the Armstrong's village. Communication towers still hadn't gone up, so they could only contact the captain through his wrist com. Bill convinced him to agree to a conference, but negotiating with the captain on who to include had been dicey. Ken holds his cards close, Jerry realized, and he won't let us in on what he's thinking. He suspected the only reason their leader agreed to talk to them was because he needed the supplies they were sharing—basic food and tools supplementing the resources of their battered sister ship. Thank goodness we didn't host them at our settlement, Jerry mused. We'd be living amid chaos. At least this way, the craziness doesn't bombard the children and most of our settlers. Although they knew about it. It was a topic of daily speculation in the established colony.

As Jerry dug through his personal box looking for clothes to throw in his pack, he heard the door open. He turned his head to see Xander hesitating on the threshold.

"What's up, Xanda panda?" he asked, grabbing a worn but clean shirt and rolling it up to stuff in his bag. He remembered belatedly that the teen-aged boy had requested he not to call him this pet name and looked up, ready to apologize. Xander's attention was somewhere else, though.

"I have to go with you, Uncle Jer." His voice was matter of fact.

Jerry stood up straight, shifting around to look him in the face. "Not this trip, kiddo. You've got school and this will take at least a week. I don't want you getting behind."

"That's what Mom said too. You think I'm too young to help, but I still have to go. Goldilocks needs me there."

Jerry's scalp prickled, and he suppressed a shiver of fear. "Hon, what's going on?"

"It's not just our group being shut out. Goldie's blocked too. She's worried. They don't understand how much they need her to survive."

"Couldn't she use me to listen in on the conversation?"

"Yeah, but she might want to say something. You can't receive as well as me."

This was true, to Jerry's consternation. He narrowed his eyes and searched the boy's face. "You're not just trying to skip out of school, are you?"

Xander shot him a withering look. "I can't get behind when I'm the only one in my class."

"Your mom will have to agree."

"If you convince Uncle Rob it's important, she'll listen to

him."

Well, he's got our family system figured out, Jerry realized. Rob's the touchstone for all of us . "OK, Buddy. This meeting is important. I guess Goldilocks should be fully present. Get your stuff together and I'll go tackle Uncle Rob."

Two hours later, as they crammed Xander's duffel bag into the bed of the Rover and sandwiched the boy between Rob and himself in the back seat, Jerry had second thoughts. They rarely took the ATV anymore, conserving precious fuel, but for this special mission they'd made an exception. At least we'll be able to get him home quickly if the conversation collapses, he thought. Why he should sense such danger puzzled Jerry. He couldn't shake it off. He looked past Xander to Rob, tapping away at his com-pad and felt grateful for his spouse's presence.

They assigned two scientists to the expedition, since the Armstrong leaders favored them: Eli, serving on the steering committee, and Rob, who agreed to go only after Bill begged off. Jerry and Sarah represented the non-scientific population, voted "most conciliatory" by their peers.

They estimated the drive would take a day and a half. The Rover wouldn't get much speed up over the bumpy terrain. They planned to travel fifteen hours, sleep for eight and then finish the trip. The new settlement stood on the plains on the other side of a long pass through the mountain range.

The first day went without incident. The winding path bounced them over the yellow grass plain, passed the camping place they had used in their first expeditions and meandered along the tree line to the head of a valley. Jerry agreed with Sarah when she said, "God, I'd rather walk this path twice than ride in this jalopy. My backside is one big bruise."

That night they sat around a campfire, protected from the brisk wind by their portable force field. They devoured sandwiches the kitchen crew had made up for them and discussed how to approach the Armstrong's leadership.

"Eli and I will lead off with what we'd like to accomplish by keeping our communities together," Rob reminded them. "By showing our hand up front, we hope they'll relax and be able to share their concerns."

Sarah leaned into the warmth of the fire, the guttering light dancing shadows on her face. "And I'll keep my mouth shut as much as possible because it's obvious that women are second-class citizens in their world."

"Well, if you do stay quiet, it'll be the first miracle we celebrate." Jerry ducked the stick Sarah threw at him in response. "Xander, can you tell us more about what Goldie wants out of this meeting?"

The adults turned their attention to the thirteen-year-old sitting with them, wolfing down not only his sandwich but part of Jerry's too. He's growing so fast, Jerry realized, viewing him with affection.

The boy straightened his back. He looked at Jerry, swallowed, then scrunched up his eyebrows in concentration. "She wants to help the new people. It has something to do with babies. Either the babies they have won't be able to sing or maybe they won't be born. She's not making much sense." He switched his gaze to his dusty shoes. "The feeling I get is very sad, and it's about babies."

Rob and Jerry exchanged glances over the boy's head. They realized it bothered Xander when he couldn't translate the planet's intentions clearly. This isn't the time for uncertainty, though, Jerry worried.

Sarah spoke into the silence. "Is anyone pregnant there yet? If so, we should ask to meet with them."

Eli asked, "It's still early, isn't it? They've only been here five months and most of them were starving when they arrived. You'd think they'd be careful that their women recovered fully before conceiving, for both mother and baby's sake."

"OK, let's inquire into any pregnancies but be discreet," said Jerry. "If we bring up our connection with Goldilocks too much it might make them dismiss us."

"Why don't we tell them Doc wants to be notified so she can help out? Deliveries are more her specialty than Doc Wilson's," said Sarah.

"Goldie needs to know too." Xander had a faraway look in his eyes signaling he listened now to the planet. "She's um... I guess she's hurt that only a few of the Armstrong's people pay attention to her, and nobody tries to talk with her. She's confused." His focus shifted back to the group watching him intently. "Why did they come if they won't be friends?"

Jerry reached over and placed a hand on the youth's shoulder. "I suspect it's unintentional, kiddo. Remember, we didn't understand Goldie until we landed. Even now she's a great mystery. Sometimes people get terrified of things they can't wrap their minds around. The way they cope with that fear is to pretend the thing that scares them isn't real."

"But they're living with her, on her, in her. How can they ignore her?" Xander's lip curled with a teenager's disgust at the stupidity of adults.

Rob said, "Hey, Bud, a little compassion here. These

people have been through hell. Their grip on reality may be tenuous at best. Will you remind Goldilocks they're still hurting and scared and we need to give them some time?"

Xander dropped his sneer and sighed. After a brief silence he nodded. "She knows. She wants to help them heal, but if they won't connect with her, she can't. She can be patient though." He looked up with wide-open eyes. "Goldie doesn't really understand time the way we do, Uncle Rob. I don't know how long she can be patient."

Rob nodded, glancing at Jerry. Then he stood and stretched. "Well," he said. "I'll volunteer to put up the tent. Who wants to help?"

The other three adults eyed the bowing trees outside their protective force field with a distinct lack of enthusiasm. Xander jumped up, laughing. "I don't mind the wind. I'll help Uncle Rob."

Knowing it was at least a three-person job to wrestle the shelter into place when a mistral blew, Sarah stood up brushing dirt off her coveralls. "I will, too. I sure wish we could wear halos when we do this though. Eli, can't you invent a modification that allows us to use them while actually working?"

"I'm trying to figure that out, but I'm not even close yet. Do you want me to give you a hand too, Rob?"

"No, you and Jerry clean up the dishes and put out the fire so we can switch the force field to the tent as soon as it's up."

As Eli and Jerry turned to their chores, they both kept an eye on the progress of those outside in the turbulent air.

"Do you think he's right?" Eli's question took Jerry by surprise.

"Who?"

"Xander—is he getting Goldilocks right? Is it something about having babies?"

"Beats me. Something's upsetting her. Xander understands her best."

"Why is that? I mean, why can't you figure out what's going on with her? You've heard her longer than anyone else."

"Again—I don't know. So many things I don't know."

T

So far, the walls around the Armstrong's village only extended ten feet from either side of the double doors across the path. Jerry saw a group of four people hauling rocks and mud to the site. They stopped what they were doing as the ATV drove up, watching but not moving closer. Instead, a big man standing in front of the gate, opened the door a crack to yell something through it. In a moment, as Jerry and his friends climbed out of their vehicle, three other men joined him and approached. Obviously these guys had been expecting them.

Eli tried to connect with one he recognized. "Hey Joe, what have you been doing with yourself lately?"

His former colleague snorted and replied, "C'mon. Ken's waiting for you."

"We brought food supplies. Can we drive in and unload at the kitchen?"

"Nope, meet the boss first—then we'll figure out the truck."

The four adults from the Glenn's settlement considered the situation over Xander's head. What was going on here? Boss? Jerry put his hand out and touched the boy's shoulder.

"Why don't you stick a couple of energy bars in your pocket in case we don't get to eat soon?"

Xander nodded and dug around in the back of the rover to find the kind he liked best. Then the five of them, flanked by the four members of the Armstrong's welcoming committee, walked through the gate into the village.

Two minutes in, Jerry realized what made this familiar scene so strange. Aside from their footsteps and an occasional command shouted on the building site, the colony was silent. No one called greetings to them or spoke to each other. There was no playful banter between people passing each other in the central square. In fact, as he scanned the thin faces of the Armstrong crew, he saw no smiles. Eyes remained hard, skittering over them as if they didn't want to draw attention. A sudden thought shook him: Perhaps the wall is not to keep us out, but to make sure that their members stay in.

Ken met them at the portal to the science orb which sat on the far side of the colony. It loomed over the fragile structures of temporary huts and the dining hall like an incongruous mountain pushed up from another reality. A path beaten in the dust led past it to their bio-dome half a mile away.

As the group approached, the frown on Ken's handsome face deepened. "Why did you bring the kid?" he asked when they stepped up to greet him.

"Xander wanted to come." Jerry said, telling the truth without revealing too much. "How are you doing, Ken?"

"I'd be better if you guys could stick to agreements. We said four representatives, not five."

"He's just here to observe, to learn." Rob's voice was calm. "He's our oldest child."

Ken, on the top step to the portal, stood a foot higher

than the Glenn's delegates. He looked over their heads and hesitated. Then he snapped, "I don't know why you think we're running a fucking school, but bring him in with you." He turned, pushing open the heavy port and leading them in.

As they mounted the stairway and entered the orb, Jerry looked over his shoulder wondering what goaded Ken into accepting Xander so easily. A group of five women congregated outside the huts, staring at him. Although he recognized none of them, he raised his hand in greeting, but they remained still, arms crossed under their breasts, faces closed. One escort took a step towards them if to chase them away as Jerry turned and followed Rob into the interior.

The detachable section of the Armstrong had landed perfectly, her machinery preserved, and every room positioned for planet-side use. It felt to the Glenn's crew like a visit to their past. The sister ships had been identical inside and out. Eli sighed. "Man, I wish we could have saved our orb in this condition. You have a treasure here, Ken."

"Yeah, you'll have to tell me sometime why you crashed your unit. Conner was a good pilot. I can't see him screwing a landing up that badly."

Even in this innocent exchange, the captain's voice dripped with disdain. Jerry frowned and closed the gap between himself and Xander. Anxiety skittered through him and he wondered—are we walking into a spider's web?

As they entered the bridge's meeting room, they recognized two other scientists from the Armstrong's original landing party. Brent Briarwood and Tom Snodgrass rose to greet them, nodding in their direction. They arranged themselves around the table, the visitors on one side and

Ken sitting between his men on the other. Sarah spoke up for the first time since they arrived. "Where's Phoebe? I thought she'd be with us today."

Ken grimaced and snapped back at her. "She's leading an expedition to explore the northern shoreline of the ocean. That's what she is—an oceanographer."

"Oh... I didn't realize you were sending out explorers yet. Well, she's very competent. I sorry she's not here though. I enjoyed meeting her when you landed." The rabbi tried to back away from the touchy subject. She glanced Jerry's way, with a minute shrug of her shoulders.

"Let's get to business," Ken settled into in his padded chair. "I don't have a lot of time to give you. We're still in the building phase, you know. Every hand needed on deck. Why did you want to meet?" He studied Rob and Eli, ignoring the other three.

He's throwing down a gauntlet, Jerry realized, taking in his abrupt movements and clipped speech. If we don't steer him onto a different path, we'll just end up yelling at each other.

As they had planned, Rob began. "Ken, we'd like to be close to your community. We believe we need you and you need us to survive. Specifically, we hope to keep our relationship healthy because we appreciate that down the line, if we can't re-establish contact with Earth, our children should intermarry to gain enough genetic diversity for a healthy community."

To Jerry, his spouse's voice sounded mild and rational. Ken's reaction, though, shot out as if under attack. "So why are you here bothering me? The best way for us to maintain a 'healthy relationship' is to get on with building our village.

What do you want from me, Rob?"

Eli responded as Rob rocked back in his chair. "We were blocked out of your settlement last time we visited. You're erecting a wall when no predators or dangers exist on this planet. We want to understand what's up."

"I'm not obliged to tell you anything. You've got your little fiefdom and I've got mine. We'll each develop them as we see fit."

"But why the isolation, Ken? Why not work together?"

While Eli spoke, Jerry watched the men on either side of the Armstrong's boss. Brent glowered as if the Glenn's group held guns at his head. A thin sheen of sweat glossed Tom's forehead, and his lips pressed tight, as if worried he'd let out a secret. They're afraid, Jerry realized. Scared of us or Ken. What's going on here?

Xander, sitting absolutely still as no thirteen-year-old should be able to, slid his hand over to grasp his uncle's. There it was—the heightened connection with Goldilocks. Jerry sensed her confusion, approaching panic, coursing through him and struggled to maintain the boundary distinguishing his feelings from hers. In a moment he sorted it out.

The speaking continued while Jerry retreated into himself, but he picked up the gist as he turned his attention back to the table.

"Look, don't you get it?" The Armstrong's leader spat the words at them. "Your obsession with this planet will kill you and we don't want you to drag us with you. You're right we have to survive, and that means holding on to our sanity and acting like the humans we are."

"You don't consider us human?" Sarah asked, keeping her voice soft and her eyes wide.

"You all are deluded—infected with a group psychosis. You've given up the foundation of rational society. That's not happening here." Ken delivered this judgment with a half-smile, cutting off any significant dialog.

Jerry spoke gently, looking at the three men across from him. "Perhaps what you perceive as delusion is evolution. All living things must change or they'll die."

"We'll see who survives. If you disappear, I guess it will prove I'm right."

Rob said, "Ken, if we disappear, you will too eventually."

The thin smile widened, slicing through the bottom third of the boss' face, while icy eyes nailed Rob. "When your crew falters, they'll know where to look for safety. That's how it worked in space. That's how it's going to work here. People need security, strong leadership. Our doors will open when they're ready to join us."

Jerry's stomach roiled. A threat hid in this man's confidence, a snake wound into a knot of arrogance they couldn't unravel. Brent, on Ken's right hand, smirked, lapping up their fear. Tom, however, looked at the table. He's ashamed, thought Jerry, and afraid. Maybe there's not as much support as Ken believes for his brand of security.

Striving to keep his tone neutral, Jerry said, "Well, Ken, our agreement was that any member of either of our communities can move to the other. That stands. I'm happy to hear you're still open to any of our people wanting to join the Armstrong's settlement. Please remember that we will be just as glad to welcome any of your crew."

Ken's lip curled. "Don't count on anyone from here defecting to your insane fantasy show. I'm building a real earth colony here." He glanced over at Brent slouching beside him. "I think we're done."

Brent pushed up and Tom followed his example. The four adults from the Glenn's village exchanged glances and stood. Xander hesitated, still holding Jerry's hand, but then dropped it and got to his feet. Without speaking another word, they moved as a unit towards the door. The men who had escorted them to the meeting waited there, ready to lead them back to their ATV. Ken remained seated at the table, making no move to say goodbye.

At the exit from the orb, Joe, Eli's former friend, stepped forward to spin the hatch lock. As he pushed the port open, Jerry noticed movement on the outside—bodies jostling in front of the stairs. The Glenn's group descended the six steps into a small bunch of people congregated at the bottom.

"Get back to work. There's nothing to see here." Joe shouted at the group of the women who had watched them come in, and a few new male faces. The clutch of onlookers held their ground.

Jerry stepped off the last riser into the little crowd, his hands on Xander's shoulders. The boy trembled but moved with him. Eli's solid bulk, shoulder to shoulder with Rob in front, created a safe wall. Sarah stationed herself at the rear of the group, head swiveling to assess the danger. A small hand reached in from the side and touched Xander, fingers brushing his bright dark hair. Everyone froze. Xander turned to the woman, no taller than himself, who caressed him.

"Hello," he said, looking wide eyed into a face filled with so much yearning Jerry's heart constricted with the pain of it. Then Xander's shoulders stiffened and Jerry felt a frisson of hope zither up from him. The boy cocked his head under the woman's fingers.

"Your babies are hungry," His soprano voice sang the words.

The woman dropped her hand and rested it on her flat stomach. "The baby…" she whispered.

A man looming over her protectively said, "Babies?"

Xander's gaze shifted up. "Yes. Didn't you know she was having twins?"

The man looked at his wife who stared at Xander with brown doe eyes, panting. Around them the crowd had gone silent. Even the guards froze in their tracks.

Xander frowned. Then sticking his hand into one of the many pockets of his jumpsuit, he brought out the energy bars stowed there that morning. He held them out to the woman, smiling reassurance. "You can have these." He pressed them into her limp fingers and, grimacing with concentration said, "Don't be afraid to dream. Dreaming will help the children." Then he gave himself a little shake and grinned his boyish smile at her.

The group exploded with movement, the other women reaching out, shoving to get near Xander. "Touch me."

"Please, I want a baby too."

"Help me, please, help me too."

Jerry's arms gathered him in, shielding the youth with his own body. The escorts came to life, pushing back the throng, herding them forward. They hustled through the crowd, across open ground, and past the wall, arriving at the Rover.

As the guards pulled the gate closed, shutting off the village to them, Sarah called, "Don't you want the food we brought?"

The great doors hesitated, but then at a barked order resumed their movement and clanged shut.

"Let's leave it anyway." said Rob. "If that woman is pregnant with twins, they'll need it."

They took only fifteen minutes to get the boxes stacked against the mud walls. Then they climbed into their vehicle and headed home.

Six months passed with no sign that the Armstrong's leadership would change its mind about cooperating with the Glenn's colonists. The discovery of Dee and Jaime Rodriguez's pregnancy convinced Ken to allow Doc regular visits, but it also increased his confidence in the viability of the new village. In the original colony, people settled in to wait, not knowing what else to do. Then, in a day, the atmosphere changed.

The children, restless during the night, continued strange behavior into the daylight hours. Parents and teachers watched them periodically stop their games, pausing in unison to listen to a voice beyond the adults' capacity. Jerry sensed the tension too. During the afternoon rest period, when he asked Xander what it meant, the youth stammered. "It's now and not yet, Uncle Jer." He crossed his arms, clutching his shoulders in opposite hands, guarding his heart. "Something bad is happening now and not yet. We have to wait."

They sat in the area between the bedrooms in their apartment, leaning against pillows piled on a couch. Jerry narrowed his eyes, then opened them wide trying to relax and connect to what Xander heard. The small living space vibrated with the wind outside mounting to a gale. He saw the taut strain of the stiff fabric that formed their window. The very air he breathed tasted electric. He searched for a reason. "Could it be the twins in the Armstrong's village?"

Doc had come home a week ago after assisting in the birth. Mother and children were fine, she assured them, but the father had been nowhere in sight. "When I asked Dee where he was, she shook her head and cried. Dr. Wilson told me they had assigned him to an explorer's party. He insisted that I not bring it up again because it upset her so much. I never got a second alone with Dee to find out more."

Xander paused for a long time, his eyes focused inward. Then he sighed. "It's in that direction. Goldie loves the babies. She's worried about them. But that's not it."

Jerry's heart sped up responding to the familiar surge of adrenaline that hit him whenever one of their children fell or got sick. "Should we go there? Do they need help?" His voice rose, mirroring the tension in his body.

Xander cocked his head. "It's now and not yet. We have to wait." He looked his uncle in the eyes. "Someone's very sad. I've never felt anyone so sad. It's the mother. Shouldn't she be happy?"

Suddenly Jerry couldn't stand it anymore. He had to do something, anything. "Come on, kiddo. Let's see what Doc says."

They left the apartment and trotted together down the hall, past the great commons square covered by its own vibrating roof of plastic, and took the sharp right to the clinic. They burst through the door, and emptiness met them. The outer office held neither patients or doctor. From the inner sanctum came a wail overlying several adult voices. Jerry headed back, Xander trailing.

Two-year-old Suzy sat on the table of their tiny examining room keening like a woman in mourning. Doc, a thermometer in one hand and her eyebrows knit together in consternation, was shaking her head. Suzy's mom, Abby, appeared to be crying too, her eyes as red as her hair. Both women turned to Jerry as he entered.

"I can't get her to stop." Abby panted. "Darren's been holding her for hours, but had to go into the lab. The minute he put her down, she started howling."

"There's nothing physically wrong." Doc addressed Jerry over the din. "Is something going on with Goldie? This is the third hysterical child I've had in here today."

Before Jerry could respond, Xander slipped in front of him and between the women, positioning himself face to face with bawling toddler. He reached out touching her knee and said, "Suzy."

The child's hazel eyes flew open. She took a gulp of air and threw herself into Xander's arms. He stumbled back and to his knees, bringing her safely with him. As the adults hovered over them, the thirteen-year-old kept his engulfing hold on the little girl, bending his head over her auburn curls and whispering in her ear. Jerry knelt too and wrapped them both in his embrace. The sobbing ebbed into hiccups as Suzy quieted. Only when she squirmed did Jerry, then Xander, release her.

Her mother crouched in front of her, relief and worry fighting for an upper hand on her pale face. "Oh sweetie, are you OK? Can you tell mommy what's wrong now?"

The swollen eyes, ringed with still dripping lashes, considered her mother's distress. "Cookie, please. Please, cookie," she sang with a slight lisp.

"All this crying for a cookie?" Abby's expression slid towards outrage as panic receded.

"That's not why she cried," Xander said. "She's hungry now but before she was hooked into Goldilocks. She's too little to block Goldie, but she knows what Goldie's feeling."

"The other kids I treated today suffered from the same thing." Anne rubbed her forehead. "Luckily they were three-year-olds, and I got them back on track by distracting them. They weren't screaming, either—just hyper-sensitive and jumpy. What's going on Xander?"

Before he answered, the weary mother, holding her toddler in her arms, said, "Anne, if you think she's OK, I'll go get her something to eat."

"Yeah, that's the best thing you can do for her, dear. Let me know if she shows any other symptoms."

Abby, half out the door, made eye contact with the boy. "Xander, may I call you if she gets out of hand again?"

"Sure, no problem."

Doc laughed. "You're going to put me out of business, kid. Seriously, this is the worst I've ever seen the little ones. Can't Goldie get a grip on whatever she's projecting?"

Xander scowled, frowning at the floor. "She's sorry. Sometimes she forgets we can hear her. She was alone for so long, you know."

The boy's reflection brought Jerry up short. The planet had been alone for countless centuries, millennia even, before they showed up. *What does she understand of us?* he wondered. Suzy's cries sounded like a mourning keen and

Xander said the mother, Dee, was sad when she should be happy.

"Xander, does Goldie realize we can die?"

"You mean like my dad?"

"Yeah, and Janice and Conner. Does Goldie know we're more like the fish and the bilbugs than she is?"

Xander cocked his head. Then he paled and reached out his hand to find his uncle's. An image flooded Jerry's brain: A long lumpy person-sized object wrapped in a blanket being rolled into a hole in the ground. His breath stopped in his chest.

The boy said, "He's not dreaming. Goldie's waiting for him to change. Maybe she means to grow back. She doesn't understand why he won't talk to her anymore."

Jerry had no doubt, but he asked anyway. "It's Dee's husband, isn't it? What's his name? Jaime?"

"Yes. He dreamed Goldie even on the spaceship. He's her first friend on the Armstrong."

Other than the two captains lost in the early crash of the science orb, no one had died on Goldilocks. They had never explained their greatest mortal fear to this alien entity they now took for granted. How can a planet comprehend death? Jerry mused. The falling of a tree, the growth and decay of grasses, the life cycles of the fish and little insects which populate her create the heartbeat of her own Life. Why should she, who never knew another sentient being before their arrival, contemplate death? Jerry groped behind himself for the doctor's stool and sank onto it, still holding Xander's hand but putting his forehead in his other palm.

"He's gone, Xander—like your dad. He won't ever speak to Goldie again. Can you tell her that?"

A moment of absolute stillness engulfed him while the planet received this news. Then a swirl of confusion, anger, fear and loss hit Jerry, threatening to swallow him. He dropped the boy's hand, pulling him into a full body hug. "Breathe, Xander. Hold on to yourself," he whispered. The sound of wailing erupted in the hall as the sorrow they unleashed hit Suzy before she got her cookie.

The Steering Committee, with the addition of Doc, Rob and Xander, met as soon as they convinced Goldie to contain herself and calmed the children. They had to act, but what threatened them? What could they do? Without communication between the two villages, everything appeared so nebulous. Bill said, "Maybe we wait it out. We've lost people before. Grief is terrible but life goes on. The death probably was an accident and Dee will adjust."

"No." Jerry shook his head. "Dee's not getting the support she needs. That's what alerted us to the crisis. Goldie's so worried that she transmitted Dee's despair, even before she understood what it meant."

"Do you think she's in real danger?" Sarah asked.

"Yes, and the twins too." Doc frowned. "Babies that young need their mother concentrating on them. A shock this big might distract her from their care."

"Why aren't the Armstrong's people helping her?" Kathir's outrage spoke for everyone in the room.

Jerry took a deep breath and looked at the table. "Here's a dark scenario. I'm not sure this is true, but it feels like it might be and it scares the crap out of me." He paused and glanced around.

Sitting next to him, Rob nodded encouragement. "Go ahead. We need to consider every possibility."

"OK. Remember this is tenuous. I don't have any hard evidence." Jerry noticed a slight tremble in his fingers. He clasped his hands together. "I think they murdered Jaime. Ken doesn't want his people to connect with Goldie and Jaime dreamt of her in space and then communicated with her when they got here. It's been over a year now. Of the Armstrong's crew, only the Rodriguez' have children. Even before the twins were born, we saw how some of their members reacted to Xander's connection with Goldie—wanting him to help them conceive. My fear is that Ken eliminated Jaime to keep control of the community and he wants Dee to fail with the babies so he can take them away from her."

The room grew silent. Ahdam said, "Jerry, that is too dark. Do you think Ken's that evil?"

"No. He's that scared. We know he's capable of sacrificing individuals for the good of the whole. He ordered his crew to mine a radioactive planet with full awareness that those miners would die. They weren't volunteers, Ahdam. They didn't realize they courted death on that job. Ken may have killed one more man believing it necessary for the success of the colony."

Heads around the table nodded. Eli said, "I agree that this might be the case. I saw Ken in action and Jerry's right. He's both fearful and in dictator mode. But if we don't have proof, and we can't talk to them, what can we do?"

Miriam spoke up. "We save the babies. That's always the first step. We get Dee and the twins to safety."

Tamara nodded. "I agree. But is it possible? We can't even contact her."

"Goldilocks can." Xander exuded confidence, but the adults eyed him skeptically.

"You mean communicate with her in a dream, kiddo?" Jerry asked.

The boy tilted his head, a puppy listening for direction. The gesture made him look younger than thirteen, open and vulnerable. Jerry shivered.

"The mom is so tired and sad Goldie is the only thing that's real to her. She's kind of dopey right now. So Goldie gets in around the edges."

"Shock." Doc nodded. "Perhaps she's so traumatized her usual psychic defenses aren't in place. If that's the case, it would be easier for Goldilocks to communicate with her."

Bill said, "Even if Dee listens to Goldilocks and we get instructions to her, what will we tell her? That wall must run around the whole village now. Were you able to scope it out when you were there, Doc?"

"Yeah, it's in place. The only gaps are right next to the science orb. I don't know if they miscalculated or plan to integrate it later into the ship but the barrier stops a few feet from the curved surface on both sides."

"If she sneaks out that way, she'd be going in the wrong direction." Eli frowned as he tried to remember the layout of the Armstrong's colony. "The orb lies on the side of the village directly opposite the path to our place."

"Yeah," said Kathir, "but at least no one would suspect her of escaping if she wandered through the settlement on that course."

Jerry drew in a sharp breath. "The bio-dome. It's outside the wall. I saw the track leading to it right behind the orb. Could she hide there with the babies? We'd sneak in at night and rescue her then."

"Anyone who sees her going for a stroll in the middle of the day will wonder why she hasn't come home after an hour or so." Miriam tapped the table, trying to drum out the solution. "She'll have to slip out after dark, find the path to bio-dome and get as far away as she can. They'll search for her when they discover she's gone, but waste time questioning the guards at the front gate. We could meet her at the dome and guide her here by a different route."

"It'll take weeks of bushwhacking to break another trail." Eli looked unhappy, his fists balled in frustration. "And longer coming back with two infants and a woman still weak from giving birth."

"Yeah, not optimum conditions for mom and kids," Doc agreed.

A tense silence fell on the room, punctuated only by Miriam's continued drumming. Tamara, sitting next to her, reached out and covered her hands, restoring quiet. Jerry sensed their ten hearts continue the beat.

"Let's take the shuttle and pick them up." Xander tossed the solution onto the table.

Faces shuttered around the circle. They appreciated that they only had enough fuel for one flight to the Glenn in orbit above the planet. If they needed something from the main ship, more plants or metal or anything—if they needed to escape—one more trip.

Jerry looked at the haunted eyes of his friends. *We'll do*

this, he realized. We might argue all night, but in the end we'll act on what's best for the babies now, no matter the consequences for the future.

"Can the shuttle land near the Armstrong's green house?" He directed the question to his spouse and Eli. They looked across the table at each other, paused, then nodded.

"When we ran the first explorations around this quadrant, I landed on a bald hill close to their village site," said Rob. "I'd say it's half a mile straight west of the bio-dome, right Eli?"

"Yeah, we can check the maps but definitely within walking distance. And we have the coordinates in the computer so we could fly it blind, in the dark."

"They'll hear the shuttle," Kathir pointed out. "We'll need to be ready for their reaction."

"That's for sure. It won't be pretty." Jerry said. "Let's vote first on using the shuttle. Then we can concentrate on preparing to cope with any resistance to Dee's resettlement."

They voted unanimously. Then the hard work of planning began.

CHAPTER 14
PLANET KOI-3284

DATE: 2079 CE/3

Jerry sat with his back up against the Armstrong's bio-dome wall, staring into the vast darkness of the forest. Lily and Xander cuddled together for warmth on his right, but he couldn't distinguish them from the deep shadows. The wind, blowing at mistral strength all day, died to a stiff breeze an hour ago, but he heard nothing over the staccato slap of leaves and branches above him. He pointed his face towards his companions.

"Where is she now, kiddo?"

"Dee's almost here. Goldie thinks she's moving slow because of the babies. She dropped her flashlight a couple of times."

"No one's following?"

"I don't think so."

"OK, let's move to the front and meet her. I'll shine my light on the ground so we can see but keep yours off until we're back in the woods. I don't want anyone from the village to spot us."

"You hold onto Uncle Jerry's shirt," Lily said to her son. "I'll hold onto you."

They crept single file around the curved wall until they intersected the path leading up to the door. Then they squatted in the darkness again, huddled against the wind, the air tinged with the spicy scent of the woods behind them. Finally, they spotted a feeble beam bobbing up the track. Jerry stepped forward silently and when she was almost upon them, whispered, "Dee."

The woman jumped, dropping her flashlight which went out. "Who's there?" Her voice squeaked in a high tremble.

Jerry flicked on his light, pointing it at the ground. He wouldn't have recognized her as the same person he and Xander encountered on their last trip. Sunken, dark-ringed eyes stared wildly out from under a rat's nest of hair further blown up by the wind. Her coat stuck out in front of her. Jerry supposed for a moment—my God, she's still pregnant. Then he realized she had bound one twin around her belly, freeing her hands to carry the other baby and the flashlight. Neither of the infants made a sound.

Xander stepped into the little pool of light and reached for her empty hand. "It's OK. We'll take care of you and the twins."

The wild woman focused on him, letting out her held breath in a whisper. "Xander."

Jerry said, "Dee, the shuttle is here and can fly you to the Glenn's colony. Is that what you want to do? Would you like to join us there?"

A high cracked laugh broke from her lips. "Yes, yes, yes. I have to get away. Jaime's dead and they want the twins. I have to escape."

Lily stepped forward and said, "I'm Xander's mom. I'll carry one of the babies. You hold Xander's hand, follow me. Jerry will come last, make sure we're safe."

Dee looked down at the tiny Asian woman confidently

giving orders. "Xander's mom?"

Lily nodded and held out her arms. The mother calmly deposited the bundle she cradled into them and then, hitching up the little one under her coat, let the youth lead her forward. Jerry followed, pointing his cone of light up the path. Between the beacon Lily carried ahead and his, creating shadows under their feet, they could just make out the faint line in the undergrowth which was their lifeline to the shuttle.

They advanced haltingly, without speaking. Jerry strained for any sound of following footsteps but sensed nothing except the wind. They tramped on until the trees ended at the hulking shadow of a hill blocking their way. Lily stopped and turned back. "Not long now. The shuttle's just up here. Watch for loose stones though. Don't trip."

Far ahead and above a beam, yellow as warm butter, spread out. They know we're here, Jerry realized. They opened the door. The path got steeper but the little troop sped up. In a few minutes the glow illuminated the boxy outline of the shuttle. A ladder dropped out from the light and hands appeared to help them up. Jerry glanced through to the pilot's cabin where Rob and Bill prepared for take-off. Isaac and Saphir, strapped into their seats and ready to go, waved at Xander as he grinned ear to ear. The youngsters had come along to amplify Goldie's message to Dee and strained to catch a glimpse of her. Jerry called to them, "Kids, please ask Goldie to inform the others we have the family and are heading to our village. No one is shadowing us. The campers should move to set up their tents now. We'll be back in four hours, before the sun comes up."

The pre-teens grinned even harder as they nodded and

then concentrated, both looking off into space. Xander caught Jerry's eye and whispered, "I'll make sure Goldie understands."

His uncle smiled, feeling his tension ease. He thought, maybe we can pull this off.

Doc, hunching up from the back, accepted the bundle from Lily. The baby at once began a thin wail. A muffled answering cry rose from the sibling still wrapped and covered by Dee's coat.

"Strap in," Anne said, heading to the rear again with her charge. "These little guys sound hungry. I'll get the milk warmed."

Lily turned her attention to the weary mother while Jerry pulled up the stairs and secured the door. She eased Dee's bulky outer layer off and unwound a shawl, freeing the infant. Handing the baby to Jerry, she sat the exhausted woman on a fold-out seat and strapped her in without protest.

"Xander, you sit here on this side of Dee. Jerry on the other."

While Jerry cuddled one twin to his chest, Lily fixed the restraints and then checked to make sure her son was belted in before she settled across from them. Doc came back, a baby in one hand and two bottles in the other. She handed Jerry a bottle and sat next to Lily.

Rob's voice on the intercom buzzed. "Ready for take-off. Is everyone secure?"

Lily, closest to the pilot's cabin, leaned over and banged twice for affirmative on the door. The shuttle filled with the reverberations of the engine. Looking over, Jerry observed Dee's head resting on the vibrating wall, eyes closed but streaming tears. Over the noise of lift-off, he couldn't offer comfort, so he concentrated on the baby instead, rubbing the bottle's nipple over its quivering lips. A few drops of warm formula found their way into the wailing mouth and instantly the crying stopped. The infant mastered the artificial breast in a second, sucking away like a pro. Jerry glanced over at Doc to see the other twin feeding just as enthusiastically.

As the shuttle leveled off and sped towards home, the noise in the cabin decreased. Jerry leaned toward the babies' mother. "What's this one's name?"

The sodden eyes opened a crack and her head turned to the greedy little bundle suckling in his arms. "Jaime," she whispered, tears welling up and spilling over again. "I call him Junior. I can't say his father's name without hurting."

"Hey, Junior. You'll be OK. Everything's all right." Jerry crooned to the baby, hoping the words reached Dee, too. "Your children are beautiful. They're going to be fine now."

She looked at him, desolation in her eyes. "Their father is gone. They killed him. They said it was an accident, but it wasn't. I know it wasn't."

Jerry nodded considering—this isn't the time to interrogate her, but we need to discover who she suspects soon. Although he didn't think it was much of a mystery. Right now he wanted to help her get a grip, concentrate on the lives she still had. "Here, can you hold Junior for a while?" he asked, handing the furiously sucking infant into her arms.

As he passed the baby across, Junior lost the nipple for a moment and howled until Dee got it back in his mouth. In this act of mothering, her tears stopped.

"You need to burp them more when they're taking a bottle," Jerry told her. "When he's half way through with that, make him take a break or he'll have gas pains and keep you up tonight."

She nodded, bending her head over the baby. "I don't have enough milk for them both. They cry all the time."

Doc leaned toward her over the other twin. "Don't worry, dear. When you feel better and eat some healthy food yourself, more milk will flow. In the meantime, we have plenty of formula we make and store for our own kids. Your babies still need you whether or not you give them the breast."

Jerry searched Dee's face to see if these words comforted her, but she showed an expressionless profile. He settled in to wait out the rest of the trip home.

"They'll try to get the twins back."

Jerry couldn't tell if she addressed this whisper to him or herself, but reached over and placed a hand on her knee. "We know. Don't worry. We have a plan."

But how's the plan progressing? Jerry sealed his lips, refusing to voice this question, sensing tension grip his spine again. The steering committee spent hours going over it and then their whole community weighed in. To put their children out in front of the Armstrong's village, vulnerable to any violence Ken might throw at them, sounded stupid tonight—the height of overconfidence. He, however, had been the biggest advocate when they hatched the crazy idea. He'd said, "Consider it a peaceful children's crusade, a sit-in where instead of shouting slogans at our opponents we just live our lives out in the open where they have access to us. If they see with their own eyes we're not the awful monsters that Ken has painted us, they'll think twice about following his orders."

"Yeah, but why risk the youngsters?" Shelly had asked to the bobbing heads of gathered adults.

"Because Ken tells them we're changed, and he's right. Our kids are different here on Goldilocks than they would have been if born on earth. What we need to prove is that it's a good change, a positive evolution. They'll see our wonderful children. They'll hear them sing."

Jerry bent his head into the palms of his hands, his elbows resting on his knees. Oh God, I hope I'm right. Please let this work. He had witnessed the longing for children in the eyes of the women when Dee connected with Xander so many months ago. That same desperation haunted him even before he had known about Goldilocks. The desire for a child—no other ache resembled it. He counted on the fact that, unlike coveting personal possessions or an exclusive lover, hoping to be a parent opened a person to a destiny unknown, uncontrolled. That's what had happened to him. Please God, he prayed, let them love our children and the future they represent more than their fear.

Right now eighty of their adults and youngsters hunkered just beyond sight of the Armstrong's great wall. In fact, after getting Isaac and Saphir's message, some of the group were sneaking in to set up tents directly under the rock barricade. When the guards looked out in the morning, it would appear that these families had sprung up like mushrooms overnight, spreading from the rough road that led to the Glenn's village around to their own bio-dome's path. It would be impossible to ignore or hide these visitors from the rest of the Armstrong's population.

In their former lives, all the adults had gone through standard training for dealing with a terrorist's attack in their earthbound elementary and high schools. Before they left for the new village, they reviewed those long ago lessons, practicing communal confrontation tactics which would momentarily confuse a single attacker. But they realized they were vulnerable if a mob descended on them in anger. They understood the risk. Their plan depended on surprise and most of the Armstrong's people joining up with them before their leaders could forbid their interaction. *Thanks goodness there are ten hours of darkness to operate in,* Jerry reflected. *We have just enough time to prepare.*

As the shuttle sped home to deposit Dee and the babies into the safety of their own science orb, Jerry went over the plan again and again in his head. It had to work. There was no other way.

Ken signaled them ten minutes after they ushered Dee into the Glenn's medical clinic which they had moved into the more secure science orb. "Too soon, too soon." Rob cursed through clenched teeth. "Stall as long as possible, Bill."

With trembling fingers, Bill fumbled for his wrist com and accepted the call. He said, in a voice feigning sleep, "What is it, Ken? It's the middle of the night for goodness' sake. Is something wrong?"

"Don't play games with me, you idiot." Ken's anger flashed out of the device. "You kidnapped Dee and the kids and took them out in a shuttle. Get them back now or there'll be hell to pay. Don't think we won't retaliate."

"I don't know what you're talking about. Who's been kidnapped?"

Rob flicked on the audio of his wrist com. He made a rolling sign with his hands, encouraging Bill to keep Ken talking, before heading out to fire up the shuttle again. Jerry, at the counter behind him, wrote out a message: Make him wait for morning before taking action. Bill nodded nervously, trying to hold up his end of the conversation. As Jerry bolted out the door to follow his spouse, he heard him say, "Slow down, Ken. Let me get this straight. Who stole what?"

In front of the portal, Jerry saw Doc waiting.

"Hurry. Lily and Xander are already on board."

"You think they'll be OK?" he asked, nodding towards the interior of the orb where the mom and twins had disappeared.

"Yeah, Jane Dahl's back there with her baby and Sally. They'll be fine if Saphir and Isaac behave."

As if summoned by their names the preteens appeared, thundering around the corner of the hallway, skidding to a stop before them. "Uncle Jer, can't we go with you?" Isaac whined.

Jerry faced the gangly youngsters, studying them. "C'mon, you two. We need you here. In fact, can one of you wait with Bill in the meeting room and let Goldie know what happens with that com call?"

"Xander doesn't have to stay." Saphir pouted. "He always gets the best jobs."

A very pregnant woman waddled into the hall and said, "Hey you guys, you heard Uncle Jerry. Let's go to the offices."

"Thanks, Sal," Jerry smiled as she handed him a bulging cloth bag with an aroma akin to pumpkin pie wafting from it. "What's this?"

"Muffins for Suzy's birthday. She turns three tomorrow. Everyone loves a kid's party." She gave him a wink.

"Well, that's something to focus us. Thanks again."

"Do we get a muffin?" Isaac asked as the gravid woman

steered the kids away.

Doc pushed open the hatch. "Let's go. I want to be on hand if events turn nasty."

Back in the shuttle, Jerry listened to the continuing conversation between Bill and Ken playing out on Rob's wrist. Eli stuck his head out of the cockpit to ask after his wife and the baby they had waited so long to have. "Did you see Jane and Hannah?"

"They're doing fine," Doc said. "Nothing can hurt them if they stay in the orb. Let's go finish this."

Jerry pried the treat bag away from Xander's inspection and helped Lily strap in, before taking the seat closest the door for himself. Rob leaned out of the cockpit.

"Bill can't hold Ken off until morning. He's threatening to send their two shuttles over here and burn down our settlement."

"Could Goldie fire up high winds to discourage them?" Jerry said.

"Well, then we can't fly back to the Armstrong's village," Rob pointed out.

"Right. Xander, put Goldie on notice—we may need her to increase the wind in a few hours. Maybe it will take them awhile to get organized and we can land before they get off the ground."

The boy nodded and focused on the floor as the shuttle shook. Jerry closed his eyes against the clamor of lift-off only to find his inner state just as noisy. It's going wrong already, he worried. We'll lose the element of surprise if Ken sends out shuttles and they look down to see tents right under their noses. He could send men out tonight to attack the sit-in without realizing we have children in the camp.

As soon as the shuttle leveled off, Rob unbuckled and came back to sit beside his spouse. Bill was doing a fine job of stretching out an argument over whether Dee left voluntarily with her babies but the Armstrong leader's thin line of reasonableness was fraying. The wrist com crackled: "God dammit, Bill. Get Rob on this com now or I'll toast you. I bet he's behind this with that fagot husband of his."

Jerry said in a low voice, "Could you convince him we're coming back on the shuttle and will talk to him in the morning? Just don't tell him Dee isn't with us."

Rob nodded and taking a deep breath, punched the mute button off. "Hey Ken. Rob here."

The com stuttered in shock and then all the viciousness being directed at Bill came pouring out towards their beloved Rob who radiated calm and goodwill. Jerry balled his fists and bit his tongue to keep from responding. Lily's face reddened with indignation. The target of the vitriol, however, just rolled his eyes and winked at Xander whose mouth hung open listening to the avalanche of abuse.

"Yeah well, Ken, sorry you're so upset. Seems we might have made a slight miscalculation, but no harm done. We're headed back to your place right now."

As Jerry hoped, Ken assumed Dee and her twins were on board.

"Smart decision, Rob. Set down inside our compound. We'll clear the plaza."

"No need, man. I'll land on that little hill behind your bio-dome. It's easier for me to touch down there."

"We'd have to bushwhack in the dark to meet you there. You can manage a landing here."

"OK, how about a compromise: I'll land on the hill and

we'll meet you at the bio-dome as soon as it gets light? You want everyone safe, don't you?"

"You're the one putting our people in jeopardy. I don't trust you an inch. I'm sending a shuttle up right now to intercept you and make sure you're headed this way."

Rob hit the mute button as he looked at Jerry's stricken face. Eli, listening in from the cockpit, called, "Remind him he's got radar for God's sake. He doesn't need to send anyone up."

Jerry said, "Stand by, Xander. If he won't buy it, Goldie will have to increase the wind."

Rob unmuted. "Ken, can't you track us on radar? We must be within range. We're headed straight for you. Should arrive in an hour or so."

Background rustling and voices told them the scanning system was being turned on and consulted.

"OK, asshole. Land that shuttle on the hill and get my woman and kids here at the crack of dawn. I'll be watching you."

"See you in the morning, Ken." Rob signed off.

"Has the sit-in crew set up their tents yet?" Jerry asked Xander, who after a moment shook his head.

"No, but they're almost ready. Another fifteen or twenty minutes."

"Ok, as soon as they have the force fields up, ask Goldie to increase the wind as much as possible without blowing us out of the sky. We've got to make it uncomfortable enough that Ken doesn't send people out to check on us."

Another pause. The teen looked up mischievously. "Would you like rain, too? Goldie thinks she can manage that."

Jerry glanced at Rob who said, "Yeah, we'll be OK in a little weather. The campers might be miserable but if they put their force fields up they should be able to get some sleep."

"I think it's our best chance to keep the Armstrong's crew inside tonight, then. Tell Goldie to give it all she's got short of killing us." Jerry told Xander. "And ask her to alert the sit-in."

The storm began shortly. Ninety minutes later, Rob and Eli landed the shuttle with a few extra bumps but nothing too rough. Then the planet let loose. No one was going anywhere in the tempestuous dark. The Armstrong's boss tried calling again but neither Rob nor Eli answered. They messaged Bill not to respond either. They figured they would let Ken stew, thinking the weather had knocked out communications.

That didn't mean they slept, though. Xander curled up on a blanket in the corner while the six adults hashed and rehashed their plans in the few hours left before dawn.

"We have to get Doc, Xander, Lily and you over to the nearest campsite before Ken and his men reach our shuttle," Rob told Jerry. "They'll be furious when they discover Dee's not here. I don't want Xander exposed to more of his foul mouth."

"Well, I don't want you having to listen to it either." His spouse frowned with consternation. "Why do you and Eli have to stay?"

"We're the pilots, Jerry," Eli said. "It's no good having a craft standing by for an emergency if you don't have someone to fly it."

"Hide in the forest and don't let those creeps see you," Lily said. "They'll leave if no one's around."

"More likely they'd come in and wreck the instruments."

Eli sighed. "No, this is our last shuttle and we need to protect it. Rob's right. We have to stay. We can always seal the door."

"OK, I agree, but I should be the one to remain," said Jerry. "Doc has to be close to Xander so he can alert her if anyone gets hurt, and Lily should hook up with Ayisha who's caring for Emma, but I'm not needed."

"Yes you are, dear heart." Rob's mouth quirked up in a half smile. "Our boy needs you to be brave and everyone else needs you to keep them calm. You go to the sit-in. Eli and I will be all right. In fact, I bet we'll be bored to death, so make your victory snappy, OK?"

Rob gets his way as usual, stewed Jerry as he eased down the ladder an hour later in the dark predawn. The problem is he's always right. His lips warm from a goodbye kiss, he visualized a light around his Love, offering a quick prayer: Oh God, the sea is so wide. Our boat is so small. Keep him safe for me this time.

The moist air hung still and heavy now after the fury of the night's storm, smelling crisp, with a whiff of pumpkin emanating from the bag clutched in Xander's fist. He couldn't see the boy or the two women who descended before him until he flicked on his flashlight. Then they set off to find the sit-in camp.

Years afterward everything else about that day blurred in Jerry's mind except the dark walk through the spice scented woods all the way to the bio-dome path and around the perimeter of the wall. They glided precariously between the world destroyed when they rescued Dee and an unknown future. All his senses—sight, hearing, smell—strained to hold him in the present. He focused his attention on the faint crunch of his companions' footsteps, the soft breath of the boy in front of him, and Lily's black hair catching the scant light of stars.

Then the first tent loomed out of the gloom, a muted glow inside throwing shadows up on the translucent wall which stretched to a peak like a miniature circus pavilion. More tents were in a line between here and the main gates: Twelve shelters with four adults and two children each. They needed to gather up the inhabitants and get them to a common area before Ken found out they had duped him. At least they would be together if his outrage spilled into violence. As they ducked inside the tent's entrance, Jerry noted that Ayisha and Kathir were already preparing for the day, gathering up supplies and cooking utensils as quietly as possible to allow the kids a few more minutes sleep.

By the time all the campers congregated in a clearing near the gate and the path home, the sun warmed the air. Someone started a fire and the scent of coffee promised resuscitation to the tired travelers. As breakfast porridge bubbled and the whining music of hungry small children blended into the wilder song of excited older kids, Jerry looked up to the wall.

Two faces peered at them, mouths gaping as they took in the scene below. "Good morning," Jerry called. "Come join us for coffee."

The heads disappeared without returning his greeting.

Around him, the Glenn's adults paused in their tasks and shifted around, looking towards the gate with expectant eyes. Abby, clutching Suzy's hand in her fist, said, "They didn't look friendly. Shall we round up the kids?"

"Not yet," Jerry replied. "I think they were just startled. They'll probably gather more people before they venture out. Let's stay cool and have as normal a breakfast as possible."

Suzy emphasized the wisdom of this decision by breaking free of her mother's grip. She ran over to greet Xander and pull him into a game of tickle. The adults nodded and returned to their work although Jerry noticed several keeping an eye on the doors that loomed in the wall.

He bent to pick up a toddler who wobbled too near the fire and when he straightened up caught sight of movement on the main path. Are more of our crew arriving? he wondered. That wasn't in the plan. He handed the child over to its mother and walked towards six backpackers emerging from the forest. One of them waved.

"Jerry? Is that you? Are all these people from your village?"

"Phoebe! What are you doing out here? We expected you to be inside."

"Out on another exploration. We should have been here last night, but that storm stopped us in our tracks. What's the occasion? Has Ken finally come to his senses?"

What do I say? Jerry wondered. The answer came promptly: Tell her the truth and we might have an ally to end this nonsense.

"Can you sit a minute and have breakfast with us? I'll catch you up on the latest news."

Phoebe dumped her pack and settled on a log for a hot meal. Another woman from the explorers sat too and Jerry looked twice before he recognized Janey Monroe, the psychologist assigned to the Armstrong so long ago. Sharp cheek bones on her face plumped as she smiled at him and he gave her a quick hug before handing her a mug of coffee. She wrapped both hands around it, taking eager sips of the caffeinated ambrosia. The other four travelers torn between staying with them for breakfast or reuniting with their spouses, finally opted to go inside the walls. They promised to return soon.

Jerry reviewed the events of the last few days with the women, careful not to mention his suspicions about how Jaime died. They listened in silence, but Jerry noticed they darted knowing glances at each other during the recitation, as if he confirmed something suspected by these two. As his story ended, neither of them responded right away.

Finally, Phoebe sighed. "You know Ken and I married right before the first jump, don't you?"

"No, I didn't." Crap, he thought. Have I insulted her? His face must have shown his confusion.

"Don't worry," she said with a wry smile. "I'm just telling you so you realize I understand how difficult he can be. He's brilliant—but also self—centered and stubborn. He refuses to accept any reality he can't wrap his mind around. Frankly, Ken's always tended toward manic depressive symptoms and I'm afraid they're getting worse."

Beside him, Janey snorted in amused agreement. "That's putting it mildly. We've been talking this through, Jerry. He's sending us out on missions because he's avoiding our questions. What he doesn't grasp is that we dream of Goldilocks too, even more when we're outside the village. We've experienced that she's real. So we already decided that this was the last time we'd go without challenging him. Something has to change here."

Phoebe said, "Your sit-in is better than anything we planned. This is such great timing. We'll bring our people out to meet you and start our relationship over again. If Ken's looking for your shuttle, we need to round everyone up before he returns."

"He's bound to uncover what's going on soon." Jerry frowned.

"If he shows up, I'll deal with him. Arguing with you will only fuel his arrogance. Ken's not completely unreasonable. I'll get him to listen."

Jerry noticed Janey's face didn't mirror Phoebe's confidence, but let it slide as the women stood up. "Be back soon," he told them. "We're celebrating a three-year-old's birthday and you don't want to miss that."

Just as they turned toward the gate though, it emitted a low groan and swung open a crack. The adults huddled against the brisk morning around the campfire faced around to watch, tensing. Through the gap squeezed two big men. Jerry recognized them as Brent and Tom, who stood behind Ken on the day he had visited the colony so many months ago. Are they still acting as the boss' henchmen? he wondered.

"Hey, Phoebe. How was the trip?" One of them called as they sauntered closer.

Jerry noticed their swift glances to left and right. They're as nervous as we are, he realized.

"Good," Phoebe said, smiling. "We found new plant life you're going to want to study, Tom. And Brent, there's a stratum of earth around the southernmost bay we explored that's fascinating. I couldn't figure out where it came from. I need you to go with me next time we're out. You know my geology's rusty as hell."

The men relaxed as they took on their scientist identities and questioned Phoebe eagerly about her expedition. Jerry grabbed two mugs of coffee and they accepted them absent mindedly, focused on the women from their ship. Soon everyone sat around the fire again. Only then did Phoebe ask about her husband.

"So did you guys finally graduate from babysitting or is Ken waiting at the gate?"

Sheepishly, the men glanced at each. Then they faced the woman anticipating their answer. Brent reached under his coat and pulled out a tiny microphone. Phoebe leaned over and took the cylinder between her thumb and forefinger, bending her head close.

"Hi, Honey, I'm home. Why don't you come to the party? These people aren't threatening us. It's time to play nice." With a practiced hand she disconnected the mic from its wire. Turning to Tom she said, "Do you have a backup?"

The man nodded and pulled out an identical unit, offering it to Phoebe who deactivated that one, too.

"OK, now tell me—how's it going?"

"He's getting more paranoid every day. We haven't seen him sleep more than a few hours a night since you left. He's carrying a gun around even when we're alone with him. And Phoebe," Tom's voice dropped to a whisper, "he engineered Jaime's death."

"A gun? What did he do—shoot Jaime?" Janey, sitting forgotten beside Phoebe, forced her shocked cry in the conversation.

Brent picked up the story. "No, nothing that straight forward. Ken assigned him to explore a mountain east of here, sixteen kilometers out. Two others traveled with him, carrying their own packs and food. Second day out, Jaime got sick, too sick to move. Before his partners could bring help, he died. Doc Wells says he ate one of those army supply meals, an MRE, that had a faulty seal and spoiled. But here's the thing: Ken personally destroyed that batch of tainted rations, or at least he said he did. The other MREs were fine. It could have been a coincidence, but it's made everyone nervous. Jaime's dead, and now Dee and the twins have disappeared too."

"Well, that's our doing." Jerry shrugged. "You might say we liberated them when it became clear that Dee feared for her life and the babies weren't thriving."

"How did you know? Only the doctor's seen them since Dee gave birth."

"Goldilocks alerted us. She was worried about them."

Tom snorted at this while Brent frowned.

"Why haven't you guys done anything about Ken?" Janey's voice sounded thin and sharp, barbed with accusation.

Tom looked at her, eyes dull. His friend sparked anger though. "You heard what we said. He has a gun, a magnum—something or other he smuggled on board before we took off from Earth. He started waving it around right after you left on this expedition. And remember, lots of people still think he can pull us through this situation, just like he did in space."

"And you two?" Phoebe asked.

"We're getting too old to have children." Tom's voice, leaden with sorrow, pronounced the verdict. "Dee is thirty. The rest of our women are that or older. It's clear now that Ken's lying. He doesn't know what to do. We need help and he won't admit it."

"So why don't you choose new leaders?" Jerry bit his tongue as soon as the words slipped through his lips. Four pairs of eyes, with varying degrees of annoyance, focused on him.

Phoebe said, "Think, Jerry: Just a year ago, Ken was our savior, our god. He pulled us out of complete disaster, imminent death, and found a way to safety. Sure, he was dictatorial, sometimes even cruel, but he understood how to play the odds and got most of us here alive. To put him aside now... Well, it feels disloyal and frankly, I suspect it would kill him. He's so identified with the hero role; he won't be able to be something else."

"Jerry's right though," Janey said. "Different contexts require different leadership. Ken's refusal to work with this planet is jeopardizing both our colonies. He has to step aside and let us connect with the Glenn's settlers and Goldilocks. That's our only hope."

"Agreed." Phoebe gave a sigh. "Brent and Tom, will you help us get everyone out here to meet these lovely co-inhabitants of our planet? If their sit-in works and our people feel comfortable with the way they're developing, we shouldn't have much trouble getting them to stand up to Ken."

Brent's face eased into the only smile Jerry had ever seen on it. "Hell, most of them will switch sides for a cup of this coffee."

Beside him, Tom nodded as they rose to the challenge. "Let us go in first, Phoebe. He still has that damn gun."

They couldn't find Ken. He appeared to have retreated and within an hour most of the Armstrong's settlers emerged from the confines of their village to mingle with the Glenn's sit-in. More coffee brewed over the open fire and cups materialized out of nowhere to be filled and filled again. Little Suzy played hostess, handing out her birthday muffins from the bag five-year-old Emma carried behind her. So many people had arrived that she broke each into pieces before she handed them out, so everyone would have a taste. "Happy birthday cake," she piped in her pure child's soprano as each guest accepted her offering.

Jerry noted with satisfaction that the kids captivated the attention of the villagers. Some grown-ups sat and gazed at the littlest toddlers, while others allowed young soccer players and fort builders to pull them into their play. Clutches of scientists formed, discussing the challenges of this unique environment. He paused by one such group, hearing Doc Wells speculating on why the children born on Goldie sang instead of talked. Their own doctor seemed bent on challenging his theory. That's right, guys, he thought. Share the excitement of what's new. Don't dwell on what's gone. Conversation, he fervently hoped, would bring them close, binding them together into a true community. As morning wore into afternoon, even the air felt charged with hope. He reached out to the planet and sensed a wave of contentment.

Jerry settled in front of the fire to catch up with Janey. She smiled, scooting over to make room for him on the log she occupied and spoke of the journey she'd just returned from. "We made it to the south shore of the sea this trip," she said, "I can't get over how gorgeous the coast is. Why didn't you settle there, Jerry?"

He stirred the fire, and as he sat to answer her, noticed that Suzy dropped her new birthday doll. Then the child stiffened, her head arched back, and screamed. Adults scrambled to help her but Jerry's focus skipped to the other children, frozen where they stood, eyes wide in shock.

"Xander!" Jerry jumped up, turning around, trying to locate the boy.

"The shuttle. Quick. Get to the shuttle." The thirteen-year-old barreled out from between a couple of grown-ups and headed towards his uncle, as an explosive bang echoed in the distance. Before Jerry took another breath, two more shots rang out, shadowed by sharp pings.

Phoebe appeared at his elbow, catching his arm and pointing him through the gates. "It'll be faster to go straight through to the bio-dome. We'll pick up a Rover."

Doc joined them and together the four of them ran to the doors. Brent, in the driver's seat of an ATV, turned around, waiting for them. Oh, God, don't let us be too late, Jerry prayed.

He wanted to run but riding was quicker. Jerry made himself sit still, refusing to think of what might happen, or already happened. Behind the dome he piled out with the others, leading them through the forest, branches slapping at their hands, their faces—ignored. Are we too late? Fear filled his mind.

They burst out of the woods, the bare hill rising before them, the shuttle solid and still, planted high on its side. Jerry charged up the path. He saw Ken standing, facing the shuttle's closed door with two bright scars on it. Then, as if time ticked differently for him, Ken rotated leisurely and brought the gun he held in both hands up to point at Jerry.

"Ken, don't!" Phoebe's scream hurtled past Jerry and the pistol wavered, the tall man's concentration broken.

Jerry realized his feet had stopped of their own accord as Phoebe came up next to him. He was aware of scrambling behind them and hoped Doc had caught Xander and gotten him out of the way. He didn't dare turn his head to look.

"I heard you out there, Phoebe—every plan you've made

against me. You didn't think I'd trust those two idiots to spy for me, did you? I permanently opened their wrist com links months ago." Ken's voice, flat and hard as the stones under their feet, slapped down on them. "All of you partying in that camp of freaks, plotting against me."

He raised the volume to include the big man coming up behind Jerry. "Et tu, Brent? You better hold it right there."

He turned his focus back on the trembling woman in front of him. "This is your fault. Brent and Tom wouldn't have betrayed me if you hadn't undermined me, Phoebs." The nickname became a slur in his mouth, pushing his wife aside.

"Kenny, it's OK. Everything will be OK now. They're not freaks. You'll see. They're just like us."

Her husband's calm shattered, and he shouted, "I am not like them. I'll never be like them. I'd rather die. They're not even human."

"Hey Love, it's OK. We'll go away then. Somewhere by ourselves—by the sea. I've seen the southern shore, Ken. It's lovely. We can go there, OK?"

His mask snapped back in place as Ken drew a deep breath. He said with a tinny laugh, "I know that voice. It's your 'humor him' voice, Phoebs. You don't mean a word of it. I should kill you now for deserting me." The cruel barrel of the pistol aimed at his wife.

"Kenny, please..."

Jerry reached out to pull Phoebe from harm's way, gasping for air.

"Don't you touch her."

The gun swung towards him and he froze. He tried desperately to remember the training. Attack—the word appeared in his mind like a sign. I need to take the offensive. Talking won't stop him. Maybe Brent will notice what I'm doing and help. He cast around to find something to throw but observed nothing useful.

"Get down on your knees, fagot, and stay where I can see you."

As Jerry eased one knee down to the path, he bent forward to break his descent, right hand on the red gravel and dirt in front of him. He scooped some up as he straightened his spine.

"Ken, please..." Phoebe's voice shook with tension and the gun swung back to her.

"Yes, beg for life. There's no real humanity here, though. Why should you care? You've given in. I'm the one who doesn't belong here now. It's not fair. It's not right that I'm the only one who has to pay the price for the mission's failure. You should come with me."

The glint of metal sparkled as the gun rose, leveling at the frozen woman. Jerry sprang up, tossing the dirt at Ken's face, as hard as he could, while pushing her out of the way. Around him the air exploded, and he slammed to the ground. He rolled to his side in time to see Brent's boot hit the path in front of him, running forward. Then, in the slow motion of shock, he focused on the shooter.

The handsome features distorted, possessed by rage and frustration. His hand holding the gun still moved back in recoil. As Brent reached out for it, Ken reeled away, shoving the barrel into his own mouth.

A second shot and a scarlet wave blossomed, filling Jerry's sight. Phoebe screamed. She stumbled around Jerry as she ran to the prone figure, calling, "No, no, no," echoing the blast.

Pressed into the gravel, the scent of mingled dust and blood filled Jerry's nose. He rolled over onto his back to let his eyes point upward, seeing only the flawless turquoise sky. Still in slow motion, a stray thought wandered in: How beautiful. Fill me up with blue—no more red. He took note that breath entered and left his lungs in the familiar rhythm of life.

A distant whir of machinery caught his attention. The shuttle door was opening. Rob...

He closed his eyes, cautiously curling up to sitting, and turned towards the aircraft. Only when he was sure that he no longer faced the path did he open them. Rob paused in efforts to deploy the boarding ladder, shouting to him. Jerry raised his arm to wave and called back, "I'm OK. You?"

"I'm fine, Jer. Eli's been shot. I've got a tourniquet on it but it's serious."

Doc materialized in front of Jerry, flying past and jumping onto the shuttle's steps before they hit the ground, then disappeared into the ship. He saw his husband's pale face and a bloody hand as he waved her in and followed back. Only then did he sense his heart beating. Only then did he search for Xander.

The boy knelt alone on the rocky path, staring toward the still figure that Phoebe cradled in her arms. The wind picked up, blowing his straight black hair around his face, so Jerry couldn't catch his expression. He observed the shaking though—a whole body quiver that threatened to topple the youth over in the dirt. Jerry walked back to him and lowered himself to the ground. Carefully he hugged him. "It's OK now, kiddo. It's going to be OK."

Xander pulled away to look into his uncle's eyes. His own held a depth of betrayal and bafflement Jerry knew belonged not only to him but to the planet as well. "We don't understand, Uncle Jerry. What happened? Why did he hurt Eli? Why did he shoot himself?"

Jerry smoothed the ruffled hair. "I don't know, dearest. How about we don't ask, 'why'? Let's ask, 'what's next' instead. That's a question we can build an answer to together—a good answer for all of us, even Goldilocks."

Xander nodded as he tucked his head back into Jerry's embrace.

EPILOGUE
PLANET KOI-3284

DATE: 2095 CE/7

Fog wrapped around, blinding and protecting. The wind started up at once. The song in the distance was insistent. Something was happening and wanted him alert. He lumbered toward the hidden singer. Where was she in all this mist? Was her voice nearer, getting more encouraging? Surely, tonight he would find her. She needed him and he needed her. Gusts howled but the fog never quivered. He reached up to touch the gale. It brushed his fingertips, an icy kiss.

Jerry woke from the dream, his right hand dangling outside the blankets, freezing. Rob stirred beside him, pulling the quilt up over them both, but he shrugged it off and sat up.

"What is it?" Rob whispered, careful not to wake the rest of the household. His head, bald now for several years, reflected the night light glowing on the small bedside table.

"I have to talk to Xander. I had the dream. Something's happening."

"OK, it's almost time to be getting up, anyway."

"Can you come with me? I think you should be there."

Rob looked at his husband's face, scrutinizing whatever could be read there. Jerry didn't hide. He felt a familiar urgency.

"Sure, dear heart. Let's go. No one may be awake there yet. Shall we get Lily up?"

"No, I don't want to wake her. Her arthritis is making it hard to sleep. She needs her rest."

The two men dressed hastily, pulling on warm boots and wrapping padded coats around themselves before venturing out through the low doorway of the rounded hut into the sunken courtyard. The wind blew over their heads, moist with the coming dawn. Stars bright as ice chips studded deep darkness in the sky overhead. They looked out over a rippling field of shadowed grass to other humps of roofs scattered here and there over the plain and headed towards a small grouping. They walked silently, following an almost invisible path through the knee high growth.

When they reached a circle of five huts a quarter of a mile away, they threaded their way into the middle of the cluster. Then they descended a ramp into the yard of the first one on their right. Jerry knocked on the door and pushed it open, ducking to miss the low lintel.

A young woman sat on a cube in front of an open hearth. She stood to greet them, swollen belly preceding her, arms wide to embrace.

"Jerri-o. Robbi-o. Welcome, welcome to our home," she sang. Rob coming up behind Jerry joined them in a three-way hug.

"Suzy-luv, sweet girl, so glad to see you." Jerry crooned in response as Rob hummed his pleasure. Standing back arm's length, Jerry looked at the woman, noticing several strands of gray streaked her long auburn hair, and several wrinkles radiated out from the bright hazel eyes softened by firelight.

"Daddy-o's!" A high voice trilled. The owner rocketed up to them, grabbing both men around the knees, threatening to topple them.

"Softly, softly son-o-mine," sang the woman, laughing as they tussled the hair of the child, who looked so much like a young Xander that Jerry's throat constricted with the memory.

He took a deep breath. "Suzy-luv, where is that boy-o-mine? Goldie's singing but I can't quite heed."

"Boy-o-yours, man-o-mine's out listening to the wind. He's heard the message in the night. Soon, soon he will return."

"Daddy-os, daddy-os, let's go, let's go—out to the dark and stars. Let's listen to Goldilocks out in the gale. Daddy-os let's go." The youngster caught their hands and tugged them towards the door.

"Darling boy, Mistral-luv, quit your pleading now. Daddy-os have just arrived. Food and drink must be prepared. Pause and stay awhile."

Jerry smiled, amused at how parents of this world sang reprimands to their children which, even as they pleased the ear, got the message across. Mistral scampered off to find cups and plates, taking his role of host seriously.

"Suzy, are you well?" asked Rob. "We thought you'd still be in bed this morning."

Rob rarely tried to communicate like the youngsters, but since they understood him they accepted his prose in the same way he respected their warbling. It was the space children—the seven born before the landing—who slipped back and forth between speech and singing unconsciously. Suzy, native to the planet, sang all of her first words and gradually transformed the speaking pattern into an operatic composition.

"Thank you, Rob." Suzy spoke now, limping her speech along. It was impolite to sing to a person who couldn't sing back. "This baby jumps and kicks, wanting to be delivered. Not much sleep for me or Xander."

"It's due soon, isn't it?"

"Yes, a brother or sister for Mistral. We are pleased."

Mistral now came up and reached around his mother's belly as far as his arms went, hugging her and his new sibling. He sang, "Baby-luv, baby-luv come out and play. When you are ready if not yet today."

The adults chuckled, then moved to sit at a plain wooden table with benches by the far wall. As they settled in for breakfast, the door blew open. A tall man of thirty, lean and strong with wind-blown hair straying out of its tie back, strode through. He didn't seem surprised to see the guests.

"Jerry-o, Robbi-o, daddies of mine. Just who I need in just the right time." His wide smile and cheerful tune left no doubt of his pleasure and affection.

Everyone stood and exchanged hugs, along with humming, singing, and tossing Mistral in the air for good measure. When they sat again, Xander reverted to speech in deference to the visitors.

"So, you tuned in to Goldilocks' dream too, Uncle Jer?"

"Yes, I can tell something important is happening, but I didn't quite reach her. Do you know what's going on?"

"She's senses a connection with the communications array on the abandoned orb in the Armstrong's old settlement. She can't see inside, so one of us needs to trek over there and inspect it."

Suzy frowned, "Shouldn't Eli go? He's the most experienced mechanic."

"It's a three-day walk, Suz. Eli would never make it with that bum knee of his."

"Who then?" she asked, although they all knew the answer. Xander connected best with Goldie, even better than the children born on the planet.

"I'll come with you, Xander," Rob offered. "I should be able to figure out what's triggering the array. If it's a signal, I can send one back."

"And I'll stay here with you, Suzy-luv." Jerry said. "Lily will come too and help with Mistral. If the baby should arrive before they return, we'll have our bases covered."

Suzy stared at her plate and rubbed her belly. "I don't want Xander leaving right now. It should be a while before the baby comes, but..." She looked up. "How long will you be gone?"

"Seven days, tops." Rob smiled encouragement. "Three there and three back with one to figure out the problem. Most likely it's nothing. Perhaps moisture's gotten in and caused a short somewhere."

Suzy nodded, accepting the inevitable but trying one more tactic. "Don't you think this could wait until after our child is born?"

"I was arguing with Goldie about that," Xander said, "but she's convinced this is urgent. Don't worry. She'll monitor you and let me know if I should head home."

"You need three days to travel back, no matter what's happening here." Suzy muttered, with a hum of discontent under her breath.

Xander looked at her sadly and then at Jerry and Rob.

"Come on Mistral," Rob said. "You can help me pack for the trip."

"Yeah, and we'll get Grandma Lily up and going this morning, too," laughed Jerry. The men grasped the boy's hands, swinging him out through the door. As they left, they caught the sound of Xander crooning reassurance to Suzy.

Three nights later, lying in Xander's hut on a makeshift mattress before the fire, Jerry thought he would never fall asleep. He was glad to be there for Suzy and Mistral, but he missed his warm bed and Rob at his side. His body ached with the extra exercise of chasing a youngster around all day. I'm getting to be a grouchy old man, he decided, as he tossed and turned. Only a few more days until they get home. The smoky smell from the banked embers lulled him into relaxing.

Suddenly the dream enveloped him. Fog glowed with a rosy light. The wind whispered urging him to move. The singer spun music calling him on. He walked forward without constraint, still blind. Soon. He would see the singer soon.

Mist directly in front of him dissolved. A communications console stood there. He sensed Rob and Xander nearby. This was the Armstrong's orb, long abandoned. The controls lay silent, cold and dark. The singer sang a longing, calling song. He realized that the air was still.

In the darkness, a green light blinked. He looked hard to make sure—yes. There it flashed, stabbing again and again. A hand reached out, Rob's right. He flicked a switch above the tiny bulb. Static came crackling over the intercom system. Even the singer held her breath now. And then they all heard the words:

"Earth to Armstrong. Do you read? Earth to Glenn. Come in, please. Is anyone still out there?"

THE END

ACKNOWLEDGEMENTS:

Writing a novel, at least one that will be published, is not a solitary creative act. This simple truth came as a revelation to me when I began this endeavor. Now, as I near the end of my work, I want to acknowledge those who shared in the labor and made it possible.

Thanks to:

Joseph Campbell who read my first draft, gave me very helpful critique and even more helpful encouragement and then (surprise!) became an editor and wanted to publish the rewritten novel.

Mary Billiter, a wonderful writing teacher who shared generously from her own writing and publishing experiences and so graciously urged all her students onward.

All my writing class buddies, who became a writers' support group: Pat Buck, Mary Burton, Dana Curtis, Jana Kegler, Teresa Gutwein, Gayle Irwin and Dana Volney ...

And especially Nurieh Zarrin who found me wonderful beta-readers (herself included), helped me get the first draft copied and generally wouldn't let me quit!

Pat Greiner and Ron Richard who also read through the rough first draft.

Chuck Babcock, my wonderful husband, who spent a whole summer listening to me read chapters from my second draft and insisted he loved every minute of it.

9 781608 641468